Tales of the Kashallans: Volume Five
Prey of the Umwira
Celu Amberstone

Kashallan Press, 2022

PREY OF THE UMWIRA

First edition. April 7, 2022.

Copyright © 2022 Celu Amberstone.

ISBN: 978-1990581007

Written by Celu Amberstone.

Prologue

F ace composed into a serene mask, Enaju Dingay, the High Matri of all Timorna, sat at the head of the High Council table and ignored the drone of debate going on around her. Even with the braided coils of her mane to act as a cushion, the heavy metal headdress of her office was giving her a headache. In brightly dyed kilt, her arms adorned with polished crystal bracelets, she was a regal figure sitting in her carved chair. Tall for an Avairei woman, her graying pelt and haughty dark eyes enhanced by the power invested in her by her office, she knew she was a personage to be reckoned with.

Until recently the massive wooden doors at the far end of the chamber had been open to the air and light of the courtyard beyond. But one of the clan elders down at that end of the table complained that Hunt Leader Segoi's Warlinga, training in the courtyard beyond were making too much noise, so the doors had been closed.

Now in spite of the keep's thick stonewalls, and the vaulted ceiling of the Council Chamber, Enaju felt like she was suffocating, and desperately tried to control the rage that threatened to overwhelm her reason. Would these fools ever quit yammering?

Well, it wouldn't be long now. After this Sorin confinement—in the Renewal—all the Master's planning would be realized. The beautiful Yeyen Banai Valley would belong to the Real People once more, and there would be no need for this charade. No, they would all bow to the will of this world's true and rightful rulers—or die. Thinking of the delicious tortures that one day these bickering, contentious slimeworms would endure in payment for their rebelliousness made her almost smile. She would enjoy their pain very much.

Weary of the meaningless chatter, Enaju was considering the unwise move of closing the day's proceedings, when a commotion in the outer

1

courtyard caught everyone's attention. Shouts of alarm and excited cries could be heard even through the heavy doors. What was going on out there? Enaju drummed her fingers impatiently on her chair arms waiting for a messenger to come to her.

After a tense wait, the doors opened a crack and an excited priest squeezed through the gap and quickly closed the door again. He hurried to the High Matri's side, and bent close to relay his message. Enaju's eyes widened for a moment, and then her face resumed its controlled mask. At her murmured response, the messenger bowed and hurried from the room.

Enaju rose, all eyes around the table now focused upon her expectantly. "Honored Councilors," she said, "A party has just reached Riath from Sulas Keep. They are quite distraught, and have some wounded with them. I have instructed my people to get them settled and see to their injuries. I suggest that we close for the day and reconvene tomorrow morning, when we can consider this new report at our leisure."

The head of clan Meh'gach rose and bowed to her. "High One, if there are injured, there must have been some fighting. That can only mean that the Umwira are raiding in the south again. I suggest we send for Ima Sagas, to give us a brief account of the facts, so that we—"

Enaju shook her head, cutting him off. "The Ima Sagas is not among the supplicants seeking refuge here today, honored Warlinga." Giving that interesting little fact time to sink in, she paused, and then continued, "I have already learned from my own people that the cause of their flight from Sulas is a priestly matter, not one that will need your attention, most esteemed Yargal.

"Now if you will excuse me, Honored Councilors, I understand that my grandson is one of the injured, and I must see to him. Until tomorrow." Bowing to them stiffly, Enaju turned and swept from the room.

Out in the corridor, her brother Persig caught up to her. "What's going on?" he murmured, matching his pace to hers.

"I don't know exactly," she said, "but I intend to find out soon enough."

"Is he really injured?"

Enaju laughed. "He had better be, and have a good reason for disobeying my orders and coming back here so soon after I sent him away. The rumors of scandal haven't settled down yet. If he's bungled things once again—" She fell silent as a group of Maveth clansmen drew near and passed them in the hallway.

Inside her own apartments, Enaju set aside the heavy metal-adorned headdress and collar that were the official signs of her office. With a sigh of relief, she ordered her maid to bring refreshments, and sank into a comfortable wicker chair, waving to her brother to do likewise.

She glanced at the opulent furnishings of her chamber, and felt a shiver of apprehension run down her spine. Nothing must be allowed to interfere with all this.

When they were served and once more alone, Persig drank, and then repeated his earlier question. "What has happened?"

Enaju set down her bowl and sighed. "The messenger babbled something about Sulas being destroyed by Umwira sorcery."

Persig choked, hastily setting his bowl back upon the tray. When he could speak again, he said, "Sister, is that possible? Would the Master—"

"Hold your tongue, fool!" Enaju hissed. "Even in here it isn't wise to speak of such things." Then she paused, considering. "No. I don't think so; there must be some other explanation, some other answer—if Sulas has indeed been destroyed, and this is not some stupid scheme Combaron has dreamed up to cover another of his little *problems*."

Persig gulped down the last of his tea and rose. "Perhaps I should have a word with your Hunt Leader, sister. It wouldn't be wise to allow anyone free admittance to our uninvited guests; talk of that kind could be very dangerous."

"Mm, then come back to me. I may need you later." Enaju looked down at her hand. She extended her tiny claws and dug them into the grooves of the chair arm. "I've already sent for my grandson. Injured or not, I will squeeze the truth out of him—and soon."

NOT LONG AFTER PERSIG'S departure, a disheveled Combaron was ushered into her presence. His braidlets snarled, his kilt dirty and uneven, he swayed glassy-eyed before her. Enaju's nose wrinkled at the pungent smells of blood, unwashed fur, and alcohol. Drunk. How dare he come here like this!

When she continued to stare without speaking, Combaron shifted nervously. "Grandmother, please," he whined, "I'm sick—and injured. Can I sit down?"

"You're drunk," Enaju snapped, still continuing to glare.

"Oh, Grandmother, please—I've had a little brandy, but only because my head hurts so bad—see." He turned, displaying the blood-matted tangle of his braidlets for her inspection. "Sagas Caltia and her demons tried to kill me, Grandmother!"

When she lapsed back into silence without comment, his eyes became pleading. "Please, Grandmother, I know I am disobeying your command, but I had to come back—there was nowhere else to go."

His expression suddenly sly, he said, "Grandmother, when you hear what has happened and why I've come, I'm sure you will be pleased with me."

I doubt it, Enaju thought and continued to glare. At last, noticing that he really was about to fall over, either from the liquor he'd drunk or from his wound, she motioned imperiously for him to sit on the floor at her feet.

What a disappointment this child of her bloodline had turned out to be. Bred of Avairei and Ghostlander parentage, like herself, he was a changeling, and they had all had such high hopes for him. But, to her eternal shame, all that had come of the Ghostland wizard's manipulations had been this incompetent piece of filth, with an insatiable appetite for sexual perversions.

Combaron didn't actually know the facts about his mixed parentage—he was far too stupid and weak to be trusted with "family secrets." He was a useful tool at times, however. What really *had* happened at Sulas? And, what was this talk about Sagas consorting with demons? That was absurd; the woman was blindly loyal to the Khutani. But Combaron was too afraid of her to come back here without good reason.

Damn him, her mouth curled in disgust—look at him—he was sitting there like a whipped Begta, holding his head in his hands and staring at the floor. "Look at me," she demanded.

Startled, he jerked his head up, trying to focus his eyes upon her angry face. "You have come here against my direct order to stay at Sulas. You sent word that the Caltia woman had gone to the pools against my orders. Not only do you return without Sagas Caltia, as you were instructed, you come here with some crazy story about Sulas being destroyed by the Umwira.

"And then you have the nerve to suggest to me that I will be pleased! Well, sniveling filth, make me pleased with you, if you can—or the pain in your worthless head will be nothing compared to what I will give you."

Part One: Meh'gach Keep

Chapter One

D unnagh-Tani shivered, his breath coming out in lavender puffs of smoke as he pulled the hood up over his long red braids, and tightened the fur cloak around his shoulders. Dressed in black kilt and combat boots, he'd added a tunic, leather vest and the fur to his usual bare-chested Timornan attire, but he still felt the dawn's chill.

After months cooped up indoors, smelling the keep's stale cooking odors, and its inhabitants' sweat, it was a relief to be outside, no matter what the temperature.

He took in another breath, filling his lungs with the crisp clean air. No snow today. Overhead the Timornan sky was a deep wine, streaks of crimson radiating out from the eastern horizon. Once the sun was up for a while it should be quite pleasant. The Sorin Storm Season was *officially* over, but that didn't mean the weather had improved much. It was still uncomfortably cold to his way of thinking.

Every year when the Sorins ended, the kavay-rich snows that followed when the winds changed direction, helped to cleanse the land of its latest deluge of poisoned debris blown south by the storms. Glancing around the courtyard, he could still see patches of the blue slush hiding from the sun in the deepest shadows.

Around him, the Warlinga lizardmen of Aju'an's hunting pack moved with a quiet efficiency, checking gear and packing last minute supplies for the trip. There wasn't much, of course; they would need to travel hard and fast if they hoped to reach Meh'gach before Aju'an's father and older brother left for the Renewal Ceremony and the High Council meetings at Riath.

He sighed, looking back wistfully at the inner keep behind him. His goodbyes were already said, to his human and Avairei wives, to the Khutani, and other friends in the keep; they should get going.

Waiting with him beside the gate, Commander Tizu misinterpreted his look, and said, "Don't worry, Ce'awn, (chieftain) I'll do all in my power to keep them safe, while you're gone."

Startled, Dunnagh-Tani turned to him and smiled. Dressed in the remnants of his black, Lann Gheal uniform, salt-and-pepper hair tied back with a cord, Tizu had been Dunnagh's commander—before they'd been stranded on this forgotten world, and he'd accepted a kashallan bonding with a Khutani symbiont.

"I know you will, Hunt Leader. I have complete faith in you, but it's still not easy to go. The babies are so young, I wish—" He shook his head, then fell silent, turning back to stare blindly at the activity in the courtyard.

Aju'an's twenty-man hunting pack was assembling in their traveling order just inside the open gate. Behind them, the five human guards that Tizu had assigned him were mounted atop their shaggy, Loti riding companions. The Warlinga all wore solemn expressions, but he could tell by the occasional tail flick, or stifled laugh that the lizardmen were glad to be out of the keep and eager to get moving.

Almost as tall and muscular as the Warlinga, Nathan studied the assembled warriors with a critical eye. He said something to Aju'an, then motioned for the Kashallan's Loti, Mashen, and two others to follow him. A ghost of a smile curved the corners of Dunnagh's mouth as they came near. Nathan was his oldest, and dearest friend; they'd been through a lot together.

Though officially the Lann Gheal corps had been disbanded, and a new fighting unit of Timornan Warlinga and humans had taken its place, Nathan still wore his patched uniform and his long brown hair twisted into a warrior's braid as before. When he was close enough not to shout, he said, "We're just about ready, if you are. Where are Ima Ngeal and Arishim?"

"I still don't like the idea of those two going with you," Tizu grumbled. "It's a crazy idea; the trip will be a hard one for seasoned warriors, let alone two old women. And if they fall ill, or slow you down, you might not reach Meh'gach Keep in time."

"I don't like it either. All of us are worried about the added responsibility. But we have no choice, have we? They took their argument to the Khutani before telling us. The Makers agreed with their reasoning so there's no point in arguing with them further about it."

"Well I still don't like it," Tizu muttered, and scowled ferociously at the approaching Loti, as if it were their fault.

The Kashallan chuckled. "Now you know how I felt when you went over my head—"

"That was different; I had a good reason."

"So do they—by their reckoning."

Ngeal never completely recovered from the shock of her niece, Nona's heartbreaking death. Nona had been Tomina Dingay's maid, and the changeling had managed to corrupt the innocent girl's mind and body with her Umwira master's power. Nona died during an attempt to kill the Kashallan's wives, and Ngeal blamed herself for the near tragedy.

Deciding to retire after that, she handed over the command of Ticca Keep to Sagas, in spite of the younger woman's pleas to the contrary. No amount of entreaties from the Kashallan, Hobral, or her other councilors would budge her.

Then, only last night, without warning, she informed the Kashallan and his commanders that she and the human clan elder, Meldra Arishim were also coming with them. Ngeal was so determined to go that she agreed to ride a Loti, in the unconventional way the humans had adopted, rather than risk being left behind.

"It's my duty to go with you," she'd told him. "I am a clan elder of the Maveth clan, and with me along to answer questions about what happened at Sulas and Ticca, I feel the Maveth, and other Avairei clans in the Yeyen Banai Valley will be more likely to believe the truth of your assertions. You will have a better chance of persuading them with me by you than you might have on your own, even with Meh'gach backing"

Arishim's reasons for going were equally compelling. Being brutally honest, she told the bondmates that neither of them was skilled in diplomacy, and that fact might have far-reaching and disastrous consequences for all of them. She had been a highly skilled politician in her old life, and, because of her background on the Dymarian ruling council, she should be there to advise him in such matters. Well, she had a point, and he had to admit it. Neither bondmate cared for politics, and they knew they probably needed her.

The sound of the inner keep door opening made the Kashallan turn. Three shrouded figures were approaching, their hoods up and cloaks held tightly about their bodies to keep out the cold. The Kashallan frowned—three? There was Arishim, a bit taller and plumper than the Avairei—and that one was Ngeal; he recognized her by her determined walk, but who was the other in the long woman's kilt?

"Amril! W-what are you doing out here?"

Halting in front of him, the Avairei pushed back the hood of his cloak and stared up at the Kashallan, in that determined way that was so like his sister Sagas's when she was being stubborn. "I am coming with you, husband."

Dunnagh-Tani let out a long-suffering sigh. "Amril, we talked about this last night—and I thought we agreed that I needed you to stay here and take care of your sister-wives in my absence. There is no reason for you to make this difficult journey, and after so long apart, I thought you'd want to be with Pela—" He broke off as Amril began shaking his head.

"We didn't agree, actually—you agreed—and I do have a reason. It is my duty to come," Amril insisted. "You will need someone to take care of you. Both my sister-wives and the Khutani agree. I can give you the blood gift when needed, and as your wife," he looked down shyly, "I will be there if you need other things."

Behind him, he heard Tizu make a sound that was somewhere between a snort and a laugh. Dunnagh-Tani swung round, glaring at him. Tizu gave him a wide-eyed innocent look.

Nathan on the other hand had a more unreadable expression. Was that hurt or jealousy he saw in those iron gray orbs? Damn him—how many times did he have to tell him about why he'd married Amril. When Nathan saw him watching him, he rolled his eyes and grinned. Growling a curse under his breath, Dunnagh turned back to his "wife."

"Amril, this is a very kind offer, and I appreciate it, but I think you should stay at Ticca—Pela and Sairsa will need—"

"My sister-wives have informed me that if I stay, I stay in disgrace. I will be sleeping alone. They feel that since neither of them is able to come because of the babies, it is up to me to go and see to my husband's welfare on their behalf."

Seeing the Kashallan open his mouth to protest, he said quickly, "And besides, husband, there is another reason why I should go with you." He held out the satchel he had been carrying under his cloak. "You have no medic traveling with this hunting pack. I don't have a lot of experience, but I am healer-trained. It is right that I go with you."

"He has a point, Ce'awn," Tizu said. "Best give in gracefully and let him go with you."

"He won't slow us down, Dunnagh-Tani, and we might need him." Nathan's eyes flicked to the women being helped onto their Loti by a couple of Aju'an's men.

Then, with a mischievous gleam in his eye, he added, "And besides, you might need your—uh—wife along, just in case you get lonesome." At the Kashallan's blush and murderous scowl, he grinned. "Come on, Amril, I'll put you up behind Oglas till you get used to this new way of traveling."

Amril followed the big man over to the line of warriors by the gate, leaving the Kashallan to stare after them in helpless frustration.

Shaggy chest held high with the importance of his responsibility, Mashen tentatively touched the Kashallan's arm. "Are you ready to go, Kashallan? I think they are waiting for us."

Dunnagh grunted and pulled himself atop the Loti's shaggy back. When he was settled, Mashen looked over his shoulder, the heavy brow ridges of his simian-like face contorted with his nervousness. "Tell me if I go to fast, or if you need something—"

Dunnagh-Tani patted his shoulder. "Don't worry, Mashen. The Khutani say I'm nearly all healed, so don't fret." Dunnagh urged the centaur-like creature forward with his knees. "You are right; they are waiting for us."

Chapter Two

Leaving the lake and the stone causeway that connected Ticca's island with the mainland behind, Aju'an lead the warriors through the borders of the reedy swamp and up into the higher land around Shaden Falls. At first the band traveled easily, excited to be on the trail at last. They called out rude jokes to one another, both human and Warlinga joining in the banter. Over the Sorins both lizardmen and humans had gained respect for one another, and a rough camaraderie had developed among them.

After the noonday rest the trail worsened and the teasing stopped. Everyone settled down to the grim hardships of the climb. On this side of the falls the land had fishered into barren gray canyons whose inky depths rarely saw the sun.

As they climbed to the portage, the trail wound its way over gravel-strewn slopes and along rocky cliffs that loomed over the foaming water. The Shaden Portage was a nightmare, as Aju'an had said. Narrow, and treacherous, it demanded all the Warlinga and the Loti's skill. In places where the ice hadn't melted, a careless step could have meant a deadly fall into the river below. Along other segments of the path, where the sun had melted the ice, greasy, ankle-deep mud also threatened to fling them into the canyon.

It was rough country, every inch of Dunnagh's body could attest to that by the end of the day. Sliding off Mashen's back that first evening, he would have fallen to the ground if the Loti hadn't steadied him.

Leaning against Mashen's flank a thin smile curved his lips as he watched some of the others having a little trouble walking as well. His long, bony legs sticking out an odd angle, Ross walked as if he had Fi'ac's shaggy barrel still between his thighs. The freckle-faced Oglas wasn't doing much better, nor were Joan Ellis, Harris or Marti.

"Are you all right, Kashallan," Mashen asked.

Dunnagh nodded. "I will be; just give me a moment. My legs haven't remembered what they were made for yet."

"I could carry you over to those rocks and—"

"I'm fine; don't fuss—see." Dunnagh stepped away from the Loti and plastered what he hoped was a reassuring smile on his face. His legs still felt a bit rubbery, but he didn't want to tell the anxious youth that. Mashen was so nervous about the great responsibility he'd been given that he probably wouldn't sleep well, in spite of his tiredness, if he thought the Kashallan's discomfort was somehow his fault.

Dunnagh glanced anxiously over to where Ngeal and Arishim were being untied and lifted off their mounts by two of Aju'an's hunters. He should go check on them. He slapped Mashen companionably on the back. "Come on; let's go see how the Ima and clan elder Arishim liked their first day of travel."

They'd stopped to camp in a sun-warmed hollow walled off by a sheer stone cliff and thorn scrub. The sun was behind the cliff, the long russet Renewal twilight bathing the ridges in a bloody afterglow. Below in the purple canyon, the river boomed, churned into an ice blue froth by the massive boulder strewn along its path.

It was getting cold again. Two of the Warlinga gathered deadfalls for a fire, while another and a couple Loti collected water in polli-plastic jugs from a seep among the rocks.

When he and Mashen approached the women, they were seated on the moss. Amril knelt beside Ngeal, a flask of water and a bowl in his hand. Arishim was leaning her head against the rock-face, her eyes closed. Deep grooves of weariness furrowed the lines around her mouth and nose.

Dunnagh-Tani sat down beside her, leaned back against the same rock and took her hand. Arishim opened her eyes and glance down at his hand as he formed the link. "I'm all right, Ce'awn, just a little tired. I'll be fine after I rest a while."

<<She's not fine,>> Tani said into Dunnagh's mind. <<But she isn't in as bad of condition as I feared. I'll give her a restorative, and something to ease the aches of riding, and she should sleep well tonight.>>

<<Mm, that's good to know, Shalla, I hope Ngeal has fared as well. I suppose that if we have to send them back, this is as good a time as any to find it out.>>

A soft mental chuckle, <<Ima Ngeal would have to be very ill indeed to let us do that, Kasha, I wouldn't count on it.>>

The travelers ate a hasty meal of dried meat and masa cakes, then curled up in their blankets to sleep. No one felt like lingering over the tiny fire to talk. Aju'an would have them up before first light and on the trail as soon as there was enough light to travel.

NATHAN TIGHTENED HIS fur cloak around his shoulders and peered down into the camp. There wasn't much to see; several dark lumps huddled together near the waning fire or up against the rock wall at the far end of the hollow. He yawned, wishing his sentry duty was over so he could get some sleep himself.

There was little danger of them being discovered by Enaju's hunting packs this early in the Renewal, but there were other predators, equally dangerous, that would have awakened from their Sorin hibernation by now. Ravenous, they would be looking for a meal, and could present a problem if the warriors were caught off guard.

"Stay awake, sweet cheeks," Marti cooed, as she passed him on her way to the privy hole. She gave him a lazy smile, her fine white teeth a sharp contrast against her warm brown skin. He grunted but refused to rise to the bait. Would the woman ever give up?

Big boned and as tall as many of the men, she was a woman in whom the feminine attributes had reached the proportions of a Valkyrie. Heavy-breasted and wide-hipped. she had strong facial features, a halo of curly dark hair and a booming laugh. She wore an air of predatory sensuality about her that both attracted and repelled most men.

Commander Tizu had picked her for this mission because she'd been partnered up as mentor to Aju'an's sister Chelka. The two women worked well together, and had formed a loose friendship that benefited them both;

but if she was going to start pestering him again, he wished Tizu would have kept her back at the keep.

Not far from the rock where he perched, two figures huddled together, making his heart lurch. Dunnagh was down there and his "wife." He listened to the low-voiced murmur of their conversation. Amril was urging him to finish his bowl of tea and get some rest. Dunnagh was telling him to stop fussing—he was all right, but Nathan guessed that he secretly was enjoying the attention. He was like that—always pretending to hate pampering, but purring like a big cat when you ignored his protests and gave him what he really wanted.

He watched the two curl up together under a single blanket, and a wave of longing came over him so strong that he could hardly breathe. Dunnagh was his dearest friend; they'd grown up together. They'd sworn the oath of the Ca'Companachda (battle companions) and those emotional ties had endured even after their physical relationship had ended a few years back. Dunnagh had been the only one there for him when his family died, and no matter how many other lovers they each had or where they'd traveled, they'd always been close.

They'd been close, until Bennett's ship was destroyed and they'd been stranded on Timorna. Dunnagh had taken up this kashallan bond thing, and now was married—three times over, and though he constantly assured Nathan that it made no difference to how he felt about him; there *was* a difference.

They were never alone together any more. Even when there was only the two of them, there was always the symbiont, like a wedge between them. And with each responsibility laid upon him in his role as the Kashallan the gap grew even wider.

For a time Tessa had been there for Nathan. She'd helped to relieve the emptiness after Dunnagh became the Kashallan; but when she became the host for the demon spirit things changed. He'd clung on to their relationship at first, hoping it would get better—hating what the demon was doing to them both—yet too afraid of the loneliness to end it. But at last that decision had been taken out of his hands, and she was gone, too.

Gods, Dunnagh, he thought, *what a tangled mess it all is*. No matter how much he wanted to resume their former closeness he resisted Tani's eager invitations, because it was all too crazy, and somebody was going to get hurt. But it was so hard.

When the symbiont looked at him with Dunnagh's warm blue eyes and gave him that sweet inviting look of Dunnagh's, that look that made his heart melt, he wanted to say, "to the black abyss with everything." If he could just take Dunnagh in his arms taste, that full ripe mouth and—

A hand on his arm startled him out of his reverie. He jerked his arm away and swiveled round. Marti was standing over him, her white teeth gleaming. "You could have got yourself shot coming up on me like that," he muttered.

She gave him a low throaty laugh and sat down, uninvited, beside him. "Nah, I got excellent reflexes. I would have jumped to the side if you'd reached for your sidearm."

Nathan grunted and returned his attention to the hollow below them, trying to ignore her. He wished she'd go away and leave him alone, but he knew from past experience that the more he fussed at her the bolder she became.

They sat without speaking for a long time, each listening to the distant roar of the falls. The night breeze ebbed and flowed around them. The surrounding countryside was quiet; a few snores drifted up to them from the sleeping camp. Nathan resumed his contemplation of the two huddled together under the blanket. Was it only for warmth that they clung together like that?

Why was the thought of him making love to Amril so much more painful than the thought of Dunnagh sharing his bed with Sairsa and Pela? Dunnagh had assured him that it wasn't like that—that he was the only man who he'd ever cared about in that way—and that he'd only married the young priest for Pela.

Watching them sleeping together, Nathan had to be honest with himself, he'd been secretly hoping to have Dunnagh once more alone on this trip—or as much to himself as he could with Tani always there. He sighed, so much for *his* sharing Dunnagh's blanket—and his secret dreams.

"You don't have to sleep alone, you know."

Nathan jumped. Damn he'd forgotten all about the woman, and like a witch, she'd read his thoughts as clear as glass. He sighed again. "Marti, won't you ever give it up. I've told you before, no."

"Yeah, you've told me know before—but that was then, and this is now—so I'm just saying, you don't have to sleep alone."

"I'm not looking to become another notch on your belt, Marti, so the answer is still, no."

Her voice taking on a soft throaty resonance that he'd never heard before, she said, "It wouldn't be like that with you, Nathan, truly."

He grunted, not convinced. "What about your woman? What would Marnez have to say about this?"

She was silent for a long moment, just listening to the river, finally she said, "Like you and Dunnagh, Marnez and me swore the Ca'Companachda Oath, and I hope that will never change between us, but things are different now. Her baby will be born, probably before I get back to Ticca—and then there's her new man Dilwin. Things are just different—you know what I mean, different."

Gods, he did know what she meant. On Timorna, everything was different—and there was no going back to what once was—not for any of them.

ON THE OTHER SIDE OF the Shaden River Falls, the tawny land fell away into jagged washes and jumbled rocky hillsides covered with shrubby purple thorn thickets. The slopes weren't as steep on this side of the portage, but it was still very rugged country, and Aju'an pushed the travelers hard, in spite of the terrain. They had no choice—they had to reach Meh'gach in time.

K'San Yargal, Aju'an's father would start for the Capital once the blue snows were gone and the Loti families were escorted back to their holdings to begin the planting. A lot depended on gaining Yargal's assistance with their plans, and it would cause a great deal of trouble if they couldn't reach him in time.

As the days passed the travelers kept up their grueling pace. Grim and determined, the women were a marvel to everyone and had won the respect of the warriors. They rode all day, and camped in the cold and damp without complaint.

He glanced over at Arishim, who was riding her Loti just behind him. Most of her gray braid had come loose from the pinned crown on top of her head. She looked exhausted, the lines of fatigue etched deep into her sallow face. When she saw him studying her, she gave him a crooked smile and looked down, adjusting one of the straps that tied her to the Loti's back.

Dunnagh glanced at his own strapped legs and sighed. Though he put up a fuss every morning when Nathan or Chelka insisted he wear them, he was secretly grateful to lose that argument. After his convalescence these long days of riding had him nearly as exhausted as the women, by the time they camped at night.

He hated to admit it, but Amril was proving to be a welcome partner on their journey. Young and fit, after a Sorin Season exercising with Timma, he was able to care for Ngeal and Arishim in the evening, thus freeing the Kashallan of that chore, so he could rest. He prayed, with every aching muscle in his body that the journey would be over soon. Hopefully they would give him hospitality at Meh'gach so he could rest.

Chapter Three

Aju'an growled deep in his throat, and his tail lashed the ground behind him as he paced. They had arrived in the hollow below his families keep with the rusty twilight. He peered cautiously through the scanty foliage of the tree. Silhouetted against the darkening sky, the high walls of Meh'gach Keep crouched atop the hill. He scowled, tail moving faster. By the Great Hunt Leader, what was keeping Mar so long?

They'd arrived in the late afternoon. Instead of going on to the keep, however, the weary travelers had concealed themselves in a nearby thicket to wait for nightfall. It would be safer if they stayed hidden in the grove, and approached the keep in darkness, Aju'an reasoned. His cloaked and hooded charges would be less likely to cause an outcry in the gloom.

He was well aware of how his family would view the strangers, unless properly prepared for the first contact. They would take one look at their hairless, flat alien faces and want to kill them. Umwira Mutant. That's what they would think—that's what he himself had thought, when first he saw the people from the stars that called themselves, the Speir'dina.

His tail raised tiny dust devils in his agitation. Ugly mutants from the Ghostlands—enemy. But they were not mutants or enemies. These creatures come down from the sky could host the sacred Khutani's symbiont children. They were his people's salvation—and it was up to him to keep this first bonded pair, the Kashallan alive, even if that meant killing some of his own kin to do it.

After some further discussion with the Kashallan and Nathan, Aju'an decided to send his cousin Mar in as a scout. He was to alert the keep to the fact that Aju'an and the pack would be arriving soon. But he also had instructions to find out as much as he could about what had gone on in the fortress over the Sorins while Aju'an and his hunting pack had been at Ticca.

If his father, Yargal was there, Mar was to ask him to come out to the grove, for a talk with his son. If he wasn't there, Mar would have to decide for himself what to do in that case.

In spite of the weather and the terrain, they had made the journey to Meh'gach quicker than Aju'an had believed possible. Atop the Loti peasant's backs, the strangers and the old priestess, Ngeal, were indeed able to keep up with his hunting pack of warriors as Ticca's Hunt Leader, Tizu had promised him. They were all tired, but they had made it to Meh'gach just as the last stubborn patches of snow were melting away.

Aju'an doubted if his family had left yet for Riath. With some luck, maybe his father would have waited to hear from him before sending Ngeal's ill-fated message on to the Capital. He prayed it was so, but dared not depend on it. Yargal had always been scrupulous about doing his duty, as he saw it, and a message directed to the High Matri would warrant his immediate attention.

Mar was supposed to have returned to them with news before now. What if something had gone wrong? He fingered the Speir'dina machete at his hip; would he be forced to defend the Kashallan against his own kin? By the Great Hunt Leader, where *was* the man—

"Aju'an, sit down, and stop fretting," Chelka hissed, her patience finally snapping. "If there's anyone up on the wall, you'll only draw attention to this thicket with your pacing."

Aju'an gave his twin sister and irritated grunt, but he did as she suggested, and sat down on a rock beside her.

Chelka sat as composed as a picture in a book. Her stone-bladed spear lay by her feet and a woman warrior's bone-scaled apron covered her lap. She'd come on this trip as one of the Kashallan's personal guards—over Aju'an's protests.

The Kashallan owed her a great debt for saving his womenfolk; so he had agreed without hesitation when she defied her brother's wishes and asked for the assignment. She certainly was competent enough, so there were no grounds to refuse her, but Aju'an was afraid that her presence would only make more trouble for them when their father learned of it.

Unable to help himself, Aju'an still fidgeted. He hated to admit it, but Chelka was right, the trees had barely begun to leaf; it might be possible for a sentry atop the wall to detect them in this grove if they weren't careful. And if his father or Fergannal sent a hunting pack to investigate, well, their presence in here would be hard to explain, even without the Speir'dina and Ngeal.

"K'San," the Speir'dina, Oglas said in a low voice, "there's two Warlinga with a lantern coming around the side of the wall on the right. I think they're heading our way."

Aju'an leapt up and stepped closer to the edge of the thicket, peering out into the gloom. "That's probably Mar, but who's with him?" a low voice asked at his elbow.

Aju'an started. He had been so intent on the approaching figures that he hadn't heard the Kashallan and Nathan approach. He peered out into the dimness once more. They were closer now; he was almost sure—yes. . . . His head crest drooped, and he sighed. It wasn't his father as he'd hoped. "The other one is my father's Hunt Leader, Fergannal."

Voicing Aju'an's own fear, Nathan asked, "Does that mean San Yargal has already left for Riath?"

"I don't know, San Nathan, but I hope not," Aju'an murmured, his heart sinking.

"No point in speculating; they'll be here soon enough," the Kashallan said, "We had better follow the plan we talked about earlier, and conceal ourselves until you find out what's going on."

"Yes, Dunnagh-Tani, that would be most wise."

Nathan gave a low-voiced command, and the Speir'dina and the Avairei covered themselves with their cloaks, and along with the tired Loti, faded into the darker shadows under the trees. With a last reassuring word, the Kashallan joined them, leaving the Warlinga to greet the newcomers.

Aju'an watched them go, with a troubled heart. Where was his father? He felt Chelka rise and come to stand beside him. The tip of her tail twitched with nervousness, but she gave him an encouraging smile nonetheless. His head crest rose in gratitude. Convincing Fergannal wasn't going to be easy, and they both knew it. Around him the Warlinga of his hunting pack fanned out, tense and alert. Saying a silent prayer, he stepped forward to meet the Hunt Leader and Mar.

As they came into the grove, Mar called out a cheery greeting; but to Aju'an's sensitive ears, his voice sounded strained. "It's me, cousin. Your father isn't in the keep at the moment, so I have brought Hunt Leader Fergannal to speak with you about our guests."

FERGANNAL'S HEAD CREST rose in relief as Aju'an and his sister stepped into the small circle of light made by the lantern he carried. Thank the Great Hunt Leader, they were safe; all during the Sorins, he had been so worried.

When Yargal returned from Riath and found his two youngest children, along with one of the keep's best hunting packs, gone to Ticca with the storms due any day, he had almost torn Fergannal to pieces in his fury. When he calmed down enough to listen to reason, however, he conceded that after reading Ngeal's message, sending reinforcements to Ticca was important.

If Aju'an chose to take on that task himself, the Hunt Leader had had no choice but to let the headstrong young fool do what he would. In spite of that, Fergannal had felt his K'San's displeasure throughout the Sorins, and was glad to see the pair safely come home.

Angry now in his relief, he said, "Young Aju'an, it is well that you have wasted no time in returning to us after the storms. Your father has been worried—and is very angry with you for taking your sister on such a dangerous journey. He will want to talk with you as soon as he returns."

"Where is my father, Hunt Leader?" Aju'an interrupted. "Has he gone on to Riath so soon?"

Irritated to be cut off in mid-rant, Fergannal blinked, then, shifting his attention to Aju'an's question, he grumbled, "No, he's not gone to Riath. He's out with your brother and some of the packs, hunting the vistri. He should be back any day now."

"Vistri? But why would he want to do that?" His head crest lifted. "Ah, I remember that pack of vermin. We saw where they attacked and savagely killed a Loti family on our way to Ticca. I recall thinking at the time that something would have to be done about the beasts first thing in the Renewal. Evidently father felt the same, and has taken charge of the hunt."

Beside him Chelka breathed a sigh of relief. "That was a terrible thing, Fergannal, truly. I'm glad father is seeing to their destruction."

"Yes, it was, Child; something that you should never have had to witness." Fergannal said, giving Aju'an another angry look. Then, resuming his interrupted scolding he said, "Young Aju'an, what is all this nonsense about important guests—and why are you out here in the dark, instead of coming to the gate?

"This is most childish and dangerous. Did you think to forgo your father's wrath by sending Mar in to spy things out for you?" The Hunt Leader snorted. "Well, it will do you no good when Yargal finds out—"

"Fergannal, enough," Aju'an snapped. "I will explain to my father when it becomes necessary. Until then I will remind you to have a care when speaking to me. I am not a child to be scolded by you any longer."

Fergannal opened his mouth then closed it again with a snap. There was a note of authority in Aju'an's voice that had not been there when he left Meh'gach before the Sorins.

Chelka whispered , "Aju'an, please."

He glanced at her sharply, then, softening his tone, he addressed the old Hunt Leader again. "Forgive me, Fergannal. I did send Mar in to find out the news, but not to evade my father's punishment, as you implied. I didn't know about Chelka's leaving the keep with old Overn before it happened. They met up with us after we were too far from home to turn back.

"I saw that vistri kill, and I felt it would not have been wise to split up the pack to escort her and the old man home. If my father is angry with me for taking her —well, that will have to be settled between us. I am sorry that he and you were worried, and I will talk to him about it when I see him. But that isn't my reason for being cautious about entering the keep—"

"If that isn't your reason, then I assume you are referring to these mysterious 'guests' Mar mentioned."

"In a way, yes."

"And what kind of guests are these that you fear to bring them to your father openly—when you know as well as I that, under the laws of hospitality, K'San Yargal wouldn't refuse bed and food to any decent traveler? What is this *really* about, San Aju'an?"

Aju'an sighed. "It's just that I have some concern about their welcome before I have a chance to speak to my father."

Fergannal flattened his head crest, his red eyes glowed with outrage. "I am your father's representative, in his absence. Are you trying to insult me? Of course we will welcome them."

"That is most agreeable news, Hunt Leader," a cool voice from the shadows said. "But Aju'an's caution is commendable under the circumstances. Such a generous welcome might not apply to me and my companions without some prior explanation."

Startled, Fergannal swung round as three cloaked and hooded figures stepped into the lamp light. One was short, probably an Avairei, but the other two were almost as tall and bulky as Warlinga—though he doubted that they were. Something about the way they carried themselves was different.

When they were close enough to be illuminated by the lantern, the two taller figures threw back their hoods and allowed him to have a good look at them. At the sight of those flattened, ugly faces, Fergannal snarled a curse, and leaped to attack.

Anticipating his response, several pairs of strong young arms grabbed him and wrestled him to the ground. He fought them until he was winded, then cursed them with a single-minded intensity. "Let me up you pack of half-bred Begta," he roared. "What by all the Gods, do you think you're doing?"

One of the cloaked figures motioned for the Warlinga to let him up. Fergannal rose, quivering with rage. Red eyes blazing, he glared at the stranger, then at Aju'an, but made no move to renew his assault.

"That's better," the stranger said. "I'm sorry my hunters had to do that, but unfortunately, I am well aware of the effect our alien Speir'dina features have on Timornans who don't know us."

"Fergannal," Aju'an said, "your reaction just now is exactly why I wanted to send in Mar for information, and to talk to my father, before we came to the main gate."

Tail tip flicking, Fergannal folded his arms across his chest. He looked at each of the men surrounding him, his lip curling with angry scorn. Returning his attention to Aju'an once more he flattened his head crest, but remained obstinately silent, waiting for Aju'an to explain further.

"Fergannal," Chelka said, "I would like you to meet Dunnagh-Tani, the first of the new kashallan-bonded. To his right is his Speir'dina kinsman San Nathan, and the other person beside them is Ima Ngeal Maveth."

At the mention of Ticca's matriarch's name, Fergannal gaped. Ima Ngeal—here? His eyes flicked around the grove. There were a few Loti peasants huddled by the main tree, but where was the Ima's covered litter and entourage? Fergannal's head crest rose in horror. Was this bedraggled old woman Ima Ngeal? Had she come alone with these strangers and the hunting pack? How was that possible?

But if Ngeal was with Aju'an and his sister, these strangers must be some of the outlaws that they had been warned about. As Aju'an suspected before he'd left to rescue Ticca, the Ima Sagas and her band of Umwira mutants must have sought refuge at Ticca. But why, if he had been in time to aid Ticca's defenders and capture the outlaws—why had Aju'an brought them here, instead of going straight on to Riath?

Then he reeled as the truth hit him like a hammer blow. These demon Umwira wizards weren't prisoners—they were free, and Ngeal, Aju'an and his sister must have been ensorcelled by them.

As if reading his mind, Aju'an said, "It's not what you think, Uncle. We haven't been tricked or put under a spell by some Umwira magic. The Speir'dina aren't mutant Umwira; they are the new host species. They were brought to our world from the stars by the Khutani Makers for their symbiont children."

Fergannal shook his head in disbelief. Kashallans, people from the stars—the boy was a fool to believe such absurd notions. How could Aju'an be so naïve? And, more to the point, how was he going to save his young charges from these demons?

"You don't believe us, do you, Hunt Leader," Nathan challenged.

Fergannal glared at the wizard defiantly. "No, I don't believe you—why should I? This is all a bunch of lies and trickery used to take advantage of young Aju'an and his sister. You may have ensorcelled them into believing your fancies, but I am not so gullible." Then, ignoring all of them, he turned to Ngeal. "Ima, are you all right?"

The Avairei were normally a slim-built people; but after the hardships of the last few days, Ngeal seemed gaunt and shrunken, her grizzled fur grayer, her braided mane tangled with dried leaves and other debris. She looked up at Fergannal with tired brown eyes. "Yes, Hunt Leader, I am all right. I am tired from our journey, but—"

Then, catching his meaning, she shook her head and gave him a sad smile. "You misunderstand, Warlinga. I am not being held prisoner by these people, nor is San Aju'an. I have come along with the Kashallan to speak to K'San Yargal. I want to try, if I can, to prevent a terrible tragedy from befalling all of us. It is as the children claim—the Speir'dina aren't Umwira, but blessed by the Holy Ones themselves."

When Fergannal remained unconvinced, Aju'an sighed. Ignoring the older man, he turned his attention back to the Kashallan. "It is as I feared, Holy One. If my father's Hunt Leader is any indication of our reception here, I fear we should remain outside the keep until my father has returned."

"Mm, perhaps." Then turning to Fergannal, the Kashallan continued, "I don't really care if you believe that I am a demon from the north, or the first kashallan as I claim, because it isn't you but your K'San who we must convince. Is that not so?

"I think the question that needs to be answered here and now is: whether you will uphold the laws of hospitality, in Yargal's name, and give us protection and shelter. Later, when K'San Yargal returns, questions of truth or trickery can be sorted out, hmm? We want no trouble. I give you my word on that. All we want is for him to hear our story before we continue on to Riath."

Fergannal's head crest rose in surprise at that. Going on to Riath indeed—did the demon take him for a total fool? He glared at the strange creature angrily, looking for the first time into his eerie blue eyes. He shuddered and dropped his gaze—*Umwira Filth!* What to do? If he said no, these outlaws and their blue-eyed leader might kill him, then leave with Aju'an, Chelka, and the Ima still under their magic spell.

But if he allowed them into the keep in Yargal's absence, what kind of harm would they do to Meh'gach's people before Yargal's return? By the Great Hunt Leader, what should he do?

"All right," Fergannal grumbled at last. "You have a point—this *is* something that needs my K'San's attention. It is obvious to me that over the Sorin Season you have done some foul magic upon my young kinsman to addle his wits. What guarantee do I have that if I give you the hospitality of Meh'gach, you won't try some of your tricks on us?"

The Kashallan gave him a feral grin, his sharp white teeth gleaming in the lantern light. "None. And for that matter, what guarantee do I have that the moment we are within your walls, you won't abandon your honor and try to kill us?"

The Hunt Leader snarled, baring his own teeth and flattening his head crest at the implied insult.

"I meant no offense, Hunt Leader; I am merely making a point," the Kashallan assured him. "We shall have to trust one another, do you not agree?"

"Dievris wouldn't like this," Nathan murmured in a low voice, placing his hand unconsciously on his sidearm.

The Kashallan shot him a silencing look, then returned his attention to Fergannal. In a voice as cold as ice, he demanded, "So, Hunt Leader Fergannal, what is it to be? Do you offer us hospitality, or do we make other plans?"

"Fergannal, please," Chelka begged. "I'm tired and cold, and I could use a bath. The Ima and the other elder with us have had a long hard journey, as well. Give the Kashallan your word that we will all be safe, and let's go back to the keep. I'm starving."

Yes, no matter what his personal opinion was, he would have to do it, Fergannal thought. For the sake of his K'San's children and Ima Ngeal, he would have to give these outlaws safe conduct, food, and shelter. Yargal would never forgive him if something were to happen to his favorite daughter or the Ima.

He nodded. "All right." Bowing grimly to Aju'an and the Kashallan, he intoned, "I offer you the protection and hospitality of Meh'gach. You have my word of honor: no harm will come to any of you while Meh'gach is in my care. When my K'San comes back, however, it will be up to him to decide what to do about you."

The Kashallan bowed. "Fair enough. Shall we go?"

Grimly, Fergannal nodded. "One other thing." At Aju'an's growl of disapproval, he smiled, then addressing the Kashallan directly, he added, "To prevent any *misunderstandings*, as you put it, you must agree to be confined and guarded while within the keep—until my K'San returns."

"What are you saying, Hunt Leader? This is outrageous—" Aju'an spluttered.

Ah, Aju'an, you will thank me for this later. When you are taken away from this wizard, and once more among your own kin, I hope that this demon's power over you will wane.

Laying a hand on Aju'an's shoulder, the Kashallan silenced him. "In this matter I agree with the Hunt Leader, so calm yourself, Aju'an." Turning back to Fergannal, he said, "You're right. It would not be wise for my Speir'dina kin and me to wander around Meh'gach, until we have had a chance to speak to K'San Yargal.

"I consent to your terms for my kinsmen and myself. But what of Ima Ngeal, our Loti companions, and my hunting pack? It is important to me to know what will be done with the rest of my people, if I am to be confined and can't see to their welfare."

His people—his hunting pack—mutant filth! We shall see about that. I must have a talk with old Neyal to see if there is some counter spell he can use to break the sorcery this creature has placed upon my kinsmen and the good Ima.

"The Ima will be treated with all possible respect, of course," he said indignantly. "As to the hunting pack, they belong here; they are free to come and go as they choose. And as for the Loti, they may sleep and eat in the servants' quarters. It is of no concern to me what peasants do."

"All right," Aju'an said, rounding on the older man. "I'm not sure what this is all about, Fergannal, but if the Kashallan is to be confined and guarded, the guarding will be done by my pack, or we go nowhere. And just where had you planned to keep them?

"If it's a cell in the lower keep—think again. I will not allow you to disgrace our house by offering such an insult to one of the sacred Khutani and its host. So just what do you have in mind, hmm?"

A cell was exactly where he had planned to house his unwanted "guests," and damn the young man for being so quick about figuring it out.

"They can stay in my suite," Chelka said into the tense silence.

Fergannal's head crest rose in outrage. "Sa Chelka, no that would not be acceptable."

"Of course it would," Chelka said reasonably. "My quarters are spacious enough to fit all of them. In there, we can offer the Speir'dina some of the comforts, at least, to which they are entitled. And it is away from the part of the keep where the hunting packs are housed, so there will be less chance of trouble."

"B-but where will you stay, my Sa?" Fergannal spluttered.

Chelka shrugged. "Oh, I'll find somewhere. Don't worry about me."

"But—"

"Yes, an excellent idea, Little Sister," Aju'an beamed.

"My San, no! This would not be seemly," Fergannal roared, his head crest flattening.

Aju'an grinned and folded his arms across his chest. "Would you rather it was *my* suite?" he countered. "It is much closer to the main part of the keep, but I'm sure we can arrange some explanation as to why a guard will be posted outside my door, even when I am elsewhere in the keep."

Giving Aju'an a black look, Fergannal started to protest, then decided it was pointless and conceded his defeat. "Very well, it will be as you wish; they can stay in Chelka's suite."

He gave the Kashallan one last angry look, then motioned for them to follow him back down the trail to the keep.

As they left the grove, Fergannal hoped that Yargal's hunt for the vistri would be speedily concluded. He was needed here more than he was needed to supervise the slaughter of the vermin.

Chapter Four

By the time they reached the tiny side gate to the keep, an evening fog had rolled in, adding to the concealment afforded by the dark. Hidden among the Loti and Warlinga of Aju'an's pack the Speir'dina walked into Meh'gach unnoticed.

Except for the sentries by the gate, Meh'gach's inhabitants were eating the evening meal. The smells of roasted meat and fried mushrooms wafted out to greet the weary travelers from the outdoor kitchen at the far end of the courtyard. Flickering torchlight spilled out the half-opened doors of the hall turning the mist in the courtyard into a luminous amber cloud.

Inside the hall they could hear the clink of bowls and the boisterous shouts of the men as they joked and boasted with one another. It was the Renewal Season, and an air of excited expectation seemed to permeate everything.

To avoid drawing unwanted attention to the part of the keep where the Speir'dina would be staying, most of the pack went off to the main hall to have their meal with the rest of the household. They had orders to eat and gather news, then report back later when a guard schedule would be drawn up. They were also warned both by Aju'an and Fergannal to say nothing about their stay at Ticca,

While one of Aju'an's men took the Loti to the servant's quarters, Chelka led her cloaked and hooded guests to her suite via the back stair. This early in the renewal season, the keep was still in transition; its inhabitants in the process of moving from the underground rooms they used during the Sorins, to the airy quarters above ground they occupied the rest of the year.

After a hasty conversation between Aju'an and herself, Chelka decided to take her guests to her underground rooms. No one liked the idea of being cooped up underground again, but as Fergannal confirmed, her furniture and other belongings were still there, so those rooms at least could be readied to receive them without much fuss.

And, they would offer an added bit of safety, since most of the Warlinga would have already moved into the upper keep, and only a few servants would be traveling through those dingy halls. Fergannal agreed with her plan when told, but trailed after them nonetheless.

The keep had been alerted by Mar to the imminent arrival of Aju'an and his pack, so there was less confusion than might have been expected at their arrival. The Speir'dina, Amril, and Ngeal waited in the shadows of an unfurnished room near Chelka's suite while servants were hastily summoned by Aju'an to bring wash water, extra bedding, and food for their elusive company.

The servants were intensely curious about the identity of the mysterious visitors. But Fergannal gave strict orders that no one was to enter Chelka's suite until K'San Yargal returned. Once the visitors were installed in the suite, all needed supplies were to be left outside the door, for the guards to bring into their guests. The Loti were confused by these odd instructions, but they bowed and swore to do as he commanded. By morning, of course, the strange goings on would be the talk of the keep, but it couldn't be helped.

Only after all the servants were gone, did the Hunt Leader allow the weary travelers to come out of hiding. Though hastily readied for occupancy the suite would do, Aju'an thought. The lamps were lit, their green flames illuminating the brightly colored tapestries that hung on Chelka's walls. All these weavings were done by his Aunt and the women of the accavett; they were of excellent quality, and would do honor to their clan. The large braided rug that covered most of the room's stone floor, was thick and well swept; it would keep their poor, naked, Speir'dina feet warm.

Chelka's neglected loom and other unwanted pieces of furniture were hastily removed to make room for the pile of moss-filled mattresses and blankets that were stacked against the far wall. A large table from an abandoned room down the hall had been placed near the center of the rug, and loaded with steaming bowls of hot stew, fresh baked masa root cakes, and watered-down mushroom beer.

To Aju'an's relief his guests greeted these preparations with tired murmurs of appreciation. But Aju'an himself was too nervous for his guests' comfort to leave. Along with Mar and Chelka, he stayed to supervise their settling in.

In spite of all entreaties to the contrary, Ima Ngeal refused to take accommodations elsewhere in the keep. Secretly fearing perhaps for the Kashallan's safety if she left him, she said firmly that "It was her duty to stay with the Kashallan," and no one could persuade her otherwise.

Finally it was agreed that Ngeal and Arishim would have the comfort and privacy of Chelka's bedchamber, while the Kashallan and the rest slept in the outer room.

Aju'an breathed an exhausted sigh when at last his guests sat down eagerly to eat their first hot meal in days. Feeling suddenly exhausted, now that things were settled to his satisfaction, Aju'an looked longingly at the outer door.

Catching his eye, Chelka mouthed, "Go ahead; I'm on first watch."

He gave her a slight nod, then went over to the Kashallan and bowed. "If everything is to your liking, Kashallan, I should go see to some other matters."

Dunnagh-Tani looked up, then set down his spoon. "Everything's fine, Aju'an, so don't worry about us. I doubt if your father's Hunt Leader will bother us tonight. And you have assigned Mar and a couple of the lads to stay here in case we need anything. You go on and get some rest yourself."

He gave Aju'an a sly smile, his eyes suddenly alive with a secret amusement. "But before you leave—I have a little something for you." Turning to Amril, he asked, "Would you find my gift to Aju'an in my pack and bring it to me, please."

Setting down his bowl, Amril nodded. Walking over to the packs stacked against the wall, he rummaged around inside one of them for a moment and returned carrying a tightly wrapped bundle. Handing it to the Kashallan, he smiled at the Warlinga shyly.

"In spite of all that has happened since the night when we shared that fine lamra brandy together, I did not forget the promise I made you, Aju'an," the Kashallan said, holding out the bundle.

The conversation around the room fell silent as all eyes turned to the Warlinga. Puzzled, Aju'an took it, then, at the Kashallan's urging, he unwrapped the heavy cloth. When the content of the bundle was revealed, Aju'an stared in stupefaction at what he held. In his hands lay a beautifully carved marriage bottle. He looked up, eyes blinking.

"There is more red kavay that my cousins made for Meh'gach in our packs," the Kashallan said, "but as I promised, I made this for you myself."

Aju'an's hand began to tremble. Hastily he tucked the precious flask into his belt before he dropped it. By the Great Hunt Leader, Tani had done this for him—with everything else there had been to think about and plan. "Thank you, Holy One."

"Best wishes to you and your bride, my friend. Now go on—it's getting late. We'll be fine I'm sure."

Aju'an bowed then headed for the door. As he reached it, Nathan called out, "Hey, Aju'an, don't forget to sleep at some point tonight. We've had a long day, remember?" Aju'an stared, then laughed as he took his meaning. He opened the door, a chorus of best wishes following him down the hall.

LATIYA BENT OVER HER embroidery hoop, trying to hide her distress from the others. The sunroom was still warm from the day's heat, because the heavy shutters on the big windows were closed to keep out the night's chill. Bright lamplight flooded the large room. The day's work was over, the massive looms were pushed against the wall. The children were put to bed, and now the women of the keep sat on padded stools drinking spiced tea, or reclined on comfortable cushions on the rug in the center of the floor playing a board game.

The women chatted excitedly about the day's news, but Latiya paid them little attention. When the servants brought them the evening meal, they reported to the accavett that Aju'an and his pack were expected at any time. She had been ecstatic hearing the news. Desperately she had hoped to see him at least one last time, before K'San Yargal took her back to her family.

Latiya had wanted to make herself beautiful for him—even though she feared, deep in her heart, that it was hopeless. But in spite of her fears, she secretly went to her small room, washed, and then opened her clothes chest, her tail flicking nervously. She looked longingly at her bridal apron. It was a masterpiece of bright colors and intricately woven geometric designs. A Warlinga woman's bridal apron was something to treasure, and pass on to her eldest daughter when her time to marry came.

This one had been handed down in her family for three generations. She fingered the rich fabric. A tear splashed onto one of its russet diamonds. She sniffed; she didn't dare put it on, the others would look at her with their pitying eyes and talk about her when they thought she couldn't hear.

Latiya picked up another apron from the chest. This one was her second-best, and one she had made herself. The apron's bold patterns of yellow and blue spirals were a little fancy for the evening gathering; wearing it would cause some talk, but she didn't care. Its bright colors cheered her, and she needed to feel good about something.

When she went back to the sunroom to wait for him, her heart was pounding. She hoped Aju'an would come to her straight away, but he hadn't. And now—well, she wasn't sure she could bear it if he did come. Latiya knew he had returned—one of the older children came with the news. But when Aju'an failed to appear, she suspected that someone must have told him about the plans to send her back. Maybe it would be best to leave it like this.

They said their goodbyes before he went to Ticca—best just to leave it at that. It was late—she should stop trying to pretend to herself that things would be different than they were. She should go to bed.

Startled out of her reverie, Latiya jumped, pricking her finger, as a loud knock came at the Accavett's outer door. Muttering under her breath in annoyance, K'Sa Eilith, Aju'an's aunt, who had been mistress here since Aju'an's mother died, hauled her bulk off her stool, retied her massive apron, and went to answer it.

Latiya froze, her embroidery dropping to the floor unnoticed. "Aju'an!" she breathed. Getting to her feet, she started towards him, ignoring the pitying stares of the other women in the room. He saw her at about the same instant, and head crest high and smiling, he moved towards her.

Before they could touch or say anything to each other, Eilith stepped between them, putting out her hand to stop her nephew's progress. "Aju'an, no. It's late, and this isn't seemly."

Startled, Aju'an stopped, his head crest dipping in surprise. "Greetings, Aunt, I know it's late, but we just got in not long ago—and then I had responsibilities—but I came as quickly as I could." He gave her a puzzled look. "And besides, what matter the hour Latiya is my wife. It isn't improper behavior for me to come to her after such a long time away—"

Eilith shook her head, her eyes compassionate, but her voice firm. "Aju'an, my child, I'm sorry—I wish Yargal had been here when you returned. It should be him that tells you this, not me."

Aju'an glanced from Latiya's stricken face to his aunt's stern one. "What are you talking about, Aunt?" he said, his red eyes suddenly hard. "Latiya is my wife—what could my father possibly have to tell me about that?"

Eilith sighed in resignation. She glanced around at the avidly listening audience. "Come into my quarters where we can talk privately."

Aju'an nodded. Then, before his aunt could send Latiya away, he took her possessively by the arm and headed towards Eilith's room. Eilith sighed again and followed them down the hall.

Inside her living-chamber she motioned them to stools beside her worktable, then sat down heavily herself and faced them. "Aju'an, you should have waited to talk to your father first before coming to the accavett. I didn't want to make a scene out there in front of everyone, but I wish you hadn't come like this, or brought Latiya with you. The poor child has suffered enough as it is."

Aju'an stared at her blankly, his tail twitching with his agitation. "What are you talking about, Aunt? Speak plainly."

"Very well I will. When your father returned from Riath, he brought with him an order from both the High Matri and the Serath clan to bring Latiya back to her family when he returned to the Capital in the Renewal Season."

Aju'an blinked. "What! Why?"

"Aju'an," Eilith said, "don't be dense; I think you know why. The marriage hasn't been consummated. Her family wants her back—and the Khutani feel—"

"The sly old Umwira witch," Aju'an snarled. Face contorted with rage, he sprang to his feet, jaws clenched tight. Trembling violently, he turned his back on them while he fought for control. In a fierce voice, barely above a whisper, he spoke more to himself than the women. "Ah, Enaju, you clever, Clever Old Hag. Sending that message back with my father—and with no red kavay to consummate our marriage, you hoped I would have the exquisite pain of it to torture my soul throughout the Sorins. How very cunning. And what a sweet revenge for my insolence, hmm? Ah, but it didn't work—only my poor love was here to suffer—and you'll pay for that."

"Aju'an, mind your tongue. You are speaking of the high Matri," she snapped. Then, in a gentler tone, "I know that you are quite fond of Latiya, and this is a great shock to you, but that's no reason to talk like that. The High One must have her reasons, and it's not your place to rebel in this matter. Breeding alliances aren't decided by you, or any young person.

"I am sorry for your pain. This whole situation is unfortunate, but perhaps in a while, the sacred Khutani will agree to another match—"

"No!" Turning to face her once more, he repeated, "No. Latiya is my wife, and I will not give her back, because you see the Khutani *do* approve, Aunt."

Taking the marriage flask from his belt, he held it out to show her. "It's only the lying Dingay who don't want this marriage—who want me to suffer. This refusal is nothing more than a cunning way to pay me back for my insolence and make sure I behave myself in future."

Eilith gasped, and stared at the flask, stunned. "Where did you get that?" she demanded.

Aju'an smirked. "From the Khutani—where else?" Then, turning to his beloved, he looked deep into her frightened red eyes as he spoke to both of them. "It was given to me by one of the Khutani who made it personally for us, to bless our union."

"B-but that's impossible! How?" Eilith stammered.

Aju'an removed the stopper, allowing the kavay's rich fragrance to fill the room with its heady promise of desire fulfilled. He re-capped the bottle and handed it to Latiya. "It was a gift—Tani made this for me, as it promised."

Head crest high, eyes feverish, he broke off. The scent of the red kavay still in his nostrils, he stared at his bride with mounting excitement.

"I-I don't understand this," Eilith stammered. "Warlinga talking with the Sacred Ones? How is that possible? The Avairei would never allow—and besides the Dingay aren't denying it to us. Your father brought red kavay back with him from Riath. The priest gave a dosage to Varrod's wife, Ainna, so she could conceive again—but he said the Khutani disapproved of your match."

Her eyes narrowed with suspicion. She glanced at the bottle Latiya held again, and when she spoke, her voice was rough with emotion. "Aju'an, I know you care for this woman, but where did you really get that? If you traded for it with some renegade priest, the Great Hunt Leader alone knows what's actually in it. Don't be a fool!

"You come here with a crazy story about Warlinga talking with Khutani and claim that the High Matri—the High Matri of all people is lying because you can't have your way?" She threw up her hands in despair. "I can understand why my brother is so frustrated with you.

"Will you ever learn? You're going to get yourself—and maybe some of the rest of us killed if you don't stop!" Eilith's scales were turning a dangerous shade of green by the time she finished her diatribe. She sat back, chest heaving. Latiya rose and picked up a leather fan and began waving it in front of the gasping woman.

"There's nothing wrong with the kavay, Aunt," Aju'an said into the silence. "I didn't trade for it with anyone. As hard as it may be for you to believe right now; it was a Khutani gift as I said. I don't know what's been going on here in my absence—and, frankly, right now, Aunt, I'm too tired to puzzle it out. But in the morning you can talk to Ima Ngeal herself; perhaps she can convince you that I'm telling the truth."

"Ima Ngeal! What are you saying?" Eilith cried and sprang to her feet, her massive bulk quivering. "Is the Ima Matri of Ticca here? Why wasn't I told?"

"You'll have to take that up with San Fergannal."

Her eyes hard and head crest flattened, she said, "I will indeed. But where is she?"

"She's staying in Chelka's underground suite." At her appalled look, he smiled. "Don't worry, she's fine where she is—for tonight. She's quartered with the rest of the people that I brought with me from Ticca. Traveling with the pack as she did, the poor woman's exhausted, I'm afraid—but she was determined to come and speak to father, so we had to bring her."

Scandalized, K'Sa Eilith shook her head in bewilderment and sank onto her stool with a thump. Picking up the discarded fan, she began fanning herself again. "But why wasn't I told, and why is she in Chelka's suite? There are plenty of guest rooms here—"

"She wouldn't leave the others; Fergannal was being difficult. I think she was afraid for them, so she refused other accommodations. But she and the other clan elder that came with her are fine, aunt, truly. Chelka and I saw to their needs personally. They've washed and eaten—and I think the Kashallan, or Amril, gave them something to ease their aches from our journey so they can sleep. They'll be fine till morning—you needn't worry."

K'Sa Eilith's tail curled and uncurled on the floor behind her as she studied her nephew for a long moment. There was more to this matter than the young man was saying—a lot more. But she might as well question the door as Aju'an right now; he had other things on his mind tonight.

"I don't know what you're babbling about, or what's going on here, Aju'an, but I will take your advice and not disturb her tonight. And why should the Ima fear for the safety of her traveling companions at Meh'gach? Hunt Leader Fergannal is definitely going to have some explaining to do in the morning."

Aju'an smiled grimly then pulled Latiya up beside him. "Aunt, if you'll excuse us—"

Eilith started to protest, then waved her fan in dismissal. *Let them go.* He had the red kavay, and the marriage contract had been legally signed. Yargal was going to get a surprise when he got back—but the young couple had waited long enough for this night, so why deny them? Suddenly feeling exhausted and a little frightened, she decided to go to bed herself. There would be a lot to see to in the morning.

Chapter Five

"Chelka, get out of my way!" Eilith said. "What is all this nonsense about not allowing me in? Fergannal has been avoiding my inquiries all morning and now you are doing it, too. I want to assure myself that such a distinguished guest as the Ima Matri of Ticca is being well taken care of. And what, by the Holy Mother, is she doing in your suite anyway? Now let me in to see her."

"Aunt Eilith, please," Chelka begged, her body wedged tightly against the tiny crack in the open door. "She's fine, I promise you, we've—"

Tired of Fergannal's evasions and her niece's arguing, Eilith wasted no more time on words. She rammed her ample mass against the door. Caught off guard by her aunt's direct approach, Chelka staggered backward, and Eilith pushed her way into the room. Just inside the door she looked around for Ngeal, and froze.

"Mother!" Mar yelped. Dropping the dice cup he was holding he scrambled to his feet, and sprang to her side. "What are you doing in here?"

Ignoring her son for the moment, Eilith stared at the unsettling tableau before her. There were several people in Chelka's outer chamber—none of whom was Ngeal. The only Avairei in the room was a young Ata dressed, of all things, in an Avairei woman's kilt, and carrying a marriage flask at his waist. Mar and another man from Meh'gach were here, as was Chelka, but what caught and held her attention were several flat-faced creatures the like of which she had never seen before.

At her entrance, everyone in the room stopped what they were doing and watched her with a single-minded intensity. Behind her she heard Chelka close the door. Eilith shuddered at the sound.

One of the strangers was dressed like an Avairei, in kilt and cloak, but the rest were dressed in black clothing of an unfamiliar type. Most had long manes of hair on the top of their heads, twisted into one long braid that hung down their backs. But it was their flat, ugly faces, bare of fur or scales that shocked her most.

Unable to look into their alien eyes, she stared in helpless fascination at their *five-fingered*, naked hands. Umwira Mutants? Her chest heaved, and suddenly she could hardly breathe. By all the Holy Ones in the pools, what were they doing here? Taking a deep breath but looking at no one in particular, Eilith said, "I-I came here to see Ima Ngeal."

After a long pause, the large male with a red mane and startling blue eyes said, "Mar, give your mother a stool to sit on, then bring her a bowl of that fresh tea. Finding us here has been a surprise for her, I think."

"Yes, Kashallan," Mar mumbled. Grabbing a stool from against the wall, he placed it near Blue Eyes, and gently eased his mother down upon it.

K'Sa Eilith sank onto the offered stool gratefully. Her breath still coming in heavy gasps, she kept her attention focused on the blue-eyed male in front of her. Surprise? That was an understatement. If she wasn't trying so hard at the moment to catch her breath, she'd be laughing hysterically. One of the dark-clad strangers placed a warm bowl of tea into her hands. She took it without thinking and drank.

Blue Eyes nodded to himself as he saw her relax, then turned to the Warlinga. "Perhaps one of you lot would care to introduce me to our visitor, hmm?"

Chelka cleared her throat. "This is my aunt, K'Sa Eilith, Kashallan. She is my father's sister, and has been mistress here at Meh'gach since my mother's death."

"Ah, thank you." He rose and gave her a deep bow. "I am Dunnagh-Tani, and I am very glad to make your acquaintance, K'Sa. Seeing us so unexpectedly for the first time has startled you, I'm sure, but let me assure you we are not Umwira, and we mean no one in this keep any harm. I am a healer. I have sworn an oath to my Khutani kin to protect and serve Timorna and her peoples—not try and destroy them."

A healer? Eilith blinked. Not sure she'd understood him, she gave him a noncommittal nod, and took another sip of her tea, stalling for time to compose herself. When she could speak again, she returned to her earlier inquiry. "I understand that Ima Ngeal is here. I wish to assure myself of her welfare, and see if she needs anything."

The Kashallan smiled. "You are a most conscientious hostess. I'm sure the Ima will be honored." He glanced towards Chelka's closed bedroom door. "She is awake, I believe. I had my wife take a tray in to her and clan elder Arishim about an hour ago. She may be up to having company—for a while—but try not to tire her too much.

"As I'm sure you can imagine, our trip across the Shaden River portage was difficult for one of her advanced years. She will need to rest for a few days before she is quite herself, I'm afraid."

"I would still like to see her, if I may."

"Shall I see if she is awake, husband?" the priest in women's clothes offered.

"Yes, please do that, Amril. Tell her K'Sa Eilith would like to see her, if she feels up to a visit."

Amril rose, walked to the bedroom door, knocked then disappeared inside.

Dunnagh-Tani gave her a lopsided smile as he noticed Eilith's shocked expression. "Yes, it's unconventional, but Amril is indeed one of my wives. How that came about is a long story, which I'm afraid will have to wait until another time."

Then he frowned as if another thought had just come to mind. "K'Sa Eilith, I am curious. It was my understanding that Hunt Leader Fergannal didn't wish anyone in the keep to know of our presence here. How did you find out about Ima Ngeal?"

She sighed. "My nephew Aju'an mentioned it, when he came for his wife last night."

The Kashallan chuckled. "Ah, that explains a lot. I had just given him the red kavay gift I made for him, and his mind must have been on other things than being discreet."

"So it was you who gave him the red kavay, but how—"

"Dunnagh-Tani is the first of the new kashallans, Eilith," a familiar voice said from behind her. "These people are not mutants, but the new host race for the Khutani symbionts. Dunnagh here is the first of his kindred to agree to host a child of the pools."

"Ngeal—Ima—how are you?" Eilith bowed, then studied the woman with growing concern. Ngeal had aged quite a bit since she had last seen her. The fur of her face and chest was almost silver, but the stern countenance and determined jaw were the same as she remembered. And yes, she was tired, Eilith could tell that at a glance, as the stranger had warned.

But there was something else wrong—a deep sadness in those dull brown eyes that spoke of her suffering a great tragedy—that had nothing to do with her journey here.

On impulse, Eilith stepped forward and took her hand, feeling her own heart reach out to the troubled woman. "Ngeal, what's wrong? I've no idea what could possibly be so urgent that you had to come here like this. What can I do to help?"

Ngeal grimaced. "It's that obvious, is it? Well, I guess you're right. I am getting too old for this kind of thing, but our news was that important. I had to come." Ngeal opened the door to the bedroom a little wider, and Eilith noticed for the first time a gray-maned, naked-faced female, standing at Ngeal's elbow. She motioned to the bedroom behind her. "Come in, K'Sa Eilith. I'll introduce you to clan elder Arishim, and we can talk."

Eilith nodded, took one last look at the strangers, and followed Ngeal into the bedroom.

When the door was closed behind them, Nathan let out a sigh of relief. "Gods, that was close," he said. "I hope Ngeal can convince her to help us."

"I do too, because I suspect the K'Sa is a force to be reckoned with around here, and it would be just as well to have her on our side."

SOMETIME LATER, ARISHIM and Eilith reemerged from the bedroom. Arishim closed the door firmly behind them and came over to the Kashallan, the Warlinga matron at her heels.

Dunnagh-Tani rose. Addressing Arishim he asked "How is Ima Ngeal, Meldra?" His eyes flicked to the closed bedroom door. "Do I need to go to her?"

Arishim shook her head. "No, I don't think that's necessary, Kashallan. Amril left a sleeping tea for her earlier." She glanced companionably at the Warlinga. "Eilith and I bullied her into taking it, so she'll be asleep in minutes, most like. Check on her later if you feel you need to, but I think all she needs is some rest at the moment."

"Mm, and she's not the only one who perhaps could do with an afternoon nap," he suggested, studying her with a critical eye.

She grimaced then chuckled. "I'm sure you're right—and I will, but first I think K'Sa Eilith may need your help, and we should talk to you about that before I go rest."

"All right then." He motioned them to stools near a small table in the corner farthest from the activity in the room. When they were seated, he smiled his encouragement.

Glancing at the Warlinga, Arishim cleared her throat and began, "Ngeal and I have told Eilith about the new kashallans, and a little about the events that happened at Ticca over the Sorins." She smiled at her companion. "I know it is hard for her to take in all at once, but she has a lot of respect for the Ima, and isn't willing to dismiss the children's trust in us out of hand, as Hunt Leader Fergannal seems to have done. And she has a problem that desperately needs your attention, if you're up to it."

"Problem, eh?" He grimaced then laughed. "First tell me what's needed then I'll know better if I'm up to it."

Eilith hesitated, and glanced around at the men in the room, her tail tip nervously flicking. Coming to some inner decision, she swiveled round on her stool so her back was to them, lowered her voice, and said, "Ima Ngeal assures me that you are not a mutant—that you are a sacred kashallan, and if that be true I do indeed need your help, Holy One." The Kashallan nodded, but remained silent, waiting for her to explain further. Eilith glanced once more at the warriors.

"This is so embarrassing to speak of where men might hear." She turned to Arishim, her eyes pleading for help.

"Ce'awn, it's about Aju'an's brother's wife, Ainna," Arishim explained. "When K'San Yargal came back from Riath he brought with him red kavay—enough to allow Varrod and his wife to have a mating once more.

Ainna has conceived, but the confinement isn't going well, and Eilith would like you to come have a look at her."

"Has the child progressed from the inner passage to the breeding pouch yet?"

"Yes, the mating was at the beginning of the Sorin Season, but the child isn't maturing as it should, in spite of all our care. And lately the mother herself has begun to sicken."

"I see." He fell silent for a long moment, twisting one of his long red braidlets as he considered the problem. At last he said, "I would definitely do my best for the woman, of course, but I have also given my word to Hunt Leader Fergannal that I will not leave these rooms until given permission to by K'San Yargal. Perhaps it could wait, or you could bring the woman to me—"

Eilith shook her head. "Your first suggestion is perhaps not wise. Her condition has worsened in the past few days to the point where I fear for her life. I don't think we can wait. And secondly, *because* of her condition, it would be difficult—and definitely not appropriate for her to come to you." She glanced significantly around at the warriors in the room once more, head crest dipping.

The Kashallan eyed the warriors as well, taking her meaning. Everyone in the room was trying to act natural, and doing a bad job of it. Chelka was standing guard by the door, Nathan was checking over his gear and the dice game had resumed, the players speaking in subdued tones in the opposite corner, but it was clear to him and the women, that they were all straining their ears to listen.

"I understand, but that does leave us with a problem. I would come, but I happen to agree with Fergannal—our alien Speir'dina faces might frighten your people unnecessarily. If I were to walk the halls unauthorized. It could cause some unwanted violence, which I would like to avoid."

Eilith's tail lashed in her agitation. She looked down at her hands unconsciously twisting her apron, then back to the Kashallan's solemn face. Chest heaving, she said, "Men! Fergannal might like to think he rules here when my brother is absent. But in matters concerning the accavett, I am mistress, and what *I* say is law," she told him, her voice ringing with self-satisfaction.

"There are ways to go from here to the accavett that are forbidden the men of the hunting packs. Chelka and I can get you to Ainna without attracting unwanted attention. If that is your only worry—never fear. My question is, will you come?"

The Kashallan stood, and bowed. "I am yours to command then, my K'Sa."

Amril handed him his hooded cloak; then looked up at the Kashallan with an unspoken plea in his eyes. The Kashallan chuckled. "All right, you can come. I might need you, so get your bag and your cloak."

As they started for the door, Nathan put himself in their path, and folded his arms across his chest. "And just where do you think you're going, boyo?"

"There's a sick woman in the accavett, K'Sa Eilith wants me to—"

Nathan shook his head, cutting him off. "Sick woman or not, you're not going anywhere without me."

Scandalized, Eilith's head crest flattened. "No, absolutely not! The accavett is a sanctuary for women. No unattached males from a hunting pack are permitted within its halls."

"Nathan, please, I'll take Chelka with me if that will ease your mind, but I have to go. The woman is Aju'an's sister-in-law and she may be dying."

Nathan remained where he was, still shaking his head stubbornly. "I got my orders too—from the Maker—and, I have no plans to try and explain to Dievris how you got yourself in trouble again because you were being stubborn."

"Nathan," Dunnagh-Tani warned, his eyes taking on a dangerous gleam.

"No," Nathan snapped, planting himself more firmly his gray eyes becoming as hard as steel. "I got my orders. You're not going anywhere without being properly guarded."

His face reddening with temper, the Kashallan took a deep breath and let it out very slowly. He glanced at Eilith, who was watching this little by-play with growing impatience. An idea suddenly coming to him, he gave Nathan a toothy smile.

"All right, if you've gone over my head and got your orders to keep me guarded, I'll take Ellis. She's competent, and she's a woman, so the ladies won't be disturbed. And, she has an implant so she can relay messages back here to Ross if I need help. Will that satisfy you?"

Nathan grimaced then stepped aside. "Wipe that smug grin off your face, Dunnagh. I don't like it—but you know it. You get your way this time, but you take Marty too. And, you keep in touch, or oath or no oath, I'll come looking for you. Got that?"

Dunnagh's grin widened. "I got it."

Nathan grunted, and motioned for the listening women to get their cloaks.

Women warriors? Eilith's head crest shot up in surprise. She hadn't been aware until that moment that the small yellow maned warrior and the tall brown-skinned one with curly black hair were women. Yes, she could see it, now that it had been mentioned. They were dressed like the men of their species, but their hips were rounder, and just like Avairei women, their suckling tits were on their chests for all to see. Her eyes flicked to the bone apron her niece wore; its significance finally registering. Warrior women. Oh, Yargal wasn't going to like this at all.

Chapter Six

The Kashallan sank down upon the edge of the moss-filled mattress on which the sick woman lay. "Hello, Ainna. My name is Dunnagh-Tani. I came here from Ticca with Ima Ngeal. I am a healer, and K'Sa Eilith has asked me to check on you."

Ainna blinked, then looked up at Eilith who nodded. Ainna blinked again and returned her sunken, red-eyed stare to the Kashallan. In a slightly slurred voice, she said, "You don't look like a priest."

He chuckled softly. "No I am not an Avairei priest. I think perhaps you are too tired for me to explain in detail so let's just say for now that I am a new kind of healer, and I want to help you if I can. Will you let me try?"

Ainna gave him a tired nod. "Yes, I guess so."

"Thank you, I know you are tired; this won't take long."

Before forming the link, he sat back and surveyed her critically for a moment. Yes, Eilith was right; she was definitely in a bad way. Ainna was lying on her side facing him. Her scales were a dull lusterless gray. Her breath wheezed in painful gasps and her breeding pouch was barely rounded by the child. Judging by the size of her pouch, this babe should have been barely old enough to crawl from the inner passage and continue its growth by attaching itself to a waiting nipple within the breeding pouch. Certainly it was far too small to be of the age that Eilith claimed. No question, there was definitely something wrong.

"Ainna." Capturing her attention, he took her hand. "I am going to form a kashallan link with you, so I can taste you and try to find out what is causing the trouble. Don't be frightened. You will feel a little prick when I make the contact, but that is all."

"Will it hurt my baby?"

"No, not at all," he assured her. "In fact, there is a special soft spot in your scales right here that was bred into your people by the Khutani Makers for just such a touch as mine." Holding up her wrist, he showed her, as he extended his tentacles and formed the link. When he was sure she had accepted his touch, he closed his eyes to make his diagnosis.

TEARING HER EYES AWAY from the scene on the bed at last, Eilith glanced at Amril, and her head crest rose in a silent inquiry. Amril caught the look, but shook his head and lifted his hands in a helpless gesture. Eilith's tail flicked anxiously.

Amril returned his attention to the Kashallan. What *was* wrong—and why was the exam taking so long? Dunnagh's face had taken on such a rigid mask of controlled fury. He shuddered, suddenly afraid of what the Khutani had found. Lowering his eyes to the bed, Amril could see that the woman was asleep again. Her breathing was far more relaxed now; whatever he had done for her, it seemed to have relieved some of her suffering.

Then without speaking, Dunnagh-Tani stood. Face dark as a thundercloud, he walked stiffly from the room, leaving Amril, Eilith, and his guards to trail after him in bewildered silence. In Ainna's outer chamber, he walked to the far wall, where he remained staring at a tapestry, his body rigid as a spear-shaft.

Amril could see his fists clenching and unclenching; he shivered. He had only seen the Kashallan this angry once before. That was the day he learned about the death sentence that Enaju Dingay placed upon all the outlaws. Catching K'Sa Eilith's eye, he shook his head again, silently warning her not to speak to him just yet.

They waited, for it seemed like hours—but probably wasn't. When Amril noticed Dunnagh's muscles relax, he caught Eilith's eye and stood. Amril approached the Kashallan hesitantly and placed a hand on his shoulder. "Husband? What's wrong?"

The Kashallan remained silent, but covered Amril's hand with one of his own. When he finally had his voice under control he asked without turning, "K'Sa Eilith, was it your household priest who gave this woman the red kavay?"

"Why, yes, old Neyal gave her the kavay, as he has always done for Meh'gach folk. Why?"

Ignoring her question for the moment, he asked another of his own. "Has anyone else been given some of that particular batch?"

She considered for a moment, a clawed finger scratching her heavy jaw. "I believe a few of the Loti women were due to breed this year. They may have been given their bottles, but I have been so worried about Ainna, that I haven't supervised things as I should.

"No one else in the accavett is breeding this year. Yargal didn't bring home much, so most of the Riath kavay would have been set aside to germinate this year's seed."

The Kashallan let out a strangled curse and swung round to face them at last. "What is the clan affiliation of your household priest?"

One look at the barely controlled rage plain upon his alien face and Eilith gasped as if frightened. "H-his name is Neyal D-Dingay," she stammered. Then, her face flushed an angry green. She straightened her shoulder and her lips curled back over long yellow fangs. "Why do you want to know?" she demanded and this time there was a tone of authority in her voice that expected an answer.

"Neyal has been in this household for many years. He is a trusted member of this keep. What has Ainna's condition got to do with him giving her red kavay?"

"I don't know—yet—but I intend to find out. Have you asked him to look at her since she sickened?"

"Oh, naturally, he has seen her. As our healer, I sent for him when I first suspected things weren't progressing as they should. But he says there is nothing more that he can do for her. Whatever happens now—it is the Goddess's will. He says we must accept."

In a voice thick with emotion, the Kashallan said, "The will of the Mother indeed. Chelka, I want him. Go find this *Dingay* priest. Bring him to me. Now!"

Chelka stared at him in confusion for a moment, then her eyes widened and her head crest shot up, and she saluted. "Yes, Kashallan." Hand on the outer door she hesitated, turning back to him. She glanced around Ainna's sitting room, then at the closed bedroom door. "Shall I bring him here?"

The Kashallan sighed then addressed the bewildered and angry Eilith. "K'Sa, I know my behavior isn't giving you much confidence in me at the moment, but a terrible crime has been done here, in the name of my kin. I won't know its extent or who is to blame until I talk to the priest. Please bear with me until then."

Eilith considered him, her tail tip flicking. She looked at Ainna's closed door for a long moment. At last she sighed and said to Chelka. "Go find Neyal, Child, and bring him to my suite. We'll wait for you there."

Back in Eilith's rooms once more, the Kashallan sat upon the stool he was offered, back rigid, hands knotted with tension. He remained silent, refusing tea, eyes staring blindly at nothing, his face a bloodless mask. When pressed, he told the worried matron that Ainna was resting comfortably for the moment. He had been able to ease her pain so she could sleep.

About anything else Eilith tried to ask him, he remained uncommunicative. After a few more futile attempts to draw him out, she gave up, and the room lapsed into a strained silence.

Amril held his hands between his knees to stop them from trembling. He was afraid, so very afraid. What awful thing had the Dingay done now? *Oh, Holy Mother, please protect us*, he prayed silently. K'Sa Eilith was still annoyed and maybe even more frightened. He feared that at any moment she might lose her patience, and call for guards to take them to a prisoner's cell.

He tried to catch Dunnagh-Tani's eye—tried to make him understand. But the bondmates were lost in their own dark reverie, and were unreachable. And Amril didn't dare disturb them—not now—when he also suspected that the Kashallan was barely keeping himself under control.

Sometime later, Amril jumped as a knock sounded at the door. Marti and Ellis flattened themselves against the wall behind the door, as Eilith rose to answer it. "Come in, Neyal," she murmured, and stepped aside to let him enter.

"K'Sa Eilith, what is this all about?" he whined. "I could get nothing out of young Chelka here, but I am very busy. The Loti families are leaving, and I have to—" A gnarled stick of an Avairei with untidy gray braids and a dusty brown kilt came fully into the room, and looked around. When he saw the Kashallan, he let out a yelp of surprise. He would have bolted, but Chelka closed the door firmly behind them, blocking off all chance of escape.

Neyal's eyes grew round with fear as he searched frantically for a way out. "K'Sa, please, let me out, I will get help," he begged Eilith in an undertone. "The Hunt Leader has warned me about these creatures—they are Umwira—"

"I have heard that too," Eilith said. "I don't happen to believe it, however."

The Kashallan rose, crossed to the priest, and loomed over him, his face contorted with his pent-up emotions. "Umwira am I? You of all people, Dingay slime, should know the falseness of that claim, hmm?"

"I-I don't know what you're talking about, Demon," the priest stammered.

"Don't play games with me, Umwira Filth, I'm in no mood," he said. "I want to know what you put in the red kavay you gave the Sa Ainna, and I want to know it now!"

Neyal's eyes widened with fear and he took a step backward. "I-I don't know what you're talking about, Mutant. Leave me alone!"

The Kashallan's hand shot out and he grabbed Neyal by his necklaces. Twisting them tight, he pulled the trembling priest up on tiptoe, staring down at him. "I'll ask you only one more time, Priest—what did you put in the kavay?" Extending the tentacles of his free hand, he showed them to the frightened man, then jabbed them viciously into his exposed arm. "And have a care how you answer me, Dingay. I will know if you lie, and I will punish such disobedience with pain."

K'Sa Eilith opened her mouth to protest, but Chelka laid a hand on her shoulder and shook her head. Reluctantly, with Chelka's low voiced urging, she sat down; Neyal remained stubbornly silent.

"I'm waiting, priest." When Neyal still refused to speak, Tani sent blinding pain down the link they shared.

Neyal screamed. He writhed in Dunnagh's grasp, then slumped forward as Tani eased off. Grim-faced, the Kashallan steadied him. "Don't try my patience, Ata. I will kill you right now if I have to. What did you put in the red kavay?"

Neyal glanced over at K'Sa Eilith, his eyes pleading desperately for help. When she refused to look at him, he shuddered. Turning his attention back to the Kashallan, he licked his lips and swallowed. "I-I only did what my Ima told me to do," he stammered. "S-she said in her note th-that it was the will of the Holy Ones—Meh'gach's people needed to be taught that they must obey the will of the sacred Khutani and—"

"You filthy Slimeworm, none of my kindred would ever have told you to poison an innocent woman. No matter what 'lesson' the men in her family might need to learn. Damn you Dingay!" Tani cried. "Your clan claims its guidance comes from my kin in the pools—and the people believe your lies, but you and I know that it is the Ghostland wizards whom you truly obey."

"N-no," Neyal cried. "That is a filthy lie! My Ima is the High One herself—she would never—" Neyal glanced over at Eilith. "K'Sa Eilith, I'm sorry about the woman, but I had no choice—I had to do what the High One commanded.

"She said it was only a 'little lesson.' If K'San Yargal bowed to the Khutani's will, what I did now would save everyone here from a great disaster later. I didn't want Meh'gach to be destroyed—I had no choice—please try to understand!"

Within the link, the bondmates could tell that the man truly believed what he was saying. <<He is only a tool to be used by the changelings, not one that would be trusted with family secrets, Shalla. So ease off a bit,>> Dunnagh said.

<<What does it matter, Kasha? The woman may die because of him—and to claim that it is Khutani will—>> Tani broke off as another spasm of rage flooded through their shared flesh.

<<Calm down, Shalla, this isn't helping the situation when you make us so upset that neither of us can think rationally,>> Dunnagh chided. Tani refused to answer, but did try to calm itself.

"You still haven't answered my question, Dingay. What did you give Sa Ainna?"

"I don't know," Neyal mumbled.

Losing patience with the reluctant priest, Tani once more sent pain down the link. Neyal screamed again, writhing in agony. "Please—oh, please—I don't know! The packet came with the kavay—I was to put it in her dosage. That's all I was told—please believe me."

"And what about the rest of the kavay you were sent? To teach Meh'gach a *lesson*, what other foul crime were you to perform?" the Kashallan demanded. "And don't lie—I will know it. You have already done enough harm to deserve a kashallan's justice—I should kill you right now, so don't tempt me."

Neyal's head jerked up at the mention of the sacred bond. He stared wide-eyed. "Kashallan—you?" The Kashallan fixed him with his ice-blue stare and nodded. "B-but that's not possible—h-how?"

"My Khutani kindred don't like how you Avairei have handled your stewardship," Tani told him grimly. "The Makers' have brought a new host species to Timorna, to set us free. Kashallans like me have been created to cleanse this land of Umwira changeling filth, and the puppets, like you, who blindly serve them."

Neyal let out a strangled cry, and slumped forward. "No, oh, please, Holy One, I didn't know. I thought it was the will of the sacred Khutani that I served—my Ima—I didn't know!"

"What does it matter now," the Kashallan said. "The crime has been committed. Now tell me what else you have done. What about the rest of that tainted brew? Have you given it to others, or mixed it with the grain?"

Before the priest could stammer out his reply, Eilith's door was flung wide, and Hunt Leader Fergannal burst into the room. Catching sight of the Kashallan and the frightened priest on his knees, he let out a roar and leaped for the Kashallan's throat.

Drawing her sidearm, Marti fired. The Hunt Leader hit the floor with a loud thud and lay still.

Eilith glanced from the black-clad warrior woman to the prone body of the Warlinga sprawled on her rug. She shivered. Turning to her niece she breathed, "What kind of magic is this? The woman just pointed something at him—she didn't even touch him. Is he dead?" Her frightened red eyes flicked anxiously from Chelka to the Kashallan.

Retracting his tentacles, Dunnagh-Tani jerked the terrified priest to his feet. He shook his head. "He's just stunned, not dead, K'Sa. He'll be awake again in a few moments, so no need to worry." Maneuvering Neyal over to a nearby stool, he sat him down, then motioned for Ellis to come over and watch him.

When she was near, he said quietly, "You had better let Nathan know what's happening here, but tell him to stay put for now. There are too many people disturbing the peace of this place already. Tell him we'll be coming back to Chelka's suite shortly—and have one of the lads find Aju'an, if he hasn't reported in. I'll need him."

"Yes, Ce'awn."

As the Kashallan predicted, the Hunt Leader sat up in another minute. Fergannal shook his head, his eyes still slightly unfocused. Finally, spying the Kashallan, he snarled and tried to rise.

"Better not," the Kashallan warned. "If you come at me again, next time you might not be so lucky. I don't want to have to kill you, but if you push me, I will have my armachd change the setting on her weapon so that next time—" He left his threat unvoiced, fixing the man with his hard blue stare.

"Fergannal, please, we're not in any danger—except from your stupidity," Eilith said.

Head crest flattened, Fergannal stared murderously at the Kashallan, but stayed where he was. Returning his attention to Eilith, he grumbled, "Someone heard screaming in here, and called me—and what is this mutant slime doing in the accavett? Eilith, don't listen to his lies." He glared at the bondmates. "Umwira Filth, I knew you couldn't be trusted to keep your word—"

Head crest high and red eyes blazing, Eilith leaped to her feet and loomed over the man on her rug, her ample body quivering. "Fergannal, I will remind you to keep a civil tongue in your head when speaking in my presence. Dunnagh-Tani is here because *I* asked him to come. And you will also show more respect for a sacred child of the pools when in its presence. This man is no Umwira mutant, you fool, but the bonded host of a young Khutani symbiont."

Fergannal blinked. "What are you babbling about, Eilith?"

"Fergannal, that's what we've been trying to tell you since last night, but you wouldn't listen." Chelka said. "The Speir'dina aren't Umwira mutants, but the new host species for the Khutani's symbionts."

The Warlinga shook his head angrily. "Have you all gone daft? This is crazy talk. Do you think I'm a fool to believe such nonsense?"

Eilith snorted. "Fool. That's an understatement. If you will just stay put and listen for once, instead of acting like an obeylem bull in rut, we will explain what's been happening here." Eilith turned to the Kashallan, her head crest lifted, her eyes flicking to the priest slumped upon his stool.

"Tell him, Dingay, tell him what you've done," the Kashallan commanded.

All eyes turned to the dejected priest. The story came out in bits and pieces; Neyal sat, his face buried in his hands. He refused to look at any of them. In a listless monotone, he related Enaju's instructions and answered the questions they put to him.

When it was finished Fergannal rose slowly to his feet and crossed to the cringing priest. "I should kill you for this. You betrayed us!"

"It would be better to wait, Hunt Leader, K'San Yargal should hear this man's story from his own lips. Then it will be up to him to decide his punishment."

Teeth bared and tail twitching Fergannal spun round on the Kashallan, sinking into a fighter's crouch. The Kashallan eyed him coldly, unmoving. "Don't push me, Hunt Leader," he said in a dangerous voice. "I repeat; we must wait for your K'San's return."

Fergannal hesitated, his eyes flicked to the two warrior women. They stood, grim-faced, their strange weapons pointing at his chest. At last he relaxed, and eased out of his fighter's stance. "There is some wisdom in your words," he said stiffly, "it will be as you say."

Reaching down he hauled the weeping priest to his feet. "I will put him in a cell in the lower keep until my K'San returns."

AS FERGANNAL MARCHED Neyal from the room, Dunnagh sighed and rubbed a hand across his face. Sinking down on a padded stool he accepted the bowl of tea that Amril shoved into his hand.

Learning the truth about some of his Dingay clan members—people whom he had always respected and served without question—had shattered the old man. If what he had done wasn't so terrible, Dunnagh could have felt sorry for him. Neyal, in his way, like so many others, was another victim of Umwira malice and treachery.

Handing the empty bowl back to the young man, he surveyed the worried faces of the women. He felt emotionally drained, and wanted to go to bed, but there were some important tasks still needing his attention. The sick woman and her child were in danger.

Becoming aware of the frightened voices in the corridor outside he turned to the shaken Eilith. "K'Sa Eilith, I'm sorry that the peace of the accavett has been disturbed in this way. Perhaps you should go speak to the people gathering in the hall. They must be very frightened if they heard the commotion and then saw Fergannal dragging the priest out of here."

Eilith stared uncomprehending for a moment, then nodded and rose. Hand on the door she hesitated and turned back to him. "What about Ainna; will she be all right?"

Avoiding her eye, the Kashallan glanced down at his hands. Extending the tips of his tentacles he eyed them uncertainly. At last the symbiont said in a brittle voice, "I don't know, K'Sa. I am very young, and the drug he gave her isn't one that I am familiar with. It must be of Umwira origin. I will do all that I can for her of course, but without knowing the poison or its antidote—I don't know."

Head crest flattened Eilith slumped against the door, then she straightened and took a deep breath. "I see. It is a terrible thing, but I know you will do your best for us, Holy One, please don't blame yourself, if you are unable to help her."

"Husband, would your Khutani elders know this drug and its antidote?" Amril asked. There must be a small pool below this keep—Neyal would have needed to consult the Khutani from time to time—if there is such a place we could try to call them—ask their help. Surely they knew where we were going, and can be summoned."

Eilith's head crest rose hopefully. "There is such a place, Kashallan—the spring and the pool are small—I doubt if anyone but the priest has been down there in years, but it is there."

The Kashallan gave Amril a grateful smile, and patted his arm. "Already I can see that I will be glad of your coming along with me on this journey, My Dear."

Amril dropped his eyes and murmured shyly, "Thank you, Husband, you do me honor with your praise."

The Kashallan patted his arm again then returned his attention to the expectant women. "It is worth a try, of course, but first we need more information." Turning to Chelka he said, "Go and search the priest's rooms, see what you can find. If there is still some of the poison among his things, it will be helpful to my elders to know exactly what she was given."

"Husband, perhaps I should go as well. I can read his papers, see what instructions he was given."

"Good idea, bring anything you find back to our suite so we can examine it further."

Marti cleared her throat. "Ce'awn, maybe I should go too. Marnez and me were the ones that searched Tomina's room. I know what to look for, maybe better than anyone else here." She glanced at Chelka, and asked, "Is there a way to take me with you without attracting too much attention?"

Chelka considered. "I think we can manage." She glanced at the Kashallan. "If you agree, Kashallan, that is."

"Go ahead and take her; if it can be done quietly and safely. She has a point." Then he returned his attention to the Warlinga matron again. "K'Sa Eilith, if you please, speak to your people and clear the halls. Ainna will sleep for several hours yet; I should go back to Chelka's suite and wait there till we have the information we need, then we can go down to these pools of yours and call my kindred."

Chapter Seven

K'San Yargal sighed and threw the last of the bones from his meal into the fire. *I'm getting too old for this*, he thought. He had awakened in the tree thicket this morning with every bone in his body aching. After another night spent on the cold, hard ground he could hardly move. He glanced around cautiously, but no one was paying him any attention. He edged a little closer to the fire's warmth and sighed. Yes, definitely too old, he decided, and drained the last of his beer from his bowl.

The blue snows were gone, but a taste of their chill still clung to the land, especially in among the rocks and kavalpa thickets where the Warlinga liked to camp. They had come out on the hunt this early in the Renewal to catch the vistri while they were still sluggish from their long hibernation. During his frequent absences at the Capital, the beasts had been allowed to breed too freely. Now his people were paying for that neglect.

Oh, he could have left this hunt to Fergannal; the man was competent enough. He could have gone on to the Capital, if he chose, but that enigmatic message from Ngeal made him uneasy. Yargal felt a strange reluctance to leave his lands without hearing from Aju'an. This hunt had been his reason to justify a further delay, both to himself and his men.

Meh'gach had lost two Loti families to the savage vermin after the harvest. The vistri posed a real threat to all the peasants returning to the land. They must be taken care of before he could leave for Riath once more—or, so he told himself. If left alone, the pack would undoubtedly cause more losses over the next year. And, he thought grimly, the way things were going, Meh'gach couldn't afford that. No, they could not.

It had been hard enough to win from the High Matri the small amount of red kavay that he had, after the trouble between Aju'an and Enaju's degenerate grandson, Combaron, got out. Only his quick action in disciplining the boy himself saved them from a worse fate. But Enaju wasn't pleased, and she made that fact known to him in many subtle ways.

They were given the red kavay they needed to get them through this growing season—just barely. Yargal gritted his teeth in frustration. When Aju'an returned from Ticca, he was going to have to punish the lad severely, and publicly, to prove his loyalty to the Dingay, or there would be worse to come.

Damn the stupid young fool. He hated being put in this position. He hated being forced by Dingay spite, and Aju'an's own stupidity, to use him as a sacrifice to prevent further trouble. Especially when Yargal knew, in his heart, that what the young man claimed was true. Aju'an saw the situation clearly enough; he'd give him credit for that.

But what the idiot didn't see was that—at least for the moment—Yargal had no choice but to obey. By refusing them the red kavay and other essential medicines, the Dingay could destroy them all, if they so choose.

By the Great Hunt Leader, how had this state of affairs come about? He shook his head in bewilderment. Meh'gach and the other great clans had all been too insular, too apathetic—they had never dreamed one clan could become so ruthless—and now, it was too late to do anything about it. They must surrender and obey, or be destroyed—

"My K'San."

Yargal looked up as one of his men approached and bowed. "Yes, what is it?"

"My K'San, your son Varrod wishes you to come. There is a group of Loti peasants on the trail, escorted by a few men from the keep. The men say they have been ordered to find the Loti families who left early and return with them to the keep."

Yargal rose to his feet. "What are you talking about? Who gave such an order, and why?"

The Warlinga shook his head. Eyeing Yargal's twitching tail and raised head crest with alarm, he stepped back. "I'm not sure, K'San. Perhaps that's why San Varrod wishes you to come talk to him." Yargal growled a curse then motioned for the hapless man to lead the way.

Brushing aside the trailing black branches of the tree, Yargal stepped out of the thicket; his clawed feet making a crunching sound on the frosty moss. His nostrils flared as he automatically tested the air for the scent of their prey. Nothing.

Above, the rusty sky was streaked with the amber clouds of dawn. The gray rolling hills with their trampled grasses and shrubby purple thorn thickets lay shrouded in mist, silently awaiting the sun's warmth. He cursed again and hurried to catch up with the hunter.

On the main trail, a large family of bewildered Loti, laden down with children and possessions, waited anxiously with their escort. Stepping up to the leader of the guard detail, Yargal demanded, "What's this all about? This area has been cleared of the vistri—the season is getting late—these people should be about their planting. Who gave such an order?"

The man had been talking to Varrod in a low voice as they approached. He broke off his explanation, and bowed. "My K'San, your son Aju'an gave the order, officially, but the Hunt Leader agreed with his command. It was Fergannal himself who sent us to collect the peasants before they got too far—"

"Father," Varrod interrupted. "There's trouble; perhaps we should—" He motioned with a jerk of his head to a place down the trail where they could talk privately.

Yargal growled a curse, then stalked off down the path, the others trailing in his wake. When they were out of earshot, he rounded on the guard and demanded, "All right, what's going on—you say my son is back from Ticca? Why would he order the return of the Loti—and what's this about trouble?"

The guard's head crest dipped. "I don't know all of it, my K'San. Those of us who were sent out to collect the peasants were only told a little. But there are strange things happening in the keep that await your attention, K'San, that's for certain."

"What sort of things?" Yargal growled impatiently. "And, when did Aju'an return?"

"San Aju'an, Sa Chelka, and the pack arrived several nights ago. They also brought with them Ima Ngeal, and several mysterious strangers, who few have seen. It is because of what the Ima and the strangers told Fergannal and the K'Sa Eilith that the Loti are being called back."

"Father, De'ul here also told me, before you came up, that old Neyal is in a prison cell. There seems to be something wrong with the red kavay you brought back from Riath," Varrod said, his tail twitching with his unease.

Yargal glanced at the guard sharply. The man nodded, head crest flattening. "That is what the rumors claim, but the Hunt Leader will not confirm or deny it. He sent us to get the Loti, and that's all I know, K'San. I'm sorry. The Hunt Leader did say that if any of us came across you while on our mission, we were to urge you to come back to the keep as soon as possible."

Yargal grunted and turned away, trying to bring his emotions under control. His blood ran cold at the mention of the red kavay, and he saw the worry in Varrod's eyes too.

It wasn't possible! Surely the Dingay wouldn't dare do this to his house—not after so many years of loyal service—surely not. *Ah, but, they haven't been pleased with your lukewarm support of their causes of late,* a small voice in his head reminded. *And Aju'an's rebellion is only one grievance among many.* Did Enaju think to bring him to heel by a display of Avairei power, as the Dingay had to so many others? Gods, he felt his guts twist into knots at the thought.

Trying to push down the fear that was threatening to choke him, he turned back to the waiting Warlinga. To the guard De'ul he said in a strained voice, "Continue on as you were directed." Then, turning to his son, he added, "The hunt is almost completed. Assign enough men to finish it up, then get the rest ready to return to Meh'gach. We leave as soon as possible."

YARGAL'S PACK MADE good time, reaching Meh'gach Keep just before dark. The K'San himself was exhausted, but he knew he couldn't rest until he learned the extent of this trouble. Going straight to his chamber, he sent for wash water, a meal, Fergannal, and his youngest son, in that order.

After seeing that his father was taken care of, Varrod took his leave—to go see his wife, Yargal assumed. But Varrod returned to his father's suite, his head crest flattened with worry, not long after Yargal finished his meal. One look at his son and Yargal snapped, "What's wrong?"

Without answering, Varrod walked over to the table and poured himself a bowl of ale, then sat. He took a long drink. "They won't let me see her."

Yargal poured himself some more ale. He sipped it slowly. Now he regretted the large meal he had just consumed, suddenly fearful of what Varrod might say. He forced himself to take a long swallow of the strong brew, then making an effort to keep his voice neutral he asked, "Why not?"

Varrod looked down at his bowl, and swirled the dregs to a lavender foam. "Aunt Eilith told me that her condition worsened after we left." Then, slamming down the bowl, he stood up and walked over to the far wall. He gazed blindly at the tapestry hanging there, claws extending and contracting as he fought for control. "—She says not to worry; a healer from Ticca is with her." He laughed bitterly. "She also says that everything possible is being done to save her, but the child—"

He growled a curse, then swung round to face Yargal again. "Damn Aju'an! This is his fault—why can't he learn to keep a civil tongue in his head, the insolent slimeworm? If he weren't my brother, I'd—"

"Calm down, Son, you're assuming that the Dingay have done something deliberately to harm your wife because of Aju'an, and that remains to be proven. He isn't totally to blame—"

"Stop it, father, I won't listen," Varrod growled angrily. "Of course he is. The Dingay are doing this to me to put us in our place, and we both know it. But this is a big part of the problem—you're too soft on Aju'an, and you always have been. He speaks his mind too freely, and now look what's happened," he complained.

"You've never disciplined either him or Chelka properly, and now my wife—" Uttering another growl of frustration, Varrod flopped back upon his stool and poured himself more ale.

Yargal looked away. The man was upset, but he had to admit there was some truth in his oldest son's claim. He had indulged them. And now—Chelka was running wild, playing at being a warrior. And Aju'an was indiscreet—and so outspoken about it that he may indeed be the cause for their misfortune.

At that moment there was a knock at the door then Aju'an himself stepped into the room. He bowed to his father and older brother, his face and head crest a neutral mask. Only the rapid assessing movement of his eyes betrayed his unease.

Varrod glared at him murderously, but at a look from his father held his tongue. "Sit down, son, you have some explaining to do. You can start by telling me why you called back the Loti from their planting," Yargal said. "I never gave you, or Fergannal, the authority to do something like that." Yargal glanced at the closed door in annoyance. "And where's Fergannal? I sent for him—"

"He'll be along in a moment," Aju'an said as he took a stool. "I told him to get the priest."

Yargal's head crest flattened. How dare this young whelp countermand his orders? He was about to reprimand him, when Aju'an spoke again. "I'm sorry, father, I know such a decision about the Loti should have been left up to you, but you weren't here, and there was no time to waste—"

Varrod snorted. Barely able to contain himself, he snapped, "And what was so important that it couldn't wait for our return, Little Brother? Since when have you become so wise that you can judge the importance of things better than our father?"

Aju'an's eyes flicked to his brother's angry face. His head crest lowered slightly, but he didn't rise to the bait. Turning back to his father, he continued, "Neyal admitted, after some intense questioning, that he had been ordered by Enaju Dingay to 'teach us a lesson.' He put some foul poison in the red kavay. I had to recall the peasants before they mixed the stuff with the seed. There was no time to wait for your return."

Yargal glanced sharply at Varrod, their eyes met, Varrod lifted his lip in a silent snarl. Yargal shuddered, feeling that knot of dread tighten in his gut. What was Aju'an talking about? Old Neyal poisoning the kavay—how absurd!

Is it? The tiny voice in his mind asked, *is it really? Such things have happened before to those who have earned Dingay disfavor,* the voice reminded. *Why do you think Clan Meh'gach should be treated any different?*

Enaju was unhappy with you, and has been for some time. It is all too possible that she might do such a thing. She could order her kinsman to do it, to make sure that Meh'gach obeyed Dingay will in future.

Yargal's tail flicked back and forth with his growing agitation. This couldn't be happening to them. Damn the insolent young fool—had his rash actions brought them all to ruin, as Varrod claimed? Oh, Great Hunt Leader, no, please not that!

Before he could voice his thoughts, however, there was another knock at the door. Aju'an rose and answered it. Fergannal came in, pushing a hollow eyed and dispirited Neyal in front of him. Crossing the room with the man's filthy braids held firmly in a clawed hand, the Hunt Leader pushed the unhappy priest to his knees in front of Yargal.

Neyal looked up briefly, then hung his head. One look into the priest's despairing, haunted eyes, and Yargal knew that Aju'an had spoken the truth. They were doomed.

Unable to contain himself any longer, Varrod sprang to his feet. His eyes flicked from Aju'an to his father. "Aju'an, if there is trouble in this keep, it is your fault—your insolence and caustic 'wit' is what has brought down the wrath of the High One upon us, you stupid fool. Why must we all suffer for your indiscretions? It's your fault—"

"Varrod," Yargal roared, "sit down and be quiet!"

Varrod glared defiantly at his father for a moment longer, then subsided, and sat. He said nothing further, but continued to glower angrily around at everyone.

Yargal sighed. In the past, he knew that Aju'an would have been quick to defend himself against his brother's accusations. They might even have resorted to a real fight in Yargal's presence; it had happened before. He gave his younger son an appraising look. Aju'an was watching his brother with a wary intensity, but gave no outward sign of agitation. *He's changed,* Yargal thought, unsure how to respond to this cool, self-assured stranger.

The young man waited a moment longer for Varrod to gain back some control, then said, "Varrod, I'm sorry. I know worry for Ainna prompted that outburst—and you are right. My actions have brought Dingay displeasure down upon us in part," he glanced at his father.

"My thoughtlessness has probably brought matters to a head more swiftly than they might have otherwise. I regret that the innocent have suffered for my indiscretions. Enaju and the rest of the Dingay have a lot to answer for, and I intend to see that they do."

"Aju'an," Yargal said, "what are you saying? We have enough trouble without you causing more. When I go to Riath, I will speak to Enaju—ask her to—"

Aju'an shook his head, cutting him off. "Neyal," Aju'an said, turning to look at the priest for the first time. "Tell my father what you were ordered to do."

Roused out of his misery by Aju'an's command, Neyal licked his lips and gave Yargal a pleading look. "My K'San, I didn't know—by the Holy Mother, I swear I thought I was doing the will of the Holy Khutani in the pools when I put what my Ima sent in the kavay. She said it was for your own good—to teach you a lesson. I'm sorry about Sa Ainna, but what could I do? She is the High Matri—I had to obey."

With a roar, Varrod sprang to his feet and leaped for Neyal's throat. Aju'an and Fergannal seemed to have been expecting such a move, and grabbed him before he could reach the priest. Varrod fought like a man possessed, in spite of his father's roared commands to stop.

Finally, getting a clawed hand under Varrod's jaw, Aju'an put pressure on a nerve point and Varrod collapsed like a corpse in their arms. Motioning for the surprised Fergannal to help him ease his brother down to the rug, Aju'an sighed and straightened. Before his father could speak, Aju'an assured him, "He'll be all right in a moment, father."

"What did you do to him?" Yargal demanded.

"Nothing much. A little trick Ticca's new Hunt Leader showed us in our training sessions during the Sorins," Aju'an said.

Yargal detected a hint of smug satisfaction in his voice as he said it. Well Varrod had certainly got the better of him many a time while they were growing up. The young man had changed, truly. What had happened to him while at Ticca—did he really want to know?

As Aju'an predicted, it wasn't long before a dazed Varrod sat up, putting a hand to his jaw. Aju'an gave him a toothy smile. Varrod bared his own teeth as if he might continue the dispute, then seemed to reconsider the idea, and remained where he was on the rug.

"As you so recently informed me, dear brother, it isn't for you or me to make our father's decisions for him," Aju'an said. "Father needs to hear all of what the Dingay priest has to say before you kill him, hmm? So, if you try that again—"

Aju'an left his threat unfinished, but the menace was there in his voice and Varrod heard it. He blinked up at his younger brother in surprise.

Once he saw that Varrod was all right, Yargal dismissed him from his mind. He slumped on his stool, head crest flattened. Suddenly he felt a wave of despair overwhelm him as the priest's words finally sank in. They were doomed. In spite of all his efforts to appease the Dingay, he had failed. Like so many others who offended that powerful clan, they would be destroyed. With no red kavay, they would be wiped out in one generation. He sighed heavily. He was so tired. It had been a long day, and now this—

"Father," Aju'an spoke quietly, breaking in on his morbid thoughts, "it's not as bad as you believe. The Dingay can't break us to their will any longer."

Yargal's head crest shot up. He stared at his son incredulous, tail twitching. "You stupid young fool, don't you know what has happened to us? Are you too full of your own importance to see what you've done? A barren house, outcast and despised—without the red kavay and the Holy Khutani's blessing, we are doomed—"

"Father," Aju'an interrupted in that quiet tone of authority that was so unlike the old Aju'an that his family had known. "Let me finish. It is not as you fear, because we do *have* untainted red kavay and Khutani blessing—or at least my pack and I do," he qualified. "As to Meh'gach itself—that will depend on you."

Khutani blessing? Yargal blinked, his head crest settling. "What are you talking about, Aju'an? You're not making sense."

Aju'an came over and poured himself a bowl of ale. Sinking down onto a stool he swallowed some of the brew then set the bowl down on the tray. "It's a long story, which I can tell you more about later—when you're rested. For now let me say that when we came to Ticca, my pack and I were taken by the keep's new defenders down to the pools.

"One by one, we were forced to go into the water, where one of the Khutani Makers was waiting to taste us."

He shuddered and took another long drink. He met his father's shocked look, and nodded. "Yes, into the pools—me, a Warlinga, that was one of the most awesome and frightening things that has ever happened to me, Father, believe me."

"I don't understand, Son, why would the Avairei at Ticca do that—Warlinga are almost never allowed into the sacred sanctum of the Khutani—why?"

Aju'an barked a mirthless laugh. "The Avairei had no say in the matter. The Khutani Maker, Dievris, demanded it." At his father's puzzled frown, Aju'an gulped down another swallow and continued, "Just prior to our arrival, a Dingay priestess had tried to kill the first of the new kashallans, and the keep was in turmoil.

"The Maker Dievris wrapped me in its coils, and demanded to know why my family had betrayed our breeding and were supporting the Dingay. I had no answer to give it, Father."

Yargal shivered. A Maker—a Maker had touched his son. Not since the days of the new beginning had a Warlinga been touched by a Maker. He gave his son a probing look; was this true? "Tell me what happened."

"I was given only one choice. I could give my oath of fealty to the Khutani and their new kashallan-bonded children, or all my pack and I would die. It was that simple, and that final. I chose to take the oath."

A stunned silence fell upon the room when Aju'an finished. At last, Yargal cleared his throat. "I—I don't understand—a new kashallan?"

"I know; it was hard for me too at first. Finding out that everything that I had believed in all my life was a lie was terrible." He shook his head and drained the last of the ale from the bowl. "Ima Ngeal or the Kashallan can give you more of the details.

"But I'll tell you that the Khutani are not happy with the way Avairei clans like the Dingay have been doing things. Much of what the Dingay claim to be the will of the Holy Ones is not.

"Until recently, the Khutani could do nothing about this state of affairs, confined to their pools as they have been. But all that has changed.

The Makers have used their power, and they have brought a new host species from another world to Timorna to set them free."

At their incredulous looks, he laughed. "No, I'm not crazy; truly I'm not," he assured them. "The Khutani have been freed once again from their pools. Inside the new host species, they can walk amongst us again. We don't have to depend on the Avairei for what we need any more."

"Hardly, little brother," Varrod scoffed. "This is all very nice in theory, if it's true. But if the red kavay has been poisoned, as you claim, what will we do for the germinating of the seed this year? Or for the consummation of your marriage, for that matter. Kashallans, if there were any—how could we get help from the Khutani in time?"

Yargal nodded. "Your brother has a point, Son. We still must try to regain the favor of the powerful Avairei clans; we will need—"

"You're not listening to me; damn it, Varrod, I said we have red kavay. My marriage to Sa Latiya has already been consummated, Father." When his father and brother only stared, still not seeming to grasp the implications of his words, Aju'an growled in frustration.

"Oh, Father, think! It doesn't matter that the red kavay that you brought from Riath was spoiled. We have some from Ticca. If we need more, Dunnagh-Tani, the first kashallan, will make it for us. We're free. We don't have to bow to the Dingay anymore.

"The Kashallan and some of his Speir'dina kin came here with me. The new host was a warrior before he made the bonding. Oh, their ways of fighting are different from ours, but he understands us, father. And he has told the Khutani Elders about our troubles; they are very angry.

"He came to see you, to offer his help to us, and ask for ours in return. There are Umwira changelings in Riath. My pack and I have taken the oath, and we must go with him to the Capital to rid our land of them. But we need your help, father, and that of other clans to do it."

Varrod snorted and poured himself more ale. "This is quite a story, little brother, but what about Sulas?"

Yargal leaned back resting some of his weight on his tail. "Yes, what about Sulas—is it destroyed as the Dingay claim—is Sagas Caltia here with you?"

Caught off guard Aju'an hesitated. "No. we left her back at Ticca—her brother Amril is with us though."

Varrod growled a curse. "Do you see what comes of spoiling him, father?" Varrod jumped to his feet and pointed an accusing tail at his brother. "See how he has repaid your indulgence? He has turned outlaw. Soon the entire Yeyen will be against us!"

Aju'an remained on his stool, that new look of understanding on his face. "I am an outlaw, Varrod, I freely admit it, but I am not a traitor to the Khutani. Sulas is dead as the Dingay claim, but It was the Khutani themselves who destroyed it after Combaron tried to kill the Kashallan."

From where he huddled forgotten on the floor, Neyal wailed, "Oh, my K'San, I didn't know it was all a lie—that the Umwira were the ones guiding her—" The old man's voice broke on a sob. "Oh, my K'San, I swear I didn't know about the Umwira!"

Yargal's head crest flattened at the mention of the Hated Enemy. "What are you babbling about, old man? Umwira—who?"

Neyal trembled, afraid to answer. The priest only looked at him, his eyes clouded with despair. At Yargal's impatient growl, he opened his mouth to speak, but only a hoarse croaking came out.

"He's talking about Enaju, and the Gods alone know how many of the rest of the Dingay clan, being Umwira-bred changelings," Aju'an answered for him.

Yargal swung back to his son. "Who says so? What kind of despicable lie is this? The Dingay have their faults, but to make such a charge—not even you could be fool enough to claim that, where it could be heard publicly, without proof."

"Oh, there is proof, Father, I assure you, and I will say that most publicly, for all to hear," Aju'an insisted. "And I won't be alone when I do."

"Who? Who else would dare such a thing?"

"Ngeal Maveth for one," Aju'an shot back, growing angry now himself.

Too stunned to speak, Yargal just stared at his son. Aju'an laughed. "Yes, Ima Ngeal. She's here at Meh'gach, father. After what happened to her niece at the hands of the Dingay and their Umwira Master, she wanted to tell you herself. She felt so strongly about it that she rode atop a Loti, and traveled with my hunting pack to get here in time to see you before you left for Riath.

"Ngeal is still exhausted from the journey, but she wants to see you as soon as possible. She is with Aunt Eilith right now, along with some of the Speir'dina that you need to speak with as well."

He stood up. "Will you come? They are waiting."

Chapter Eight

"Dunnagh-Tani?"

"Hmm?" the Kashallan mumbled. A hand touched his shoulder. He blinked and looked up. Chelka was crouching over him. "What is it?" he murmured, his voice still thick with sleep.

They'd let him rest in a tiny alcove off Ainna's bedroom. The spot was a hastily vacated maid's room refitted with a thick moss-filled mattress and several embroidered blankets that nearly filled the tiny enclosure. At his back, a furry body groaned, then settled back into sleep.

Chelka lowered her voice, not wishing to wake the exhausted Amril. "My father has returned. I am sorry to wake you, but my aunt wishes to know if you could join her and Ima Ngeal. They would like you to speak with him—if you aren't too tired."

"I'll come right away." He yawned and reached for his discarded kilt. Chelka helped him fasten his belt and adjust some of the pleats.

"Husband? What's wrong?" Amril asked, and started to sit up.

The Kashallan pushed him down gently, and re-covered him with the blankets. "Go back to sleep; it's nothing. I'll call you if I need you."

Amril grunted and drifted back into exhausted slumber without another word. *Poor man*, the Kashallan thought. *He's probably gotten less sleep in the past few days than I have.* Chelka handed him his cloak. He adjusted the hood to conceal his face and followed her out into the hallway.

"How is Ainna?" Chelka asked as she closed the door behind them.

The Kashallan stifled a yawn. "The last time I checked she was sleeping soundly. Her maid is sitting with her. She has orders to let me or Amril know if there's any change in her condition."

"I'm sorry I had to wake you; you must be exhausted too."

He stifled another yawn and chuckled. "I think I could sleep for a ten-day, but this is important too. You did right to come for me."

Meh'gach was like all the ancient stone keeps built not long after the Khutani reintroduced life to the surface world. Its deepest tunnels contained a small pool that connected with the system of underground waterways the Khutani traveled. Though the Khutani were not usually present in a Warlinga keep, if there was need, the household priest could summon the ancient race to aid him—and for Ainna's healing they definitely had needed help.

When the problem was explained to them, the Khutani instructed the Kashallan to have the Warlinga bring the ailing woman on a litter to the pool. It had been a long and difficult healing, even with the Khutani's aid, and both Dunnagh-Tani and Amril were exhausted by the time it was over. Working together, they managed to save the mother, but the child had been lost.

Losing the baby was a great tragedy, but it was only Amril and Marti's quick work in finding more of the Umwira drug that saved the mother's life. Without a sample of the poison, even the Elders would have been unable to heal her. This death, like so many others, was just another charge against the Hated Enemy that would need to be paid.

As they hurried down the corridors the keep's inhabitants they passed, stole sidelong glances at his heavily wrapped figure, but no one raised an outcry. He could feel their eyes upon him, however, long after he passed and it sent unwanted chills down his spine. Chelka wore her bone–scaled apron and carried her spear with a grim determination that boded ill for anyone who dared stop them.

Nearing the public areas of the keep he heard the boisterous men in the main hall, and pulled the hood down even lower to shadow his face. "How much does your father know yet?"

Chelka slowed so she could look into the shadows under his hood. "I'm not sure. Aju'an and Aunt Eilith have been keeping me busy elsewhere." Her lip curled in a mocking little smile. "To spare father the sight of me perhaps—or them the problem of having to explain my new status; I'm not sure which."

"Mm, yes, we will have to work something out there, won't we?"

"Father and Varrod have been with Aunt Eilith and Ima Ngeal for a while now, so I suspect that they know the basics. Clan elder, Arishim is with them too I believe, so your appearance won't be a shock to them if that's what's worrying you."

Dunnagh stifled a yawn, and chuckled. "Maybe it was a little; I'm too tired for vigorous exercise at the moment."

Reaching the entrance to one of the smaller public chambers, Chelka grinned and knocked. Mar opened the door, and stepped aside for them to enter. Once inside the Kashallan flung back the hood of his cloak and paused to get his bearings.

The room was furnished with brightly woven tapestries and well-padded stools with embroidered covers. A geometric design of brown and orange tiles lay atop the stone floor. Carved stone lamps hung from hooks on the walls bathing the room in a silver-green light. Most of the people already in the room were seated round a low table laden with refreshments of various kinds.

Sighing with relief, Dunnagh noticed that K'Sa Eilith, Ima Ngeal, and Clan-elder Arishim were here. Good, as Chelka suspected, they'd probably filled the Warlinga in on the basics. That suited him fine. As tired as he was at the moment, he would be lucky to speak a coherent sentence let alone give a full accounting of their experiences.

With some amusement, he also noted that Nathan had managed to have himself invited to this little party. He was lounging against the wall near Aju'an and Hunt Leader Fergannal. Near them, the Dingay priest Neyal slumped on a stool, his eyes downcast, looking at nothing.

Next to the women sat two Warlinga. The elder, a grizzled, well-muscled veteran with an air of authority about him, was eyeing the newcomers coolly. The other, a much younger man with flushed green scales, must be Varrod, Aju'an's older brother, and Yargal's heir. The Kashallan sighed, remembering that he was also the husband of the poor woman he had been treating.

Idly, Dunnagh wondered if he had been told about his wife's condition yet—then decided he had. Varrod's green flush and the way he eyed him with a sullen, worried look made it clear to Dunnagh that he knew something.

Stepping forward, Chelka bowed to her father and her brother. "Father, Varrod, may I present to you Dunnagh-Tani, the first of the new kashallans."

CHELKA. BEFORE HE COULD focus on the stranger just behind her, Yargal felt his attention drawn to his willful daughter. This was the first time he'd seen her since arriving home, and he didn't like what he saw. She was wearing her warrior woman's apron and carrying a spear, like any guardsman on duty.

Aju'an had already warned him that at Ticca, Chelka had gotten her wish to be trained as a warrior and she'd given her oath of service to the Kashallan. Oath of service—like any lowly hunter—damn the girl. His guts churned with a wealth of conflicting emotions.

While they waited for the others to arrive, Aju'an had told his father briefly about Chelka's conspiring with Overn to secretly leave the keep ahead of his pack. By the time Aju'an and his men caught up to the runaways, they were too far from Meh'gach to be sent home without splitting up the pack. And with the vistri kill along their back trail, Aju'an had felt it was too dangerous, for all of them, to do that.

Reluctantly, Yargal had had to agree with Aju'an's logic. Especially having just returned from hunting those very same beasts, he knew what a danger they would have posed to a small party traveling alone.

Next, the young man gave them an account of their journey across the Shaden portage with the Sorins at their backs. He praised his sister's courage on that trek, and shocked his father further by saying that she had the admiration of Ticca's defenders for both her beauty and her warrior's skills. On one occasion, which he didn't elaborate upon, he said that Chelka had even fought and killed one of the Hated Enemy. Aju'an ended his account by saying that she like himself, was now a member of the Kashallan's household.

That bit of news didn't please Yargal. He would have allowed his temper to get the better of him, but at that point they reached the chamber where Eilith and the other women were waiting, and that cut him off in mid-rant. Yargal was still angry with Aju'an, however, and he would have more to say about the matter later, when he wasn't so tired.

He didn't approve of such crazy notions as women warriors. A grown woman's place was in the accavett, not in a hunting pack. How would he ever find her a suitable bridegroom if this got out? Inwardly he seethed, but decided to let it pass for now. There were more important matters to be dealt with first; his daughter could wait.

So, this was the new kashallan. Fergannal warned him, about the appearance of the Speir'dina. He had already seen and spoken with the one called San Nathan, as well as one of their female clan elders. This tall, well-muscled male in the doorway had the same ugly, flattened face that Yargal had noted in the others of his kind. The host wore his long red mane in the Avairei style, but his most striking feature, the Warlinga K'San decided, was his kavay-blue eyes.

And right now those eerie blue orbs were watching him as intently as he had been considering the other man. At last, realizing he was being rude to the Khutani, Yargal cleared his throat and invited, "Come in, Holy One—please sit down and join us."

The Kashallan bowed, then crossed and sat down on a vacant stool. When he was seated, Chelka poured him a bowl of tea, then took up a position at his back. He took the drink gratefully, stifled a yawn behind his hand and waited for Yargal to begin.

Did this man host one of the Holy Ones in his body—truly? Yargal felt overawed at the prospect of actually speaking to one of his people's revered "Makers." He had no wish to appear ignorant or foolish. What could he say to this creature that was half alien stranger, half Khutani symbiont? For the first time in his life he felt choked with emotion and at a loss for words.

They sat quietly for a long time, the Kashallan sipping his tea, Eilith glaring at her brother, Ngeal distant and composed, San Nathan, and the clan elder watching him and Varrod warily. Yargal himself was looking down at his bowl, his face and head crest position telling them nothing about what he was actually thinking.

It was Varrod who at last, unable to stand the suspense any longer, broke the spell. Looking into Dunnagh's eerie blue eyes, he said with a note of challenge in his voice, "The Ima and my aunt claim that you host a child of the pools. If that is so, then I would like to know what's wrong with my wife."

The Kashallan sighed. "As you probably have already been told, your household priest was instructed to add a slow-acting poison to the draft of red kavay that was given to you and Sa Ainna. I am sorry, San Varrod. All that was possible was done for her. My Khutani relatives and I were in time to save the mother's life, but only at the expense of aborting the child."

Varrod looked away. "So I was told. Does she know?"

"No, not yet. At the Khutani's advice, I am keeping her sedated for the present. She is very weak and the shock would be most upsetting to her. I think it best if we wait until she is stronger before someone tells her."

"That's probably wise. Will I be allowed to see her?"

The Kashallan toyed with a long braid as he studied the man and considered. Making up his mind at last, he tossed the braid over his shoulder and said, "That is possible. I will have someone come for you the next time she wakes, if you wish."

"Yes, I want to see her." He looked down at his hands, slowly extending and retracting his claws. "Aju'an says that you can make the red kavay that this keep will need for the coming year. If that is so—when she is better, will you give us some of the kavay gift, so that another child can bless our union?"

The Kashallan rubbed a hand across his face and sighed. "I hadn't planned to speak of this other matter—not just yet—but since you've asked me directly—well, you have the right to know. I have already told Aju'an and the K'Sa Eilith that whatever Meh'gach needs I will provide, but for you and your wife things may not be quite that simple. My kindred have warned me that there may be side-effects of the drug that we aren't aware of yet."

Eilith scowled at her brother and Varrod. Catching Yargal's eye, she glanced significantly over at the Speir'dina and Warlinga lounging against the wall. When Yargal returned her look with a puzzled frown she snapped, "This is hardly a subject for such mixed company, brother. Men. You can be so insensitive at times."

Yargal grunted then ignored her. Returning his attention to the Kashallan he asked, "In spite of my sister's injured sensibilities, you are correct; we have the right to know. What are you referring to, Holy One? Is Ainna still in danger?"

"This Umwira poison, my elders remembered from long ago. It is a very evil thing. The drug's most striking and immediate effects, of course, were upon your wife and unborn child. I doubt if they were intended to survive this ordeal. But since Sa Ainna has, she may suffer from temporary, or more long-lasting, sterility—as may you yourself, San Varrod."

Eilith gasped. Her face turned a murky green and she reached for the leather fan on the table. Breathing heavily she fanned herself, her head crest flattening in dismay.

Yargal glared at the Kashallan angrily, as if such a horrible fate was somehow his fault. "Do you mean to say that not only my daughter-in-law but my son and heir may be temporarily or permanently infertile?"

"I am sorry, K'San Yargal, but that is what the Khutani think."

Varrod sprang to his feet, upsetting the table between them in his rage. "Damn you, priest," he roared, "I'll kill you for this—"

Varrod lunged for the frightened Avairei, but before he could grab the cowering man, Aju'an was between them, wrestling his brother back to his seat. Varrod fought him savagely for a while, then abruptly slumped back on his stool, all the fight gone out of him. The stricken man looked down at his hands, extending and contracting his claws, unwilling to meet anyone's eye. His head crest lowered in shame.

"San Varrod," the Kashallan said into the shocked silence that followed his outburst. "None of this is your fault. Please believe me. You and your wife are the victims here, as is all Meh'gach. Just as in battle, when the Hated Enemy uses the mind magic to torment and confuse us, the better to break through our defenses, so is this, another of their ploys.

"This was done deliberately to humiliate you—a diabolical threat designed to make sure that in future you and your family would be intimidated into obeying Dingay will, for fear of suffering much worse at their hands. And as in battle, you must fight them—don't let them drive you to despair."

Varrod looked up, but made no comment; then he let his eyes drop once more to his hands.

Yargal watched his daughter and clan elder Arishim right the table and pick up the wreckage of their refreshments. Suddenly he felt so very, very cold. It was like his brain had been enclosed in a block of ice. He couldn't think. How could these horrible things be happening to him and his family—it wasn't possible—it was too terrible to believe. The Kashallan had a point, yet still—how could they fight them? He didn't know.

"K'San Yargal, I can guess how you must feel. It is hard to believe that anyone could be so cowardly and so cruel. More than once I have tasted the bitterness of the Umwira and Dingay malice. It is one thing to fight an enemy face to face in open combat; I have fought the Umwira and Combaron Dingay so. In such a struggle, a man may live or die according to his skill. He accepts that as a part of the oath he takes when he becomes a warrior. But it is another matter entirely when the enemy shuns open conflict and seeks to gain his ends by means of fear and treachery.

"This last time, the Umwira tried to destroy me by striking at the innocent around me, not coming at me directly. Two of my wives and my youngest son almost died in that attempt. I owe your house a great debt, for if it hadn't been for your daughter's courage and quick action, I would have lost them.

"Ngeal's niece did die in that tragedy, when she became the innocent unwitting tool of one of the Ghostland wizards. He used her without mercy to try and achieve his ends. It is the way of these warped and terrible creatures to care nothing for the innocents they destroy, or the pain they inflict on all whom their malice touches. Their goal is to obliterate all that we have accomplished, and they rejoice in our torment."

The Kashallan's eyes suddenly burned with blue fire. He met the Meh'gach K'San's gaze, and said fiercely, "So many innocents have suffered. These Umwira and those whom they have corrupted must be stopped. As a kashallan, I have pledged my life in service to the land and peoples of Timorna. And as a kashallan, I give you my word that I will do all that is in my power to stop them. That is why I have come."

For a long time, Yargal sat, his body and mind still numb, unable to grasp the awful truth of what he had learned. At last he said, "You say you want to stop them, but can you? Many of the clans follow the Dingay's lead.

And how do you even know that the Dingay have been corrupted? Can you fight so many—how will you make the people believe what you claim?"

"To answer your question about the Umwira changelings first," Tani said. "My Kasha and I were sent by my Elders, because I am the only one of us who is free to move upon the land who has tasted the taint of the Umwira. When my people escaped Sulas after Combaron tried to kill me, we fought a warband of the Ghostlanders. During the battle, I tasted the enemy when my Kasha physically attacked their war leader.

"When I made the link with Tomina Dingay at Ticca, I tasted that same taint about her. My elders and I believe that the Umwira have corrupted the Dingay clan. I will know more when I taste others of that family in Riath."

Tani saw the Warlinga's eyes flick to the priest. "No, Neyal is no Umwira changeling. I have tasted him. He is but a tool, and in his way as much a victim as any of us."

After Varrod's attack, Neyal became more aware of what was going on around him, and he was watching the Kashallan intently now, his expression unreadable. "I don't excuse him for his crime," Tani said as it saw the Warlinga's tail flick in irritation. "He is guilty, but he also believed what he was told by his clan superiors—just as any hunter in your packs would follow your orders without question. I think he honestly thought he was doing the will of my kin."

The Kashallan's lips curved into an ironic smile. "For as you yourself have pointed out, K'San, it is almost impossible to believe that the High Matri herself could be a servant of the wizards. It is Neyal's superiors that are the true targets of my wrath—as they should be yours."

Yargal shook his head in bewilderment, his head crest dipping. "But how is that possible? An Avairei clan—the High Matri's seat itself corrupted—it's too unbelievable!"

"Oh, Father, think. It *is* possible, and knowing that they have had Umwira help would explain a lot of things," Aju'an said. "Dingay traditional clan holdings are near the Jeban Pass; it would be easy for the enemy to sneak over the pass. Especially after that drunkard Gormach Tragar inherited the border patrol from his father.

"The Ghostlanders and the Dingay could have come and gone as they pleased, without that fool being aware of anything. How else would they have managed to rise to power so quickly? How could they strike so much fear into the rest of us, so that we dare not oppose them—no matter what crimes they commit? How else, but with Umwira backing?"

Aju'an leaned forward, his face and head crest animated by his ardor. "Oh, no one wants to believe that the Umwira have grown so strong, or that we have become so complacent or vulnerable—but that doesn't change the facts, or mean it isn't true!

"Father, I asked Dunnagh-Tani to come to Meh'gach with me, to talk to you, because we need your help. With the coming of the kashallans among us again, not only are the Holy Ones freed from the pools, but we are freed, too.

"We don't *have* to do whatever the Avairei want us to do. We don't have to be afraid to oppose the Dingay and their followers any more. If we don't do something to stop the corruption, the Khutani have threatened to abandon us, father—don't you see? We must help him!"

Yargal glanced sharply at the Kashallan. "Is this true?"

The Kashallan nodded gravely. "The Makers have talked of it," he admitted.

Yargal shuddered, and took a long drink of the beer that Chelka had brought to them. He nodded thoughtfully as he drank. Setting his bowl down at last, he said, "It has never been my desire to go against the Sacred Ones of the pools.

"I didn't understand much of what has been done in the name of the Khutani these last years. And my son is right—we have allowed our fears to overrule our good sense. How can I be of help to you?"

"That I fear is not a simple question to answer, K'San. It is getting late, and all of us need our rest, so let's save that discussion for another day. But there is one other thing that needs to be settled between us before we part tonight, K'San."

Yargal's head crest rose. "What is that, Holy One?"

"You have agreed to help us, and for that I am most grateful, but my elders have required that all those who take up my cause and wish their favor must swear an oath of fealty to me and my kin. I must take this oath while you are in the link with me, so I can taste your sincerity. Your honesty isn't in question here," he hastened to add.

"In your case it would be a mere formality that my elders insist upon but you should also understand that—should we fail, Meh'gach will become outlawed, like the rest of my followers. Your son and daughter and the men of Aju'an's hunting pack have already sworn this oath to me, but only you and your heir can speak for Meh'gach. So I must have your pledge, K'San, before we can proceed."

Yargal looked at his oldest son. Varrod had been listening half-heartedly to the conversation. Sensing his father's regard, he looked up. Yargal's heart almost failed him as he saw the haunted, despairing look in his son's red eyes. Varrod's head crest dipped in agreement, then he looked down at his hands once more.

Inwardly Yargal raged. By the Great Hunt Leader, the Dingay would pay for this, he vowed, as he knelt before the Kashallan and held out his hands.

Part Two: War Plans

Chapter One

"K'San Cousin?"

Tobrach looked up from the scroll he was deciphering; in the doorway to his private suite stood his battle-scarred Hunt Leader, Warega. Framed in the blue glow from the fungus lantern in the hall, Tobrach could see the troubled look in the man's red eyes. What was wrong now, another fight? He laid his scroll down on his worktable and sat back on his stool, tail tip quivering. His head crest rose in inquiry. "What is it, kinsman?"

"Trouble, K'San; the hunting pack from Riath has been sited."

Across the table from him the Avairei priest, Thon, gasped. Beneath his trembling four-fingered hands the scroll he was reading rolled itself up with a snap. Thon looked from one grim-faced lizardman to the other. "So soon? Surely not this early, the blue snows must still be in the passes yet. Are you sure, Hunt Leader?"

Warega's eyes flicked to the priest, but he remained silent. Ignoring the Avairei's question for the moment, Tobrach motioned his kinsman to come in. The Warlinga stepped inside, closing the door firmly behind himself. He crossed to the table and stood stiffly at attention in front of them. Warega glanced at the reading materials on the table in front of the priest and Tobrach, then focused his eyes resolutely on his K'San's face.

"One of the sentries I posted on the heights has just come in. There is a large, well-armed hunting pack headed up the eastern trail towards the keep."

Tobrach sighed, glancing wistfully at his studies spread out on the table. Like the priest, he wished that the pack from Riath wouldn't have been so eager to brave the hostile weather.

This past Sorin Season had been a busy one, but an unexpectedly happy one as well. In exchange for his service to the kashallan and the Khutani, the Maker Gladdris granted him one of his most secret wishes. Thon was teaching him to read.

"How much time do we have before they get here, Warega?"

The Warlinga scratched his jaw and considered. "They have a covered litter with them and several Loti packers. An Avairei of rank must be with them, which means they won't be traveling as fast as a pack on the hunt would be. But this close to Tragar, they will probably try to reach the keep tonight; rather than spend another cold night on the trail.

"My guess is that they will be here by the evening meal, K'San, at the earliest, or tomorrow morning if they are slowed for some reason. The trail is still quite icy in patches. They will have to be careful with the litter or risk an accident."

An accident, one couldn't happen to a more deserving bunch. "Mm, that will give us a bit of time to prepare at least." He glanced down with regret at his slate and scrolls once more; he was going to miss his hours of study with the old priest. No Warlinga, to his knowledge, had ever been taught the priestly glyphs; the Avairei were jealous about their secrets. But books had always fascinated him, and now, when he had the Khutani's favor, and a priest willing to teach him...

He sighed and turned to the priest. "Ata Thon, You had best clear away these things and gather your people as we've planned."

His braid ornaments clicking, Thon's furred hands shook as he picked up the scrolls and writing implements from the table, and began putting them back in his case. Slade in hand, he paused. "But, K'San, what if they don't believe your story about The Umwira attacking and killing K'San Gormach as he was bringing the Ima Sagas and the rest of us to Riath."

Tobrach gave him a reassuring smile, but his eyes remained troubled and the priest saw it. "You will be safe in the deep tunnels until the men from Riath are gone, Ata Thon, no matter what happens in the keep above. They will not look for you there—even if they don't believe our story."

Thon pushed his braidlets off his shoulder; he sighed, nodded and finished his packing. When his things were stowed away in his case he stood and bowed to Tobrach. "K'San, we are all grateful to you for your kind treatment of us. When Gormach brought us here from Sulas, bound like criminals we despaired of ever seeing another Renewal. I wish I could have followed the Kashallan and the Ima Sagas into outlawry, but my duties required that I stay behind.

"I fear the Dingay spite, but I also don't want to repay your kindness by having you face execution in my place. We have talked about this among ourselves and all agree that perhaps you should give us to the High Matri's men, as your cousin would have done. It could be dangerous for you, if you lie to them."

Tobrach bowed. "Your offer is very generous, Ata, but one I can't allow. As long as there are young Khutani in the pools below this keep needing your care, I can't permit you and the others to do that. You are needed here. My kinsmen and I have taken the oath; we will protect and take care of you as the Holy Khutani wish us to do."

Coming around the table Tobrach put an arm around the old man's shoulder and ushered him to the door. "Go now, Ata, there is a lot to do before our 'guests' arrive. And try not to worry all will be well." He smiled down at the Avairei as he opened the door for him. "If the Gods are willing we will see an end to our unwanted visitors soon, and then perhaps we may continue with my studies, hmm?"

The priest nodded solemnly, the frightened look still in his eyes. "I would like that, K'San, truly. I would not have believed it of a Warlinga, but you are an excellent pupil—you have been a delight to teach. I wish all my students were so eager. I will look forward to resuming your instruction when time permits."

Giving the two Warlinga a last bow the Avairei settled the strap of his satchel on his shoulder, stepped out into the hall and disappeared into the gloom.

From the doorway, Tobrach watched the kilted figure of the priest until he was out of sight. At last he shook himself and turned back to his Hunt Leader. His voice low and introspective, he said, "If something should happen to me—if they take me, see that Ata Thon and the others are cared for, Warega."

"It will be as you say, San Cousin—we will defend them to a man, if need be." His tail curled and uncurled itself with his unspoken agitation. "You think they will take you then? Truly, you think even the Dingay will risk angering our clan by arresting you?"

Tobrach stepped out into the hall, motioning for his Hunt Leader to follow him. "There is a good chance that they will take me, yes. Hopefully not under arrest and bound, but I suspect that it is Enaju's grandson Combaron in that covered litter. The High One must be in a great hurry to get her claws into Ima Sagas—and perhaps the Kashallan too.

"She would give a great deal to have her Caltia enemies destroyed, and tying Sagas Caltia with the Kashallan, whom she considers to be an Umwira mutant, would be too tempting a prize to let slip through her fingers. And, I doubt if she would trust my late cousin to bring such a treasure to her unaided."

He barked an ironic laugh. "I doubt if Combaron himself would have come out on his own in such weather, without his grandmother's urging. And when he arrives here, and finds out that K'San Gormach is dead and there is no Ima Sagas to placate his grandmother's wrath—yes, I think you can count on them taking me."

Warega's jaw tightened. "I see what you mean. I never understood what Gormach was planning with the Dingay priest, but whatever their game, things have changed now. The slimy little pervert will not be pleased, true enough."

"Truly, he will not, and if they take me; it will be up to you to carry out the patrols. After the Ghostlanders' raid near Sulas last season, I expect they will try their luck again. Because of Gormach's negligence, they have gotten far too bold in the last few years."

Warega growled deep in his throat, his tail swishing with pent-up emotion. "If they try again to get over the pass they will learn that a new K'San now rules at Tragar Keep. The packs are ready; we will show them. I will have the hunters out and patrolling never fear, K'San. The kindred are eager to challenge the Hated Enemy."

Tobrach smiled. "I am glad of that, cousin." He studied the older man in the lantern light as they climbed the stairs to the main hall. Warega was a seasoned veteran of such border skirmishes. He would probably do better leading the packs than he would himself, if it came down to a real fight.

It hadn't been easy to break the cycle of lethargy and drunkenness that his cousin Gormach had encouraged among the men during his time as K'San of Tragar. But Tobrach and Warega had worked the men mercilessly over the Sorin Season. Discipline was strict and punishments harsh, but hopefully it had been enough. As Warega insisted, morale was high, and the men were eager for the hunt. Which might be a good thing. If the Kashallan needed him—if the Umwira attacked—he might need all his fighting men at his back.

Chapter Two

Amril tied in the last ornament, swept his braidlets back over his shoulder and tightened the sash at his waist. Nearby the Kashallan made a few minor adjustments to his apparel and reached for his cloak, where it lay across the foot of their bed. Catching the young man's eye as he did so; he smiled.

While the Kashallan and Ngeal were speaking with K'San Yargal the night before, the rest of the Speir'dina and their possessions were moved to other accommodations further down the corridor from Chelka's suite. Ngeal, Arishim with Marti and Joan Ellis to guard them were given one set of rooms, while the Kashallan, Amril and the rest of the men another.

The Kashallan would have preferred to sleep in the outer chamber rather than this tiny bedroom, Amril suspected, but the servants had prepared things in their absence and he'd been too tired to put up much of a fuss when he was shown to the new suite. He'd only scowled at San Nathan when he wished him pleasant dreams and closed the door in his face.

Amril looked down at the carved marriage bottle hanging at his waist and fussed anxiously with the pleats of his woman's kilt. It was a beautiful kilt. Dyed a moss yellow, it was made of the finest fabric. Blue and brown diamonds formed an embroidered border around its hem. It had been a gift from K'Sa Eilith; one of the finest garments her women had produced—

"You don't have to wear that thing if you don't want, my dear," the Kashallan said quietly. "I can imagine how hard this is for you, facing all those strangers, wearing women's clothing. I never wanted it to be like this—it'll be fine with me if you put that kilt aside."

Startled, Amril looked up. "No, it's very beautiful—I don't mind, truly. It's my duty—I'm your wife. It will please K'Sa Eilith if I wear it—and Ima Ngeal—" he broke off. Glancing down at his kilt, he made another imaginary adjustment to its folds.

The Kashallan threw his cloak about his shoulders and fastened the leather clasp. "Yes," he agreed, "you are my wife—in name at least, but we both know that was the only way for you and Pela to be together without shaming her. Now that the legalities are taken care of, there is no need to continue in this charade, to my way of thinking. And as for Ima Ngeal," he smiled showing predatory white teeth. "I'm sure I can talk her round to seeing things my way, if you don't want to wear it."

Amril hesitated, taking a moment to gather up his own cloak and set it about his shoulders. This would be their first meal in the main hall of the keep. Beyond the door of their tiny bedroom, someone laughed in the outer chamber then there was a knock at the door.

It was time to go. Amril shook his head. Taking a deep breath he faced his spouse, jaw set stubbornly. "No, I thank you, Dunnagh-Tani, you are very kind." With only a slight tremor in his voice he added, "I appreciate your concern for me, but I will do what is my duty. I am your third wife—and that is a great honor to me and my family.

"You have given me what I always wanted when you let me be with Pela, I am not ashamed to be your wife for the rest of the world to see." He spun round allowing the kilt to flare out for Dunnagh-Tani's inspection. "I might also insult our hostess if I don't wear it." He glanced at the rich green of the Kashallan's own new apparel.

The Kashallan glanced down at his new kilt and grunted. "You have a point there. And, I appreciate your courage—you honor me." As another thought came to him he smiled and put an arm around the Avairei's shoulder, steering him towards the door.

"And besides we have our reputation as wild uncouth outlaws to consider, we might as well give people in the Yeyen Banai Valley something really juicy to talk about, now hadn't we?"

Amril stared up at him confused then catching his meaning, he smiled. The Kashallan laughed softly, gave him a quick one-armed hug and opened the door.

In the outer chamber Nathan and the rest of his Speir'dina guards had stacked up the mattresses and were readying themselves for the same ordeal. Chelka stood by the open door to the hall waiting for them.

As the bedroom door opened Nathan glanced around. When he saw Amril's bright yellow kilt, he gave Dunnagh a toothy smile. "My, Amril looks nice today. You and your—uh—wife sleep well?"

Dunnagh blushed, and scowled. "Yeah, we did—have a good sleep that is."

Nathan's smile widened. "Right, glad to hear it." Nathan sobered when he saw Amril's anxious look toward the open hall door. Changing the subject he said, "Chelka over there says that K'San Yargal has spoken to his people; they're waiting for us. If you're ready we should go and get this over with."

The Kashallan gave him a crooked grin then nodded. "I feel a bit like an exhibit at the zoo, but I suppose it can't be helped."

Nathan laughed and fell into step beside him as they walked out into the hall. "You better get used to it, boyo, For the next few months, kashallans and Speir'dina are going to be the most interesting curiosities around—provided we live that long."

The Kashallan grunted. "There is always that to consider."

As they continued up the hallway, Chelka collected clan elder Arishim and Ima Ngeal from their suite. The Kashallan studied the two women covertly as they joined him. They still seemed tired from the journey, but otherwise looked in good health. If there was time after the coming strategy meeting with K'San Yargal, he would examine them more thoroughly.

It would seem that K'Sa Eilith had shown her gratitude to everyone. Ngeal had a new kilt of a deep red color. All the Speir'dina wore cleaned black uniforms, and sported their own gifts from Meh'gach's inhabitants. Nathan wore a new leather vest over his black shirt and Marti had a brightly colored headband across her forehead to keep back her black curls. Suspecting how much time and energy had gone into making these handmade items, he felt humbled by Meh'gach's generosity.

Hiding a smile he noticed that, as always clan elder Arishim had refused the long kilt and bare-chested Avairei style of clothing. She was dressed in her mended and cleaned Dymarian robe, the deep blue poli-fiber garment showing off her golden skin and crown of gray hair to advantage. She had made one concession to Timornan custom, however. A Warlinga woman's apron woven in orange, light blue and brown was tied around her plump waist. Zoo exhibits maybe, he thought, but well-dressed ones at least.

Hewn out of the stone of a cliff face, as were all the old keeps, the main hall at Meh'gach was a large open chamber with arching support columns disappearing into the gloom of the ceiling above. Sputtering reed-and-tallow torches hung in brackets along the walls, and beautiful tapestries, woven by the women of the accavett, decorated the inner wall behind the head table.

This morning the doors to the outside of the hall were flung wide to take advantage of the light and the growing warmth of the day outside. It was early, but even at this hour the stools around the long wicker tables were crowded with men from the hunting packs. Loti servants and a few Begta slaves bustled about serving out the morning meal to the waiting men.

At the entrance to the main hall the guests paused for a moment as the hall went deathly quiet; all eyes in the room focusing on the newcomers. Beside him the Kashallan could feel Amril begin to tremble. Without looking at him Dunnagh took his hand and squeezed it reassuringly. From his other side Nathan mumbled, "Zoo animals on display maybe, but at least they aren't leaping for our throats."

From his place at the head table, K'San Yargal and his son Varrod stood; and offered them a formal greeting. Just in front of him, Ngeal and Arishim bowed and started forward. With Amril's hand still engulfed within his own, the Kashallan bowed to their host and followed the women down the long isle to the head table, Aju'an's hunting pack clustering proudly around them.

Chelka escorted the Kashallan, Amril, Nathan, and the two women to the head table; Mar taking the rest of the Speir'dina to a lower table where Aju'an's pack was sitting. For a few moments longer the hush remained, then the need for food and drink took over and the hall lapsed back into its earlier bustle and chatter, with only the occasional glance directed towards the newcomers.

When the guests were seated, Chelka took up her place at the Kashallan's back. Dressed in her scaled bone warrior woman's apron she held her spear ceremonially at her side, her eyes forward, refusing to meet her father or older brother's eye.

The Kashallan saw Yargal give his daughter a disgusted look; then he sighed and took another sip of his morning tea.

"I'm sorry that you do not approve of your daughter's place among my hunting pack, K'San, but she really is a very capable member of my guards and I honor her greatly." He motioned to the Speir'dina sitting among Aju'an's men. "As you can see Women warriors are not uncommon among my host's kindred. Under Ticca's Hunt Leader's tutelage, Chelka has trained very diligently over the Sorins."

Yargal grunted, took another swallow of tea and said a bit stiffly, "So Aju'an has informed me—but I still think that a woman's place is in the accavett. How will I ever find her a husband if this goes on much longer."

On the other side of the table Aju'an choked with laughter. Both his father and his sister gave him a murderous glare. He took a swallow from his tea bowl and said, "I'm sorry, father, but if you could have seen all the adoring looks my little sister received from the men training with her at Ticca, you wouldn't be so worried."

"Shut up, Aju'an," Chelka mouthed, but Aju'an only smiled, his red eyes a light with mischief.

"She was really quite well favored by Ticca's defenders, especially Second Hunter Fadir, isn't that right, Little Sister?"

His father gave him a disgusted look and growled, "Enough. Men of a strange hunting pack indeed, hold your foul tongue and don't disgrace your sister further with your impudence."

Aju'an stared at his father defiantly for a moment, then looked down at his half-finished bowl of porridge and began eating again.

"I'm sure Aju'an meant no offence to his sister, K'San Yargal, nor do the men of Ticca who hold her in such high regard," the Kashallan said. "But if a marriage alliance is what is troubling you I'm sure that when the time comes round to that, her status as a hunter in my pack will not present a problem. I can think of at least one young K'San at the moment who might make a good match for her."

Behind him Chelka let out a startled gasp, he turned and gave her a conspiratorial wink then said to her father, "But now is not the time to be considering such a topic, as pleasant as it might be. When our affairs in Riath are concluded, we can speak of this further."

Yargal made a noncommittal sound, and changed the subject to a neutral topic. "I trust that your new accommodations are to your liking, Holy One."

Dunnagh blinked then nodded. Tani said, "Yes, thank you."

"Your hospitality is most satisfactory, K'San," Ngeal said smoothly. "Meldra and I slept quite well in our new suite last night."

Arishim nodded her head in agreement and picked up the bowl of tea that a servant set on the table in front of her.

The Kashallan glanced over his shoulder as a shaggy arm laid a bowl of porridge and a platter of meat in front of him. Recognizing the Loti serving him he smiled. "Mashen, they put you to work, did they? How are you and the others doing?"

The Loti's heavy-browed face creased into a smile. His yellow eyes alight with excitement, he said, "This isn't work, Dunnagh-Tani. I told them in the kitchen to let me do this. I am your Loti companion; it is my duty and my honor to serve you. We are all fine. We were very worried about you and the other Speir'dina at first, but now everything is good."

Overhearing him, Nathan chuckled. "I guess you and the rest of the outlaw Loti from Ticca must be pretty popular at the moment in the servant's quarters. Have you told them all our adventures yet?"

Mashen swished his feathery tail and beamed. "Not so many, San Nathan. The people here are curious, but to tell them everything would take till the next Sorin Season—or even longer."

Nathan laughed and took another mouthful of porridge. "You got that right, but no harm in telling a few stories to impress the women-folk, now is there?"

Mashen smiled. He laid his arms familiarly on the two men's shoulders, then leaning forward he confided in a low murmur. "Capric thinks he has found someone his family might wish to mate him with. There is this girl who works in the kitchens, but Fi'ac says he is crazy to think about such things now.

"But Capric says that he has to think about it because if he doesn't the girl's family may make other arrangements for her before his mother has a chance to come back later—" Mashen broke off and looked at the Kashallan imploringly.

The Kashallan's expression remained neutral, but he said kindly, "It is nice of you to speak up for your friend, Mashen, but I think Fi'ac maybe right. If I have time later I will come taste the pair and see what the girl's elders think of such a mating, but I won't make any promises."

"I think they will approve, Kashallan. Now that the K'San here has agreed to help us, Meh'gach's people hold us in high favor as San Nathan said."

Then changing the subject he leaned even closer and said, his voice just above a whisper, "I know you are very busy, but if you could find the time to come to the servants corrals it would be a good thing."

Looking anxiously sideways at the Warlinga he said, "Holy One, the high K'Sans of the Yeyen can offer you the fighting men you may need against our enemies, but there are things that my people can do to help beyond just the duties of a servant.

"There are many things the high K'Sans don't know about us—hidden things—like ways to travel through the Yeyen without being seen by the Warlinga and the Dingay's spies. Perhaps you should come speak to these elders, hmm?"

"I think you may be right." The Kashallan straightened then reached up and patted the Loti's shaggy arm. "Good lad, I'm glad you are thinking while you're out in the corrals; keep it up. You do your mother and your family proud. Come see me later, in my suite and I'll go with you to talk to them."

Mashen bobbed his head, and with a final anxious glance at the Warlinga, he hurried away.

Becoming aware of Yargal's shocked eyes upon him and the retreating Loti, the Kashallan took another mouthful of his cooling porridge then asked, "Is there something wrong, K'San?"

Yargal's head crest dipped. "No, Kashallan." He hesitated, then added stiffly, "But I am surprised that you would allow a peasant-servant to act towards you so familiarly. If that man was one of mine he would be disciplined for his insolence."

The Kashallan's mouth tightened, his blue eyes freezing the Warlinga like glacier ice. Yargal's head crest flattened in a mixture of confusion and irritation. It was clear by the rhythmic flicking of his tail that he was not accustomed to anyone giving him such a hard look.

For a long moment the Kashallan remained silent, staring; finally he said, "There are many things that have changed in the last seven hundred years, K'San, and it would appear that this attitude towards the Loti is but another of them. Mashen is the son of one of my dearest friends; I am not insulted by his ways.

"It was never the intent of my Khutani elders to create this segregation of the species that has developed in Khutani absence. In future this shameful system will have to change."

Arishim put down her tea bowl and gave the kashallan a despairing look. Into the uncomfortable silence that followed his remark she said, "As hunted outlaws traveling across the Great Swamp we learned to depend on and relate to one another in rather unconventional ways, K'San Yargal. I think that the people in the Yeyen are going to find us a bit hard to get used to at first. But with the Khutani's guidance, I'm sure we can learn to understand and accept one another, do you not agree?"

Yargal bowed stiffly to her and to the Kashallan, then turned his attention to something his son Varrod asked him.

The Kashallan sighed and gave Arishim a grateful look and busied himself with his meal. Politics, how he hated this little game they had to play. He knew they needed this Warlinga K'San's help, but he hated always having to watch what he said, especially when he heartily disliked how the other races treated the Loti and Begta. Ah well as he himself had said to Amril before entering the hall; they were an unconventional bunch.

AFTER THE MEAL THE people at the head table retired to a private chamber to further discuss their plans for destroying the enemy threat to the Yeyen Banai Valley. When they were all seated round a long work table, the Kashallan cleared his throat and said, "As you may have guessed, K'San Yargal, I must go to Riath. I must root out the corruption and destroy it, or there will be no safety for any of us—not in the Yeyen Banai or over the Rim Wall in the Great Swamp.

"But as an outlaw, with a death sentence on my head, it would not be wise for me to go there without support, either, as your son has also pointed out to me. It would be too easy for the Dingay to claim that I was an Umwira mutant and have me tortured, then executed. If that were to happen, I fear the reprisal of my kin would be most terrible."

"Dunnagh-Tani is probably talking about the Khutani abandoning you, K'San," Nathan said, "But that warning would have to apply to his Speir'dina kin too. We were warriors in our old home before we came here. We may not look like much, by Timornan standards of what a hunter of the enemy should be, but we still have with us some of the weaponry from our old life."

He brought out the hand blaster from the holster on his hip and laid it on the table for emphasis. "The priests tell me that our weapons are similar to the armament the ancients used before the great wars. I have my orders from the Maker Dievris—if Dunnagh-Tani is harmed or killed—"

At Dunnagh's frown, he left the rest of his thought unvoiced, but Yargal took his meaning. He nodded slowly. The man was right; his people seemed defenseless, but the way they carried themselves, and the worshipful way Aju'an deferred to them, let Yargal know that their appearance was most deceiving.

"I am not sure what I can do to help you stop them, but I am willing to hear your plan. What is it you require?"

"K'San Yargal, after the death of my niece, I too felt as you must. I didn't see how I could fight them," Ima Ngeal said. Along with the others, Yargal turned to her. He could see that she was tiring and should go back to bed, but as if anticipating his suggestion she waved her hand in dismissal.

"To have a changeling as my trusted councilor for years, and not even know it, then to have her wizard master overpower an innocent child entrusted to my care, within Ticca itself—I despaired. I even resigned my position as Ima Matri, because I felt so ashamed and unworthy. I am not sorry that I have done this, even though I no longer feel I am to blame, as I once did.

"I feel I am needed elsewhere now. I made this journey because I want to tell other clan elders about what has been happening to us. And that is where you can help too. We need your support. You are on the High Council, and I know there are other families that have tasted Dingay malice, but they are too afraid to do anything on their own. With your support, however, others will listen and join us.

"Once the clans understand that the kashallans have truly come amongst us again—and that the Dingay don't have the favor of the pools, as they claim—then surely with Maveth, Caltia, and Meh'gach backing we can bring Dunnagh-Tani to Riath to confront them.

"If you will help us gather other clans to our cause, we will have the strength we need to go to the Capital."

Yargal sat silent a long time, considering. This was a bold plan the Ima suggested. From the looks his youngest son and the Speir'dina gave him, he could tell that they had talked of this before among themselves. The idea had its appeal, and it might work, if his peers weren't already too cowed to challenge the Dingay. And it would most likely come to open conflict, he thought grimly. There were those who had curried favor with the Dingay, and would fight to keep the privileges they had gained by their sycophancy.

No, it would not be easy, and he suddenly realized that part of the price he and his family would have to pay, in order to gain that support from the other clans, would be to make his son's humiliation public. Just as the Ima had done, they would all have to share their stories.

True, the taste of their revenge would be sweet if they succeeded—yet it was a hard draft to swallow, nonetheless. Ah, but it was also a fitting penance for their complacent apathy all these years. For the Kashallan was right; these evil creatures must be stopped.

"All right," he said finally, "I see the wisdom in your plan. I will send out runners tomorrow to those K'Sans I know I could count on for their support. We can meet here—"

"K'San," Ngeal cut in, "to avoid Enaju's spies alerting her too early to our plans, may I suggest that we meet with these other K'Sans at a neutral spot, such as Shaden Keep, rather than here? Ima Urinia is a kinswoman of mine by marriage, and her Ata Leyas is Ronnan Caltia. As a dear friend, I am sure she will give us her support.

"As soon as I am rested I will go to her and tell her about the new kashallans. I will also explain to her our plan, and what happened to us over the Sorins.

"To make Ronnan her Second, over Dingay disapproval—you know that she has already dared much. Urinia is very courageous; she will not be intimidated or betray us, I believe. Inform whomever you think you can trust, but let her call the meeting. Shaden is a far more central location than Meh'gach is, as well."

"True, though perhaps not as secure," Yargal added upon reflection. "There are other unaligned or even hostile clan members there, who would surely learn of our intent and warn the High Matri."

Ngeal nodded. "That is a possibility, though I doubt if there are many spies in a place like Shaden at the moment. Urinia would have discovered and sent them packing by now, if I know her. Still it is a risk, as you say. But I believe it would be best to gather there, because of its closeness to the Capital.

If Urinia herself calls both the Warlinga and Avairei clans we feel we can trust to this meeting, it may look less ominous than if you should suddenly do so.

"The Dingay will be watching Meh'gach carefully after what they have just done to your house. Enaju will want to know if you have been broken to her will, or if you still harbor rebellion in your heart. She may even send K'San Drucas Segoi and his hunting packs against you if she fears you are plotting behind her back.

"For that reason, I suggest that you return to the Capital, as always, to allay any suspicions. Because of Sa Ainna's illness and Aju'an's disgrace, it would be perfectly understandable, under the circumstances, if neither of your sons accompanied you.

"That will leave them free to carry out any orders you may have in secret. Let Urinia and I arrange the meeting. We can give as a pretext the planning of a great feast and celebration for the solstice."

Yargal scratched his jaw thoughtfully. The woman was shrewd; such a plan might work. And she was right about Meh'gach—Enaju would have her eye on him after what she did. Any attempt to rouse the clans openly would draw Warlinga hunting packs from Riath to crush them swiftly, with few the wiser once their destruction was completed.

He nodded. "I can see the wisdom in your suggestions, Ima. It will be as you say. I will let you and Urinia call the clans, and I will return to Riath and," He grimaced, "pretend to be suitably cowed."

Chapter Three

Following Mashen out into the courtyard a while later, the Kashallan breathed in the damp Renewal air and sighed with pleasure. The sky above the keep was a crystal clear amethyst, the yellow sun warm upon his up turned face. To the right of the massive main gate, near the Warlinga warm-weather barracks, an old veteran shouted commands at a class of young hunters who were sparring with one another in a roped off oval.

To his amusement he saw Nathan and Ross over there, with the other onlookers. It hadn't taken Nathan long to get himself immersed in the thick of things. Not wanting to be side tracked into watching the bouts he hurried Mashen along to the servant's area. At the back of the outer courtyard the store houses and Loti corrals were arranged in orderly rows near, or along the outer wall.

When Dunnagh and his squad were captured and sold to the Warlinga at Tragar Keep he became personally acquainted with such accommodations. It was not a time he cared to remember—and the poor Loti at Tragar had been mistreated shamefully. Their lot had not been much better than his had been as a slave. As they strolled among the outbuildings, Dunnagh was pleased to see that things were much different here at Meh'gach.

Oh, compared to his suite within the keep, the Loti's corrals were lacking in many of the *civilized* comforts, but the shelters against the keep's outer wall were clean, sturdy and newly thatched with last year's liru reeds stored away for that purpose. The low stone fences that enclosed the larger family shelters seemed to be there to keep the younger children confined rather than to imprison their occupants, as had been done at Tragar. As he walked among the corrals, the air seemed to vibrate with the sounds of excited children who kicked and bucked playfully in the mud, grateful to be once more outside.

Around him Loti adults laughed and joked with one another while they packed their belongings. Because it was still so early in the Renewal season, the corrals and courtyard were more crowded than they would be a ten-day from now when most of the families here would have returned to their villages to plant the Sun-Time's grain.

The Loti he and Mashen passed were curious, The Kashallan could see that, but they didn't seem to be frightened of his alien Speir'dina looks. They knew who he was, of course, and greeted him shyly when their eyes met, but then they went back to their own business, with less concern than the Warlinga in the hall had done.

Mashen walked confidently to a large corral at the back of the outdoor kitchen. Here the smells of spices and roasting meat were a fragrant perfume in the air. Pausing just outside the fence, the Kashallan took in a deep breath and let it out in a wistful sigh. Mashen smiled and held open the corral's gate for him.

"I think I heard someone say that one of the hunting packs killed an obeylem bull last evening, that's probably what you're smelling."

Dunnagh laughed softly. "Whatever it is, it smells wonderful. I can hardly wait for our next mealtime; give my compliments to the head cook when you see him or her."

"You can tell her yourself for it is old Suki'a that I am taking you to see," the young man explained.

Inside the fence, the Kashallan saw Capric, Tli and others of Ticca's Loti helping their hosts with their chores. When they saw him the outlaws hurried over with excited cries. He greeted them warmly then walked with them towards the thatched hut at the back of the enclosure.

The shelter was a large rectangle. On three sides, the walls consisted of rolled-up woven screens that could be lowered at night for warmth. Peering inside the doorway he saw a large mound of clean dry moss piled against the stone that formed the house's fourth wall. Two small children lay sleeping in its cottony golden mass, their long colty legs tucked tight against their shaggy flanks.

Near the entrance a large loom had been assembled; a half-finished piece of russet kilt-cloth hung upon its frame. Two matrons stood nearby gossiping, their drop spindles whirling. They were twining yarn made from their own ragged coats, while a third woman wove some of the finished thread into the cloth.

Just outside the door to the kitchen an older Loti woman with grizzled fur stood with four feet planted solidly on the stone; her tail swishing gently, like a fan as if to cool herself. Her heavy brows were drawn down with concentration as she stirred a sooty clay pot hung over a smokeless peat fire. She looked up as they approached, then handing her ladle to a younger woman she hurried forward to greet her guest.

Mashen beamed, then announced proudly, "Aunt Suki'a, I told you he would come. This is Dunnagh-Tani, the first kashallan."

Bending her forelegs, Suki'a allowed her upper torso to nearly touch the ground in her obeisance. "You do us a great honor to visit us, Holy One."

Taking her hand the Kashallan helped her to rise. "On the contrary, Timornshaya, it is I who am honored."

The old Loti's yellow eyes filled with unshed tears at the sound of the ancient title. She wiped at her eyes with a furred arm, sniffed, and smiled. "Thank you, Holy One, I-I have never been called that, in my life time. I didn't even know anyone but my own Loti people remembered that form of address."

Still holding on to her callused hand he smiled, his blue eyes soft with his own emotions. Tani said quietly, "My Khutani kin have not forgotten, nor have I, Elder, and it grieves me sorely that so many others treat your people with such shameful disrespect."

Suki'a blinked, sniffed again, then motioning to a pile of grain sacks she said, "Yes, well, we get by—the K'San here treats us good enough. Come sit, may I offer you something to eat or drink?"

The Kashallan lowered himself onto the sacks, but shook his head. "No, thank you, I can see that you are busy so I won't stay long. I wanted you to know that, as a kashallan, I am here to serve all Timorna's people, not just the great Warlinga K'Sans and the Avairei. If there is something I can do for you and your kin; you need only call upon me."

Suki'a ran her hands through her tangled fur considering. Outside the fence a Loti man with a large pack strapped to his back shouted for someone in the kitchen to help him unload it.

"There is nothing that comes to mind at the moment—save for the kavay needed for the grain—but you already know about that, and have provided for us, so I'm told."

"Aunt Suki'a, I have told Dunnagh-Tani a little of our secret ways—if he should need our help—I thought he should know he could count on us, too."

Suki'a's face took on a guarded expression, her tail flicking with her unease. She studied the Kashallan thoughtfully for a long moment, then nodded. "This young one is a bit rash, but perhaps he is right. If you should need us, we will be there to help you if we can, of course."

The Kashallan raised a hand and brushed back a stray wisp of red hair; then he folded his hands in his lap, and looked her squarely in the eye. "I thank you for your trust, Elder. It is a comfort to know that I have so many loyal followers to rely on. But I am a little confused, have the Loti become warriors in secret?"

Suki'a laughed, shaking her head. "No, nothing like that, I'm afraid. You will have to look to the Warlinga for your warriors. But we do have our ways."

"I told him about the secret network," Mashen prompted, tail swishing with excitement. "If the enemy were to kill all his loyal Warlinga—and we had to hide—or travel in secret to protect the Holy One—I thought—."

Suki'a glanced around the courtyard and lowered her voice, even though there were no Warlinga close enough to hear them. "The network usually only passes on news from one Loti village to another, But Mashen is right, it could do much more than that. We do travel pathways from village to village, that the Warlinga and Avairei seldom use—or even know of. Because they pay us so little attention we can travel pretty much as we please, if we need to."

"That is a good thing to know, Elder. I would appreciate it if you would have the network spread the news of my coming. Let them know that the kashallan bond has been re-formed, so that if I need to I can call upon your people for help and advice as I journey to Riath."

"We will do that for you with pleasure."

"Thank you." The Kashallan fingered one of his long braidlets, twisting it between thumb and forefinger thinking. Over by the loom one of the women laughed. "The hunting packs from the Capital will be on the lookout for us, I suspect. My guards and I may need to use these secret trails of yours."

Suki'a's mouth tightened, and her expression became circumspect. "If you are in danger, by all means use the network; but we have guarded our secrets jealously for so long we would prefer to keep them from the Warlinga and Avairei—can you understand that?"

The Kashallan sighed, and nodded. "Yes, I guess I can understand. I will honor your wishes, elder. We will only use the network, if it becomes necessary—I promise you."

"Thank you."

The Kashallan stood and stretched. "I should get back; I have kept you long enough. The meal you are cooking smells wonderful. Is there anything else I can do for you before I go?"

Suki'a combed her thick hands through the long fur of her chest not looking at him. Finally she nodded and looked up her eyes, under her heavy brow ridges troubled. "I hope this will not seem to bold of me to ask, but there is a small favor that you could do for me personally—if you would."

"If I can, certainly, I will do it. You need only ask."

She took a deep breath. "This may not be to your liking, if the stories Mashen here has been telling us are true, but I would like you to do something about old Neyal. Basically, I believe he is a good man. I'm sure it was very hard on him to do what he did, and now—"

She lifted her hands in a gesture of hopelessness. "They are still keeping him in a damp cell in the lower tunnels, and the guards, when they remember him at all heap abuse, and sometimes worse upon him. He is in a bad way, and I fear he may die, if something isn't done soon."

The Kashallan's face clouded. For a time he said nothing staring blindly out into the courtyard. Finally he sighed. "I will see what I can do. You shame me with your compassion, Elder. In truth, I have been trying to forget about the man, but you are right in a way, it is his superiors in Riath who are to blame.

"It is to this house that he is bound, so I'm not sure what I can do. Ultimately it will be up to your K'San to decide his fate, but I will promise you that I will go see him, and see that he is not mistreated."

"That will be enough, Young One, and I understand. Thank you"

As the Kashallan followed Mashen back to their suite, Tani said to Dunnagh, <<Everything is much different than my encoded memories led me to believe, Kasha. Only the stone rooms of the keeps seem to have remained much as my ancestors remember them>>

<<Well that's to be expected, Shalla, it has been hundreds of years since your ancestors walked the surface world.>>

<<Mm, it has been that. You know, Kasha, out of the four intelligent species the Makers bred, I think the gentle Loti have remained the most faithful to the Makers intentions for them.>>

<<That is often the way with people who are close to the land, Shalla,>> Dunnagh said. <<It is a shame that the others can't see more value in them.>>

<<Mm, I can remember that they were once on the High Council—as were the Begta, I might add. I would like to see their seats re-established again, when this is all settled. I think I will speak to our kindred about that when there is time.>>

<<Do that, Shalla, it is a good idea.>>

Chapter Four

Chelka paused and looked back at the Kashallan, her head crest rising slightly in inquiry. Just a head of them the flickering light of the guardsman's torch revealed a heavy wooden grate set into the floor. About them the ponderous weight of the stone seemed to press down like a smothering shroud.

"Is this where he is being kept?" the Kashallan asked quietly. Grim-faced the guard nodded. The Kashallan sighed and motioned for the man to remove the covering. The air in the lower tunnels was clammy upon his skin, though not overly chill. It was too close to the heat of the underground pool for that. This could be an unexpected luxury to anyone imprisoned down here, he thought.

Handing his torch to Chelka, the guard crouched down and heaved the grate aside, revealing a gaping maw of blackness. Standing once more his head crest rose; his eyes flicked to a ladder propped against the wall, then back to the Kashallan's face. The Kashallan nodded and he slid the ladder into the pit below.

Dunnagh-Tani started forward, but Chelka put an arm out to stop him. "Let me do this for you, Kashallan, there is no need for you to go down there."

He shook his head. "No I promised; I will go."

"Then, I will come with you." Before he could open his mouth to protest she stepped to the edge of the pit and with torch in hand sprang into the darkness. Dunnagh rolled his eyes in exasperation and followed her more slowly down the ladder. Did she think the old man was going to attack him with tooth and claw? His guards' over protectiveness was starting to get on his nerves.

As he descended an overpowering stench hit him like a hammer blow. Blinking in the torchlight at the base of the ladder he could see where

106

uneaten food and rotten garbage had been flung down through the grate to add their perfume to the smell of the overflowing bucket in the corner. Dunnagh's mouth tightened in disgust.

The cell had been hollowed out of the living rock at some time in the distant past. It wasn't very large. A rotting heap of moss was piled carelessly along the farthest wall and upon it the shrunken figure of the old Avairei lay curled in a motionless ball. The Kashallan frowned. Since their arrival the man had given no indication that he was aware of their presence.

Muttering a curse under his breath he crossed to the old priest and crouched down beside him. "Neyal?" When the man made no reply; he reached out and took one of the man's hands in his own and formed the link. He gasped as a wave of bitter despair and hopelessness came crashing down the connection they now shared. Damn.

The poor fellow hadn't eaten in days, and glancing around at the garbage that had been flung down to him, the Kashallan couldn't blame him. As Suki'a had predicted; the old man was in a bad way, both physically and mentally. Sending a restorative into the man's blood stream; he waited.

Finally Neyal opened a crusty eyelid and stared up at him. The Kashallan released himself from the link. "Feeling a little better?"

Neyal licked his lips with a swollen tongue. "K-Kashallan?"

"Ah, good, you know me at least." He patted the priest's shoulder reassuringly. "There is no reason for you to be treated like this; I'm going to get you out of here." Neyal stared at him blankly for a moment more then closed his eyes, drifting back into his delirium.

The Kashallan stood and turned to Chelka. "Can you carry him out of here? Perhaps I'm overstepping my authority, but I see no sense in this meaningless cruelty. If he is to die for his crime against your family then let it be done—and cleanly." He gestured in disgust at the filth around them. "Not like this."

Chelka hesitated; she looked at the dying man, then nodded. "I can carry him; where would you like me to take him?"

He scratched his jaw, thinking. "Take him back to his room; he will rest better in his own bed, and he is too weak to go anywhere. We'll have one of the servants clean him up and feed him. Later when he's rested, with your father's counsel, we can decide what to do with him."

Chelka nodded and handed him the torch. Bending over she cradled the old man in her arms, stepped beneath the whole in the ceiling and leapt easily out of the pit. Grim-faced, the Kashallan followed her up the ladder, without looking back

THE FOLLOWING AFTERNOON the Kashallan was resting in his suite when he was summoned to K'San Yargal's chamber. Last night he had explained to Yargal at dinner what he had done, and why. The Meh'gach K'San hadn't been overjoyed at his interference, but he said very little about it at the time. Now he approached the K'San's rooms with some trepidation, wondering what Yargal's mood might be.

Aju'an opened the door to his father's chamber, then stood back and allowed him to precede him into the room. K'San Yargal and his heir, Varrod were there seated on padded stools. A low wicker table with bowls and a pitcher of beer upon it stood between them. To his surprise, Ngeal was also present; sitting in a comfortable chair to Yargal's right. Two of Yargal's guardsmen stood on either side of the door, their eyes alert. On the braided carpet near the K'San's feet a dejected Neyal crouched.

Neyal looked up, as the door opened, his haunted eyes following the Kashallan's progress across the room to the stool Yargal invited him to take.

The Kashallan bowed, and seated himself. The old man certainly looked better than he had yesterday, he thought, though his sunken chest and listless appearance told their own story of mistreatment and despair.

When he had accepted the bowl of beer Aju'an handed him, K'San Yargal set down his own bowl and said in a gruff voice, "Before I make my final decision about what should be done with this man, he has asked to speak to you."

The Kashallan nodded. Trying to maintain a neutral expression he focused his blue-eyed stare upon the priest and asked, "I am here, what is it you have to say to me?"

Neyal raised his eyes from his contemplation of the carpet, scooted closer to the Kashallan and held out his hands palms downward in the ritual gesture, inviting the link.

Startled, the Kashallan took his hands automatically and established the connection. Neyal licked his lips, then in a trembling voice he asked, "If you will permit, Holy One, I wish to offer my fealty and take the oath of service to you and the Khutani."

The Kashallan jerked back, almost breaking the link in his surprise. Narrowing his eyes he glared at the man suspiciously, but he could taste Neyal's sincerity through the link they shared. "Why would you want to do this, Dingay? You should know by now that I have no love for your clan."

Neyal swallowed hard, he was trembling under that cool blue gaze, but he met that look honestly. "I know that," he murmured, "yet all the same I am offering myself to your service. I wish to make amends—in part for what I did. I will not betray you, I swear it."

"Dunnagh-Tani," Ngeal said into the silence. "Neyal has asked me to speak for him." She glanced at Yargal, including him in her plea. "I believe him when he says that he thought he was honestly doing the will of the Khutani, no matter how misguided his attempt might have been.

"I also believe that allowing him to live, and taking his oath will be of some service to our cause."

Yargal's head crest rose in scornful disbelief. "How can such a loathsome little worm help us, Ima? I fail to see how this can be."

"As a member of the Dingay clan, he will be able to tell us many things about his clan members that cannot be found out in other ways, K'San. Also it will add some weight to our cause when one of the Dingay clan's own Atas tells his story and denounces the High Matri for her crimes.

"To have openly proclaimed what could not be proven, only suspected before, is of great advantage to us—believe me—we can use him."

Varrod sprang up and began pacing the room, muttering to himself under his breath. Turning angrily to his father and the Kashallan, he snarled, "This is nothing but a lie—a way to worm his way out of the death he deserves so he can betray us all later. I say kill him and be done with it."

"I understand, and sympathize, with your anger, San Varrod," the Kashallan said, "but through the link I share with him, I can tell you that he isn't lying. His offer is sincere."

Varrod glared, at the room in general, but returned to his stool and sat heavily upon it. "Would you have me spare his life so that he may give you his oath?" Yargal asked quietly.

The Kashallan rubbed his free hand tiredly across his face, trying to decide. The man was making a sincere offer to help, but did he want that—could he accept his pledge?

"Dunnagh-Tani," Ngeal said, leaning forward in her chair to catch his eye. "You told me once that you held no ill will against the Dingay family in general. That first night at Ticca when I stepped into the pool with you and the Maker Dievris; you said that if members of that clan would give you their oath, you would welcome them as you would any other of your followers."

The Kashallan sighed. His mouth twisted into an ironic little grin. "So I did, Ima, and maybe you are right. Turning to the Warlinga he said, "K'San Yargal, Ima Ngeal has a point; we can use his help. If you have no objection, I will take his oath."

Varrod glared at them all angrily. Yargal glanced at his son, then took a long swallow of his beer, studying the priest on the floor as he did so. At last he said. "I don't like it, but I see the wisdom in the Ima's suggestion—provided he can be trusted." He glanced at the Kashallan, head crest raised. Dunnagh-Tani nodded. "Very well, take his oath. But know this too. He can't stay here; I will not have him as a part of my household any longer, no matter what oath he gives."

"He can go with me to Shaden Keep," Ngeal said. "All I ask is that you guarantee his safety till then."

Yargal gave his son a stern look then nodded.

Chapter Five

Trotting amidst an honor guard of his kinsmen Tobrach glanced over his shoulder for a last sight of Tragar Keep as they rounded the bend in the trail. The massive stone fortress crouched like a hungry predator on a barren ledge facing a maze of deep canyons and tawny ridges that lead into the gray-shrouded peeks of the Ghostlands to the north.

Hidden now by the cliff wall and the thorn brush along their back trail, Tobrach was surprised by the feelings of loss that came over him when he thought of the old pile of rock. Was he viewing it for perhaps the last time? How ironic, he thought. A couple of years ago he would have given almost anything to be leaving the lonely border keep and heading back to the comfort of his clan's apartment in the capital at Riath.

He'd been sent out to the border, as his cousin Gormach's heir when he finished his training, because the Ima Sagas had refused Gormach the red kavay needed for breeding. The drunkenness, the apathy, the despair, he had found when he arrived, had made him grow to hate the place. Ah, but that was before the Kashallan killed Gormach and remade the world.

Tobrach glanced to the north again, eyeing the jagged peaks with a tendril of unease twisting in his belly. What was the enemy planning? His instincts warned him not to leave. Every bone in his body cried out against it. He should be taking his hunting packs north to patrol the border, not heading south for a Sun-Season of luxurious confinement in the Capital. Not that he'd had much choice in the matter, he thought bitterly. At Combaron's insistence, and with one of K'San Drucas's best hunting packs to back his veiled threat, Tobrach had had to come along peaceably or risk terrible consequences.

If he had resisted—even killed Combaron and his escort to a man, the price would have been a high one. He would have lost many of his kinsmen in such a battle. And, as an outlawed keep he would be caught between the enemy and fresh hunting packs from the Yeyen sent to investigate and punish such an outrage.

It hadn't been worth it. He might be sacrificing his own life by agreeing to come so meekly, but with his hunt leader, Warega in charge, the Khutani and the border would still have what protection he could offer, and that was what truly mattered.

The column of hunters and the Loti peasants carrying supplies and Combaron's covered litter were strung out along the steep trail for some distance. As Tobrach used both his clawed hands and feet to negotiate a particularly treacherous section of the path, he could hear the priest's whining curses as the Loti climbing behind him tumbled the priest about in their efforts to traverse the slope. Tobrach gritted his teeth and tried to climb a little faster. The man's voice grated on his nerves.

Combaron had changed since last he'd seen him. His face still had that sly sharpness about it, but over the long Sorin confinement he'd grown a paunch that hung in a blubbery fold over the belt of his kilt. His pelt too was different. It had taken on that odd sickly mottling some of the Dingay assumed in middle age.

He'd staggered into the Tragar's main hall that first night, a small, disheveled figure surrounded by the massive, hard-eyed men of his escort. He'd looked so pitiful with his tangled mane and muddy kilt, but Tobrach couldn't find it in his heart to feel sorry for the man.

Reeking of lamra brandy he demanded to see Gormach, and when he learned that neither Gormach nor his prisoner, Sagas Caltia were at the keep he had worked himself into such a rage that he'd dropped to the floor in a frothing fit.

After they'd gotten Combaron settled in a bed with his apprentice Dar to look after him, Tobrach told Drucas's hunt leader his prepared story over a meal in the hall. The man's hard eyes never left Tobrach's face as he recited the tale. Tobrach could almost taste his skepticism as he rambled on about the Umwira finding them, killing Gormach and escaping with Sagas, Blue Eyes and the other prisoners.

When he fell silent at last, unnerved by the hunt leader's stare; the man only took a long drink of his beer and smiled in a way that gave Tobrach an impressive view of his fangs. "I think my K'San and the High Matri herself will wish to hear this tragic story, K'San Tobrach. When the Ata has recovered his health we shall start back to the Capital without delay so that you may tell them your news."

Tobrach swallowed some of his own beer, hoping to hide his unease. As he'd feared, they were going to take him back to Riath—and then. . . . Making a last futile attempt to avoid the inevitable, he said, "Surely your memory is a good one, hunt leader. I have told you all there is to tell. The priest can write it down if you wish, but the Umwira's Sun-Season raiding will begin soon. I am needed here with my hunting packs."

The hunt leader took another long swallow of his beer and flashed his threatening smile again. "Oh, I think there is time for a quick run to Riath, K'San. It is still early yet. The snow will be clogging the passes further north for many a ten-day yet. You have time—and it is such an *interesting* story. I'm sure they will want to hear it. Do you not agree?"

Tobrach hadn't agreed but felt it better to come along without too much resistance lest he risk arousing more than this hard eyed man's vague suspicions.

They would have left that next morning, but a storm yesterday delayed their departure. High winds and blue sleet roared down off the eastern peeks, covering the ground with a coating of treacherous ice and forcing them to remain within doors. Listening to Combaron's complaints and the rude jests of the hunters in the hall, Tobrach had fretted, praying that a fight between his men and the Riath pack wouldn't start, or that the hunt leader wouldn't get bored and decide to go exploring into the deeper tunnels of the keep where Gormach's former prisoners hid.

By the time the day ended, Tobrach was actually looking forward to getting out of the keep just to relieve the tension. The following day dawned clear and warm; the storm taking out its spite on the Begta warrens in the canyons further west. Yesterday's ice already was melting into chilly rivulets by the time the Loti were packed and Combaron pried from a drunken stupor into his litter, so they could start.

The Riath hunt leader set a fast pace and kept it up till the sun was well past its zenith. Coming to a wide portion of the trail with some shelter out of the wind, he finally surrendered to Combaron's cursing and threats and allowed the exhausted Loti and the rest of the men to rest for a time.

Tobrach crouched, leaned his rump against a boulder and took out a strip of dried meat from his pack. His cousin, Chi'am crouched beside him, the rest of his men nearby, forming a casual but protective circle around him. Chi'am rummaged in his own pack and said in a low voice, "If that whining little pervert doesn't shut up soon, I'm going to topple him and the Loti off the side of the next cliff we pass."

Tobrach grunted and bit off another mouthful of the salty meat. "Better not, or we may all join him in the canyon. It wouldn't take much provocation for our *escort* to decide we were too much trouble to bother with."

Chi'am sneered, his head crest flattening. "Let them try."

Tobrach shot him a warning look and he lifted his crest and began eating again. "I want no trouble, Chi'am," Tobrach murmured. "Officially Clan Tragar is neutral in this veiled struggle between the Caltia and Dingay clans, and I have no wish to change that position—not until I have a chance to speak to my grandfather and the other clan elders about the Kashallan. No trouble; do you understand?"

"I understand, K'San, and I will obey."

After his meal, the salty taste of the meat lingered in his mouth so Tobrach decided to go down to the creek for a long drink rather than drinking from the tepid pool in the rocks where he'd filled his water flask.

Climbing down the embankment he walked along the rocky bank allowing the water's cool breath and joyous babble to ease his troubled heart. Thorn bushes grew along the opposite shore, pink buds, like furry pimples clustered on the tips of their thin black branches. Last year's moss crunched under his feet as he wandered along the creek looking for a way down to the water. If they kept up this pace they would reach the Jeban Pass in two more days he reckoned.

At last finding the low place he wanted, he slipped down to the creek, and squatted in the shallows, looking into the luminous indigo water. He lowered his head and drank. The icy flow made his teeth ache, but he buried his face in the rush of it and sucked in great mouthfuls of its coppery sweetness. There was nothing like the threat of doom to make the simple pleasures of life seem so important, he thought.

As Tobrach raised his head and started back towards the camp his eye was snagged by the outline of a large footprint in a patch of unmelted snow a little ways further up the creek. The print lay in the shadow of a big rock where a mound of snow and frozen mud had collected.

Upon closer inspection he could see where someone, like himself had come down from the path and stopped to drink and relieve himself in this out of the way place before returning to the trail above. Tobrach crouched, reached out a finger and scooped up a fragment of the muddy gray mound of dung, and brought it close to his nose.

He sniffed. It was old, but not as old as dung left here before the Sorin confinement. Had the Riath pack stopped here on their way to Tragar? Perhaps, but something about this aroused his instincts in a way that the find of another Warlinga would not.

He wiped off his hand in the snow and studied the footprint more carefully. It was blurred and half eroded away by the melting ice, but he doubted if the print was made by one of his people. The foot that had made it was large, but it was broader and the claw marks were positioned oddly for a Warlinga. Tobrach hissed, his tail lashing the ground behind him. Umwira, he was almost sure of it. A warband of the enemy had traveled over this path just after the last Sorin storm blew itself out.

Tobrach rose, still staring at the muddy footprint. His body trembled, every nerve in his being wanted to answer the ancient call to the hunt. The enemy had been here; they were plotting, he must—

"What are you doing, K'San?"

Tobrach whirled, claws extended, his body sinking into a fighter's crouch. Masked by the sound of the creek, the Riath hunt leader had managed to steal up on him without his notice. Except for the flicking of the tip of his tail, the man gave no outward sign of aggression, but his hard eyes watched Tobrach carefully.

"We are ready to leave, K'San, why do you remain down here? Are your bowels griping you?"

The tone of the innocent question set Tobrach on the defensive. Was the half-bred Begta mocking him? He stepped to one side and pointed to the footprint. "My bowels are fine, but this proves that it is not wise for me to go with you to Riath. I am needed on the border. A warband of the enemy has been here since the Sorin confinement I must—"

The hunt leader's head crest rose, the motion of his tail increasing. He brushed past Tobrach and glared down at the print, managing to deface it more as he did so. After a long moment he laughed, the sound deep and mocking. "Very clever, but I think not. You will not squirm out of your meeting with the High One and my K'San so easily."

He pointed back up the slope with his tail, his eyes never leaving Tobrach's face. "It is time to go."

Tobrach felt the threat, but held his ground. "The Hated Enemy is abroad; it is my duty—"

"Duty? Ata Combaron, as the High Matri's representative entrusted your cousin Gormach and you with the duty of capturing the renegade Sagas Caltia and her blue-eyed mutant demon. A duty, which you failed to accomplish—I might add. Now you have the nerve to babble to me about trailing an enemy warband, because you found where one of my men relieved himself on our journey here?"

"If the enemy is indeed abroad, it would seem to me that you and your drunken, lazy kinsmen are not to be trusted to undertake such a charge."

He gave Tobrach a toothy smile. "Trust, K'San, hard to win back, once it has been betrayed. Do you not agree, K'San?"

Tobrach's head crest flattened; he remained in a crouch, his whole body trembling with rage. The hunt leader pointed again with his tail up the slope. In a voice barely above a murmur, he said, "If you think you can take me; do it now. Otherwise get back up that trail, or I will leave your bones here for the scavengers."

Tobrach quivered, his instincts goading him to try—and if he did? He was no match for this seasoned warrior. The man would indeed leave his carcass to rot in this lonely ravine. And what good would that do anyone? His death would be just another foolish, pointless killing that would leave his keep without a K'San and the Kashallan and the Khutani with one less defender.

He'd been a fool, and now he would have to swallow his pride and endure the man's contempt. Straightening Tobrach bowed to the other man. "As you say, hunt leader, it is nothing. I will go now." Brushing past him, Tobrach hurried down the ravine and climbed back onto the trail.

With a lowered head crest and tucked tail, Tobrach ignored Combaron's angry questions and took his place among his honor guard, enduring the smirks of the Riath pack as he passed them. Refusing to answer his kinsmen's anxious questions, he strode out at a brisk pace following the hunt leader's barked command.

For the rest of the journey, and if necessary in Riath too, he resolved to play the cowering Begta if he must. But at the first opportunity he would send a runner back to warn Warega about the Umwira warband, and perhaps another on to his grandfather. The pack was making good time, but the litter would slow them down going over the pass. A lone man could make better time, and he needed a little safe guard—to avoid any convenient accident before he reached the Capital. He would have to be very careful, however, if the Riath hunt leader found out...

Chapter Six

"Hunt Leader, I'm sure it's them. Open the gate," Ronnan Caltia said.

The priest stood in the advancing shadows near Shaden Keep's side gate, looking up at the big Warlinga, with a phony air of assurance that didn't fool the Hunt Leader for a minute. Pagrich stood refusing to be hurried. The Ata didn't know any more than he did who was out there. He left the rest of that thought unvoiced, even to himself. They were all living on borrowed time; Ronnan should know that and not be in such a hurry to invite trouble in.

The knock came again; Pagrich's tail lashed the ground behind him in a menacing arc. His three subordinates waiting nearby glanced at one another uneasily, careful not to draw attention to themselves. Were the people out there really Urinia's mysterious visitors?

Then his head crest flattened as he saw two Loti servants carrying a large vat of stew hurry from the kitchen towards the barracks open door. Damn. He had told them to clear the courtyard.

"Kir, see to that," He jerked his head in the direction of the noisy barracks. "I want this courtyard cleared and kept clear. They can wait a while longer for their meal, damn them. Nobody is starving round here. Those half-bred Begta better listen to my orders this time, or I'll know the reason why."

Kir saluted with a clawed hand to his chest and loped off. Some moments later the frightened Loti were hustled out of the barracks, minus the stew pot, and hurried into the far kitchen. Pagrich grunted.

The howl of a vistri somewhere out in the darkness, drew Pagrich's attention back to the barred gate in front of him. His lip curled in a silent snarl. If these travelers at the gate were the ones they were expecting, as

Ronnan and his Second claimed, then they were early. He'd given the messenger specific instructions to wait until the keep was a bed.

The knock came again, more insistent this time. Motioning for the priest to remain where he was, Pagrich continued on to the gate alone. He glanced at his kinsmen, tall bulky shadows in the gloom and gave them a hand sign to be ready in case of trouble. Pagrich pulled back the window in the door and growled, "This is Hunt Leader Pagrich; who is there?"

"San Aju'an Meh'gach," said a low voice from the night beyond. "I come with the travelers from Ticca. Open the gate damn it, Ima Urinia is expecting us."

Pagrich grunted, his natural instinct warning him to go carefully here, in spite of the Meh'gach name. As usual the arrogant Avairei had told him very little. He didn't like all this secrecy—and they were early. His red eyes narrowed as he tried to see into the dimness.

Outside the road was a carpet of silver flowing off into the evening mists. Closer to the gate he could see the shadowed figures of a well-armed hunting pack. They stood with head crests raised and their spears gripped in their hands, anxious to get themselves and their charges within the keep now that night had fallen. And, that too was understandable. All manner of vicious hunters prowled in the darkness beyond Shaden's walls.

Pagrich tried to make out the details of several heavily wrapped figures clustered together within the warrior's protective ring. Catching a glimpse of a shaggy Loti torso within their midst, he scowled. Loti? By the Great Hunt Leader were these fools playing some kind of joke—why would the Ima want to see peasants in such secrecy? His head crest flattened and he let out a low hiss of displeasure.

The Meh'gach Warlinga leading the pack glanced down the road behind him and stepped a little closer. "Well Hunt Leader? I can appreciate your desire to be cautious in these times, but we're being followed by a pack of vistri. Are you going to let us in, or do we have to stand and defend ourselves at your very gate?"

As if to emphasize the young man's words, a high-pitched howl rang out, this time much closer than the one Pagrich had heard not long before. A moment later others of its kind answered it in the surrounding darkness.

Pagrich growled deep in his throat in an instinctual response to the vistri hunting cries, yet still he hesitated. It was one thing to rescue weary travelers from death at the jaws of the vermin; it was another to be tricked by foul Umwira magics into allowing an even worse enemy within Shaden's gates.

He had heard the stories about Sulas Keep—and who knew what was abroad even in the Yeyen Banai Valley these days. Better to be safe than sorry.

While he was still trying to decide, Pagrich felt a touch on his forearm. Head crest dipping, he turned his head. He'd forgotten about the priest. The slim figure of the Avairei stood now at his elbow, looking up at him, an expression of quiet authority on his face. "Open the gate Hunt Leader. I heard the man give you his name, these are assuredly the travelers Ima Urinia and Ima Ngeal are expecting."

Pagrich grumbled under his breath, "On your head be it, and stepped back, motioning for his kinsman to throw open the gate.

What's this? Pagrich blinked, not sure if his eyes were playing tricks on him in the dim light. The creatures the pack was ushering through the crack in the gate appeared to be half Loti, half something else. Once inside the courtyard the strange Loti-like creatures began to "come apart."

The Warlinga gaped, at last realizing that the travelers they were expecting had been sitting astride Loti peasants in a most unusual manner. Once more he felt the worm of doubt stirring within his gut. By the Great Hunt Leader, he'd never heard of such a thing.

The travelers dismounting from the Loti's backs varied in size, but all remained wrapped in their heavy cloaks with their hoods pulled up to conceal their faces in spite of the mild night. "More damned secrets," he grumbled and stepped a little closer to get a better look at the newcomers. A gust of wind made the torches by the inner keep door flare.

Still atop one of the peasants, Pagrich saw the anxious face of a young Avairei Ata peering out from a wide hood as if searching for someone. Spying his quarry in the increased light he smiled. "Uncle Ronnan, over here." Ronnan Caltia let out a startled gasp and hurried forward, Pagrich not far behind.

As they came near the young man was being helped off the Loti's shaggy back by one of Aju'an's men. Throwing back his cloak he hurried forward to embrace the older priest. Ronnan suffered the embrace for a moment, then held the young Ata out at arm's length. "Amril, what by all the Gods are you doing here? Whatever was my sister thinking of to let you come on such a dangerous mission?"

Amril looked down shyly and smoothed the fur on his chest for a moment then he murmured "I had to come; it is my duty—"

A soft chuckle from the figure still on the Loti beside the youth made them look up. Pagrich caught the gleam of sharp white teeth in the torchlight, then the face was once more in shadow. "I said much the same thing to him myself, before we left Ticca, Ata, but your family is a stubborn lot, and neither He nor Sagas would listen to me, so here he is."

In the next moment the figure climbed from atop the Loti's back and stood beside the young man. Hugging him against his side he said, "Stubborn though he may be, I have been grateful for both his company and his assistance already on our journey. I'm glad he is with me."

Atop the Loti the stranger had seemed gigantic, now on the ground Pagrich realized he was a couple hand-widths shorter than himself. The Hunt Leader flicked his tail nervously.

Why did he continue to conceal his face? This odd traveler was no Avairei, too big, but he was no Warlinga K'San either. Yet the priests and the Meh'gach hunting pack seemed to hold him in high regard, untroubled by his oddness.

"You honor me with your praise, Husband," the Avairei murmured.

Husband?

As the torchlight sputtered then flared again the Hunt Leader saw a furless, five-fingered hand squeeze the Ata's shoulder and a pale flat face smiled down at the two priests. So, the stories were true—the Caltia had betrayed them to the Umwira—and like a fool he had allowed them inside the gate. Pagrich's head crest flattened, as he readied himself for the attack. They would die here, he would—

Before he could make another move, a pair of scaly arms roughly seized him from behind, and a barbed tale wrapped itself around his neck choking off a roar. Pagrich bucked wildly, but by that time another Warlinga held him as well, and the tail around his neck was tightening its grip

As he felt the blackness engulf him Pagrich heard a muffled command and the pressure around his neck slackened. In the next moment he heard a low voiced cursing in a strange language and someone muttered, "Damned secretive Avairei. Dunnagh, is this going to happen every time we enter a new keep? If it is, the joke's going to get stale really quick."

There was a low chuckle. "I hope not, but this kind of welcome does keep you and the pack awake, that's for certain."

Out of the corner of his eye Pagrich could see that his kinsmen were also helpless. This pack was well-trained and good. Silently cursing his bad luck, he decided to try again anyway. Pagrich opened his mouth, but before he could make a sound the pressure on his throat increased again. Another of the cloaked strangers stepped in front of him and said, "Easy, Hunt Leader, don't do anything stupid. This Keep is in no danger from us. I would hate to have to kill you, but I have my orders from Maker Dievris—"

"Nathan. It's all right, I think our friend here was just a little surprised to see me that's all." He gave Ronnan a reproachful look. "Why didn't you tell him?"

Ronnan stammered a hasty apology, which the stranger barely acknowledged before coming over to Pagrich. Pulling back his hood he allowed the Warlinga to take a good look at him in the flickering torchlight. "Take a good look at me, Hunt Leader. The instinct to always be on guard against the enemies tricks was bred into you by my Khutani ancestors, so it would be natural for you to make the assumption when seeing my host, that I was another mutant down from the Ghostlands," Tani said. "But I assure you I am not."

The creature gave him a crooked smile. "And, with my experience of Avairei high handedness, especially towards the Warlinga, I suspect that your Ima, or the good Ata there never bothered to tell you who has really come visiting tonight. I too fight the Hated Enemy. That is why I am here."

Pagrich grunted, his head crest rising in spite of himself. Beside him one of the guards who held him let out a throaty feminine chuckle. "It is their way, Kashallan, whether by custom or breeding, I don't know."

Shocked again, Pagrich turned his head sharply and gaped at the Warlinga female holding his arm in a vise-like grip. She gave him a toothy smile. "Hello, Hunt Leader. The night is full of surprises, hmm?"

"Chelka," Aju'an warned. The woman's smile widened, but she remained silent. Stepping forward at that moment Amril bowed to his uncle and then to Pagrich. "Uncle Ronnan, Hunt Leader, let me present to you my husband, Dunnagh-Tani, the first of the new kashallan bonded."

Pagrich blinked. His head felt like it was stuffed with porridge—an Ata this creature's wife—and what was a kashallan? He'd heard that word before, but couldn't place its meaning. When the word's ancient significance finally registered, he stared at the Kashallan, jaw slack in amazement. At last he turned to Ata Ronnan for conformation.

The priest nodded slowly. "It is true, Pagrich, or so Ima Ngeal has assured us, and both Ima Urinia and I believe her, after hearing her story." Ronnan hesitated, then murmured in a somewhat apologetic tone, "I'm sorry, I guess we should have been more forthcoming with you, but—"

"Excuse me, Ata," the one called Nathan interrupted. "It's been a long ride today, and, your Ima did stress the need for secrecy." He glanced significantly towards the noisy barracks. "Perhaps we should continue this discussion indoors where we can be a little more private, and less likely to be observed."

"This is my kinsman, and one of my Hunt Leaders, San Nathan," the Kashallan said. "I believe he has a point. Perhaps we should go indoors before we attract too much attention."

Ronnan bowed. "Of course, Holy One." The priest's eyes anxiously flicked to the still restrained Pagrich, and then he returned his attention to the Kashallan with his unvoiced question.

The Kashallan considered the Hunt Leader thoughtfully for a long moment. "Before I tell my Warlinga to release you, Hunt Leader Pagrich, I need your word of honor that you will do nothing to harm me and my followers, or hinder me as I carry out the will of my Khutani elders."

Pagrich's red eyes gleamed; how dare the creature speak to him like that! But if he was indeed a kashallan, as Ronnan claimed then to do ought else but submit would be the greatest sacrilege. He thought about it a moment longer then sighed and nodded his agreement. "You have my word. If you are as you claim a sacred kashallan, then you are deserving of my loyalty. I will do nothing to hinder you, unless I learn otherwise."

"Good," The Kashallan said and motioned for the Warlinga holding him to step away.

The Warlinga female gave him another toothy smile as she released him, but Pagrich noticed her hand stayed very close to a long bladed knife she wore on her right hip. He gave her a murderous scowl, then ignored her. *Insolent female*, he thought. *Who was she anyway—and what was she doing here?*

Ronnan cleared his throat. "Holy One, if you and your people will come with me I'm sure there will be no more trouble." He glanced significantly at Pagrich who gave him a sullen nod.

As he headed for the inner sanctum, Ronnan became aware that the entire hunting pack of Meh'gach Warlinga and the Loti peasants were also following him inside the keep. Horrified, he paused and cleared his throat nervously again.

"Holy One, the suite isn't that large, and, Warlinga aren't usually housed within the keep itself—it will cause talk if they come with you."

"You have a point, Ata." Turning to Aju'an he said, "You should stay in the barracks as usual, I will keep Chelka with me, but it will cause unnecessary talk if you all come inside. I will be fine; my Speir'dina kinsmen can protect me if need be. If anyone asks why you are here, just say you are doing some errands for your father. No one will think that unusual."

Aju'an flattened his head crest as if he wanted to argue the point, then he gave Pagrich a calculating look and thought better about it. He smiled and slapped Pagrich companionably on the shoulder.

"Come on Friend, your eldest sister married a cousin of mine I believe; show us and the Loti where to put our gear. I could use some food, and I'd be glad to fill you in on what's going on over a jug of cool mushroom beer."

Pagrich grunted, then giving Ata Ronnan one last reproachful look he led Aju'an and the pack towards the Warlinga barracks.

When he was gone, Ronnan let out a long sigh of relief and led the way into the inner sanctum of Shaden Keep. Turning to his guests once they were inside, he said, "The halls should be fairly empty at this time of the night, but it might be wise to pull up your hoods as we pass through the main corridors. Your suite has already been prepared; your clan elder, Arishim, is there and waiting. When you have refreshed yourselves I know my Ima is anxious to speak with you."

"Mm, and I her. I take it there wasn't any trouble with my kinswoman arriving in the closed litter with Ima Ngeal then."

"No, Holy One, she arrived with no trouble. We were—uh—a little shocked to find her with the Ima and Ata Neyal, but both Urinia and I have enjoyed the K'Sa's company while we waited for your arrival. She is a most fascinating woman."

The Kashallan laughed softly. "That she is, Ata, that she is. I am very grateful that she was willing to undertake this long journey on my behalf at her age. I know it hasn't been easy for her."

"It hasn't been an easy trip for either of them, but we have done all we can to see to her, and Ima Ngeal's comfort while among us," the priest assured him.

"I never doubted it, and thank you."

The group continued on in silence, past the dining hall and the darkened library. From the main chapel, the sound of a low rhythmic chanting drifted out to them as they rounded a bend in the passage, but the few Avairei they encountered paid them no attention.

As they neared the hallway that led to the pools a spicy odor filled the air. The Kashallan stopped abruptly, nostrils flaring. He took in a deep breath and let it out in a long sigh. With some surprise the priest saw his hand tremble, before he thrust it back under his cloak. As Ronnan watched the alien features mold themselves into a look of such hungry yearning that he blinked, unsure if he had read the man's feelings a right.

In the next moment the Kashallan's expression changed again, this time into a guarded mask. Returning his attention to his host, he said quietly, "Ata, I'm sure your provisions for our comfort are most pleasing, but—I need to go to the pools. I can feel my kindred calling to me,; they already know I am near and want me to come to them."

Ronnan looked flustered. "But-but you can't! The healers will still be down there with their students. And the young Khutani are always fed in the main cavern at this time of night. You can't just—I-I will have to talk to my Ima—" His voice trailed off as a cold pair of blue eyes bored into his.

Ronnan swallowed hard, suppressing a shudder. "P-please, Holy One, later on would be a better time."

"I will be careful, Ata; I won't disturb them. Once down there, I will go straight to the kashallan pool surely that will be safe enough. I doubt if very many of your people go there anymore, so I won't be disturbing them." He smiled as another thought struck him. "And besides, what better place for the people of Shaden to meet me than in that pool among, my Khutani kin."

What better place indeed, Ronnan thought, *but not right now*. "Please, Kashallan, my Ima will be cross with me for not carrying out her instructions. Can't your visit wait just a while longer?"

Before the Kashallan could answer him, Nathan took a hold of his arm and spun the Kashallan round to face him. "You're not going down there alone."

Dunnagh-Tani gave him a disgusted look. "Really, Nathan, this is ridiculous. You're getting to be a real pain in the ass about your 'orders' from Maker Dievris."

Nathan folded his arms across his chest and smirked. "Too bad you think so, Boyo, but it really doesn't matter where you got a pain, I'm coming and that's that. As I told you before, I've no wish for its 'Exalted Snakiness' to take a chunk out of my ass, if something were to happen to you." The Kashallan bristled, but the other man stared him straight in the eye unwilling to back down.

Ronnan's jaw dropped open in horror. How dare this insolent stranger speak to a child of the pools this way? And to talk about one of the ancient Makers with such familiarity! Before he could frame a scathing reply to such insolence, Amril stepped between the two men. "Please, Husband, San Nathan, let's talk about this later—once we are in the suite. We could be seen if we stand here arguing much longer."

Startled, they gaped at him stupidly for a moment then the Kashallan let out a low chuckle. "He's right; we'll talk about this later." Nathan grunted, but stepped aside.

Catching sight of the shocked Avairei's face, the Kashallan gave him a toothy smile and motioned for him to lead the way. "Never mind, Ata, you'll get used to our ways in time. Hasn't Ima Ngeal told you what a stubborn, willful creature I am?"

Ronnan's lips twitched. The Kashallan saw the faint smile, and nodded. 'All right, Ata, I see the wisdom in your plan—though I don't necessarily like it."

Inwardly Ronnan breathed a sigh of relief. He didn't want to anger such an exalted personage, but he had his orders. As soon as he could get him alone, he would have to have a long talk with Amril. Catching sight of the young man out of the corner of his eye, he took note, once again of his unusual dress. *Wife, hmm.* Hiding his confusion with a deep bow, Ronnan led the way down the silent corridor. He was definitely going to have to have that talk with Amril—and soon.

Chapter Seven

The suite the Imas had chosen for him was a large and opulent one off a side passage seldom used by the Avairei during their daily routines. Its door opened onto warm lamplight and the smells of fried mushrooms and freshly baked masa root cakes. Dunnagh's eyes slid without conscious volition to the sideboard where a row of covered dishes and clean plates awaited the hungry travelers.

Ima Ngeal, Arishim and Ima Urinia were sitting in padded wicker chairs waiting for him, the habitual pitcher of spiced tea on a low table between them. As they entered Ima Urinia stood up. She seemed to recognize the Kashallan without hesitation, crossed, and stopped in front of him, her sharp dark eyes meeting his without any sign of uncertainty.

Urinia bowed to him, and held out her hands, palms downward, in the ritual gesture, inviting the link. "Welcome to Shaden Keep, Holy One. I hope you are well and not overly fatigued by your journey."

Urinia was a tall woman for an Avairei, Dunnagh thought. She was also a bit rounder of figure than most, but she carried herself in that haughty, authoritative manner that was so typical of her kind. Her coloring was also unusual. Due to Khutani breeding programs, most Avairei pelts were a fairly uniform medium brown in color, but this woman's fur was almost black in its rich deep hue. Tomina Dingay had also had unusual coloring, Dunnagh remembered. Could this woman too, be a cleverly placed changeling plant? Out of the corner of his eye he saw Ngeal and Arishim watching him expectantly.

Suddenly conscious of how vulnerable they were trapped in the bowels of this unfamiliar fortress, he wondered if Pagrich had deliberately been kept uninformed. How easy it would be for her to cry for help—mutant wizards, steeling into a keep by means of foul sorcery—their deaths would be so much easier to explain that way. In his middle Dunnagh felt Tani writhe at the bitter flavor of his suspicions.

Best to find out now before a betrayal risked all their lives further. The Kashallan took her hands, extended his tentacles and formed the link. Urinia stiffened at the unfamiliar touch, then relaxed and stared into his alien blue eyes.

Dunnagh's face remained neutral, giving her no reassurance. Instead he surprised her and closed his eyes, allowing Tani's senses to dominate their shared awareness. Urinia shivered and glanced at Ngeal, but Ngeal seemed as puzzled by his odd behavior as she was herself.

A moment later, when he opened his eyes again, he breathed an inward sigh of relief, and released her from the link. "Thank you, Ima, I am well." He glanced at the sideboard and gave her a toothy smile. "And I'm looking forward to your hospitality."

Urinia seemed flustered for a moment, then taking his meaning she bowed once more and stepped away from the doorway. "I forget myself, Holy One, please come in." She waved her hand to the empty chairs near the women. "Please, you and your hunt leader join us." Becoming aware of Chelka standing at his back she hesitated again, then added, "And you as well, Sa Chelka. I will call the maid to serve you."

Dunnagh-Tani bowed. "Thank you, Ima, but there's no need to trouble the woman this late; we will just help ourselves." Giving her no time to protest he led the group over to the sideboard, picked up an empty plate and began filling it.

Urinia stared in confusion at the jostling mass of dusty men and women filling their plates. Walking stiffly back to her own chair she sat. Arishim caught her eye and smiled reassuringly. "Don't be offended, Ima," she said in a low voice. "Our Speir'dina ways are less formal than Avairei custom, but he truly is appreciative of your thoughtfulness."

The Kashallan and Nathan took seats beside Arishim and the two Imas. Chelka bowed out of the invitation for her to join them, claiming to Urinia that she was at the moment here as one of the Kashallan's hunting pack, not as her father's daughter. Bowing, she took her place with the rest of the Speir'dina guards on cushions along the wall.

Urinia's mouth tightened when she was introduced to Amril in his long woman's kilt. She'd been only vaguely aware of the young Avairei Ata among the Kashallan's party when they'd entered. Wife? She shot Ngeal a disapproving look, but the old woman pretended not to notice. Much to her relief after the introduction was completed Ronnan took a firm grip on the young man's arm and ushered him over to a quiet corner where they could talk privately.

Over the meal, the Kashallan explained to Ima Urinia that to ensure his safety the Makers now demanded that everyone in Shaden swear an oath of allegiance to the new kashallans. And this oath would be given while in the link with him.

"I mean no offence, Holy One, but this will be most distressing to many of my people."

"I'm sure it will be, Ima, I am well aware how I appear to most Timornans."

Pouring himself more spiced tea Nathan snorted. "That's an understatement." When Urinia glanced at him sharply he took a swallow of his tea and said, "You should have introduced your hunt leader to clan elder Arishim, or at least let him know more about us. I thought I was going to have to kill him at the gate when he got a good look at us."

Urinia frowned glanced at the oblivious Ronnan and Amril, then turned back to him. "What happened?"

The Kashallan waved his hand in a dismissive gesture. "It was nothing really; Nathan is exaggerating a bit. Hunt Leader Pagrich was startled, but my hunters are well-trained; there was no harm done. But the incident merely emphasizes the point that in order for the people to get to know me and trust me, they must see me and feel my touch while I take their oaths."

Urinia gave Ronnan another murderous look, unconsciously glanced down at her hands and nodded. "I understand, Holy One, it will be as you say."

Giving Arishim a teasing glance he added, smiling, "If it will make you feel any better, Ima, my own Speir'dina kindred were equally uncomfortable when made to feel my touch for the first time." Startled Urinia stared at him incredulous. He laughed. "It's true ask the clan elder there if you don't believe me.

There is nothing like a host symbiont bond among the Speir'dina. At least Timornans have their history and traditions to ease their fears. It was much worse for my host's kin than it will be for the people in this keep."

Then sobering he added, "Besides, it will also give me a chance to taste them and see if there are any spies or changelings among your people."

Urinia stiffened, her eyes snapping at the implication. "There are no spies or changelings within my keep, Kashallan. I have worked very diligently to remove them. You are perfectly safe here, I can assure you."

The Kashallan set down his plate and met her glare calmly. "That may well be, Ima, I have already tested you for the taint. Your breeding has proven true, and I'm sure you have done your best, but as Ngeal can tell you, it isn't always that simple to detect the enemy among us. The one planted at Ticca had been her trusted friend and councilor for many years."

Her eyes widened with outrage when his words about her testing registered. "It is what my elders require," he said patiently, "I mean you no offence. But by all means check with the Khutani you know and trust if you wish to confirm my words. Is there not a Maker here waiting for me? Please take counsel with it and have your fears put to rest."

"Yes, there is a Maker here," she said, "I will take counsel with it perhaps, but how did you know?"

He shrugged. "I didn't know it was here already, but it was a logical assumption. They knew where I was headed, and one of the elders would be summoned once I arrived, so I thought—" He shrugged again and smiled.

Urinia sighed and stood. "All right, it will be as you say Ima Ngeal has told me of the oath that everyone took at Ticca. I had assumed that was because of Tomina, but I will assemble my people in the main chapel after the morning meal. I will explain to them and you can *taste* them, or whatever you need to do. Ronnan and I will be the first to give you our oaths then, so they can see us make our pledges. Is that agreeable to you, Holy One?"

"Yes, Ima it is." Suddenly a wave of exhaustion slammed into him with the force of a tidal wave. The heavy meal after the long ride was making him lethargic. He could wait till tomorrow to go to the pools. He put a hand over his mouth to stifle a yawn. "I must confess I wasn't looking forward to starting in on the process tonight."

"Ima," Nathan said, "before you go one last question. As Dunnagh-Tani said, we know how native Timornans see us. The Makers have entrusted the Kashallan's safety to me. I can assume that Aju'an will square things with your hunt leader, but I need to know if I can expect trouble from others among your folk."

Urinia considered then shook her head. "If you mean violence, no. I shouldn't think so—not if Hunt Leader Pagrich assures them that all is well. I can understand your position, but my people are very loyal, Hunt Leader." Nathan's expression told her that he wasn't totally convinced, but he bowed and made no further comment.

Urinia's mouth tightened. She bowed, stiff backed, and headed for the door, Ima Ngeal and clan elder Arishim in her wake. Before she could open the door, however, Dunnagh stopped her. "Ima?" when she turned to face him once more, he looked into her smoldering eyes and bowed. "Thank you, Ima, I truly appreciate the help you are offering me and my Khutani kindred. My task would be nearly impossible if it weren't for people like you. I am very grateful."

Flustered once more by the sincerity she heard in his voice, she bowed to hide her embarrassment. "I am honored by your regard, Holy One but it is nothing more than my duty."

IT WAS LATE MORNING by the time Ronnan came to fetch the Kashallan to the main chapel. The travelers had slept in, then had a leisurely breakfast, served by Urinia's elderly personal maid, and a couple wide-eyed novices.

Not long after the meal was cleared away, Chelka opened the door to admit Ronnan and Dunnagh saw Aju'an and a couple more of his hunters standing in the hall behind the priest. He rose with a sigh of relief, his Speir'dina guards following him to the door. "Is she ready for us then?" he asked the priest.

"Ronnan bowed. "Everyone is in the main chapel as you requested, Holy One."

"Including kitchen slaves and Warlinga?" Nathan asked.

"Everyone as you said." Ronnan's mouth twitched. "They are very confused by this break in our normal routine, but they are there."

"Some of my hunters are taking over guard duty at the gate, San Nathan," Aju'an said. "All Shaden Warlinga are inside the chapel—and will stay there till you allow them to leave."

Nathan grunted. "Good."

Ronnan led them to a side passage that approached the chapel from the private entrance the officiating priest used, rather than the main doors to the chapel. Once inside the small waiting area the Kashallan could hear the buzz of talk in the outer chapel.

Urinia, Ngeal and Arishim were there waiting for him. Urinia was dressed in a long red kilt stiff with finely crafted black and gold embroidery. Around her neck she wore a leather collar encrusted with jewels and precious bits of metal. Jewel bead swung from the ends of her long braidlets, and her dark pelt shimmered like black satin in the soft light.

Before going to her Dunnagh stopped just inside the entrance, and motioned Nathan and Aju'an to come to him. "I know these people think they have thought of everything, but I'm not so sure they have. Nathan, I'd like you to keep Ross, Harris, Ellis, and Oglas with you.

"Take the pack and do a more thorough search of the keep while everyone is in the hall. Post some men in likely spots to catch any runaways. They *may* all be in there now, but once they see me and know what I require of them, any spies or changelings will try to slip out."

Nathan scowled, but before he could open his mouth to object, Dunnagh said, "I doubt if there will be any trouble in the chapel itself, but I'll take Marti and Chelka in there with me just in case. You don't need to dog my every footstep. You will be far more useful to me outside."

Nathan thought about it for a while then nodded. Motioning with a jerk of his head for the Speir'dina named to follow him he stepped back into the hall.

With Chelka and Marti in his wake the Kashallan crossed to Urinia and bowed. She'd seen the men step back into the corridor and gave him an inquiring look. "Just a little added insurance, Ima, in case someone decides to take a walk once we've started." He could tell she wasn't happy about it, but she nodded without comment.

"Please wait here behind the screen while Ima Ngeal and I speak to them, Holy One." She motioned to a large decorated partition standing just inside the chapel itself that blocked the view of the assembled people. "If you sit on that chair next to the clan elder, you can hear all that passes, and I will send Ronnan for you when we are ready for the oath taking." The Kashallan nodded and took the offered seat.

When the two Imas and Ronnan stepped out into the chapel the talk died in a gasp of astonishment. <<They must be surprised by her ceremonial garb,>> Tani said into Dunnagh's mind. <<It's not a feast day.>>

Through a small opening at the edge of the screen, Dunnagh saw the two Imas kneel by the altar and make an offering to the gods. When she finished making the blood gift, he heard Urinia rise and step to the center of the dais to address them. "My people," she began. "Though this day at present is not on the festival calendar, from now on it will be a great day of thanksgiving for us."

Ima Urinia led them in prayer and songs of thanksgiving, praise to the Khutani, and the ancient gods of Timorna. She spoke of the enemy's plotting, the plague, the Khutani's' confinement to their pools for lack of a host, and the people's prayers for a renewal of the kashallan bond.

None of this was news to her audience; the Kashallan could hear restless movements among the congregation. But like a master showman, Ima Urinia took her time, allowing the sense of excitement and mystery to build in her audience.

The Kashallan heard the sound of a commotion somewhere beyond the chapel, and was about to investigate when Urinia's next words jerked him to attention. "But the Makers, in their wisdom have used their magic and drawn a new host species from out of the sky to free them." After that pronouncement the hall erupted into a babble of confused chatter.

The Kashallan listened to the babble. His attention divided, he strained to hear more of the noises from the corridor, but whatever had distracted him a moment ago, he couldn't make out over the talk coming from the chapel. Nathan must have taken care of it—he hoped so anyway. He glanced at Marti and Chelka, but they must not have heard it, because their attention was still focused on the noise beyond the screen.

"It is true," Ngeal said, lifting her voice over the growing din. Rising from her place by the altar for the first time, she joined Urinia.

When the noise quieted once more, Ngeal told the true story of what had happened at Sulas, the Kashallan's trek across the Great Swamp and the changelings' manipulation of her young niece that ended in the poor child's unconsecrated death.

When she finished silence enveloped the chapel like a blanket. Urinia allowed it to continue for a moment then motioned for Ronnan to bring the Kashallan.

When he stepped out onto the dais with his two unusual bodyguards the assembly erupted into gasps and cries of horror. Someone spoke of Umwira magic and a novice screamed. At the back of the hall several people rose heading for the door. Pagrich and his two hunters who had already met the Kashallan, were there and physically began shoving frightened people back.

"Go back to your places and Stay calm!" Urinia shouted, before the panic could take over completely. "Do you take me for a total fool? Do you think I could be so easily deceived by the Hated Enemy's tricks? There is a Maker in the pools below as some of you already know. I have spoken to the Ancient."

She pointed to Dunnagh. "No matter his alien appearance, the Maker assures me that a Khutani symbiont coils in his middle. Do you think a Maker would lie to me!"

A middle aged Ata with gray dappled in his pelt rose quivering with rage. "I don't expect a Maker to lie, but I know *you* well enough, Urinia, to believe that you would manipulate the facts as you choose, if it will get you what you want."

Urinia's hands twisted the folds of her kilt as if she'd like to rip the man's head off. "And what exactly would that be, Ata Selic?"

"Why, to discredit the Dingay clan, of course! I warned you that choosing Ronnan Caltia was a mistake. And now you have allowed the Caltia corruption to infest this keep and blind you to a demon's lies. You are a fool to believe such nonsense, Ima."

Turning to Ngeal he added, "And I'm dismayed to see such a respected Ima as yourself, Ima Ngeal, ensnared as well in this."

Urinia's mouth opened, but no words came out, only a strangled sound of outrage.

"Corruption—mistake!" Ronnan shouted, stepping forward. "You only say such lies because *you* were not given the position of Ata Leyas. How dare you insult my family, Ata!"

"That is an outrageous lie."

Placing a hand on Ronnan's shoulder to prevent further outbursts, the Kashallan fixed the angry priest with his unnerving blue-eyed stare. "If you don't believe the Imas, Ata, when we finish our business here I will take you with me down to the pools, and you can ask the Maker yourself. You may give *it* your oath instead of me—if you are brave enough to risk its ire."

Dunnagh caught the flicker of fear in the man's eye quickly masked by his bluster. Holding up an amulet to ward off evil, he shouted, "Umwira Mutant, how dare you! Don't try to trick me with your foul magic—"

"Selic, shut up!" Urinia commanded. "You are a disgrace to this keep and your family."

"No," the angry man shot back. "The Dingay were right about you. It is you who are the disgrace." He pointed an accusing finger at Urinia. "Blasphemer! Would you allow this creature to destroy Shaden like he did Sulas? I won't stay to listen to another word." Shoving aside a frightened novice, Selic pushed his way towards the outer door.

Stunned by his accusation no one made a move to stop him. When Selic got to the door, however, the black-clad Nathan roughly pushed him back into the room. Ross and Harris with hands near their side-arms, blocked the entrance behind Nathan.

"It was Combaron Dingay who destroyed Sulas, Ata, not me," the Kashallan said. Selic shuddered, then ceased his struggling.

"You will stay until you are given permission to leave, Ata," Nathan said, "now go back and take your place, or you will be *made* to take it. So, what will it be, hmm?"

Selic gave Nathan a murderous look, and jerked out of his grasp. "Keep your hands off me, Umwira Filth!" He turned and started back to his place; then he spun round and bolted down a side aisle, heading for a side entrance.

Chelka leaped from the dais and caught the priest in her claws before he could hall the heavy door open. Dangling the struggling man by his braidlets she half dragged half carried him back to the waiting Nathan. This time Nathan tied Selic's arms behind his back and pushed him ahead of him out into the hall. "If you are in such a hurry to leave, you can join the other spy, until the Kashallan has time for you," they heard him say as the door closed behind them.

Other spy? Dunnagh-Tani sighed and glanced at the two stunned Imas on the dais beside him. Ngeal looked grim, but not surprised, Urinia was hiding it well, he thought, but he could sense that she was shaken by the open confrontation.

"I'm sorry for this, Ima," he said to Urinia in a low voice. "That man's outburst and my hunters' violence haven't reassured your people much, have they? My elders want me to do this on my own so the people will get used to me, but perhaps we should have done this at the pools."

Urinia shook her head. "No, they are right, and there are too many dark corners and places to hide and escape notice down there. But I am truly sorry about this, Holy One. Ata Selic belongs to a clan that has allied itself with the Dingay. He can be difficult but I never thought he would be so hostile and insulting."

"It is of no matter, Ima, we will deal with him later; let's get on with it."

Urinia took a deep breath and addressed her people once more. "Do any of you truly believe that the enemy is so strong that one of their wizards could walk into this keep with a Maker present in the pools below us?

"Because if you do, then you must also believe that we are doomed. I cannot except that," she said fiercely. "All my life I have fought them—and I will continue to fight them until my death claims me. This man is a bonded kashallan host. He has sacrificed much to free the Khutani from their pools. And, he is deserving of my loyalty." Kneeling before the Kashallan, Urinia held out her hands to invite the link.

The Kashallan took her hands, extended his tentacles and listened to her oath. As she rose Ronnan took her place. "Let us offer up another hymn of thanks to the Mother," Ngeal said. "Let us rejoice that we have lived to see this blessed event come to pass in our lifetime."

Though most of the people who hadn't been in Urinia's confidence enough to know about his coming were frightened, when they felt his touch and understood that he was a true kashallan they lost their fear. Dunnagh felt humbled to see the looks of rapture on many Avairei faces.

By the time he had completed the oath taking the chapel was ringing with the sounds of excited chatter and rejoicing. This reception was very different than he had encountered at either Ticca or Meh'gach, and it cheered him immensely to know that so many welcomed the return of the kashallans in the surface world.

When it was over he was exhausted, but knew he couldn't rest yet. Excusing himself from the people milling around the dais, he slipped back into the tiny chamber off the chapel telling Marti and Chelka to keep watch on the entrance.

Nathan was waiting for him with the two bound and gagged prisoners, squatting against the wall. Selic he'd expected, but the other was unknown to him. "I thought I heard you say something about capturing a spy," he said to Nathan as he came over to study the man.

The spy was a small Avairei with sharp features, wearing a dirty kilt. He looked up at the Kashallan's voice, his eyes white-rimmed with fear. "We caught him hiding in one of the storerooms off the kitchen," Nathan said. "What do you want us to do with him?"

"I'm not sure yet." Turning, he called out to Chelka, "Ask Ima Urinia or Ronnan to step in here for a moment, would you."

A moment later Urinia brushed past the screen and came over to stand beside the Kashallan. Dunnagh motioned to the unknown man. "My hunters caught him hiding in a storeroom, Ima, do you know who he is, or why he was there?"

Urinia glared down at the quivering man. "His name is Ko. I know little about him. He has been here a long time; I inherited him from my predecessor. He is a minor clerk; copies old scrolls. He has always been very quiet and well mannered, but I know little more about him." She glanced at Nathan. "All were supposed to be in the chapel. Where did you find him?"

When Nathan told her, she scowled. "Take off his gag, Hunt Leader, I would like to hear his explanation."

When his gag was removed, Ko dropped to his knees. "Please Ima, have mercy; save me from these terrible creatures. I meant no harm. I was just—"

"Why were you not in the chapel, Ata? I gave orders for all to be present."

Ko's eyes slid away from her stern face. he licked dry lips and finally stammered," I-I don't know."

Nathan snorted. "It doesn't take a lot of brain power to figure it out, Ata. Somehow you found out about us and you planned to sneak out and go running to Enaju with your story, hmm? Is that the way of it; the Dingay put you here to spy for them?"

"No!" Ko cried. "Ima, I would never do that, please tell them."

Urinia's look became even colder. "I would not tell anyone that, Ata, because I don't know that it is true. *Were* you spying on me for the Dingay?"

Ko shook his head, but remained silent. The Kashallan sighed. "There's no point in questioning him further at this time. We will let the Maker deal with him and the other." He glanced at Urinia. "I need to go down to the pools now; I will have to tell them about the oath taking and explain to them about these men."

"Of course, Kashallan, shall I take you down there now?"

"No, let Ronnan do it. You should stay here with your people to answer questions." Turning to Nathan he said, "Give me a few minutes alone down there to report, and then bring these to down." Urinia seemed shocked by his suggestion, but said nothing.

Answering her unspoken concern he added. "It's all right, Ima, I know in the past the pools have been forbidden to all but the Avairei priesthood. That will now be changing. My Speir'dina kindred and the other species of Timorna are welcomed there once more. The Maker will not be offended if Nathan and some of the hunters bring the prisoners down to it."

Chapter Eight

S till dressed in her ceremonial garb, Ima Urinia led her entourage of Avairei witnesses down the darkened stairwell and stopped on the main causeway. Trailing behind her with Chelka, Aju'an and the prisoners, Nathan stepped out onto the walkway and inhaled the moist spicy aroma of the Khutani's underground world. Shaden had that same coppery smell mixed with vanilla that he'd noticed at Ticca and Sulas.

The cavern at Shaden seemed to him a bit larger than Ticca, but from what he could tell the arrangement was similar. Near the main causeway numerous shallow ponds spread out like a luminescent, patchwork quilt. Each pond contained a separate Khutani-made medicine. A network of underwater channels and stone walkways connected the ponds, and allowed both the Khutani and Avairei access to this underground realm.

Dunnagh had told him once that the Makers had wanted to maintain their control over the society they re-created after the great wars, so much of what was made and stored here were Life's necessities. The Khutani developed a system in which the Avairei fed their young and in exchange the adults created the potions stored here, and collected by the priests for distribution among Timorna's other inhabitants.

What the elders hadn't foreseen, he thought grimly, was that by introducing this monopoly they gave the Avairei a lot of power over the rest of their society, and the temptation to abuse it.

In the misty waters beyond the lighted walkways, where the Khutani lived, Nathan could hear the young ones splashing and squealing at play somewhere in the dimness

Ronnan and another of the priests included as a witness for the encounter with the Maker, scraped some glowing fungus from the pitted walls into empty lamp bowls and handed them round. Holding her lantern high, Urinia strode briskly down the causeway away from the ponds, heading for the kashallan pool. Nathan pushed the reluctant Ko forward with a muttered curse, Aju'an beside him urging Selic forward none to gently as well.

A kashallan pool was different from the other ponds and pools in a Khutani inhabited keep because it had no rim; the bottom merely sloped upwards till it connected with the walkway. The pool had no back wall either, it simply continued out into the blackness of the channels.

On its two sides, however, low shelves and headrests had been carved out of the rock to make it easier for a kashallan's patients to enter and be treated in its healing warmth. This arrangement also allowed the Khutani to be consulted on a difficult case if need be.

When they arrived at the kashallan pool the Maker Qwaltamis was waiting for them its massive gray body coiled loosely about the legs and torso of the Kashallan. Tani's tentacles were extended, embedded in that smooth hide to form the link, and Dunnagh's face had taken on that alien look it had when the Khutani half of the bond was dominating the partnership.

Nathan shivered; just seeing his friend trapped in those sinewy coils gave him goosebumps. Giving Ko an unnecessarily hard shove, he pushed him up to stand by Selic at the water's edge.

"Untie their bonds, Nathan," Dunnagh said. "And let Chelka or one of the Warlinga bring them into the pool so you don't need to get your uniform wet. Maker Qwaltamis will want to taste them."

Head crests flattened, Aju'an and Chelka pushed the men ahead of her into the phosphorescent liquid. Excited young Khutani swam about them, rubbing against their legs. When the water became about knee-deep Selic stopped trembling so much he couldn't continue. Ko staggered as a young one swam between his legs. He righted himself with a sharp cry of fear.

At the sound the Maker's hard yellow eyes focused directly on the prisoners. Ko moaned low in his throat, but Selic remained silent, his eyes white-rimmed and shaking. Speaking through Dunnagh's mouth, the hollow, otherworldly voice of the Maker said to the prisoners. "So, you dare to doubt that this young one I am holding is a true kashallan? Do you think you are seeing an illusion, or do you question ME of being deceived by an Umwira wizard!"

With a strength born out of desperation, Ko pulled out of Chelka's grasp and stumbled towards the shore that led away into the darkness of the cavern. Chelka bounded after him, but before she caught him, Ko suddenly stopped a few paces in front of her, his body going rigid. Chelka reached out to grab him then jerked her hand back as if it had been stung.

Nathan saw what was happening and inwardly shuddered. Maker Dievris, back at Ticca, had caught him in its power like that once. Skin tingling, he'd been unable to move—frozen, like being trapped in an ice cube. He could still remember how panicked he'd felt. Dievris had been only mildly annoyed with him then—toying with him actually. But this time, the Khutani was dead serious, and no mistake.

"Step away, Warlinga, you are no longer needed," Qwaltamis said. "This one's life is forfeit." Swiveling the terrified man around to face it, Qwaltamis bared its teeth and hissed. From Dunnagh's mouth issued its words of judgment.

"I have no need to sink my teeth in you to taste your corruption. I can taste the soured flavor of your deceit from here. You have helped the Enemy not because you would want to see the Ghostlanders triumph, but out of petty spite for those you feel have slighted you. You are a lying, treacherous cull—your breeding is flawed. You are deserving of a Khutani's judgment."

The onlookers stared in horror as one of the adults in the surrounding pod, reared out of the water in front of the helpless priest and spat a black viscous substance into the man's face. Ko screamed, the sound high-pitched and jarring. Still held suspended by the Maker's power, the man writhed in his invisible shell, his face dissolving before the onlooker's eyes as the black kavay ate away the flesh down to the bone.

Ngeal staggered and Nathan put out an arm to steady her. He glanced at Urinia and the rest of the witnesses. Urinia was all right, holding herself rigidly under control as she watched the man die. Ronnan, Arishim and the other Avairei looked ill, but were coping. Aju'an and the Warlinga present had their head crests flattened to their skulls, looking grim.

He'd seen Tani kill like this before when the Kashallan had fought Gormach, but he doubted if any of the people here had witnessed such a judgment before today. It wasn't a pretty sight; it made his skin crawl.

It didn't take long before the man's screams subsided into a phlegmy gurgle and then silence. When it was over the Maker discarded the body on the empty causeway, and returned its attention to the horrified witnesses and the remaining prisoner. "The time for leniency has passed. We will no longer coddle the Enemy among us. All must pledge their allegiance to us and the new kashallans or die."

Qwaltamis focused its hard yellow eyes on the trembling Selic, being guarded by Aju'an. "What say you, Ata? Will you come forward of your own free will and give this kashallan your oath of allegiance?"

Selic took a hesitant step forward then collapsed, doubling over with pain. After a moment's hesitation, Aju'an helped the prisoner to his feet. Selic tried again, and once more was forced to his knees. Around him the water frothed with the young Khutani's agitation.

"I can't!" Selic managed to gasp out before another stabbing pain doubled him over again. "Oh, Maker, I c-can't!"

Nathan blinked; what was wrong with the man? Was the Maker doing something to him? He glanced at Dunnagh's face. There was little expression there, the Maker evidently still in control of his body, but Dunnagh's eyes were wide with surprise. So, maybe the Maker wasn't causing the man's pain—but if not then who?

"Do you doubt my word or my power, and defy me?" Qwaltamis thundered.

Nathan glanced at Ngeal still standing beside him. "What's going on, Ima," he murmured out of the side of his mouth. "Do you know?"

"No."

Overhearing him, Chelka growled deep in her throat. "I think I do." She bounded back into the pool, waded over to the floundering man, and tore off the mass of necklaces twisted around Selic's neck. With a growl of disgust, she flung them against the cavern wall. Selic collapsed, sobbing into her arms.

"Chelka, why did you do that?" Aju'an murmured.

"Yes, Warlinga, why did you do that?" Qwaltamis asked.

Chelka glanced at the puzzled faces on the causeway, then turned to the Maker, her face turning green with embarrassment and her head crest dipped. "I remembered that Ima Ngeal's niece was controlled by the

Umwira wizard who corrupted her by means of an amulet she wore around her neck. When I saw him trying to come to you—when I saw his pain—I-I thought maybe—" Her voice trailed off, eyes sliding away from the Maker's yellow-eyed stare.

"You did well, Warlinga," Qwaltamis said. "Bring the prisoner to me."

Chelka's color deepened under the Khutani's praise. She firmed up her hold on the unresisting Selic, and waded out into the deeper water of the pool. When she stood in front of the massive creature, Qwaltamis lowered its head and took one of Selic's arms between its jaws.

Selic shuddered as the Maker's teeth bit carefully into his flesh to form the link. When it was finished Qwaltamis released him and stared once more into his eyes. "You would like to give me your oath, but the compulsion is too strong, isn't it?"

"Y-yes-s," the priest stammered. "Maker, please help me."

The hollow voice was surprisingly gentle when it spoke once more. "Alas, I cannot. You believed the Dingay lies; the corruption has gone too far. I couldn't accept your oath now, even if you were able to give it."

Selic shuddered. He glanced at Ko's corpse lying discarded on the causeway, some distance away from the onlookers. "Then you will kill me, too?"

"You must die, yes."

Selic's eyes flicked to the corpse again, and trembled violently. "Must I receive a Khutani judgment like Ko? Please, ancient, mercy. I didn't know—I thought Ima Enaju—" Selic broke off, and bowed his head.

Qwaltamis studied the priest for a long moment; finally it said, "In this I will be merciful." With one quick stroke, Qwaltamis bit into the man's flesh severing his neck. Selic gagged, choking on his own blood, then fell back into Chelka's arms.

Qwaltamis raised its head and fixed her with its unblinking stare. "Take him and the other to the waste pit. Their taint is too strong to feed to the young ones in the pools."

Not long afterward, a solemn and thoroughly shaken group was about to leave the pools when Pagrich and Aju'an's cousin Mar arrived, a bloody hunter supported between them. Nathan swore under his breath and hurried to meet them. "What happened?"

"Vegar is dead," Mar said. "Clor here and Vegar were on the front gate. When Hunt Leader Pagrich sent hunters to relieve them, they found," He pointed his long brown tongue at the bloody Clor.

"Bring him to me, Mar," The Kashallan said. The Maker had freed him and he was standing knee deep in the pool eyeing them. When the Warlinga was eased down into the Water beside him he crouched to examine the semiconscious man. "Trouble?" Hiking up her ceremonial kilt, Urinia waded out to them, staring down at the wounded man. Returning her attention to Pagrich, she snapped, "What happened?"

"One of my men, a new man, named Ruhar must have slipped out during the confusion—when the Kashallan came out—before the oath taking. To my shame I didn't notice—" Pagrich took the knife from his belt and offered it to Nathan. "I am unworthy."

"Put your knife away, Hunt Leader, I can't afford to lose you," Dunnagh ordered. "I will need all my Warlinga when we go to Riath. What is done is done."

Pagrich hesitated, then sheathed his knife. "I will take my best hunting pack and go after him. I will bring him back, Holy One, never fear."

Dunnagh sighed and shook his head. "He has too much of a lead. If he left before the Oath taking he already has several sun-marks head start, and you don't know which trail he may have taken. There is little sense in following him now."

"He could know very little, Kashallan," Urinia said. "Warlinga in the packs rarely enter the inner sanctum." Her gaze wavered under his blue-eyed stare. Reluctantly, she glanced at the corpses being dragged to the waste pit, and sighed. "Unless one of the others managed to slip him some confidential information."

"We have no way of knowing that, Ima, and it's too late to worry about it now. But perhaps you could have your people check these men's rooms and also check your personal files to see if anything is missing."

Urinia bowed. "Yes, I will do that," She bowed again. "If you have no further need of me, Holy One, I will return to the keep above and report to my people what has happened here."

"Yes, please do that," he said. "I will see to Clor's wounds. Then the Maker wishes to speak with me further, so I will remain here for a time."

When Urinia and her entourage left, the Kashallan closed his eyes and allowed Tani to devote itself completely to Clor and his healing. As the Kashallan continued his exam, other Khutani encircled the Warlinga and began plastering yellow kavay over his bleeding wounds.

"How bad is he?" Nathan asked.

The Kashallan grimaced. He pointed to a jagged cut along the scales of Clor's inner thigh. "If that knife wound had been a little closer to the man's phallic sheath, he would have been dead like the other. As it is, he will be fine with several days' rest and some tonic to build up his blood again."

The Kashallan retracted his tentacles and looked up at his waiting Warlinga. "Can you help him to the barracks and make sure he rests? I've given him a sleeping substance that will take effect soon."

"Yes, of course, Holy One." Mar and Pagrich helped the semiconscious man to his feet and started back down the walkway.

"You gonna stay here?" Nathan asked.

"Yes, but I'd like to attend the death rites for Vegar, if you permit, Aju'an."

Aju'an dipped his head crest. "But of course, Kashallan, you would be most welcome."

Nathan nodded and glanced at the waiting Chelka and Speir'dina. "I'll go up too and see if I can help the Imas, or Pagrich. I'll leave Oglas here in case you need something. In the meantime, try to get some rest."

Dunnagh-Tani nodded. "I'll try to. These oath swearings take a lot out of me. I'm about done in." At Nathan's frown, he slapped him on the shoulder. "Don't worry, Mother Hen, I'll be fine. I plan to sleep while Tani and the Maker have a chat. Come get me for the ceremony."

Chapter Nine

In her opulent suite within Riath Keep, the High Matri, Enaju Dingay sat drumming her fingers impatiently upon the arms of her carved chair and gazed blindly at the far wall. She was a handsome woman with a regal bearing, the gray in her pelt seeming to add to the dignity of her office. When in public, fulfilling her duty she assumed a mask of beatific calm that made her appear to the people as the ideal of the "All Wise Mother." Now in private, however, her hard black eyes and cruel mouth gave the lie to that illusion.

Since the Renewal, there had been no word from her brother, and her grandson was dawdling over the errand she'd given him. Enaju Dingay was definitely not pleased. By the Fires, she felt so frustrated. The blue snows were gone, yet still she sat here, blind and helpless without news from the North.

She fingered the dark stone pendent that she always wore around her neck. The beloved Master had given it to her in her youth. By its power she had been bound to the will of the Ghostland wizards, then sent back south to work towards the fulfillment of their plans.

And now the promised destruction of the Khutani and their slaves was almost upon them. Only a few more game pieces need be put into play—and Sagas Caltia was one of those pieces. Her capture and public execution at the solstice high festival would signal the beginning of the end for Khutani rule in the Yeyen Banai Valley.

Ah but, the renegade priestess is not yet under your claws, a tiny voice in the back of her mind warned, *and who knows what the Masters enemies along the Shallow Sea might do to thwart his plans? They sent the mutants to Sulas didn't they? And, where is that miss-begotten grandson of mine? He should have returned to the Capital with the Caltia witch by now.*

When Combaron came to her, drunk and disheveled, after the defilement at Sulas he assured her that K'San Gormach would catch Sagas Caltia and her demons. So close to the Sorins, Enaju had had no choice but to rely on the border K'San to carry out his instructions. Gormach himself was smart enough to know better than to fail her—and yet, the snows were gone and there was still no sign of him.

As soon as the Jeban Pass cleared, she sent Combaron north with one of K'San Drucas's hunting packs, to Tragar Keep. Enaju thought she had made her instructions clear enough, even for a disgrace to his family like Combaron to understand and carry out, but it would appear not.

Grudgingly, Enaju had to admit that after the violation of Sulas Keep, from whatever unknown cause, Combaron had been clever to think of using the mutants and the Caltia witch's disappearance to the Dingay clan's advantage.

Even though the news had come so near the enforced confinement of the storms, all who heard the story were outraged. Sulas corrupted, the sacred Khutani dead by Umwira treachery, the news had spread like a plague. And with the entire Sorin Season to ferment that brew, the whole Yeyen Banai Valley should be ripe for the Ghostlanders take over by the time of the solstice trials. With Caltia power broken, all the other unaligned Warlinga and Avairei clans would fall into line—or be destroyed.

Enaju stroked the stone, her hand trembling. Should she risk using the jewel to call the Master? Enaju desperately needed information, answers, guidance. The Master expected too much of her, she thought, as a knot of fear tightened in her gut. *I'm only a poor, half-bred Khutani slave—why can't he understand?*

Enaju looked up as a knock sounded upon the outer door. A moment later her maid appeared to announce the arrival of her brother Persig. Following the maid unbidden, he came in. Enaju breathed an unconscious sigh of relief and motioned for the woman to bring refreshments.

Persig was an elegant Avairei immaculately dressed in a finely woven blue kilt, and satiny indoor cloak, with many valuable hair ornaments carefully twined into his graying braidlets. In public he assumed a cool aristocratic air that discouraged familiarity, but in the privacy of her suite he relaxed his guard and smiled at her warmly.

As her Ata Leyas, her second in command at Riath Keep, they could not both be absent from the Capital at the same time. For that reason they took turns returning to the main Dingay clan holding over the Sorin season. This year she had remained in the Capital while he returned to the keep near the Jeban pass to await further instructions from Wizard Barak.

When they were seated with refreshments and the maid once more out of hearing, Enaju sat down her tea bowl and said, "I will have to leave for the first council meeting soon, so briefly give me the news." Glancing around anxiously, even though they were completely alone she pitched her voice lower then asked, "Have you any message from our Beloved Master?"

Persig eyed her over the rim of his bowl, taking an extra moment to study her as he drank. At last he said, "You seem a bit anxious, Sister Dear, this isn't like you. What has happened in my absence to upset you. After all this time, you're not losing your nerve, are you?"

Enaju glared at him angrily. "You forget yourself, Ata. Don't waste time with foolishness, what is the news?"

Persig shrugged, and took another sip of his tea. "Sorry. You don't have to look at me with your dagger eyes; I was only teasing."

Enaju drummed her claws on her chair arm and continued to glare. Persig sighed. "Much of what I have to tell you can wait till after the council meeting. I can see that my teasing has unnerved you unduly. Before I begin, first tell me what's wrong?"

"There is a Maker here, dear brother," she hissed, "so if I seem distraught, I have good cause."

Persig choked, hastily returning his bowl to the end table. Enaju smiled with malicious satisfaction. "Yes, a Maker, but never mind that for now. You can question your underlings later for the details. Tell me the news."

When his coughing fit had passed he gave her a worried look then said, "Since you must leave soon I will give you only the most important items now. First of all, Tomina is dead."

Enaju gasped, and hastily sat down her own bowl, her hand trembling.

Persig nodded, sharing her concern. "I don't know the details; the Master didn't have time to relay them to me, but it would seem that our renegade priestess, Sagas Caltia, is not at Tragar. She and her blue-eyed mutant accomplice managed to evade the Tragar packs search for them and went to Ticca."

Enaju's claws dug deeper into her chair. "Drunken fool! I knew it was a mistake to trust Gormach Tragar with such a vital task. Damn Combaron, the sniveling—"

Persig held up a hand. "Wait, there is more. Before she was killed, Tomina had a chance to report that not only have our western *allies* betrayed the alliance, they have formed a new pact with the Khutani. The mutants that Combaron spoke of can host the Khutani symbionts, so Tomina claimed, and if that is true—"

"If that is so, dear brother, then those western traitors must be made to pay, and pay dearly for their treachery."

Persig's lip twitched in a malicious smile. "Oh they will, my dear, they will," he assured her. "For such a betrayal of the ancient pact, the Master sent his warbands west, to wipe out the clans along the Shallow Sea. They will trouble us no longer, I assure you. The Master's vengeance upon the Khutani will not be spoiled by their disloyalty—but there still remains Blue Eyes and the troublesome Caltia witch to deal with, however."

Enaju scowled, feeling that knot of fear tighten in her gut again. It was unbelievable—who would have thought they would do such a terrible thing. The western clans forsaking the ancient pact and aligning themselves with the Hated Khutani—how was that possible?

And if true, not only had they gone against all tradition, they had even bred a race of mutant slaves to barter to the Khutani to host their loathsome symbiont children. What had the Khutani slimeworms offered them that caused them to forsake their kin and their honor like this? May they rot in the black pit forever!

"Did you say Sagas and her outlaws spent the Sorins at Ticca, brother?"

"It would appear so."

Then it was a fool's errand to send Combaron to Tragar."

"Mm, perhaps, but it does have the advantage of keeping him away from the chattering tongues of the capital and that is a blessing. We can't afford a scandal now."

"He wouldn't dare."

"Oh, he has a healthy respect for your claws, dear sister, but when he stopped by Dingay Keep, I took the liberty of sending him on to Tragar anyway to fetch Gormach. The man failed in a task given him; he needs to be questioned—and a suitable punishment carried out for his negligence. We can make him an example for others who fail to carry out their assignments in future."

"Good. There is something odd going on at Tragar. I have a suspicion that he and Combaron were plotting something. I would like to have Gormach and his heir, Tobrach, here where I can keep an eye on them."

"Yes, I thought of that. Tobrach is far too clever to be left in charge of the border while Gormach is here explaining himself. I told Combaron to bring them both. Without any direction the rest of those Tragar lay-abouts won't have the initiative for anything more daring than chasing Begta down their stinking warrens. They should pose no threat to the Master's warbands when they come south."

Enaju picked up her tea bowl again and sipped, thinking. "A wise move, brother, and if the heir proves as *difficult* as his cousin, Tragar may need a new heir as well as a K'San, hmm?"

"Precisely."

Returning her attention to the main topic of discussion, Enaju said, as if thinking out loud, "Wherever the outlaws spent the Sorins, we need them—I shall have to send K'San Drucas, with several of his hunting packs to Ticca—"

Enaju broke off as another knock sounded outside. A moment later her maid ushered the Segoi K'San into the room. "Ah, K'San Drucas," Enaju purred, "we were just speaking of you." The High Matri waved him to a stool and motioned for the maid to close the door behind herself.

Drucas Segoi was a large, battle-scarred Warlinga with hard red eyes and flaring nostrils. A dangerous man to cross, Enaju thought. Like the Dingay, many of the Segoi clan were changeling bred in the north and returned to the south as tools of the wizards' malice. Drucas was as devoted to their Master as Enaju was herself, and yet the man exuded an air of ruthless menace that set even her nerves on edge.

Drucas was loyal to the Real People, but did his loyalty extend to her personally? He was also very ambitious, coveting a high position in the new order to come. With his strength and cunning he would probably get what he desired, but could she trust him not to turn on her and her family, when the day of their victory came?

Face and head crest a bland mask Drucas bowed to Enaju and Persig, then sat. "K'San Yargal Meh'gach has just arrived," he announced.

Enaju drank more of her tea before answering. "Have you seen him yourself?"

"Briefly, Ima."

"Mm, and has our most esteemed Councilor and his sons had a restful yet instructive Sorin confinement?"

Drucas lips twitched. "Perhaps, but it is difficult to say. Yargal himself seemed quite subdued when I spoke to him, but his sons are not with him, nor is Sa Latiya."

Enaju set her bowl down with a thunk, betraying her irritation. "I see. Did he have any explanation for why he has returned without the woman, or his willful brood for that matter?"

This time the Warlinga did permit himself a faint smile, though she noticed a hint of worry deep in his eyes. Was the Meh'gach clan actually fool enough to try and defy her?

"I only spoke to him briefly," Drucas repeated. "What he gave as his reason for returning to the capital without his full entourage was trouble at home. Varrod's wife is *ill*. And the Serath woman is pregnant. According to his father, Aju'an remained at home to be with her."

Enaju's jaw tightened. Had that fool Neyal disobeyed her and given that tainted red kavay to both women? If he had—her nails dug once more into the wood of her chair. She glanced sharply at the Warlinga. "Do you believe him, or is there some treachery here?"

Drucas shrugged. "Perhaps, perhaps not. Aju'an was rumored to be devoted to the woman, if the priest disobeyed—" At the High Matri's scowl he broke off, then shifted to another front. "There may be another reason for the Meh'gach brothers' absence than the health of their wives, Ima, and if what my spies tell me is true, their absence may have a far more sinister meaning."

Black eyes snapping Enaju leaned forward. "You try my patience. What have you heard, Warlinga?"

Unasked Drucas poured himself a bowl of tea from the pitcher, and drank. His red eyes watched her insolently as he did so. Finally he put down his bowl and said, "It would seem that Ima Urinia has called a meeting to discuss plans for the Solstice Festival."

Enaju snorted with contempt. "Is that all, the woman is a constant annoyance, true, but of no real threat. She will be dealt with soon enough."

"Indeed. Then it might interest you to know that the Ima has several mysterious 'guests' one of which is Ngeal Maveth. It is she who my spics say has called the meeting. And, it might also interest you to know that not only Avairei clans are coming to discuss the festivities, many Warlinga clans have also been invited to attend. And it is the Meh'gach brothers who have been sent to collect them."

Drucas's head crest flattened, his red eyes flaring with irritation. "I warned you that playing your little games with the Warlinga would be dangerous. Brute force is what is needed to bring Meh'gach to your will, not lingering poisons. Didn't I tell you such a ploy wouldn't work?"

Persig sipped his tea and eyed the Warlinga speculatively. Ignoring the challenge, he said, "Perhaps the Ima's claws aren't as dull as we assumed. But tell me, do your sources know the identity of her other guests?"

Drucas shook his head. "No, Ata. It is difficult to get news from within the keep itself at the moment. I know they are treated with the highest respect, but there was talk of everyone in the keep being forced to take some kind of Khutani supervised oath. My Warlinga source felt it wise to leave lest he risk being discovered. I haven't heard from my sources within the Avairei sanctum itself since he left, and that worries me."

Persig nodded. "I can share your worry, but your spy should likely be commended for his precaution where the Khutani are concerned. But I sense there is something else you haven't told us. Speak, K'San, it may be important."

Drucas hesitated a moment longer, then flipped his tail in a shrug. "I am reluctant to speak of it, Ata, because I can't confirm it, and it sounds too preposterous to believe, but my source claims there is a kashallan at Shaden Keep."

Drucas laughed eyeing the two Avairei warily. "It is an outrageous fabrication, of course. I had the man disciplined for his insolence."

"That is most unfortunate, K'San, for your source may indeed be correct," Persig said. "One could hope you're 'disciplines' weren't too extreme."

Drucas's head crest rose in surprise. Enaju laughed. "Oh yes, K'San—as preposterous as it may seem, the Master has sent word that his rivals to the west have indeed bred a new race of mutants who can host the Khutani. He believes these traitorous slime have made alliance with the Hated Enemy against us. If that is so, then it is our duty to stop them at all cost."

Drucas growled deep in his throat, his tail tip flicking angrily. "I agree, High One, I will make preparations to go to Shaden Keep immediately—"

Persig held up his hand, stopping the Warlinga K'San in mid flow. Turning to his sister he said, "It is in my mind that we should go carefully here, Sister. With a little patience we can perhaps ensnare all our quarry in one trap."

"How so?"

"I suggest that Sagas Caltia and her blue eyed demon are also at Shaden. Now Shaden is a formidable fortress, if we move too openly, they will merely close up their gates and wait us out. That would not suit the Master's plans. I suggest that we wait, act ignorant of their machinations, then capture all the conspirators when they come forth for the festival."

Drucas shook his head. "I see the point you are trying to make, Ata, but it would not be wise to wait too long. If they have time to gather too many of the Warlinga clans to their cause they could put *us* under siege."

"And with a Maker already here at Riath—who could guess the outcome of such a confrontation." Enaju shuddered in spite of herself. "No, it would be far better to lure our enemies out of Shaden, then separate and destroy them before they unite and become too powerful."

Smiling to herself she rose and crossed to her altar. Picking up the heavy, ornate metal headdress that was the symbol of her office from its stand, she placed it on her head, and turned back to them. "It is time for the High Council meeting," she announced.

"We will speak more of this later. In the meantime give some thought to 'traps and lures' hmm?" Holding out her hand she glanced significantly at the two men. "My K'San, Ata, shall we proceed?"

Chapter Ten

Nathan paused in the entrance to the main cavern of Shaden's pools and took in a deep breath. Tendrils of mist flowed about him caressing his face; the scent of their alien spice, a heavy presence in the moist air. Though the Khutani's watery world didn't inspire the intensity of feeling in him that they did in Dunnagh-Tani; the pools did have their allure—even for a warrior like him.

Stretching out into the shadows beyond the luminescent ponds were the pools and channels where the Khutani themselves lived. Nathan could hear the young ones splashing somewhere in the darkness beyond. He hesitated; would Dunnagh be with them? Tani was still quite young, would it be playing with its cousins out there? Maybe. But even if the bondmates were, when they tired, they would probably come back to the kashallan pool to sleep.

It was getting late, he could wait for them as easily down here, as he could in the keep above. Aju'an would want his answer by morning. Picking up an empty lantern from a pile by the entrance, Nathan scraped some of the glowing fungus off the wall into its bowl, then headed out into the darkness to find Shaden's kashallan pool.

As Nathan had hoped Dunnagh-Tani was there. He was lying on one of the side shelves immersed to the neck in the luminous, azure liquid; a pair of the Khutani cousins twined companionably about his torso and legs. His eyes were closed, his long hair floating like a russet shawl about his shoulders. Nathan hesitated, he looked so peaceful lying there, should he disturb him? Gazing at that familiar, well-loved face made his eyes sting and his heart ached with longing. Why had he let things change between them? Why had he let Dunnagh drift away—stupid, stupid, why?

Suddenly becoming aware of the light on the causeway the Khutani raised their sleek heads and hissed at him. Nathan froze. The Kashallan opened his blue eyes then smiled when he recognized him. "Ah, Nathan, I think I was just dreaming of you, and here you are. Come join us."

Nathan hesitated, his eyes flicking to his friend's two guardians uneasily. "Uh, I might want to do that, Tani, if you tell your snaky kinfolk there to let me come in. I wouldn't want to lose some essential body parts if they took exception to my being there."

The Kashallan laughed. Stretching out a hand he extended his tentacles and brushed them lightly over the smooth skin of his companions. A few moments later they relaxed their hostile stance and uncoiled themselves from around Dunnagh's body. "It's all right now I've told them who you are; they won't harm you. Come."

Nathan grunted, took off his clothes and waded into the pool, still eyeing the Khutani warily. Reclining next to his friend, he let out a long sigh of pleasure as he felt his tense muscles relax in the warm liquid. He closed his eyes and leaned his head back against the headrest. "Mm, I could get used to this real easy, no wonder you like it here."

The Kashallan moved closer to him. Running a tentacled hand across his companion's chest he laughed. Nathan shivered, feeling a stirring in his groin; that touch was so sensual, yet soothing.

"If you took me up on my offer," Tani said, "the pools could be your home too, then you could enjoy them anytime you wanted."

Nathan grabbed the hand that was continuing its exploration lower onto his belly and sighed. Still cradling the hand in his own, he opened his eyes. "Tani, don't start that again, please. I've told you no, I'm not interested in a kashallan bond, don't spoil my mood by pestering me about it now, all right?"

"Nathan, I'm sorry, I won't speak of it again—I promise."

The Kashallan fell silent lowering his eyes, but against his hip, Nathan could feel the other man's growing erection. *Damn, what's gotten into him?* Letting go of the Kashallan's hand he sighed and moved a little farther down the shelf.

Trying to assume a stern tone of voice he said, "Tani, Don't. I told you before I wasn't interested in playing the fucking game with you either. I thought we agreed that you'd stop this.

"Dunnagh, if you can hear me, will you make your bondmate behave. Stop it, all right?"

Dunnagh looked up, his blue eyes moist, his lower lip trembling. Nathan's heart gave a lurch. Ever since they were children, he'd hated it when his friend looked at him like that. But was it Dunnagh, or the alien symbiont, who was watching him from the depths of those blue orbs? No, it was almost certainly Tani.

Dunnagh , the coward, was probably hiding out somewhere in their shared flesh, and allowing his bondmate to do this to him. Damn Dunnagh anyway; he didn't want this!

Sliding over to him once more, the Kashallan pressed himself even closer against him. "Don't be angry with us, Nathan I didn't mean to upset you. My Kasha and I love you; we only want you to be happy. I can taste your loneliness you know, and it hurts us. Now that Tessa is—well, if you made a bond you would never be lonely—and with your bondmate's help, we could share even more than we do now. Won't you let me show you how beautiful it could be for all of us?"

Unable to help himself, Nathan reached up and caressed that well-loved face. "I know you mean well," he said, his voice thick with emotion, "but let it be."

"I just want you to be happy, truly." Sliding a tentacled hand over Nathan's torso and downward onto his belly once more, the Kashallan kissed him.

As their eyes met, Nathan groaned. Suddenly he felt his sex harden with awakened desire. "Oh, damn you," he breathed and wrapped his arms around the Kashallan crushing him to his chest. "Damn you," he murmured again as his mouth sought that adored other. As he and Dunnagh kissed, Nathan was startled as a bittersweet liquid poured into his mouth. He swallowed automatically. "What is that—what are you doing?"

Dunnagh's smile was lazy and self-satisfied. "You'll see soon enough."

"Dunnagh?" Nathan started to pull away.

The Kashallan reached for him, slid his hand along Nathan's thigh and stroked his erect shaft. "Oh don't make such a fuss; it was just green kavay." Lips parted he breathed, "Kiss me again, Mo Hara."

Green kavay, the stuff Singey and the priests were always daubing on their fingers to make a diagnosis. The stuff that opened up the mind and body's awareness to those other dimensions that only the Khutani could claim naturally.

As he relaxed and returned the kiss, Nathan felt several Khutani enfold them within their sinewy coils. He gasped as the world around him exploded with a wealth of new sensations. Satiny skin flowed over his, sensitive mouth tentacles brushed like delicate feathers against his body, exciting his desire to even greater heights. "Oh, Gods, Dunnagh!" he caressed that smiling, well-loved face. "This is a dirty trick, you know that—Oh, Gods—it's so beautiful."

"I know. Love, it's our gift to you; enjoy the feeling while it lasts."

Nathan thought he would drown—drown in a torrent of awakened sensations and long damned up passion. Licking, sucking, exploring, the water and air around the writhing mass of intertwined bodies seemed to vibrate with their aroused excitement.

Blurred images and alien sensations engulfed Nathan in a chaotic whirlpool of ecstatic communion. He felt, he tasted,—where did the self end and the other begin. He wasn't sure—didn't know—wasn't even sure he cared. The flavor of this new kind of loving was unbearably sweet upon his tongue. Time stood still; nothing mattered except the desire to become one with those others.

Ah, but it will not last, a tiny voice inside his mind warned. *No one you've ever loved can be yours forever—they always die or leave you in the end. No,* he begged the voice, *no not this time—please, no!* But even as his mind cried out in denial, he felt the crest of their climax take him.

Then he was fragmenting, senses once more dulled, tumbling alone, over the precipice into the blackness of exhausted sleep.

DUNNAGH PROPPED HIMSELF on one elbow and gazed, with troubled eyes, at the sleeping man beside him. Nathan lay on his back, his head resting on a gray coil of the Khutani who still wrapped itself loosely about him. Somewhere out in the darkness of the main channel a school of the cousins played a boisterous game of tag. He listened, but was glad for the moment that Tani had no desire to join them. He sighed. He'd like to bend over and kiss those sweet lips, but dare he—would Nathan like him to do that?

What is your love made of, I wonder? Time will reveal that. Which one of us will truly betray him in the end, hmm? Think on that, Kashallan—which one of us shall bind him, out of 'love,' to a course not of his choosing? Dunnagh shuddered as the demon spirit's words to him came unbidden into his mind. What had Tess-weh seen—was he wrong—

<<What's wrong now, Kasha, I can taste your unease. Why are you worried?>>

Dunnagh sighed again. <<Maybe we shouldn't have done that to him. He doesn't want to make a bond, and resuming our old affair...>>

<<Whether he makes a bonding or not is up to him. I promised you that neither our kindred nor I would do anything to hinder his freewill in the matter. We only made love to him—showed him how it could be for him, if he did make the bonding. And, he did like it, Kasha, truly, you know he did.>>

<<I know he did—we all did, and maybe that's even worse.>>

Tani made a mental sound of disgust. <<Humans. You make everything so complicated for yourselves. Stop it, Kasha. Before now, what did he know of the bonding first hand, hmm? From you he only had a taste of the fear and pain you experienced during the Transformation. I just showed him how beautiful the communion can be once the process has been completed. And his bonding wouldn't be like ours anyway—the Makers know so much more about the procedure now; they will help him, if he ever decides to do it.>>

<<I know, I just—>> Dunnagh broke off his internal conversation as he became aware of Nathan's wary gray eyes watching him. "Hello, Mo Hara." Bending down he kissed him tenderly.

Nathan hesitated, then returned the kiss. After a moment, however, he gently, but firmly, disengaged himself and sat up. The sinewy body around him shifted and a gray head sleepily nuzzled his shoulder. Without thinking, he stroked its satiny skin but kept his attention focused on the Kashallan. "What time is it?"

Trying to hide his disappointment, the Kashallan sat up too. Brushing back his russet braidlets he smiled shyly. "I have no idea. I heard the Avairei feeding the young ones a little while ago, so it's probably morning."

Nathan muttered a curse under his breath and started to stand. Then he remembered the eel-like body still coiled around his legs and flopped down with a sigh. He glanced at the Kashallan, eyes pleading.

The Kashallan laughed. "It will let you up when you want to leave, don't worry. But before you go, tell me the news; did you have a particular reason for coming down here last night?"

Nathan looked away, his hand stroking the Khutani with a distracted concentration. Under his hand the young adult squirmed with pleasure, though Nathan seemed to be unaware of that fact. "Yeah, I did. Before I got sidetracked, I did want to talk to you about a few things."

"Oh."

When Nathan continued his sudden interest in the Khutani, and made no effort to resume the conversation, Dunnagh ventured, "Nathan, are you angry with me?"

The big man froze. After a long moment he sighed, glanced at his friend, and then returned his attention to his sinewy companion. "No."

Dunnagh waited, but Nathan refused to say anything more or look at him. Muttering a curse under his breath he finally decided to change the subject. There was no getting through to him when he was like this, Dunnagh knew from bitter experience. "So what's going on up there? How is Amril? I haven't seen him in a while. The Avairei aren't giving him too hard of a time, because of his dress, are they?"

Nathan shrugged. "I don't think so, but I haven't seen much of him either. His uncle has been keeping him pretty busy. He probably hasn't had the time to worry about things like that. He and Arishim are usually with the Imas in some meeting or other."

Nathan turned and gave him an ironic grin. "As nothing more than a 'Stupid Warlinga,' however, they don't always invite me to their confabs."

The Kashallan's face darkened. "Mm, I see."

Reaching out his free hand, Nathan tentatively patted Dunnagh's arm. "Now don't get all worked up about it. You're not going to change the customs of centuries overnight. Arishim keeps me up to date, so I know what's going on."

"Mm. What have you and the rest of the Speir'dina been doing then?"

"Oh, we've been keeping busy, never fear. We've set up some bouts with Pagrich's lads; showing them some of the techniques we developed during the Sorins." Nathan made a face. "Pagrich's a bit too stuffy for my taste, but he's coming round."

"I'm glad to hear it. How is the recruiting coming? Ima Urinia warned me yesterday that some Avairei clan elders were expected any time now."

Nathan nodded. "So I hear. We seemed to be making some progress with the unaligned Avairei clans, but Varrod sent a message that many of the Warlinga are still unwilling to join us."

"Why, does he have any idea?"

Nathan shrugged, avoiding eye contact. "Evidently this K'San Drucas Segoi is a dangerous man to cross. He has most of the Warlinga clans scared shitless—which is hard to believe, but even the Meh'gach boys head crests dip when they talk about him.

"Aju'an thinks they'll be more likely to join us with a little demonstration of 'Speir'dina magic' to ease their minds. They want me to go with them to Serath Keep to talk to the K'Sans assembled there, and maybe give them a little demonstration of our weaponry."

"Mm. Do you think I should go with you?"

Nathan shook his head, still stroking the Khutani absently. "No, they believe the Avairei when they say there is a kashallan here—that's not the issue—and besides Urinia would have a fit if you weren't here when her guests arrive. No the problem is more a military one—that's why they want me, as your Hunt Leader, to go."

"Then you should go, but take Aju'an and the pack with you—and maybe Ross and a couple of the others too. You'll need protection, encase somebody decides you're really a mutant and tries to kill you."

Nathan looked at him sharply, his hand frozen upon the Khutani's back. "I don't know, Maker Dievris—"

The Kashallan scowled. "Nathan, I'm getting very tired of hearing that name. I know the Maker is a very impressive creature—and not one to trifle with, but I'll be all right." He waved an arm at the surrounding cavern. "I'm here with my kin. The Keep is loyal, and I'll still have Chelka and the rest of the Speir'dina with me. All I'm going to be doing is talking to and tasting whomever the Avairei send to me. It'll be you who'll be in danger, so if you decide to go, be careful."

Chapter Eleven

From his concealment among the thorn bushes, K'San Drucas focused his attention on the shimmering ribbon of silver roadway that stretched out from Shaden's main gate. In the cool darkness of predawn, his dozing mind had become aware of something that disturbed the stillness. Was that sound the bar being drawn back from the gate? Under his breath he hissed a low voiced command to his men in the surrounding thickets.

Senses straining Drucas peered into the gloom. Yes, the gate was opening now. Just inside the keep a sputtering torch revealed a pack of well-armed Warlinga readying themselves for a Journey.

Two unrecognizable figures wrapped in heavy cloaks also joined the men crowded near the partially opened gate. Drucas's tail twitched. Ah, this was very interesting; his hunch had been correct.

The pack filed out through the narrow gap, then took up a defensive formation on the road beyond. The cloaked figures, now sitting atop Loti peasants, in a most unusual manner took their places within the warriors' protective formation. Drucas wished the light was better, so he could see them more clearly—but no matter, he knew who they were.

Unconsciously Drucas bared his teeth in a silent snarl. Traitorous slime, what were they up to now? His claws flexed rhythmically at his sides. He would like to rip open their filthy throats right here and spill their blood upon the stone of the road. It would give him a sweet pleasure to kill them all and leave their ungrateful carcasses for the vistri to devour.

But no, there had been only two of the traitors with this pack. His spies had told him there were at least five or six of the vermin here. If he acted too rashly, the others might get away to cause trouble elsewhere. He mustn't let them know too soon, that he was already aware of their presence here. He smiled slyly to himself; no that would never do.

Nearby his Second whispered, "K'San, should we take them?"

"No. We will wait, but have them followed. I want to know where they're going."

When the hunting pack and their unseen escort was well out of sight Drucas stood up and stretched. He was tired and hungry; he would go back to their camp and rest for a while. Though he hated to admit it, perhaps it was time to introduce Enaju's little gambit into the play.

It would be to their advantage that the enemy was dividing their strength, but he doubted if the mutants who left Shaden to night were very important, in the overall picture. Messengers perhaps—no matter, they could be dealt with later. Certainly neither of them was this traitorous kashallan, he reasoned—if there was indeed such a creature. He would wait, set out his bait and see what fell into his trap.

"SIT DOWN RONNAN YOU'RE giving me a head ache with your pacing," Urinia complained.

Startled Ronnan paused midway across her braided rug; then returning to his chair, he flopped down hard enough to make the wicker creak in protest. "Sorry," he mumbled.

Ima Ngeal winced in sympathy with the chair, picked up the pitcher of spiced tea and refilled his bowl. They were in Urinia's private suite deep within Shaden Keep. Ngeal thought her friend's décor done in rust, gold and deep blues was usually a delight to behold, but right now its finely crafted tapestries and delicate wicker furniture held no appeal for her troubled mind. Handing the bowl back to Ronnan, she said coolly, "Calm down, Ata, it may not be as bad as you think—"

"Not bad!" Ronnan spluttered. "My Mother's message was quite explicit. There is plague at my family's keep—and the Dingay have caused it—we all know that. With Sulas destroyed, and Sagas outlawed, they think they now have the support they need to wipe out all Caltia—and who will dare lift a hand to stop them,!"

Unperturbed Ngeal sipped her tea before answering. "There are many who will rise up to stop them, Ata never fear. When it's time—"

Ronnan sprang to his feet again, spilling his bowl in his haste. "And by then my family may all be dead!"

"Ronnan, enough," Urinia growled.

Her fiery Second gaped, then sat back down, glaring at the women in the room sullenly.

Taking a deep breath Urinia continued in a more reasonable tone of voice, "You are upset, Ata, I can understand that, but that is still not a good reason to shout at one of our guests."

Ronnan blinked, then sighed. "My apologies, Ima Ngeal, I meant no offense."

Ngeal bobbed her head in acknowledgment. "I understand, Ata, but my point still is a valid one, we must not be too hasty in how we respond to this message it may not be what it seems."

As Ronnan began to protest, Arishim said, "Ata, please, I think I understand what Ima Ngeal is suggesting. Are you *absolutely* sure that letter was from your mother?"

Startled Ronnan opened his mouth then closed it again. Urinia leaned forward in her chair. Catching his eye she focused her predatory gaze upon him. "Calm down and listen to reason. Ronnan, the clan elder has a point. I am sure that Enaju has heard by now about our plans for the 'proposed festival.'

"Undoubtedly she knows of our many visitors, yet there has been no word from the Capital officially—or otherwise about all the activity. Perhaps she holds me in such contempt that she thinks nothing I do a threat to her, but maybe there is another reason for her silence."

"Like what?"

"A trap?"

Ronnan brushed his braidlets back over his shoulder, their ornaments hitting together in a clanging discord. He laughed nervously, waving his hand to dismiss the idea out of hand.

"That is a real possibility, Ata," Ngeal said, her aged features suddenly grim. "We have no way of knowing what Tomina told her Umwira master before she was killed. The Ghostlanders may already know of the reforming of the kashallan bond. This plague may be only a ruse to lure the Kashallan out of our protection in order to capture or kill him."

Reaching for his bowl again, Ronnan froze. Staring blindly at the far wall, he said as if talking to himself, "Holy Mother, I-I never thought of that."

"Ronnan?" Urinia said into the silence. "What are you concealing from us? I thought we agreed to keep this information to ourselves, until we could find out whether the report was genuine or not. What have you done?"

Ronnan looked up, but his eyes slid away from hers. "I have said nothing to him." His eyes flashed in challenge, but he sidestepped her question. "The Dingay have been trying to destroy us for years—why would you think this plague was a lie? Now would be a perfect time to do this to us."

"Would it? Why do it now? Why not wait till after the solstice festival—or when K'San Segoi's hunting packs have captured your sister and the rest of the outlaws. Why risk a confrontation now, when if she waits, there might be far more to gain, hmm?"

Ronnan squirmed and looked down at his bowl. He picked it up off the table and took a long drink of the tangy brew. The women's collective gaze pinned him to the wall of their suspicion. Ronnan took another swallow of tea, but remained stubbornly silent.

"Did you tell him, Ata?" Arishim finally asked.

Ronnan's head jerked up; he shook his head again. Turning to his superior, he mumbled, "No, I didn't tell him—I didn't disobey you, Ima Urinia."

Urinia waited.

Suddenly Ronnan let out a groan and doubled over, as if the tea he'd just drunk poisoned in his gut. Trembling he covered his face with his hands. Speaking through his splayed fingers he said, "Oh, Ima, my mother is old; her glyphs are a bit hard to read, but I was so sure—"

"Who did you tell, Ata?" Urinia demanded sternly.

Ronnan groaned again, his body seeming to curl up upon itself in his anguish. In a brittle voice he said, "By all the Gods, may no ill come of my disobedience. In my despair, I-I told Amril."

"You fool," Urinia snarled, her eyes flashing. "You sniveling coward! So, you wouldn't openly defy my order by telling the Kashallan himself, but you knew as his wife, if you told Amril, it would have the same result. And, I have no doubt that the young man pleaded your case most passionately. How very clever, Ata—but if something happens to him—" Urinia broke off her rage suddenly making her incoherent.

Ngeal forced herself to raise her cup and take another mouthful of tea. The stuff was as bitter in her throat as gall. Caltia... The whole clan was a stubborn, impulsive, fanatically passionate lot. What horrible mischief had this fool done in his single-minded desire to help his kin.

She had just come from the pools. The Kashallan wasn't there—and the Khutani were furious. Nor was he in his suite either. No one thought anything of his absence at first, assuming, no doubt that he was in one place or the other, but at the midday meal when it was remarked upon that Amril, and the rest of the Speir'dina guards were missing, too; they began to worry.

As Sagas predicted, Ngeal found this new kashallan and his kin to be stubborn and willful creatures. But, she also had learned that Dunnagh-Tani was very sentimental, and loyal. With Amril to argue the Caltia case, he might very well do something foolish in spite of the danger.

And the fact that Aju'an and his Hunt Leader, San Nathan were away gathering support among the Warlinga, might not dissuade him, if Amril's entreaties were poignant enough. How very, very clever, Ronnan, you slimeworm, she thought.

Catching Urinia's eye, Ngeal rose and headed towards the closed door. "I'll go see if the servants have found anything."

Urinia opened her mouth to protest, but she stepped out into the passage and closed the door firmly behind herself before the other priestess could get the words out. She had to get out of there, even if it was only for a few minutes. The growing tension in that room was about to make her go mad. She needed to be doing something—anything, to keep her terror at bay.

Sometime later Ronnan jumped as the outer door opened and a grim-faced Ngeal stepped back into the room. Taking one look at her, he said in a toneless voice, "He's gone, isn't he?"

Without answering, Ngeal crossed the room and held out a scrap of parchment to the Ima. Urinia took the missive woodenly and began to read.

"He left this with one of the Loti in the kitchens, of all things," Ngeal said into the silence. "And the stupid woman, thinking to aid him in his deception no doubt, waited until now to tell us. Forgive me, Urinia, if I've overstepped my authority here, but I ordered her disciplined for her sloth."

Urinia grimaced and nodded, not looking up from the note.

"What does it say, Ima?" Arishim asked. "I'm afraid my skill with your glyphs isn't very good yet."

Urinia put down the parchment and looked up. "It is a note from Amril to his uncle. He says that he, the Kashallan, the K'Sa Chelka and the Speir'dina guards took the outlaw Loti and went to the aid of the plague victims. Amril says not to worry, with the Speir'dina' magic and the Loti's help; they will be fine.

"Barbarians and peasants, Bah!" Urinia flung the parchment across the room then glared at her Second murderously.

Ronnan groaned. "Oh, Holy Mother, I didn't know he would do this—I thought he would send for his Warlinga, then—" His voice trailed off. He shook his head incredulously, then buried his face in his hands

"Never mind feeling sorry for yourself, Ata," Urinia snapped. "Get up! It is your duty to go and find him. Tell San Pagrich to organize a hunting pack to accompany you—and go with all haste."

Part Three: Prey of the Umwira

Chapter One

From the cover of the thorn thicket the weary travelers gazed down at the village in the hollow below them with a cautious eagerness. Like most of the Loti holdings in this part of the Yeyen, a wall of stone and mud had been erected around its dwellings to keep out the vistri and other predators.

Inside the wall the Kashallan could make out the thatched roofs of several long houses. In the center of the village the dark silhouette of a kavalpa tree raised its shaggy head into the evening sky. Farther off, the planted fields of lamra and masa root spread out along both sides of a sluggish irrigation ditch.

They had been traveling hard and fast for three days. Rising with first light the Loti had kept up a ground-covering trot, with few rests and only dried food to keep them going. Thank all the Gods the terrain wasn't as rough as their journey over the Shaden Portage. The rocky hillsides and boggy hollows of the network's secret pathways were isolated enough that there was little risk of discovery by a chance traveler, but the route was tiring for both Loti and Speir'dina.

Each night when it grew too dark to see, they'd camped in thorn thickets like this one. After a hasty meal they rolled into their cloaks, unwilling to risk a fire to alert possible spying eyes to their presence. Everyone was exhausted and the thought of a hot meal and rest was an overpowering lure that had caused them to consider stopping early at this isolated village before going on to Caltia Keep.

But by the time they reached the village, the gate had already been closed for the night. From inside the walls came the excited shouts of children at play and the lower murmur of adults going about their evening chores. A stray breeze wafted up to them bringing with it the smell of frying mushrooms and spices.

Mashen looked back over his shoulder and asked hopefully, "Shall we rest here for the night, Holy One?"

The Kashallan took in a deep breath and let it out in a long wistful sigh. He patted the Loti on his shoulder. "It is time for a rest, isn't it? Everything seems as it should down there, and those mushrooms smell delicious—I see no reason why we can't stop here." Directing his next comment to the man at his back he said, "Didn't you tell me, my dear, that we were on Caltia lands a couple sun-marks back?"

Jerking out of a doze, Amril tightened one arm around the Kashallan's waist and peered over his shoulder down into the vale. "It's been a while since I've been here, but I believe this is Mattol, it is one of the farthest settlements from the keep, but the people here give their fealty to Clan Caltia for certain."

Mashen leaned upon the butt of his traveling staff and studied the peaceful scene below them more carefully. His heavy brow ridges and protruding jaw molded his face into a gargoyle-like mask of bewilderment. "I think you are right, Ata, but if that is so, why does everything seem so normal? It doesn't sound or look like there is any sign of the plague here."

"Hmm, why indeed," the Kashallan mused.

"We are nearly a half days walk away from the keep, perhaps the infection hasn't spread this far yet," Amril said. "During the growing season there isn't a lot of travel to and from the keep, the Loti are too busy in the fields. Being so far away, these people may not go to the keep except on festival days and during the Sorin confinement."

"That's true."

Oglas shifted the position of his beam rifle and asked, "Would you like me and Capric here to go down and have a closer look?"

The kashallan considered. "I think it would be a good idea for *someone* to go down and check things out, but not you, Oglas. We don't know if the network has carried the news about us this far yet; we don't want to frighten them with our alien faces unnecessarily if they haven't heard about us."

Slipping off Mashen's back, he lifted down the surprised Amril, then said, "Let Mashen and Capric do it alone." Putting an arm on the Loti's shoulder, he said, "See if the village elders will allow us shelter for the night."

Picking up his staff Mashen started down the path, Capric following in his wake.

Amril watched them go, his face a mask of weariness. He shivered in the cool air and hugged his cloak closer around his slim shoulders. Seeing the gesture, the Kashallan enfolded the smaller man in his arms and wrapped his cloak around them both. Shyly Amril leaned back against his larger bulk to take advantage of his warmth.

"Tired?"

"A little maybe." Turning within the Kashallan's embrace Amril looked up at him and said a bit plaintively, "Can't we go on to the keep? We are so close now, if we—"

The Kashallan gave him a hug, bent to kiss his forehead, silencing him in mid-sentence. "No, My Dear, that would not be wise. It's getting late, and the Loti are exhausted. I share your worry for your kin, but we too need our rest. If the sickness is bad at the keep, it would not do the people there any good if we arrive too weary to care for them, hmm?"

Amril thought about it a moment, then nodded reluctantly. "You are wiser than I, My Husband, I guess it would be best to go on in the morning."

Down by the gate, the two Loti halted. Reaching into a small pouch slung over his shoulder, Mashen produced a bone flute, raised it to his lips and blew several high, shrill notes. From within the compound the noise suddenly quieted. Mashen repeated his signal twice more then waited.

At last the gate was hesitantly opened. The outlaw Loti crowded near speaking to someone inside. The conversation continued for a few minutes more, then the Loti turned and headed back up the hill. The Kashallan and Oglas stepped forward to meet them.

Mashen stopped in front of the Kashallan and bowed. "These people are very isolated here, Holy One, they hadn't heard the news, as you suspected, but they are curious about us, and have willingly agreed to give us lodging for the night."

"That's good."

As he drew near enough to mount, Mashen stopped him. He glanced at the waiting Amril, then murmured so only the Kashallan could hear, "Dunnagh-Tani, there is something very wrong."

"How so?"

"The headman here says he knows nothing about any sickness at the keep."

Putting a hand on the Loti's withers he swung himself onto his back. "I was afraid you'd say something like that."

By the time they reached the village, most of its population was standing in a loose semicircle around the gate awaiting their arrival. As they entered, and the people saw their alien faces for the first time, they drew back. Some of the younger children hid their faces in their mother's shaggy flanks, and the young men's grip tightened on their shovels and traveling staffs.

Spotting a grizzle-pelted elder directly in front of them, Mashen turned and murmured, "That is Elder Haru there before us."

Sliding down from his back, the Kashallan stepped forward and bowed respectfully to the old man. "My thanks to you, Timornshaya, for allowing us to shelter within your walls this night." He held out his hand. "I am Dunnagh-Tani, and as Mashen has probably told you I am the first of the new kashallans."

Haru bowed in return, his golden eyes alight with wonder. "So this young man has told us. I must confess that I never thought to see such a marvel in my own lifetime. Truly you are welcome among us, Holy One." He motioned to the kavalpa in the center of the enclosure. "Come refresh yourselves at the spring. The evening meal will be ready soon. You can eat with us and tell us your news. Then you may rest; my own family's house is at your service."

WHEN THE MEAL WAS FINISHED and the younger children put to bed, the adults of the village, and the Kashallan's party lingered over the glowing flames of a peat fire outside the elder's house. Haru sat with his legs tucked up beside his body and took a last swallow of his mushroom beer. Setting his bowl down he looked at his guests thoughtfully for a long moment. At last he said, "Your story troubles me greatly, Holy One. Poisonings, fighting, changelings in Riath, such things are beyond a simple Loti, like me. But what concerns me most is this story of plague here on Caltia lands."

Haru glanced warily at Amril, sitting huddled in his cloak with head bowed, beside the Kashallan. "You have come in haste—and perhaps, at a great risk to yourself, but we have neither seen nor heard anything of this plague."

"Your village is quite far from Caltia Keep, is it possible that you have escaped the contagion for that reason?" the Kashallan asked. Behind him he could hear the Loti shuffling uneasily. In a nearby house a child cried and a woman began singing to it softly.

"Possible surely, but I don't think so," the elder replied.

"Has there been any traveler along the network from the keep recently," Mashen asked.

Haru who had been about to pour himself more beer looked up and scowled at the young man. His eyes flicked to Amril, and the K'Sa Chelka standing at the Kashallan's back, then he returned his glare to Mashen. Around them the other Loti became suddenly quiet.

In the stillness Amril raised his head. Catching the looks directed his way he sighed. In a tired voice he said, "Don't worry about your precious secret network. Chelka and I swore blood oath that we would not speak of it to anyone; so go ahead and say what you like."

Haru's look softened. He bowed solemnly to the priest and the Warlinga, then continued, "My youngest son and two of his cousins packed a load of early mushrooms and herbs to the keep two days ago. They did some needed work for your grandmother, Ata, then returned this morning. All was well when they left there at that time."

The Kashallan sighed. "Which of course was days after we received the note at Shaden."

Startled, Amril gasped. "No, how could that be?" Then as he figured it out his eyes widened in fright. "No," he breathed, and laid a trembling hand on the Kashallan's arm. "No," he repeated, "oh, Husband, what have I done?"

The Kashallan covered his hand with one of his own. He gazed at him out of eyes suddenly soft with compassion. "It's all right; we had to know for sure, don't worry about it, My Dear." Turning back to the elder, he said, "Elder Haru, I think it would be wise for us to be moving on as soon as possible, but if you will allow us to rest for a few hours under your tree; I would be most grateful."

Haru stood up and bowed. "But of course, Holy One, but you need not sleep outside in the damp." He pointed to the sturdy thatched house at his back. "As I said before, you're welcome to my home, for as long as need be."

The Kashallan shook his head, rising as well. "I thank you, Honored Timornshaya, but we will be leaving well before dawn; it would be best that we sleep under the tree, so that we will not disturb anyone as we go."

The elder opened his mouth as if to protest then reluctantly agreed. "Your will, Kashallan. I will have my daughters bring out soft mattresses and extra blankets for your people's comfort. We will have food packages prepared for you to take along with you when you leave."

"Thank you, elder, you have been a most gracious host."

LATER WHEN THEY WERE alone under the tree, Marti swore under her breath and angrily tossed another lump of peat onto their tiny fire. "The question is where do we go from here? Do we go on to the keep and wait for Nathan and the pack to come and get us, or do we make a run for Shaden?"

Reclining on a moss-filled tick the Kashallan sighed and opened tired eyes. "I was just trying to decide that very thing."

"The keep is nearer than Shaden—and we don't know how close the enemy is on our back trail—the keep would be my choice, Ce'awn," Ellis said. An angular woman with large brown eyes and a wispy blond braid, she curled her long fingers unconsciously around the butt of the weapon on her hip.

"Sa Ellis is right; that may be our best option—especially if there is a Warlinga hunting pack stationed there," Chelka said. "But if no pack is at the keep now, it might be dangerous to be trapped there. The keep would have little in the way of reserve food stores at this time of year—if we had to wait." She left the rest of her thought unvoiced and asked Amril instead. "Are there Warlinga at your family keep?"

"Sometimes. K'San Serath sends us men to patrol for vistri during the growing season, but no one is stationed there regularly. Though with all the trouble, my grandmother may have made other arrangements."

The Kashallan glanced at their exhausted Loti mounts Huddled like large shaggy dust mops in the hollows between the tree's arching roots. Nearby the spring babbled to itself in the darkness. He was tired; he should go to bed, the others wouldn't rest if he didn't. "Oglas, did you ask the elder about setting out a few guards tonight?"

Oglas brushed back his brown hair and nodded, his usually cheerful boyish face drawn and solemn. "I did, Ce'awn. A few of the lads are going to help us with sentry duty. Me and Harris will take the late watch, the women can divide up the time between now and then how they like."

The Kashallan glanced at Marti who nodded and stood up. "I'll take first watch, Ellis and Chelka can have the mid watch." She Picked up her beam rifle and headed for the gate.

"Good then I guess we'd better get some rest. We'll leave early for the keep. Even if there aren't Warlinga there at the moment, it's our best option. The Loti are too tired to make a fast run back to Shaden. And if whoever is following us pens us down there, I think our weaponry can make them think twice before trying to take the keep. We'll wait there till someone from Shaden comes to fetch us."

As he drifted near the borders of sleep a worried voice spoke into Dunnagh's mind.

<<I'm frightened, Kasha.>>

Dunnagh rubbed a hand across his belly. <<I know, little one, so am I; try to rest now.>>

There was a long pause, then Tani said,<<Nathan and the elders back at the pools are going to be furious with us aren't they, Kasha?>>

Dunnagh sighed and pulled his cloak up around his neck. <<I'm afraid so, Shalla, and I'm not looking forward to their discipline either.>>

Chapter Two

Smoke eddied lazily up into the morning mists from the burned-out ruins of Mattol. The Speir'dina coughed, a bubble of purple blood ballooned out of his mouth. It quivered a moment in the cool morning air, then burst, splattering its contents into the moss below his chin. Panting, Oglas groaned then flopped onto his back. He was so tired; he doubted he could crawl any further.

Pain! It was a blessing in disguise, he knew, but oh, Merciful Mother, could he make it? He watched the pair of vistri eyeing him hungrily from a few paces away. Squat, piggy bodies covered in iron-gray scaly armor they waited with their long snouts raised, nostrils flaring.

If he could just roll over, crawl to where the enemy had kicked his sidearm during the fight last night; he'd finish off those scavenging vermin. He'd blow them apart, even if it was the last thing he did in this life. Oglas trembled. Oh, by all the Gods, who was he kidding? He wasn't going anywhere, and the cursed beasts knew it—they need only bide their time.

The High Matri's hunting pack waited till the exhausted travelers and the villagers were peacefully asleep; then in the hours before dawn, they attacked. Oglas himself, and Harris were on watch when it happened. They weren't caught totally off guard—though it had done them little good.

Glancing once more at the mangled corpse of his comrade, Oglas cursed under his breath. Clever Devils. Harris hadn't had a chance—none of them had. In the darkness last night it seemed like the Warlinga were over the wall and on them before they knew what was happening.

Well, why not; the wall wasn't that high. It was built to keep out vermin, not an enemy hunting pack bent on slaughter. These people wouldn't have believed such an attack possible—no Timornan would, until last night.

The High Matri's hunting pack that followed them from Shaden must have been closer on their back trail than they realized. The pack also would have known how near they were to the safety of Caltia Keep. Once assured that their quarry was inside the village, and intended to stay there; they made their plans to take them

Like green recruits, they fell right into Enaju's trap. How could they have been so stupid! The ruse used to get them out of the keep initially, had been designed to play on Caltia family loyalty and the Kashallan's compassion. How could the changelings have known their weaknesses so well? And the distraction used last night to divert, then overpower them was so cleverly conceived—damn the black-hearted devils, that they hadn't suspected a thing, until it was too late.

A SLEEPY ELLIS, COMING off watch, nudged Oglas awake as she stumbled to her blanket. When Oglas stepped out of the trees, he saw that a ground fog had settled over the village while he slept. Damp tendrils of the stuff coiled about his legs making the cloth of his trousers clammy to the touch. Oglas rubbed at his eyes and looked up; faintly luminous indigo and gray clouds massed in large clumps across the black abyss of the sky.

A few hours yet till dawn, he thought and yawned. Next he scanned the village half hidden in the mist. The disembodied thatched roofs of the houses floated above the fog like shaggy tents. Ghostly haloes enveloped the green-flamed lamps on doorposts scattered here and there around the deserted compound. All seemed quiet.

Over by the gate the sentries had made a small fire; Oglas could see Chelka and Harris squatting by it warming their hands, waiting for him. He settled his rifle more comfortably on his shoulder and walked over to them.

They looked up as he came near. Chelka pointed to a clay pot nestled in the warm ashes at the edge of the fire. "There's some hot tea left if you want it."

Oglas grinned and removed the battered, Lann Gheal issue cup from his belt. He yawned, mouth wide, jaws straining. "Good, maybe it will help me wake up." He lifted the pot with a branch and poured the steaming liquid into his cup. "All quiet, I assume."

Chelka glanced out into the darkness, nostrils flaring. "So far. A pack of vistri was making a fuss out there," she motioned with her chin to the shadowy hillside beyond the gate, "when I started my watch, but nothing to report since then."

Harris slurped his tea, blowing the steam off the rim of his cup. "Then why don't you go on to bed like Ellis has done. You must be tired; get some rest while you can. Oglas and I will take a stroll around the perimeter of the walls in a few minutes."

"I will soon." She took another sip of her tea, but made no move to leave them.

Oglas shivered and set down his cup. The dampness was chilling him to the bone. "What's wrong Sa?"

Startled, Chelka looked up, her red eyes caught the firelight suddenly glowing like angry coals. Oglas shivered again and looked away.

"Nothing's wrong really. I guess I just can't help worrying. The night's been quiet—almost too quiet, except I know that when a pack of vistri is hunting—like they were, it usually is like this. But I can't get it out of my mind that we're missing something—or that we should be doing something more than we are." She sighed and dropped her head, once more staring into the flames.

Harris laughed softly. "Well, we'll be doing something soon enough. It'll be dawn in a little while, and before that the Ce'awn will have everyone up and making a run for Caltia Keep to be sure."

"Yes, and I for one will be glad to see the stone walls of the Caltia stronghold truly. Even with your Speir'dina magics, we are in danger as long as we remain out here in the open."

Oglas grunted an agreement and sipped at his tea; the warmth of it felt good in his gut. Chelka was right. They had been so sure about the plague that they hadn't kept a proper watch on their back trail, trusting mainly to speed and secrecy to protect them. He yawned. Gods, he was tired; he wished he could wake up, but his brain felt like it was stuffed with cotton.

Across the fire Harris stood up and stretched. He picked up his rifle and turned away from the light, taking a moment for his eyes to adjust to the darkness beyond. "I'll take a walk around the village, have a look." Then he stepped away from the wall, his black-clad figure fading soundlessly into the gloom.

Oglas sighed, finished his tea and re-hooked his cup on his belt. "You should go to bed, Sa," he said gently.

"I will in a while."

Oglas started to argue, then felt his gut cramp. He stood up hastily and reached for his rifle. "If you're going to sit here a while longer, I'll have a stroll around the village as well then."

Chelka glanced up and smiled. "Go ahead, I'll wait here till one of you returns."

Oglas was coming back from the privy when he heard animal snarls and the sounds of Loti children shrieking. The tumult seemed to be coming from the far end of the village. Unslinging his beam rifle from his shoulder, Oglas headed in that direction. Suddenly out of the corner of his eye, Oglas saw a dark shape coming towards him and instinctively dropped into a fighter's crouch, his rifle aimed in that direction.

"Oglas, what, by all the Gods is going on down there?" Harris panted as he came running up to him.

"Don't know," he muttered, reslung his rifle and quickened his pace. Harris cursed and fell into step beside him. By now sleepy Loti were sticking their heads out of doorways and shouting anxious questions to one another.

"Damn, it sounds like a hundred devils are loose down there, but it doesn't seem like a fight. Can you see any Warlinga?"

"No." Almost running now, Oglas strained his eyes to pierce the gloom. He saw no attacking lizardmen; only frightened peasants and screaming children running and bucking—slowing them down and getting in their way.

Suddenly a squat, gray thing about two feet high, shot out from between two of the houses just ahead of them. In the lamp light from the doorway he saw a pig-like creature with bony spikes along its backbone. Oglas cried out in surprise. The creature turned at the sound, baring its long fangs. Still moving Oglas raised his rifle and fired. The beast exploded in a shower of white-hot sparks.

"Damn. What was that thing?

"Vistri!" Oglas panted, quickening his pace.

"Vistri?" Harris cried. "How did it get in here?"

How indeed, Oglas thought. His Caldoni intuition warned him that there was something wrong—vistri couldn't get over that wall—on their own.

"Shit!" just ahead of him, Harris suddenly stopped. Without a word he turned and sprinted back the way they'd just come.

Trying to catch his breath Oglas shouted, "Hey, where are you going?"

"Come on!" Without looking back Harris yelled, "It's a trick—the Ce'awn."

Oh, Gods, Harris was right; the vistri in the compound were nothing more than a diversion. Running flat out the two men raced for the kavalpa grove.

Then there was no more time to think—everything happened so fast. Screaming like demons the hunting pack from Riath came over the wall from several directions at once. From the kavalpa grove ahead a blinding flash of white light exploded into the night. Oglas cried out blinded by the flash. He tripped over something in the dark and went sprawling, his breath coming out in a painful grunt, his weapon jarred out of his hand.

Gasping for breath he groped for his rifle. He could hear Marti's foghorn bellow and more beam rifle fire. From somewhere a Warlinga screamed in agony. Oglas cursed, groping for his weapon. Ah, there. Snatching up the rifle he lunged to his feet and pelted after Harris. He had to get to the grove—had to find the Ce'awn!

Then in the lamplight just ahead of him he saw Harris go down, a Warlinga spear through his back. Unseen the man had been hiding in the ground fog at the side of a house, coming out to attack just after the armachd passed by. Intent on the fight going on in the grove, Harris hadn't noticed him until it was too late.

Still running, Oglas raised his rifle and fired at the Warlinga now bending over the body, but whether he hit his target or not; he never knew. Blinding pain exploded in his side and he crashed to the ground.

Coming to his senses sometime later, Oglas levered himself to hands and knees, and looked around. The night was paling into dawn, but he could see little through the mist that still hugged the ground. He groped in the dirt for his weapon.

There was no more rifle fire coming from the grove. How long had he been out? He cursed. His side ached like poison, and he could feel a warm trickle of blood dripping down over his buttocks. Damn, whoever had stabbed him must have taken his rifle—or kicked it out of reach—he couldn't see it anywhere. Well he still had his sidearm, thank the Gods. Unable to stand, he began to crawl on all fours toward the grove.

He was still crawling doggedly forward, when the sound of snarling Warlinga just ahead made him stop and look up. In the paling light of dawn, Oglas saw two Warlinga circling a third at the edge of the grove. The hunter's tails whipped and their claws slashed at their opponent. Oglas recognized Chelka by the gleam of her bone-scaled apron. On the ground nearby another Warlinga sat clutching his belly, dark blood spilling through his fingers as he tried to push his guts back into his body.

Chelka was fighting with grim determination, but she had already lost her spear, and he could see that she too was wounded. When two other Warlinga joined the fray it was over soon enough. He fumbled for his sidearm, but his hand was trembling so much he couldn't unsnap the clasp of his holster.

He fell back onto the ground panting, straining to get to his weapon. As he watched helplessly, she fell to her knees, bleeding from another deep gash.

One of the hunters shouted in triumph and drew a wicked-looking stone knife. Stepping forward he grabbed her by the head crest, jerked her head up, and put the blade to her throat. Before he could give her the killing stroke, however, an unusually tall, powerful-looking Warlinga shouted at him and he took the knife away.

Coming over to them the tall man looked down at Chelka for a long moment, then he gave her a malicious smile and said something to his men that made them look at Chelka and laugh.

Chelka spat and said something in return which made them laugh all the more. Ordering his men to hold her the tall man took some powder from a pouch at his waist and rubbed it roughly into a long gash on

Chelka's arm. She bucked and swore at them, but they held onto her and in a few more moments she slumped unconscious in her captor's arms.

Oglas swore under his breath; his fingers managed to finally unsnap the holster flap and then they closed around the butt of his sidearm. He pulled it from the holster, his breath coming in short gasps. What had happened to the rest of the Speir'dina, and where, by all the Gods was the Kashallan?

He got his answer soon enough when several limp, tightly-bound bodies were brought out from the kavalpa thicket and strapped to the backs of several terrified Loti, captured for that purpose.

Oglas aimed the gun, his arm against the dirt by his cheek, his other hand braced against his arm to steady it. That big one was obviously their leader, Oglas thought as he ignored the pain and focused on his target. "Just hold steady you devil—"

Oglas screamed as another stabbing thrust of pain slammed into his back. A clawed foot kicked the gun from his hand. Then, his strength gone, the blackness claimed him.

Oglas lingered in a dream-like state of consciousness in which it was impossible for him to tell through the waves of his pain what was real, and what imagined. He thought he saw the pack tie their drugged captives, like bleeding sacks of grain across the peasants' backs. When the Kashallan was tied upon his back, the brave, but foolish Mashen, bolted for the gate. With angry curses, several hunters bounded after the Loti, butchering him savagely not far outside the compound.

Oglas could hear the poor lad's screams echoing in his head long after the bleeding corpse was dragged back behind the walls. The bundled Kashallan cursing weakly was returned and retied onto another frightened peasant; then their leader gave the order for the pack to collect their prisoners and move out.

As a final act of cruelty the Riath pack fired the village, and left, triumphant, abandoning the dead Loti, Harris and himself to the tender mercies of the vistri.

OGLAS BLINKED, WHERE had his verminous tormentors gone. Were they trying to come at him again from behind? From somewhere amidst the rubble he heard the vistri quarreling over one of the unburned corpses. He sighed. Good, maybe they would leave him alone for a while, but if he were to fall asleep again...

WITH A HEAVY HEART Ronnan slowed his pace, looked down into the hollow, and surveyed the ruins of the village. Behind its low earthen walls the charred skeletons of the ravaged houses still smoldered in the glare of the morning sun. From the kavalpa grove at the center of the compound he could hear children wailing.

Tears stung his eyes and he wasn't sure if it was from the clawing smoke or the black despair he felt in his heart at the sight below him. The men of the hunting pack, cursing under their breaths loped past him down the trail. Head crests high, spears at the ready, they continued on to the village, while Ronnan followed more slowly.

A Loti village burned, never in living memory had such a thing ever happened. It was unthinkable. There could be no other reason for this outrage; the Kashallan was either dead, or taken. And may all the Gods curse him—it was his fault.

Once they knew for certain that the Kashallan had left the keep, the priest and his hunting pack hurried towards Caltia Keep as fast as they could. Ronnan even agreed to forego a litter and ride a Loti as the Speir'dina did. But, they made a mistake in assuming that the Kashallan would take the main trails to the endangered keep.

They had arrived at the Caltia stronghold yesterday only to find no Kashallan. His mother and the rest of the household knew nothing of either a plague, or the Kashallan on his way to rescue them. In desperation, the Warlinga at the keep and the men from Shaden split up into groups to search the nearby countryside for any signs of the missing party.

This morning the rescue party that Ronnan went out with had smelled the stench of smoke on the wind and quickened their pace, fearful of what they might find. But in spite of their haste, they were too late. One look at the wreckage had assured Ronnan that his worst nightmare had come true.

With a sinking heart, Ronnan slid down off the Loti's back just inside the yawning gate. The place reeked of, singed fur, charred meat and despair. Along the earthen wall several badly mangled corpses had been lined up in a row, their blackened remains unrecognizable. Ronnan crossed to the bodies. One, hadn't been burned, but slashed repeatedly by what could only have been Warlinga spears and claws. Ronnan recognized the man as one of the outlaw Loti from Ticca,. So, this fire had been no accident as he'd hoped.

Not all the village had burned to the ground, thank the Mother. Down at the far end of the compound a few houses remained standing their damp thatch only scorched by the blaze. Here and there sobbing peasants picked through the wreckage. Near the edge of the kavalpa grove Ronnan could see a few children huddling together, their frightened yellow eyes staring blindly at nothing. Ronnan cursed softly under his breath; why had they done this terrible thing to these gentle people? And where was the Kashallan?

Ronnan motioned for his hunt leader to join him. Grim-faced the man approached and bowed. "See if you can find me someone in charge here. We need to know what has happened, and if the Kashallan and his people were here at the time of the attack." He glanced worriedly around the village once more. "These people need help, but if we are going to find the Kashallan we won't be able to aid them ourselves. Send a fast runner back to the keep and ask for men and supplies to come as quickly as possible."

"I have already done so, Ata, and I have sent out scouts to see if they can find the enemies trail as well."

"That is good, Hunt Leader—"

"Over here, Ata," a Warlinga cried. "I have found one of the Kashallan's Speir'dina guards and he is still alive!"

Mouthing a silent prayer, Ronnan crossed to the crouching man. A black-clad man lay sprawled in the dirt, a dark pool of blood soaking into the ground under him. Yes, it was one of the Kashallan's Speir'dina guards; they had indeed been here when the attack happened. Ronnan shuddered.

How could he live with this shame? Urinia was right, he was a cowardly fool.

From his medical satchel, he took out a jar of the green kavay and applied it to his fingertips. He motioned for the Warlinga to turn the man over onto his uninjured side. Ronnan gazed down at the Speir'dina's ugly, naked face streaked with dirt and blood. The man's eyelids flickered as he touched his wounds with his green-coated fingers.

The Speir'dina was alive—but just barely. Setting aside his own guilt, he focused on his diagnosis. If he could save this one, perhaps the man could tell them what had happened to the Kashallan. By all the Gods, they needed to know—they must have more information. "Don't die, Alien Warrior," he breathed, "we need you."

Chapter Three

Drucas set a fast pace after leaving the burning village. The pillars of gray smoke climbing into the morning sky would act as a beacon to any hunting Warlinga within site of the cloud. To avoid discovery and the loss of such a "precious" treasure, Drucas turned away from the traveled roadways and cultivated lands, and headed towards the rugged terrain of the backcountry. In the wilds they were less likely to meet up with pursuit or be spotted by tattling peasants.

But the purple hills of thorn, and liru reed bogs held many dangers for the unwary. The maze of wandering paths that crossed it, led into quick sand traps or blind washes as often as not. Vistri packs also hunted the wild land, but Drucas reckoned the added risk was well worth the concealment it offered.

The pack and its prisoners made up a large, well-armed group; predatory beasts would be little threat. And with the Begta slaves they had terrorized into guiding them through this wilderness, there would be less chance of getting lost.

The High One's orders were clear; they were to take as many of the mutants and their Caltia supporters as possible alive. Then they were to return with them to Riath, for the public trials and executions that would follow at Solstice Festival. Their pace would be slower this way of course, but that would only give him more time to get to *know* his "traveling companions."

When he finally allowed his men and the exhausted Loti to rest for a few hours, Drucas judged that they were well away from Caltia land holdings. It was most unlikely they were being pursued after such a grueling run, but he sent out scouts along their back trail to make sure, before entering the kavalpa thicket and taking some refreshment.

Wraith-like, the Begta gathered water from the spring and went about their camp chores, seldom taking their frightened eyes from the lounging Warlinga. Already hobbled and tied to arching tree roots for the night, the exhausted Loti curled up, shaggy lumps of misery; their heads resting on their folded upper set of arms,.

Bowl of mushroom beer in hand K'San Drucas squatted beside a tiny fire and surveyed the catch of last night's hunt with grim satisfaction. Sagas Caltia wasn't among his prisoners, more the pity, but they would catch her; he never doubted that. He laughed softly to himself; the Caltia brat and the Meh'gach woman would go a long way to placating Enaju's disappointment.

His bound prisoners lay together at the base of one of the trees, not far away. Drucas took another swallow of beer. He wanted them near him—he like looking at them. It gave him pleasure to think about the sweet tortures in store for them when they reached Riath.

Even though they didn't have Sagas; they did have the blue-eyed leader of the mutants. And, to his way of thinking, that was even better. His red eyes hardened, his lip curling into a cruel smile, as he contemplated the man. Blue Eyes was an ugly, flat-faced brute, with a thin skin and no natural defenses; yet he was sturdy and well-muscled. It was an ideal combination for a *slave,* but why would his wizard master have wanted to breed such a puny excuse for a warrior, if he planned to send him into the heart of enemy held lands?

And yet it was rumored that this one had vanquished one of the Master's war leaders in single combat. If that were true, he must have some powerful magics indeed. Was the traitorous slime hosting the symbiont at that time? Perhaps that would account for his victory; the Ancient Enemy always had their tricks. Even the Master didn't know them all. He'd better have a care with this one.

As their eyes met, Drucas could see that he was fully conscious. The symbiont that coiled in his middle must have neutralized the drug he had been given. Though tightly bound the creature's eerie blue eyes burned into him with his hatred. Inwardly Drucas shuddered in spite of himself—what hideous, unnatural eyes.

Traitor! Drucas set down his empty bowl, flexing his claws unconsciously in his mounting rage. By the Fires this mutant and all his kind should be given a most excruciatingly painful death.

Unable to contain himself, the Warlinga rose. Drawing near the captives Drucas fixed his eyes on the Kashallan, and gave him an impressive view of his fangs. His low voice thick with emotion, the changeling promised, "When it is time, your end will be exquisitely painful, traitorous slime. I will personally see to that."

Blue Eyes blinked; his expression suddenly confused and uncertain. Then his mouth hardened and his eyes became glacial again. "I've forsaken no alliance with your Master, changeling. I am no wizard-bred mutant—as you are. Don't you and your Ima know yet, who I really am? Ah, too bad. Didn't Tomina tell you before we killed her?"

Startled, Drucas's head crest flattened, a low rumble began deep in his throat. "Lying vermin! Don't try my patience, mutant, or I shall begin your punishment here and now. We have with us your wizard's magical weapons, and I can see the Khutani slimeworm coiled within your abdomen. What is that but clear proof of you and your wizard's betrayal."

Blue Eyes met and held Drucas's hostile stare. "It is true enough, K'San, that I have made a kashallan bond. My people can host the symbionts, but we are not mutants from across the Shallow Sea. We are the Speir'dina.

"We were brought to this world from the stars, to free the Khutani from their pools. You may kill me, K'San, but you will not find my people's alliance with the ancient race so easily destroyed. We aren't the Bebech, and we will defeat you and your Umwira allies in the end."

Snarling a curse, Drucas extended a clawed foot and delivered a savage kick to his helpless captive's side. Blue Eyes grunted but gave no other indication that the blow hurt him. Drucas's lip curled with satisfaction when a moment later he saw a dark stain seeping into the debris under the man's ribs.

"Liar. Warriors from the stars indeed. Do you take me for a total fool? Enough, Insolent Slimeworm, your Master's magics have failed you," Drucas hissed. Then to further his point his tail whipped round, its tip striking a stinging blow to his face. Blue eyes' head slammed back against the tree behind him. He gasped then bit down hard on his lower lip.

In a bloodless voice, the changeling said, "I'll not warn you again, Mutant, don't try my patience with your lies. You would not like it if I became truly annoyed with you."

"K'San Dru-cas, plea-se," Amril said, his voice still slurred with the Umwira drug. "My hus-band does not lie."

Drucas spun round focusing his scalding red glare on the young priest. Amril swallowed, tried to hold his gaze, but dropped his eyes.

The changeling gave him a toothy smile and flexed his claws where the young Ata could see them. He was going to enjoy the questioning of this one, almost as much as he would Blue Eyes. "Have a care, Ata," he warned in a dangerous voice, "don't try my patience either, or there will be little left of you for the Dingay to devour."

Amril licked his lips and closed his eyes. The drug he'd been given was dulling his fear—somewhat, but the priest had understood him.

Drucas wasn't sure quite what to make of the young priest. An Avairei Ata, dressed in a woman's kilt he claimed to be wife to the blue-eyed traitor, fascinating. He smirked. Here was one who could rival the High One's grandson for disgusting perversions. Enaju was going to be terribly amused.

These Avairei were a weak and loathsome race. In the new order to come Drucas hoped the Master would rid the world of all their putrescent lives. Ah well, someday perhaps, but for now they had their uses. And, the High One should be pleased. This young Caltia's depravity could be used as just another example of the deep-rooted corruption so ripe within the enemy clan.

She should also be delighted to find Sa Chelka Meh'gach among his prisoners. Her presence with this bunch was ample proof of her father's treachery; in spite of his submissive behavior at Riath. What would the old K'San do when he knew of her capture? The woman was rumored to be one of his favorite children.

Drucas walked closer and looked down at her. Wounded and disheveled, her head crest torn, she lay in her drug induce torpor next to the other mutant women. Women warriors, bah! A female's place was in the accavett, not interfering with the affairs of men. No wonder it had been so easy to take Blue Eyes if his master could only send *women* to protect him. When there was time, he might allow himself the pleasure of teaching Chelka and the other two that important lesson.

She was watching him warily, but he could also see the coals of hatred smoldering deep in her eyes. She was no sniveling coward, he'd give her that. His eyes slid possessively over her slim, well-muscled figure. Cleaned up she would be quite a beauty—she would bear many fine children, no doubt; though she would need to learn who was her master. He met her gaze, held it, and then curled his lips into a taunting smile. He might enjoy bringing this one to heal.

Bearing her own teeth she raised her head and snapped at his leg. Drucas laughed and slapped her back down, almost gently with his tail. Still laughing to himself he returned his attention to Blue Eyes and the priest.

When their eyes were focused upon his face once more, he said "People from the stars, mutants, what does it matter. It is not up to me to decide if the babblings of traitors and slaves be the truth or lies. I will let my Ima, and her brother, Ata Persig, determine such matters.

When we get back to the Capital; you can look forward to receiving a great deal of their undivided attention, I am sure. Ata Persig is most skilled in the fine art of administering pain—as am I. You will come to appreciate our skills, before your death finally claims you."

DRUCAS FLICKED THE barbed end of his tail across the rump of the Loti as he passed him. "Move you piece of verminous filth or I'll cut off your ragged tail and stuff it down your throat for your dinner." The peasant jerked and broke into a shambling run. The yellow-maned woman tied across his back groaned as the Loti's increased pace bounced her up and down upon his back. Drucas slapped the peasant again, for good measure, and continued on up the column.

They'd wasted time backtracking out of that bog. It would be dark in a while, and they needed a place to camp. The peasants couldn't keep up this pace much longer, even with the pain he could inflict as a goad to spur them on. His eyes narrowed and he studied the line of weary Loti. Yes, after three days of this grueling pace they were nearly spent.

In the morning he would have to give them some of the stimulant he had in his pack. They would be good for nothing but the stew pot by the time they reached Riath, but that was all to the good; there would be no chattering tongues to tattle their secrets.

Searching for a campsite, they were well into a narrow steep-sided wash when a large boulder crashed down onto the trail just in front of the lead hunter. The column collided with one another, Loti and Warlinga alike, milling round in confusion. Then a high-pitched cry rang out and an enemy hunting pack charged them from the concealing brush.

Teeth bared Drucas roared in outrage and sprang for the throat of the nearest attacker. The man blocked his initial rush with his spear, and swung his tail around to deliver a hard slap to Drucas's throwing arm.

Drucas snarled as the pain shot up his arm. Whipping his own tail round, he lashed at the man's legs and felt him stumble. Before he could right himself, Drucas grabbed him with a clawed hand and yanked him further off balance. As he fell forward, his adversary raked at his eyes with gleaming claws. Drucas blocked the blow and sank his fangs into the man's neck. He jerked his head sideways, tearing the wound wider. His enemy choked on a curse and went limp.

Drucas flung the body from him and glanced around wildly. Through a haze of dust he could see snarling knots of battling men strung out along the floor of the wash. Cries of pain and roars of challenge deafened him. Curse them all to the Fires how had the hated enemy tracked them—and where were the prisoners?

Catching sight of a lone Warlinga hurrying the terrified peasants back down the wash Drucas bounded after his escaping prize. Knocking an exhausted peasant aside, Drucas leapt upon the enemy Warlinga from behind, sinking his fangs into his shoulder.

The man staggered and fell to his knees, then twisted round and drove his bone knife into Drucas's side. Drucas swore, gripped the hand and bent it backwards. A moment later he heard a satisfying snap and the knife fell from the man's useless hand.

Before he could recover and launch a counter attack, Drucas grabbed his discarded knife and plunged it into his enemy's groin. The man screamed as dark blood fountained out of the wound. Drucas jerked the knife free and spun round, searching for another enemy.

Out of the corner of his eye he saw the Loti jogging down the wash. "Come back here!" When they either didn't hear him, or chose to ignore his command, Drucas roared at two of his men, just finishing their own kills. "Don't let them escape, go after them." he pointed with the bloody knife at the vanishing Loti, and the two men bounded after them.

Drucas felt the wetness dripping down his side and grabbed some moss from the rocks by the trail to plaster over the wound. He pressed his hand to the injury till the bleeding slowed. The cut was a deep puncture, but didn't appear to have ruptured anything vital. He could see to its care later. Drucas returned his attention to the business at hand. None of this verminous slime could be allowed to live, and bring other packs down upon them. Ignoring the pain he headed back up the wash to find the rest of his men

THE LIGHT WAS FADING by the time Drucas's hunting pack left the enemy dead to the vistri, herded their charges passed the ambush site and out into more open country. Hurrying on into the deepening twilight, they finally stopped on a low hilltop when it became too dangerous to go on any further.

When the Loti were tethered and the captives unpacked Drucas squatted beside a tiny fire, and took stock of the damage. Four men were dead from this latest skirmish, and all the Begta had run off during the fighting. They would have to return to more traveled roads because of their loss, but they were more than halfway to Riath now; they would just have to make a run for it.

They could hide out during the day and travel by night, once they returned to more civilized lands. That was one advantage of the plan. A disadvantage, to his way of thinking, would be that he would have to forgo his nightly sessions with his "guests." A pity that; he so *enjoyed* Blue Eyes's company, but his screaming might alert another searching pack to their whereabouts.

He hated to admit it to himself, but his torturing of the captives had probably drawn the enemy's attention in the first place. He'd allowed himself to be lolled by the isolation of their surroundings into thinking they were alone. He'd gotten careless while indulging himself and it had almost cost him everything. It wouldn't happen again.

Chapter Four

"I never touched her, grandmother! The woman has no family of importance; I would never dream of—"

"It is precisely because she *has* no family of importance that you thought you could get away with playing your little games, useless worm, don't deny it."

Combaron fell to the floor at Enaju's feet, groveling. *Ungrateful piece of fur, how dare she come to the High One after the favor I showed her. She should be proud to accept my attentions, not go whining to her father about the pain—it couldn't have hurt that much. She is going to pay—her whole family is going to pay. I won't forget them, and when the time is right, I will have my revenge.*

They were in Enaju's private suite; the maid had been dismissed. They were alone. Combaron trembled violently waiting for her judgment. He cracked an eye open and stole a look at her enraged face. She sat in her favorite carved chair glaring down at him her claws buried in the wood.

A low whimper escaped his throat. He could already taste the pain of her punishment. His back and buttocks burned in anticipation of the lash and he felt his male organ harden and poke out of its protective sheath.

Oh, Mother, if she knew—if she saw it. The erection died with that thought as effectively as if he'd been thrown into ice water. Combaron shuddered and covered his head with his hands. Why couldn't she understand? He'd tried to explain to her about the hunger—the craving. It hurt so much he had to do something to satisfy it—

"And what about the assignment I gave you? What is Tobrach Tragar doing these days?"

Combaron blinked, disconcerted by her change of topic. "Nothing, Grandmother."

"Nothing! Sit up when I'm talking to you and answer me properly."

Combaron scrambled to a sitting position on the floor at her feet. He brushed the braids away from his narrow face. "Nothing subversive, Grandmother, truly. I have had my apprentices watching him every moment. He goes to the required social functions—as you know. Other than that he keeps to the Tragar apartments or the exercise yard. That's all, Grandmother."

Enaju leaned forward pinning him with the force of her rage once more. Combaron cringed. "And who visits him, useless Begta Filth? Can't you do anything right? WHO VISITS HIM?"

"N-no one visits—just his cousins, and other members of his family."

"What about Yargal Meh'gach—or any of the Meh'gach or Serath clan?"

Startled, Combaron said, "N-no, never—I swear." Enaju let out a noncommittal grunt and stared at the tapestry on the far wall, thinking.

Combaron gave her a speculative look. Why would she think that he would visit K'San Tobrach? K'San Yargal had been heard to say publicly on more than one occasion that the entire Tragar clan was a disgrace. What was she planning? Were there more secrets, more delicious schemes they were keeping from him?

The old hurt welled up in his heart threatening to choke him. Why didn't they trust him—he did his best—tried to please, but it was never good enough. *A disappointment, useless,* the echoes of her words and countless cruelties over the years filled him to bursting with hurt and anger.

Well, if his little diversions spoiled her schemes, it would serve her right—damn her.

Suddenly the outer door to Enaju's suite burst open. He heard uncle Persig say, "Sister, good news. We have them. K'San Drucas has done it. He has captured Blue Eyes and the Meh'gach daughter—"

Coming fully into the room he broke off when he saw Combaron sitting on the floor by Enaju's feet. He gave his nephew a hard look, but made no comment about him being there. Just behind Persig K'San Drucas closed the outer door.

Forgetting all about Combaron, Enaju rose, giving Persig and the Warlinga a triumphant smile. "Truly, you have them. Blue Eyes and Sagas Caltia?"

"Sagas Caltia was not with the bunch I captured, High One," Drucas said. "But we do have her brother Amril—in a women's kilt no less, and Aju'an's twin sister, Chelka, along with Blue Eyes and several of the mutants."

Before Enaju could ask any further questions, Persig shot her a warning look, and motioned to Combaron. Enaju scowled down at him, taking his meaning. "You may go, Filth, we will continue our discussion later."

Combaron got slowly to his feet, his eyes going from one implacable face to the other. "Grandmother, please let me stay—please let me help. He tried to kill me. I want to make him suffer, I want—"

"Ata. The High One gave you an order," Drucas said in a low but menacing voice. "I suggest you obey, or she may give you to me for my discipline. Would you like that, hmm?"

Combaron shuddered. Trying to control his chattering teeth he said, "N-no, K'San, I'm going."

As the door closed he heard Enaju say, "Did you put the crystal in his cell. Don't forget about the Maker, if the Maker discovers—"

Out in the hall Combaron leaned against the stone wall and closed his eyes waiting for his quivering muscles to relax. Damn the Warlinga for interfering. He might have been able to convince Persig to let him stay if it hadn't been for the big brute. Well no matter, he had his own spies and ways of getting what he wanted.

His heart fluttered with excitement. Blue Eyes, here, at last. His grandmother and uncle Persig could do what they wanted with the man, but he would have his own sweet revenge too.

DUNNAGH FLOUNDERED to the surface of consciousness, struggling to rid himself of the chaotic nightmare that had ensnared him. Every inch of his flesh ached. Gingerly he explored himself by touch. Ah, they had released him from most of his bonds. Only a laminated chain tether fastened him to the wall. The chain alone limited his movement—but it was enough under the circumstances. He wasn't going anywhere—he was probably too weak to even stand. Where was he? He couldn't remember coming here.

Around him pressed the weight of living stone, but no light penetrated the blackness. Were they in Riath already, a cave somewhere along the trail, or was this just the fortress of a Dingay supporter somewhere along their route. He'd lost all track of time and distance—the drugs and the torture had seen to that. He listened, but could hear nothing but water dripping somewhere out of reach in the gloom. He licked his lips. Water. Cool, sweet water, a drink would taste wonderful right now.

He stretched carefully, enjoying the limited freedom, determined not to think about what he couldn't have. *Yes, don't think—about anything.* It felt good to lie here in the blackness, his blistered back pressing against the cool stone with no one shouting at him—or hurting him.

During their journey to this place, the pack kept them all tightly bound as much as possible. Whether out of cruelty, or fear they might escape, he wasn't sure. And for him personally, being tied belly down, across the Loti, with his bulk pressing against his bondmate's coils had been an added torment for the young symbiont.

After his last "questioning" session with the changeling, his endurance had been taxed to the limit. Unable to convince his tormentor that he knew nothing about what the western wizards planned, he had lapsed into a chaotic delirium of pain and despair.

Dunnagh sighed. Nathan was going to be extremely angry with him for going off like this and getting himself captured. He choked, fighting back the tears. He would have to apologize and make amends to his friend—if he ever saw him again—if he ever saw any of his loved ones again.

An image of that last morning at Ticca came unbidden to his mind. Sairsa lay in their big bed a sleepy Tameh sucking contentedly at her full breast. She watched him with troubled green eyes, her mouth still soft from his kisses.

Oh, Sairsa, love! I don't know how much more of this I can stand—the cursed changeling was right—he is very skilled at giving pain. And he keeps assuring me that Ata Persig, damn him, is even better than he is. Oh, Gods, I think I'm going crazy, Dunnagh wailed inside his own mind.

<<Kasha?>>

<<I'm here, Shalla.>> Dunnagh sniffed, and ran his hands over his bruised abdomen. <<How are you, Little One?>>

<<I don't know—it hurts—we hurt—oh, Kasha, I'm so frightened.>>

<<So am I, Shalla, so am I.>>

<<Kasha, where are we?>>

Dunnagh sighed. He didn't want to frighten his bondmate further, but there was no point in trying to lie. Tani would know. <<I don't know for certain, but we're probably somewhere in Riath Keep.>>

<<Yes, that would make sense,>> the symbiont agreed. <<What do you think they will do to us now?>>

<<I don't know, Shalla, best not to think about it. Just concentrate on getting your strength back while you can.>>

<<I will,>> Tani assured him, <<and when they come for us again I might have a little surprise ready for them as well.>>

<<Mm,>>

<<Kasha, I'm worried about the others. K'San Drucas was almost as hard on Amril as he was on us. I wonder where he is.>>

<<Yes, I know. If you're feeling up to it let's explore a bit and see if they are here with us,>> Dunnagh suggested.

<<Good idea, I can stand it, if you move slowly.>>

The Kashallan investigated his surroundings as far as his tether would permit. There was a thin carpet of stale dry moss on which he had been tossed, but unfortunately there was no food or water within reach.

During their journey their captors were usually indifferent to their prisoners' physical needs. They fed them and offered them water, if they remembered, but more often than not, they forgot, or ignored their pleas. However, they never forgot to dose them with the drugs that made them tractable, he thought bitterly.

Exploring a little further with Tani's added senses to draw upon, the bondmates, decided that they must be at Riath. He could sense a Khutani pool somewhere deep within the rock, but it either wasn't close enough to enable him to reach out to its inhabitants, or some other barrier was interfering with the contact. There would be no help from that quarter—at least for the moment.

Anxious now, he pressed on. Where were the others? Ah, there. His groping hand encountered a scaly leg. Chelka, good, if she was here, most likely the others were too. Painfully extending a tentacle he probed under her scaly skin. Yes, she was all right, just suffering from the effects of the medication. Tani had always been able to throw off the effects of the foul substance faster than the rest of them—she would come round in time.

With a little more searching he found Marti and Ellis—also comatose from the drug. Amril was harder to locate. He was just on the verge of giving way to his rising panic when his questing hands encountered a furry arm. Relieved, he tugged, gently drawing the unconscious priest closer, till at last he could gather him into his arms.

"Amril, oh, Amril," he breathed, a tear rolling down his cheek. "What have they done to you, Dear One?"

Like himself, Amril had been singled out for the special attentions of their captors. Amril's feminine dress, plus the fact that he was one of the hated Caltia, marked him for their added cruelty.

Tenderly he ran his hands over the priest's body checking the extent of his injuries. Extending his tentacles the Kashallan formed the link, forcing what restorative he could muster back down the connection they shared. When he felt Amril rouse; the Kashallan retracted his tentacles and sighed. "Feeling a bit better, my dear?"

Amril reached out and ran his hand hesitantly over the Kashallan's chest and face. "Dunnagh-Tani? Where are we?"

The Kashallan hugged him, he could feel the slim furry body trembling in his arms. "I'm not sure. Hush now, go back to sleep."

"We are at Riath, you're trying to protect me again, aren't you?"

"Maybe we are at Riath—I don't know—go back to sleep."

Amril pressed himself closer to the larger bulk of the other man. "First tell me, how you are feeling."

"I'm fine."

Amril shook his head. "No you're not, and we both know it. When they come for us again, don't make them angry so they will hurt you. I am not worth it, your life is too precious to us—don't make them kill you for my sake, please. This is my fault anyway, let them kill me if they want to."

"Hush now. Don't talk such nonsense. This isn't your fault, Rest or I shall have to give you something to make you do so." The Kashallan tightened his embrace, tears stinging his eyes. Against his chest he felt Amril give a weak nod and drift back into unconsciousness. Dunnagh sighed. Alone once more with his thoughts, the blackness and his fear became heavy weights upon his soul. Lying down upon the moss, he lapsed back into an exhausted stupor himself, still cradling his consort in his arms.

Chapter Five

"Ah, such a sweet tableau," Combaron cooed," how very touching."

At the sound of his voice, his enemy's strange eyes flew open. Then he grimaced and closed them again as torchlight covered his face. Combaron smirked. "Ah, Poor Mutant, did I startle you?"

Sitting up the mutant blinked several times, then focused his murderous blue-eyed stare on Combaron's face. "Combaron."

"Yes, it is me," Combaron said. "I heard that you were our *guest*. I came to see how you liked your accommodations."

"I should have made sure you were dead back at Sulas."

Combaron laughed, his eyes as hard as obsidian pebbles. "Yes, maybe you should have, Mutant, but it's too late now. You will pay for that attempt, and your other crimes—we will make sure of that."

The identity of their prisoners and their whereabouts was being kept a closely guarded secret at the moment. Combaron had had to offer several large bribes to discover the prisoner's identity and their location. Ah, but seeing one of his most hated personal enemies here in this cell, filthy and wounded, was well worth the price.

Combaron slim hands curled into talons; his tiny claws extending and contracting with his pleasure. These vermin owed him something for the pain and trouble they'd caused him, and he was here to collect part of the debt. Turning to the Warlinga guard that accompanied him into the cell, he said, "Step back with the light; I want to see all of them."

Without a word the man return to a spot by the door and raised the tallow-dipped torch. The women were nothing more than comatose lumps along one wall, still sleeping off their drug induced torpor. Blue Eyes was fully awake and watching him warily, as was the Caltia brat he had been hugging a moment earlier.

Combaron's lip curled in a secretive smile, his imagination titillated by how he had found them. Amril was blood-streaked and dazed, not very desirable, still, he was a Caltia. What would it be like to take him—he had never considered that possibility. Hmm. Amril's humiliation would taste sweet upon his tongue. It might be a small compensation for what his sister Sagas had done to him.

At the moment he sat beside his mutant lover, and Combaron knew better than to approach too near that one. Even in his weakened state he was dangerous. Blue Eyes was confined to the length of his tether. The brute could do him no harm, if he stayed out of reach, and it would be great sport to toy with him in other ways. Amril could wait till later.

Pointedly turning his back on Blue Eyes, Combaron returned his attention to the women. They were blinking up at the light, but it was obvious that they were still heavily under the influence of Persig's concoctions. Warriors indeed. They were no threat—only toys for his amusement. He stepped closer, taking his time to study them as if they were sweets on a tray.

The yellow-maned mutant female was of no consequence. She was all bones and grime, moss and debris snarled in her wispy hair. His eyes widened when he recognized the large brown-skinned mutant female lying next to her. She had been his slave at Sulas. He smiled, remembering her fondly. She was a big brute, almost as large and muscular as Blue Eyes. He felt the swell of his sex press against its protective sheath.

Drugged and bound her angry eyes had spoken her hatred, but when he dosed her with the red kavay her body had betrayed her and she had begged him for more of his attentions. The delicious pressure between his legs was growing stronger. How nice it was to meet an old *friend* once more. Before his interest could be snagged in that direction, Combaron focused his regard on the other supine form.

The Warlinga guard had whispered to him excitedly before they entered, that one of their prisoners was a Warlinga female—and one claiming to be a warrior no less. Combaron had smiled and nodded, amused by the man's obvious interest. His spies had already told him that Chelka Meh'gach was here, of course. Her presence was one of the reasons he had risked Uncle Persig's wrath by coming.

Blue Eyes and Amril Caltia were an incentive, true enough, but he could have waited to see them. It would have been just as pleasurable to greet them in the secret room down the hall with its many "toys" with which to play. It was Sa Chelka that tormented his sleep and his waking daydreams. There was no rest for him; he had to disobey and come.

He had prepared so carefully for this meeting. The High Council was in session at the moment so there was little chance of anyone interrupting his amusements. He had bribed these stupid Warlinga well, and hinted that there might be more for them later if they kept their mouths shut. Combaron doubted if they would betray him to his grandmother or his uncle Persig; they had too much to gain by not doing so.

As if in a trance he moved closer, fascinated by her scaly form. What would it be like to...? Unlike the mutants who'd been only tethered, Chelka's tail and hands had been tied, as an added precaution. Yes, the guards knew who the true danger here was. Those fangs and claws could rip out his throat in a moment—if she were awake, and free to do so.

The contemplation of that risk set his blood to tingling. Combaron took in a ragged breath, forcing himself into calmness. Not yet—he would have to wait a little longer.

Combaron glanced out of the corner of his eye at the guard waiting in the doorway. He was speaking to someone in the hall, and paying him no mind. Good. He crouched beside her, and ran his hand down her flank, pausing over the swell of her hip. She was such a powerful brute. This was his most forbidden fantasy come true. He shivered, feeling the red kavay he had taken before coming down here awaken his lust in earnest, and like a caged beast it writhed, wanting to be released.

Chelka's red eyes widened at his touch, her lip curling in a silent snarl, but she was still too drugged to do anything more. She was, however, alert enough to know what liberties he was taking with her. Combaron bared his own teeth, and slid his hand lower, his extended claws, leaving silver trails in the dirt and dried blood of her haunch. She hadn't expected such an intimate gesture—not from him—and that heightened his excitement even further.

His lip twitched with a private amusement; idly he wondered if his grandmother had informed her illustrious father where she was right now, or was Enaju saving that fact for a special surprise?

Keeping his body in shadow to hide his growing excitement, he glanced toward the door again. He would have to be very careful now. The God's alone knew what K'San Drucas was allowing his men to do with the woman, but he doubted if he could buy their loyalty at any price if the guards suspected what he truly wanted here.

Combaron stood and stepped away from the women. Blue Eyes was watching him with a puzzled frown on his ugly face. In the darkness of the cell he hadn't been able to see what Combaron had been doing—and that was all to the good—he might have raised a fuss otherwise. Combaron felt his pulse quicken as he studied the man. Would he enjoy his little performance? He hoped so.

Turning to the Warlinga, he snapped in his most imperious tone, "Leave the light then get out. I wish to question these prisoners privately. They have foul secrets that the High One wants only me to hear. You need not risk being corrupted by their blasphemy." The Warlinga hesitated. "Get out I said, and don't come back till I call." The man's head crest dipped and he bowed. He placed the torch in a bracket on the wall and closed the heavy door.

When they were alone again Combaron returned his attention to Blue Eyes, his tiny fangs gleaming in a feral smile. It would be an added treat to use these women as he chose and make him watch. The mutant would be powerless to prevent it. Would he enjoy his helplessness? Combaron would. Its savor would be sweet upon his tongue.

Still keeping eye contact with Blue Eyes, he slid his hand to his sash and allowed his kilt to puddle around his ankles. Blue Eyes blinked, then his mouth tightened. Stepping out of the richly ornamented garment he laughed deep in his throat and returned to the bound Chelka's side.

Combaron's blood roared through his veins. He felt so alive, so in control—he would tame all these willful brutes to his will. Yes, he was the master now. Combaron crouched beside the bound woman once more. He stroked her possessively. Chelka shuddered under his touch. He could feel his organ swelling with anticipation. He moved a clammy hand down her torso till it came to rest on the tender mouth of her breeding pouch.

Somewhere along their journey K'San Drucas himself, or one of the men in his hunting pack had removed her apron. To the modest women of her species having a man who wasn't her husband touch, or even see her this way was unbelievably humiliating. The pack had known that of course—as did Combaron.

His fingers caressed the lips of her breeding pouch for a long moment, then buried themselves in its silken folds. He hissed in surprise. So soft, he hadn't expected that. Her skin was so tough and leathery on all other parts of her body, he hadn't expected this delicate softness within its cavernous folds. Did Warlinga men know what delicious treasure awaited them on their first mating night? He slid his hand a little deeper, and smiled.

Chelka moaned, and tried to pull away. Unable to move, she bared her teeth and growled deep in her throat.

"What are you doing to her, Dingay? Leave her alone," Blue Eyes said, getting awkwardly to his feet.

"And what will you do if I don't, hmm?" He explored even deeper, and his hand brushed against a rubbery tit. He pinched it between thumb and forefinger and felt it elongate and harden. Combaron groaned. In answer to the tiny organ, his sex burst aside its leathery casing and came fully erect. Blood roared in his ears, and he swayed in sheer ecstasy. Belly jiggling, he rocked his hips, his engorged phallus pressing against Chelka's scaly flank. Ah, so sweet, just how he had always dreamed it would be.

Chelka moaned again and tried to raise her head enough to bite him, but her bonds and the drug made that impossible. Combaron looked into her smoldering red eyes, and caressed the firm muscles of her upper arm. He gave her a toothy smile. "Would you like to tear my throat out? You may try harder if you like, but it will do you no good. You are my toy to play with—don't you understand—mine."

Combaron pressed himself against her, shuddered and drew back. Though his fantasy had always been to tame and couple with one of these powerful females, biologically he knew his limitations. Still, her mortification was equally satisfying. And as an unexpected pleasure, there was the brown-skinned mutant at hand to act as the surrogate, receptacle of his lust. She had satisfied his desires when she was his slave at Sulas; she could do so again.

Blue Eyes saw Combaron's attention shift, and he cursed him with his impotent fury. "Leave them alone, Filth, I have already sworn to kill you for your crimes against me and my kin, don't make my judgment any worse than it need be."

Combaron laughed. His black leathery organ throbbed, tiny beads of milky oil dripped from its tip. It was too soon. He must hold back or be overwhelmed by his excitement. He cupped his hand around the shaft as if to physically restrain his mounting lust. He wanted to savor the taste of this moment for as long as possible.

Needing a further distraction he said to Blue eyes, "Brave words from one who will die soon. I have little to fear from you I think. But perhaps you are only jealous, hmm?" His eyes flicked to Amril. "Your tastes seem to be as 'perverted' as you claim mine are." He turned into the light and let Blue Eyes see his hardened phallus. He caressed himself slowly, his eyes glassy with his arousal. "Would you rather I took you first, hmm?"

Blue Eyes stiffened. "You Disgusting Slimeworm!"

Combaron giggled. "No more than you, I think." Still giggling to himself he turned his back on the mutant. Crossing to the still comatose brown-skinned female, he flipped her onto her stomach, and mounted her.

As he felt her warm flesh engulf him, Combaron let out a long shuddering groan, and sank his claws into her buttocks. Never in his life had he experienced such pleasure, and the sexual act that he was now performing was only the smallest portion of it. Thrusting himself deeper he threw back his head, bared his teeth and quickened his rhythm. Suddenly he was on fire, flaming with the heat of his passion.

Then a furry body hurled itself upon his back, knocking him sideways into the moss. He cursed as his orgasm exploded onto his thigh in shuddering jets of oily blue slime. When it was over, Combaron scrambled to his feet, and let out a shriek of rage. "You Gods cursed Caltia! You spoiled it—damn you."

He had forgotten that the wounded Avairei had been the only one in the cell not confined in some way. The Warlinga had evidently held him in such contempt, that they hadn't thought him worth tying.

"You Slimeworm," Combaron screamed. "You'll pay for this!"

Amril lay where Combaron had tossed him. He blinked up at him and gave him a triumphant smile. "Good, I'm glad I spoiled it."

Combaron screamed again and kicked him hard in the side. Amril grunted and tried to crawl away, but his outburst had sapped his strength. Now he was too weak to escape the onslaught of kicks and blows the incensed Combaron rained down upon him. Covering his face as best he could, he crawled slowly away from his tormentor. Paying no attention to anyone else in the gloomy cell, Combaron followed, screaming his curses at the hated Caltia.

Suddenly he was jerked to a halt as a pair of muscular arms grabbed him, and spun him around to face their owner.

Combaron stared wide-eyed into Blue eyes enraged face. The priest froze. Oh, by the Great Mother, how had he forgotten about the mutant?

His grip tightening like an iron vice upon the man Blue Eyes smiled, displaying his white triangular teeth in a triumphant grin. "I warned you, Dingay. You have deserved a kashallan's justice for a long time."

"Kashallan—you? What amazing lies you can dream up." Combaron laughed nervously. "Let go of me Demon, or I'll have you skinned alive for your insolence!"

"I'm going to die anyway, you Stinking Pervert, so what do I have to lose, if I kill you here and now, hmm?" Blue Eyes countered, tightening his hold.

Terrified, Combaron looked into the creature's eerie blue eyes and scalding piss ran down his legs. He was lost. Abandoning all semblance of dignity, he began to cry. Flinging himself about, he tried frantically to break the other man's grip, but in spite of the mistreatment Blue Eyes had received at the hands of the Warlinga, his hold was unbreakable.

Blue Eyes laughed. "Months ago I made a promised to the Ancient Gods, that you would taste my judgment for what you have done. Now, I will fulfill that pledge." Whipping his head forward, like a striking snake, Dunnagh opened his mouth wide as Tani spat the black kavay that it had been preparing into the priests startled face.

Combaron screamed. Staggering backward, he clawed at his face trying to rid himself of the clinging acid that was eating into his flesh. Over and over his ear piercing shrieks tore apart the air in the tiny cell.

Suddenly the door was flung open, and several people rushed into the room. Just inside the door, they halted; mesmerized by the sight of the dying man convulsing upon the floor.

WHEN IT WAS OVER, PERSIG stepped past his Warlinga escort, and glanced warily at the kashallan-bound mutant. He was sitting with his head in his hands breathing raggedly. No threat there for the moment; Persig dismissed him and walked over to gaze down at the still twitching corpse.

Devoid of his kilt, Combaron sprawled in an untidy heap, his face almost unrecognizable. His features had been eaten down to the bone in places by the corrosive black goo that was clinging to his skull.

Black kavay. The words came unbidden into his mind. It was the Khutani's ultimate weapon of death. Persig sighed. It had been an unpleasant way to go, but he couldn't find it in his heart to mourn the sniveling little weakling. The pervert deserved it, coming here without permission as he had.

Unfortunately even though the mutant had done him a favor by disposing of Combaron, Persig couldn't let his adversary think he had scored a victory with this little ploy. He would have to do something to pull Blue Eyes' fangs once and for all, or he himself might be the next recipient of the Khutani's "gift."

"Stand him up." Persig motioned to his men to raise the mutant to his feet. When Blue Eyes faced him, held firmly between two of his men, he looked into the man's eerie blue eyes and smiled. "I suppose I should be grateful to you for ridding me of a tiresome nuisance. Your little surprise was probably meant for me, or K'San Drucas, hmm? Too bad; you've wasted your chance and you cannot be allowed to have another."

Persig pulled a tightly stoppered bottle from his belt pouch and showed it to him. "Along with my Master's final instructions, this and other things were sent over the Jeban pass during the Sorin confinement. My Master has prepared this little 'gift' especially for you, traitor, and all the Hated Enemy. I hope you enjoy it as well as Combaron has his." Persig saw the fear come into the man's eyes then, and his smile widened.

Directing one of the Warlinga to claw a long gash in the struggling host's abdomen, Persig opened the bottle, and rubbed some of its contents onto the bleeding wound.

Backing away, he motioned for the Warlinga to release him. Blue Eyes sagged to the moss, exhausted by the struggle. Physically, there was no more fight left in him at the moment, but his defiance and hatred was still there to be read in his unnatural eyes.

Expressionless, Persig folded his arms across his chest and watched the mutant intently. He was curious to see if the drug would have the desired effect.

One moment Blue Eyes was glaring defiantly at him; then suddenly he clutched at his belly, and began to scream. As the terrified cries continued, Persig smirked with satisfaction. Yes, the Master had been right once again; his experiment was a success.

Though not able to outright kill the hated Khutani, when dumped into the pools this substance would render them helpless. Floating belly up in their ponds, they would become easy prey for the crossbows and spears of the Master's warbands when they arrived.

"What have you done to me, Umwira?"

Persig laughed. "That is a little *gift* for you from my Master as I told you. But don't worry you and the symbiont will not die of the drug. You are still of use to us.

"When you come to your trial, Western Filth, there will be no more alliance, no more kashallan, as your supporters will claim. No, these foolish Khutani-bred slaves will see only an Umwira mutant, nothing more. With your bondmate unable to prove your assertion, who will believe such wild babblings. You have failed your wizard master and you are doomed to die along with the rest of the traitorous scum who champion your cause."

When they were gone, Dunnagh sat in the darkness, rocking himself, crying uncontrollably. <<Tani! Oh, Shalla, what did he do to you? Shalla, speak to me. What's happening to us?>> Inside his middle there was no answering voice, only a deep aching emptiness.

"Oh, Tani!"

Beside him, Amril huddled in frightened silence, but Dunnagh never noticed. His hands splayed protectively across his middle, he rocked and sobbed, trying to push away the fear.

Chapter Six

Nathan sat on his cot, blinking back his tears. He let out an enormous belch, then stared into the foamy liquid of his third bowl of mushroom beer. From somewhere outside his tiny room he could hear the Avairei singing some dirge of a chant. Gods, he wished they would shut up, or sing something else. Ah, well, a few more bowls of this stuff and he wouldn't care what they were singing.

The stupid, stupid, ass, he'd gone and done it this time, the amadan. Playing hero. How could Dunnagh-Tani have been such a fool? Leave him on his own for a few days, and what does he do? Goes off and gets himself captured that's what. Gods he'd like to strangle that shit-for-brains Ata Ronnan. Unfortunately, the fool had saved him the trouble.

After returning with the wounded Oglas, Ronnan had made his report to the Imas, then slit his own throat, and offered himself to the young Khutani in the pools. Gods, what a tangled mess! If he wasn't so pissed off at Dunnagh right now he'd probably do the same thing himself.

Nathan took another swallow of beer. He planned to get very drunk tonight, and he didn't care what the Imas thought. There wasn't anything else he could do at the moment, so why not.

Between himself and Ross they had enough firepower to make a good show at Riath—if the clans backed them—but on their own, they couldn't do anything but get themselves captured as well. No, he wasn't going anywhere—at least for the moment. Getting himself killed in some stupid rescue attempt wouldn't help Dunnagh-Tani, now would it? But it was so hard to stay here and do nothing. He choked. Oh, Gods, Dunnagh, what are those fiends doing to you!

"Nathan?"

Nathan sighed, drained his bowl and looked up. Arishim was standing in the doorway; her cloak wrapped about her plump figure, as if she were cold. Her gray hair was as immaculately braided as ever atop her head, but her eyes had a bruised look to them, and the lines around her mouth were etched deep with weariness. Just behind her stood Ross, with his beaky nose and thin lips, he looked like a stern bird of prey, until you saw the frightened look in his eyes.

"What is it?" he muttered, and poured himself another drink from the clay pitcher on the floor beside the bed.

Arishim glanced from his stricken face to the brimming bowl. She frowned. Keeping her voice even she said, "Ima Ngeal and Ima Urinia want to meet with us."

Nathan took a long swallow of his new beer. This wasn't working, he wished he could find some brandy; he wasn't half as drunk as he wanted to be. "Tell them I'm busy," he grumbled. "I'll see them in the morning."

"Nathan, please. I think I have a pretty good idea what you're going through right now, but this isn't helping. You aren't doing yourself, or Dunnagh-Tani any good by doing this, please come."

Well she was right about that, it wasn't helping—damn her. He took another drink. "Go away. Let me be."

Arishim sighed, and folded her arms across her chest. "Nathan, I don't know what the Imas want, but it must be important or they wouldn't be sending for us so late in the evening."

Nathan grunted, then turned away, ignoring her. He heard Ross clear his throat and whisper something to her, but he paid no attention. He drank his beer slowly—hoping Arishim would take the hint—and leave. But no matter how hard he tried to put her out of his mind and concentrate on his drinking; he could still feel her eyes boring into his back. She wasn't going to give it up, he finally decided. Damn these women, they wouldn't even let him get drunk in peace.

He sighed. He might as well go with her and get it over with before he was to sloshed to walk. "All right, I'm coming." He stood up, belched, swayed, and caught hold of the wall to steady himself. "Let's get it over with."

At Urinia's private suite, her maid ushered the Speir'dina in and showed them to chairs facing her mistress's worktable. Ima Ngeal was already present, her hands folded in her lap, her aged face solemn,

Nathan gave the women a baleful stare. The delicate wicker chair creaked ominously under his weight as he flopped into his seat. Urinia scowled.

When her maid left them alone Urinia sipped at her tea and studied the strangers trying to hide her unease. She was starting to get used to them by now, but she still found their ugly flat faces disconcerting and hard to read at times.

Clan elder Arishim seemed composed, but behind her bland mask Urinia suspected that the woman was as devastated by this terrible tragedy as the rest of them. Dismissing her for the moment Urinia focused her attention on the two men, for it was one of them that must come forward and make the sacrifice.

The one called, San Ross—Ngeal had supplied the name, sat on the edge of his chair, his eyes flicking here and there around the room. He was nervous; she wondered why? This man was only a common hunter in one of the Kashallan's hunting packs, maybe he just wasn't used to being in such company. Perhaps that was all that was worrying him, or maybe he already sensed her purpose —if so, he would not be reassured when she finished speaking.

The other, the Kashallan's Hunt Leader, and according to Ngeal, his closest kinsmen, sprawled in his chair watching her through heavy lidded eyes. Urinia wrinkled up her nose. Had the man been drinking? He had—the fool—and at a time like this.

She scowled, giving him a dagger-eyed glare. The insolent slimeworm only smirked and returned her look. Truly Ngeal was right these people were all arrogant, willful, barbarians.

Deciding to waist no more time, Urinia set down her bowl, folded her hands on the table in front of her and began. "I have just come from the pools. This tragedy has been a terrible blow to all of us. I felt unequal to the task of making any more decisions about our problem without involving the Khutani Elders in the process.

"When I made my offering I was surprised to find a Maker waiting for my gift. I have told it about the trap and Dunnagh-Tani's capture. It has given me certain orders, one of which concerns only the Speir'dina, and that's why I have asked you to come to me tonight."

Taking the tea bowl that Ngeal handed her, Arishim frowned. "I don't understand, Ima what does the Ancient want with us? Surely you Avairei—"

Urinia shook her head, cutting her off. "No, Clan Elder, in this we cannot assist the Holy Ones." Focusing her stern gaze upon the two men, she directed the rest of her comments to them. "In order for us to salvage this situation and unite the clans to defeat the Ghostlanders and their changelings, one of you must make the gift of himself. The Maker demands that another kashallan bond be formed."

"Oh, my God," Arishim breathed. She glanced at Nathan and Ross, then her eyes slid quickly away, dropping to explore the weave of the rug at her feet. Taking a gulp of her tea, she set the bowl on the table, her hands trembling.

Startled, the Kashallan's Hunt Leader jerked erect in his chair and stared at Urinia, his gray eyes wide. He looked terrible, she thought, like one of the Warlinga had just kicked him in the belly. Was he going to be sick on her favorite carpet? Damn barbarian, she hoped not; the smell would be impossible to get out.

"B-but, Ima, how could that help?" the one called Ross said. "Even if one of us made the bond tonight, surely the symbiont would be too young to aid us. I don't see the point?"

"Under normal circumstances, you would be right, San Ross, such a young child would be of little use to us. But in this case that wouldn't be true. The Maker, as the symbiont's parent, will be able to link itself with either bondmate.

"Through the host's eyes, it will see firsthand what is happening in the surface world; through his mouth it will tell us its will. And it will also be able to use the symbiont's body to carry out that will, if necessary. Such a powerful ally could mean a great deal to us."

Urinia leaned forward, her eyes feverish. "I know we are asking a lot from you—but we have little choice now—don't you see? That's why this bonding is so important, Speir'dina," she cried fiercely. "It will go with us to Riath and help us defeat our enemies. And hopefully save the Kashallan, if he still lives."

Swallowing hard, Nathan looked away from Urinia's intense face and glanced at Ross. The man was as white as a sheet. Gods, he probably was too! Their eyes met, and he read in Ross's frightened gaze the immanence of his doom. If it wasn't so terrible, he'd laugh. Ever since he had made that blood vow to the Gods, he'd known deep in his heart that someday this would happen.

Back on the mesa, when he had been about to fight Gormach, Dunnagh laid a Geish upon him. Nathan swore to make a kashallan bond, if something were to happen to Dunnagh-Tani. The bondmates had won the combat that day, but his blood had been spilt, and the oath given. He'd always been afraid that his words hadn't been forgotten.

Oh he'd resisted Tani's teasing invitations, but he'd always known it would come down to this. All these months he had been living a lie, struggling to resist, trying to avoid his fate, but it had come to nothing in the end. He had given his pledge, and the Gods , and the damned Khutani were determined to see that he kept it.

Nathan sighed. There was no point in resisting any longer. "It's all right, Ross," he said quietly, "this isn't your burden to bear. I've already been chosen."

Turning back to the priestess; he met Urinia's eye, and said, "I've given my pledge, and been marked as a Chosen for some time now. I swore that I would make the bond if something happened to D-Dunnagh—" Nathan choked, then blinking rapidly he stood up. Without looking at anyone, his voice thick with emotion he said, "Come on, let's get it over with. You'd better take me to the Khutani, before I lose my nerve and shame myself and all of us."

Chapter Seven

"Come on, Dunnagh, stop fighting us," Ellis growled in frustration. Giving his arm an extra hard tug, Ellis hauled him into a sitting position and propped him against the stone wall. "Ce'awn, you've got to eat."

"Please, husband, try," Amril begged in a low urgent voice. He glanced anxiously at the Warlinga standing in the open doorway and proffered the bowl again.

Dunnagh blinked. In the torchlight, his face had a dazed, vacant look, like a traumatized child. He blinked again; his lips quivered, but no sound came out of his mouth. He swallowed, and tried again. "Eat? I c-can't—no use—T-Tani isn't interested. I—" Mumbling something incoherent, Dunnagh closed his eyes and slipped sideways, drifting back into the torpor that had overcome him since Ata Persig started given him the Umwira drug.

"Ce'awn, no," Ellis said, pulling him back upright. "Wake up!" She slapped his cheek then shook him, demanding that he pay attention. "You have to rouse it then, make it eat. You'll die, if you don't, damn it."

Dunnagh raised a hand and weakly tried to push her away. Why were they bothering him like this—didn't they understand. "I know we'll die," he mumbled, "but it's no use—Tani—it doesn't want to. Doesn't matter, we're going to die anyway."

Ellis swore in and undertone and shook him again—this time harder. "Damn you, it does matter," she hissed, and glanced furtively at the open door. "K'San Drucas already had his men take Marti and Chelka out of here—and the Gods alone know what he'll do to them.

"The only reason he left us here, was to take care of you—so just what do you think he's going to do to *Amril Caltia*, and me if you die before this trial that he wants you alive for? Damn you, think! Do you want him to start torturing Amril again?"

Dunnagh's heart lurched; his eyes alert and focusing now, he glanced from Ellis's angry face to the bedraggled Avairei. "N-no."

"Well he will," Ellis predicted, "if you get any worse. I convinced him that if he let Amril stay in here with me, we could keep you alive. I told him that as your wives, Amril and I might be able to help you recover better than if he had his Warlinga force-feed you.

"He agreed, but only as long as you showed signs of improvement. The Dingay want Amril's blood so bad they can already taste it. So stop trying to kill yourself, and think of him for a change, you Big Amadan."

Amril gasped. "Sa Ellis please," he said, "my husband is hurt—you shouldn't speak to a Holy One like this."

The Kashallan patted his arm clumsily. "It's all right, Dear One, she's right. If you help me—I'll try to eat."

Assisting him into a more comfortable position, Ellis breathed a sigh of relief and reached for a water flask. "That's better. Is Tani awake? Will it accept the water, and a little food?"

Dunnagh closed his eyes. <<Tani? Please, Shalla, rouse yourself. We need some food, Shalla, or this body is going to die. Please.>>

<<I will try, Kasha, but it's so hard.>>

<<I know, Little One, but you have to,>> Dunnagh said, <<they will kill our Amril and the others, if we die. You have to try.>>

<<All right.>>

Dunnagh opened his eyes. "Yes, Tani is awake. We will try to eat."

"Do you want some water first?"

"Yes."

Holding the rim of the bottle to his open mouth, Ellis helped him hold it and he took several long swallows.

When he pushed the flask away, Amril scooted forward and held out the bowl of porridge. "Let me help you, Husband. You don't have to do anything, just open your mouth and I will feed you."

Dunnagh nodded, opened his mouth like a baby and swallowed the tasteless lump Amril placed upon his tongue. Ata Persig's little plan had backfired, Dunnagh thought with grim amusement, as he choked down the gluey mess.

His damned Umwira drug had put Tani into a defenseless stupor as he had planned, but what he had forgotten—or didn't know, was that the symbiont digested food and water for both of them. Ever since the drugging began whatever Dunnagh tried to eat or drink ended up being vomited onto the floor of his cell not long after.

As time passed and the dosages continued, there came a point when Dunnagh was unable to rouse his bondmate and so lapsed into a despairing lethargy himself. The Kashallan grew steadily weaker, until Persig feared he would die before the Solstice trial and ceased the treatments. *It would never do if I died before my execution*, Dunnagh thought, and took another mouthful.

When the Kashallan was finished, Amril got up stiffly and limped over to the waiting guard. He held out the now empty bowl for his inspection. "Tell Ata Persig he has eaten," he said.

The guard took the bowl, grunted, and then closed the hall door, plunging them once more into inky darkness. Dunnagh eased his body back down into a supine position. Not long afterwards he felt his two companions nestle on either side of him. He let out a long sigh, feeling their added warmth ease his aching muscles.

As his body sank deeper into its usual comatose state, Dunnagh for once didn't give way to despair and drift into the oblivion of sleep. Ellis's rough words had shocked him back into some sense of himself. He couldn't surrender, the other's survival might depend on him. He couldn't just give up and die, but he needed help. Tani was in desperate trouble, Dunnagh was sure of that. Though they had stopped administering the drug, Dunnagh feared the damage had already been done.

Tani was dying. Oh, Persig would probably get his wish—if he could continue to coax Tani into accepting food—they might live to be tried, but how long after that could they survive even if rescued? He didn't want to think about it—but for Tani's sake, Dunnagh knew he had to find someone who could save his Shalla.

He would have to contact one of the Khutani Makers on his own. Taking several deep breaths, he centered himself, then slipped into the psychic trance the Caldoni called the Cumarsaid.

Dunnagh felt-heard a sort of pop, and then he was free. His spirit floated in the darkness somewhere near the ceiling of their tiny cell. He looked down and in the gray light of the spirit realm, he could see the silver cord that anchored him to the body lying upon the moss. That form looked so battered and weary; the colors of its dual auras muddy and freckled with dark patches.

Poor creature, he thought, *so much pain*. It would be so easy now just to drift away swimming on and on, till the cord grew too thin and finally broke. No, that would never do—what was he thinking of—Tani needed him. He had to find a Maker—get help.

Dunnagh rose a little higher. Reaching out his ghostly hands, he probed the gray mists, searching for the channel down which he could swim to find the Khutani.

But whatever direction he took, he came up against an unseen barrier that confined him to the miasma of his cell. It was like being in cased in a huge soap bubble, a bubble that resisted all his attempts to break through it. Puzzled, he stopped his frantic swimming and just floated, trying to think. What was this thing; he had never encountered such a barrier before. What—or who had caused it?

It was obvious; it was a figment of Umwira power. This foul impediment had been erected to prevent him, even here in the void, from reaching the Khutani. He didn't know how they had done it, but he was certain that the changelings, and their wizard master, had created this obstruction, to prevent help from reaching them. What was he going to do? He was getting nowhere swimming around in circles like this. Maybe he should go back—try again later...

As he floated, considering his options, his mind automatically slipped into an old familiar pattern. He began thinking about Nathan, and the bond of the Ca'Companachda (battle companions) that they had sworn to one another so long ago. Even before their days of soldiering in Lann Gheal Nathan and he had been close. Each could always sense when the other was in trouble and needed his cousin and best friend.

Building up an image of that well-loved face in his mind's eye, Dunnagh could almost feel his presence beside him in the gloom. <<Oh, Nathan, I love you so much. I'm sorry I let Tani talk me into seducing you—and I'm so sorry. I was such a fool to go off like that. I wonder if I will ever see you again—>>

Then, suddenly, he was through the barrier and gone. The power of his love had freed him, and like a thankful traveler in a storm, he followed this new beacon straight to his old lover's side.

ENGULFED WITHIN MAKER Qwaltamis's coils, Nathan floated in his own sea of agony. At this stage in its development the Shalla was too young to understand, and compensate for, the pain it was causing its new host, while it grew and transformed their shared flesh. The Maker was doing all it could to spare him, but the pain was almost unbearable even so.

When the latest spasm had passed, Nathan leaned his head upon the Maker's sleek gray neck and tried to catch his breath. That had been a bad one. He wished the little worm would take a nap or something, so he could relax for a while.

In his mind a mental chuckle, <<It will not be long now, Young One,>> the Maker assured him. <<The Shalla is growing well, soon it will be old enough to make first contact, then the transformation will be easier to bear, even without my help.>>

<<So you keep assuring me, Amla, I just wish it would hurry up about it,>> Nathan grumbled.

Another mental chuckle, <<Courage, Child, I am helping you all I can. Ready yourself now, the Shalla's hunger isn't satisfied yet.>>

Throughout the long hours of his suffering, Nathan's mind kept returning to thoughts of his friend. Dunnagh had gone through this, Nathan reminded himself, and it had been even harder for him. Being the first, the Elders hadn't known exactly how to make a bond with an alien host. They had made mistakes.

Dunnagh hadn't even had an amla (parent) to care for him and help him through the worst of the process, like the rest of the kashallans. He had lain in that little chapel by the birthing pool at Sulas, with only Sagas and a couple frightened Atas to help her care for him

Eyes closed and gasping, Nathan writhed. *Oh Gods, Dunnagh, how did you stand it, how did you survive? Now I know what a sacrifice you made, you Big Amadan, now I understand....*

Suddenly through his torment, Nathan thought he felt the touch of a kiss upon his cheek. Opening red-rimmed eyes he glanced around to see who or what had come to him. Was it only the mists from the pool, his imagination, or did he actually see Dunnagh hovering near him. The apparition looked so frightened and lonely. "Dunnagh," Nathan breathed, "is it really you?"

The spirit ventured closer, and nodded. Though he didn't speak, the hungry pleading in his sad eyes offered its own message. "Oh, Gods, Mo Hara, are you dead?" Nathan cried. "Is it your ghost I'm seeing?"

Dunnagh shook his head. He opened his mouth to speak but though Nathan strained he couldn't hear him. Distracted by another spasm of pain, Nathan forgot about his friend for a while. When it was over, he glanced around, searching for the apparition. It was still there, though Dunnagh's expression had changed to one of concern, as if somehow he now understood what was happening to his friend.

Dunnagh held out his arms in invitation, and this time Nathan understood. To be with him, he would have to step out of the confines of his mortal flesh and enter the spirit realm where Dunnagh was waiting.

Though he had never showed the interest in the Caldoni magical disciplines that Dunnagh had, like all Caldoni of his rank, Nathan knew the basics of the Cumarsaid trance. And why not use it? Right now having his old lover's arms around him, even in spirit would be a great comfort; better than staying in his pain tormented body.

"I'm coming, wait for me," he said. Closing his eyes Nathan began the mental preparations that would take him into the Cumarsaid. Before he could totally break free, however, Nathan felt his consciousness slammed back into his body.

<<No, Chosen, you must not!>> the Maker roared. <<The Shalla will need you soon, you must stay within your own flesh, until after first contact is made.>>

<<But it's Dunnagh,>> Nathan pleaded, <<he—>>

<<No!>>

Rearing back its head the Khutani hissed angrily at the spirit, and bared its teeth in warning. Slipping into the spirit realm Qwaltamis placed its massive bulk protectively between the two humans; barring any further contact with its symbiont child's host.

<<You go away,>> it said. <<I have no wish to hurt you, Young One, but while he is experiencing the Transformation, I can't allow you to distract him. Go!"

<<Elder please,>> Dunnagh begged, <<I need help. My Shalla—"

<<No! If my child's Chosen follows you, the kashallan bond might never be formed, and both host and symbiont would die.>>

<<Come away, Chosen Dunnagh, don't despair, I am here.>> Dunnagh felt another luminous sinewy body beside him. <<Maker?>>

The Khutani coiled itself around him and began swimming away. Maker Gladdris said, <<We have been trying to contact you and Tani ever since we learned of your capture, Foolish Child. Where is your Shalla? Never mind—tell me all that has happened.>>

Qwaltamis watched Gladdris float away with the troubled host, and breathed a sigh of relief. Qwaltamis would have liked to encircle him and learn what had happened since the bondmates' capture, but Gladdris would see to him. Qwaltamis's first duty was to its own young.

As it returned its attention to the transformation process taking place in the birthing pool; it couldn't help worrying. The host was free of his body, but without his bondmate—that didn't bode well. How had he managed to break through the barrier, when the Council with all their power had failed? Truly that Speir'dina was a remarkable creature! They had done well to have chosen such a one for the first kashallan bonding.

All the Makers had contributed genetic materials to the first Shalla, Tani. But since that Transformation, the Council of Khutani Makers had recognized that this first kashallan needed an amla parent like the others. Gladdris had been at Sulas during his Transformation and agreed to assume that responsibility.

Though the link between them wouldn't be as intimate as it would with a younger symbiont—especially of its own making, it was clear to the Makers, that that pair of bondmates had suffered from the lack of nurturing and guidance. Right now the Khutani needed some link to help the hostages, and re-forming the amla bond might be their only chance.

Qwaltamis nuzzled Nathan's shoulder. <<Don't worry about your kinsman, Child, Maker Gladdris will see to him. Rest easy, the worst will be over for you soon.>>

Chapter Eight

From the darkness of dreamless sleep, Marti was awakened by furtive male voices and a pungent, spicy smell. She took in a deep breath, nostrils quivering. The scent was alluring, and vaguely familiar. Eyes still closed, she lay quiescent, resenting her unwanted return to consciousness.

Someone snickered; then the sounds of a struggle and Chelka's choked off cry. Marti's eyes flew open. Damn the scaly devils; were they back so soon to torment her again? Rolling over she pulled herself into a sitting position. Two of their guards were in the cell. One of the lizardmen held the bound woman, while the other was trying to force the contents of a small bottle down her throat.

Chelka had her mouth clamped tightly shut and was flinging her head from side to side to avoid taking the draft. Marti cursed; what were they trying to do to her? She knew something was wrong with this picture, but in her foggy state of mind, she couldn't think what it was.

It must be getting about time for the guards to give them more of the drugs that kept them tractable. Was that what they were doing? But always before, when their captors wanted to administer the foul stuff, they merely re-opened a wound on their bodies and rubbed the powder into the cut. Why were these idiots trying to make her drink it now?

Then her nostrils caught the illusive scent again. Ah, now she got it. Shit, red kavay. Marti lurched to her feet. "You Half-bred Begta, leave her alone, damn you."

The one with the bottle turned his head to stare at her. In the dim light from the torch by the door, Marti saw the dilated pupils in his smoldering red eyes. His head crest flattened as he gave her an impressive view of his fangs. "Shut up Mutant Witch, or we will give you some of this, too."

His partner snickered. "Maybe that's what she does want, Cousin. That right, Mutant, want to play with us too?"

Marti glared, her jaw tight. Inwardly, however, she was shaking with fear. If they did that—if they tried—it would be bad. She had survived rape before, it was an occupational hazard of her profession, but in this case their biological incompatibilities would truly harm her.

Marti tossed her head and bared her own teeth. "You pitiful excuse for men, take your bottle of joy and get out of here."

When they only grinned at her, but made no move to obey, Marti stumbled to the end of her tether, picked up the nearly full chamber pot and advanced on them grim-faced, eyes hard.

"I don't know where you pair of idiots got that stuff, but you'd better think again before you use it on her. What will K'San Drucas do to you when he finds out about it, hmm? Will he be pleased, or will he strip your scaly hides off your bones for you? What will he do, Begta Filth? Use your brains and think."

Head crests dipping the Warlinga glanced at one another anxiously, her words starting to penetrate their drug induced excitement. Marti let out the breath she hadn't been aware of holding. Her suggestion had been a gamble; for all she knew Drucas had sent them. They could have been just another ploy in the foul devil's game to break Chelka's spirit, but she doubted it.

Being more worldly wise than her friend, Marti suspected than in spite of his taunts and other cruelties, the changeling wanted Chelka for his own. And if these fools weren't so drug-aroused at the moment, they might have considered that too.

Assholes! Marti waited, motionless as a statue, pot in hand. If the red kavay had taken hold of their bodies in earnest; they wouldn't care about the Changeling's wrath, until it was too late. But if they had just drunk from the bottle themselves before coming in here, then maybe their fear of K'San Drucas, and their good sense would prevail and they would leave Chelka alone.

Growing impatient at last, Marti gestured with the pot, its malodorous contents spilling over the rim and splashing into the moss at her feet. She had to get them out of here—every minute they remained heightened the danger. "Get out, you Black-Hearted Devils, or eat my shit!"

They looked at one another, tails lashing nervously, trying to gather their lost courage. Finally the one with the bottle muttered a curse and stoppered it. Without looking at anyone, he walked to the door and disappeared into the gloom of the corridor. His partner released Chelka with a curse and followed; taking the light, and slamming the door hard behind him.

Marti sighed with relief and returned the pot to the corner. She laughed softly to herself as she hobbled to her sleeping pile of moss. *Stupid shits, what a way to conduct a gang rape.* Well, this was Timorna, what did she expect? With red kavay controlling arousal and fertility cycles; rape was virtually unknown among the natives. Now if the enemy soldiers had been human...

"Chelka? You all right?"

Silence.

"Chelka?" Marti scooted over and stretched out a hand; groping for her friend in the darkness. When her hand finally encountered a scaly thigh, Marti paused. The body under her hand was trembling violently. "Oh, Chelka. It'll be all right—you'll see."

She patted the Warlinga's leg clumsily. If she could, she'd take the other woman in her arms, but the way Chelka was lying at the moment, her leg was all she could reach. After a long silence Chelka said, "Marti?"

"Hmm?"

"What those men wanted to do to me—has that happened to you before?"

Marti sighed, and stopped her stroking. "It's called rape, in our language. And, yeah, it's happened to me before. It's not something I like to remember, but among my people at least, it's a warrior woman's occupational hazard. It goes with the job, sort of. It's just something you learn to accept, if you want to be an armachd."

Chelka was silent for a long moment, finally she said, in a voice choked with emotion, "Maybe my father is right, maybe a woman has no place in a hunting pack—no right to have dreams of something more to her life than babies and her friends in the accavett. Maybe—"

"Chelka, stop it. You killed one of the devils and wounded a few more before they took you, didn't you? You are a warrior woman, and part of the reason these Begta-Bred devils have been taunting you as they have is because they know it too—and it scares them shitless. Don't you see that? When we get out of this—if we get out of this—if you want to go home and have babies fine. But do it because *you* want to, not because some shit-for-brains man says you should. What they're doing to you is just another type of Umwira mind magic. You have to fight it."

In the darkness Marti felt Chelka move, coming a little closer. "Mind Magic. Yes, I guess you could call it that, but it isn't only the Umwira who use it. My own family uses it too." She choked. "And that's what makes it so hard to bear—it seems like I'm fighting everybody, all the time."

"Except the Kashallan," Marti said. "Dunnagh-Tani never doubted you, nor I think did Hunt Leader Tizu for that matter—or me, and Moraga. *Or*, Second Hunter Fadir."

"Fadir." Chelka sniffed, then chuckled softly, as if she remembered something pleasant about the man who gave her the Warlinga version of soulful, puppy dog eyes every time he saw her. "Oh, Marti, you are so good to me. How can I lie here feeling sorry for myself, when you remind me of such things."

Then she sobered, and said, "The Kashallan, he is so brave; I wish I was more like him. I thought I could handle anything, until we were captured. When they took away my apron, saw my breeding pouch—touched me—it wasn't at all like stripping down to bathe with my cousins after a practice bout at Ticca.

"It was—terrible, but I have no right to consider my own torments as being so unbearable, when I think of him. Oh, by all the Gods I wonder what they've done with him?"

"So do I, and that worries me more than our own situation, believe me."

WHEN MARTI AWOKE NEXT the first thing she saw was the head-crested silhouette of another Warlinga in their cell. From her supine position, the glowing fungus lamp he'd hung on a bracket by the closed door, made his shadowed bulk, seem over large and menacing.

She stared mesmerized—who was he? Was he even real—or was she still dreaming? He was standing so quietly—as motionless as stone, his features unreadable in the gloom. Then he crouched down and reached out a tentative hand towards Chelka's shoulder. "Sa—"

Chelka was lying on her side facing Marti, but when she felt his touch, she jerked back then rolled over with an angry snarl to face him.

Marti groaned, rolled on her side and levered herself to a sitting position. *Here we go again; don't these guys ever know when to quit? What man does, no matter what his species—where's that damned chamber pot?*

Before she could get fully erect Chelka herself swore a particularly vile barracks oath, bared her teeth and lunged for the outstretched hand.

With a startled cry the man drew back his hand and hopped out of range. Chelka swore at him again and clumsily pushed herself into a sitting position, her tied hands flexing, her bound tail tip flicking with its desire to smash into his face.

The man's head crest dropped, seemingly as surprised by her language, as he was by her attack. When she stopped for breath, he said, his voice soft, trying to placate her, "Sa Chelka, please, I mean you know harm—truly—I'm a friend. I only want to help you, if I can, please."

"Friend!" Chelka laughed mirthlessly, bearing her teeth once more. "Come closer, F*riend*, and I'll show you what I think of your offer."

Not surprisingly the Warlinga remained where he was. He sighed. "Sa Chelka, truly, I want to help you, if I can. Though, in all honesty, I may not be able to do much—I am under suspicion myself, but whatever I can do for you I will. Please, Sa, believe me."

"Liar," she spat back. "So this is K'San Drucas's new game—he wants to send me a *friend* does he? Well go back and tell your changeling master that it won't work."

The Warlinga froze, searching her face carefully, as if wondering if she were joking with him. He was quiet for a long time, at last he said, "K'San Drucas doesn't know I am here, at least I hope not, or I may be placed in a cell as well.

"Changeling. It makes sense—I wondered about that." Head crest lowered he ignored Chelka's next insult and fell once more into a thoughtful silence.

Marti shifted uneasily, there was something going on here, true enough, but was it of the Dingay, or K'San Drucas's planning, or was it something else. Could this man truly be a friend. Something about him seemed familiar. "Who are you?"

The stranger glanced over at her, then his eyes widened in surprise, as if truly seeing her for the first time. "I know you, I think," he said slowly. "I never learned your name when you were with the Chosen at Tragar, but I'm sure you were with him there. And I saw you again, that day on the Mesa when we came there to arrest the Ima Sagas."

Marti gaped. "Tobrach?"

"Yes, that's right, I'm Tobrach Tragar," the man smiled, his head crest dipping in acknowledgement. "I'm glad you remember me, too."

"Tragar." Chelka's voice dripped with contempt. "Begta Filth, Drunken lazy, Dingay sycophant—get out of here and leave us alone."

Tobrach's head crest flattened at her insult, but he made no move to go. In a controlled voice he said, "My cousin Gormach deserved your insult, Sa, but we are not all like him. I have taken the oath and am loyal to the Holy Ones, as I believe are you."

Marti stretched out a hand and touched Chelka's shoulder. "Chelka, wait. If this is Tobrach Tragar, he's telling the truth; he has taken the Kashallan's oath. Remember, we talked about it one day during practice. He was there on the mesa when the Kashallan fought Gormach. He took the oath after the fight—remember? I told you about it."

Chelka hesitated, her red eyes bored into the strangers face. He met her gaze openly, and finally it was she who looked away. "It could still be a trick," she muttered.

Marti sighed, then turned to the Warlinga. "Bring the lantern closer so I can see you more clearly."

Tobrach rose, took down the lamp and brought it to where the women sat. He handed the lamp to Marti. She stood, raised the lamp and studied him carefully. The Warlinga stared into their searching faces, his expression solemn. Unbidden his eyes traveled lower, taking note of Chelka's battered, unclothed body.

His head crest dipped and his skin greened in embarrassment hastily he looked away. When he raised his eyes to their faces once more Chelka was watching him, her eyes challenging.

Tobrach dropped his eyes, staring determinedly at the moss on the floor. "Forgive me, Sa, I-I didn't know—in the dark, I didn't see."

Chelka laughed again. Her voice brittle, she said, "Take a good look, K'San, go ahead, all the other men in K'San Drucas's hunting packs have done so, why should you be any different."

Tobrach's green flush deepened, and his tail flicked angrily, but he only said, "They shouldn't have done that to you, Sa, I am sorry."

Chelka opened her mouth, then closed it again. She looked away. Into the strained silence, Marti said, "Tobrach, what is happening, where is the Kashallan? Do you know where he is, or what they've done with him?"

"No, I don't know. I wasn't even sure he was here, until you told me just now." His head crest fell. Eyes troubled, he looked at the women solemnly; his whole body seeming to sag with his despair. With a sigh he crouched down in front of them. "This is very bad. Tell me what has happened."

As if giving a report to a Lann Gheal officer, Marti gave him a clear, yet brief account of the trouble at Ticca, their journey to Meh'gach Keep, and the bare bones of their capture by K'San Drucas and his pack. As she spoke the Warlinga's jaw tightened and his tail lashed the moss rhythmically, but he let her finish without interruption.

When she was done, he pressed her for a few more details, especially about what had been happening to them since arriving at the Capital. Finally satisfied, he lapsed into a thoughtful silence, his tail still lashing.

Chelka glanced at Marti, then she said in a more friendly tone of voice, "Now tell us a little of what's going on out there. What are they saying about us; how did you learn we were here?"

"The Dingay are keeping the true identity of their prisoners a secret, as far as I know. Until yesterday, I heard only a vague rumor, about Umwira mutants being held for trial at the Solstice Festival. I wasn't sure whether to believe the rumors at first, but last night one of my own men whispered to me that he'd overheard a man in K'San Drucas's pack telling another man about a mutant female and a Warlinga woman being kept secretly in the abandoned east passage of the keep.

"When I heard about you, Sa—though not by name, I was afraid there was more to the rumors than I thought. At any rate I had to come see. I never dreamed the Dingay might actually have the Kashallan."

He gave Marti an accusing look. "I left him with you because I thought, with your magics, you would protect him."

Marti sighed and looked down at the moss. She picked up a clump, crumbling it between her fingers. At last she said in a tired voice, "You're right, Tobrach; we should have done better. The changelings set a trap, and we stepped into it, like a bunch of new recruits—and our off-world weaponry didn't help us a bit."

Into the silence that followed, Chelka asked, "Does my father know I am here, K'San Tobrach?"

Tobrach scratched a clawed finger across his jaw and considered, "I don't think your father knows, Sa Chelka, but I can't be sure of that." His lips twitched in an ironic smile. "Like yourself, Sa, your father doesn't have a high opinion of my family. The few times we've met socially, since I've been here, he has ignored me."

Chelka's skin greened and she dropped her eyes. "Forgive my rude behavior earlier, K'San, I thought you were another of K'San Drucas's men come to torment me."

"After what you have told me, it is understandable. I will try to see that such behavior stops in future."

Chelka shook her head. "Don't endanger your own liberty on my account. You need your freedom, in case the opportunity arises for you to rescue the Kashallan. What they do to me is unimportant. But could you get a message to my father?"

Tobrach sighed. "Possibly, if I were careful. You see my situation here is very—precarious at the moment. When Combaron came looking for Gormach's prisoners and didn't find them; he escorted me,, here for questioning.

"I am not *officially* under arrest—my grandfather has seen to that, but I am not allowed to leave Riath either. As far as most people know, I and my clan are friends and allies of the Dingay, but I am watched."

He chuckled softly. "I don't think Enaju believed my story about Gormach and the outlaw prisoners being killed by an Umwira warband."

Marti laughed. "Considering that the Kashallan thinks Enaju is half Umwira herself, I'm sure she does not. But she's also in the awkward position of not being able to let on why she knows that story is a lie." Marti looked up at him solemnly. "Be careful, Tobrach. Watch your back. If they can get proof that you are with us, they'll kill you."

"I know that already, but thank you for your concern."

A knock on the cell door interrupted any further conversation. The women glanced at the door anxiously. Tobrach picked up the lamp and stood. "I have to go. My cousin is replacing a man who was injured in a fight last night. I will come back when I can—if I can."

His eyes focusing on Chelka's face, he said, his voice thick with emotion, "Don't despair. I will do what I can, Sa Chelka, by my life's blood, I swear it to you. I will do all in my power to help you and the Kashallan.".

"I believe you, K'San Tobrach, and thank you."

Chapter Nine

K'San Drucas pushed his way passed the maid and bowed to the High Matri and her brother. The Avairei were sitting in comfortable wicker chairs, in Enaju's private chamber. On the low table between them lay empty tea bowls, and scrolls stacked in untidy heaps. As he entered Enaju put down pen and parchment and gave him a questioning look. Drucas dipped his head crest, and her expression relaxed.

Motioning for the servant to set a stool near her, then leave, Enaju waved for Drucas to take a seat. The Warlinga crossed to the stool and lowered his bulk onto it gingerly. When he was settled to his satisfaction on the flimsy thing, he dipped his head crest again and began his report. "It has been done, Ima, K'San Yargal's 'gift' will be there waiting for him upon his return from today's council session."

Enaju smiled, but there was no warmth in that look; her eyes glinted like obsidian pebbles. "That's good, K'San, I hope our worthy councilor understands, and appreciates our concern for his welfare."

Persig glanced up from his reading, and gave her a perplexed look. "What gift are you talking about, Sister?"

Enaju smirked and reached for the tea pitcher, making him wait for her answer, while she poured herself, and K'San Drucas a bowl. "I thought it was time we stopped coddling K'San Yargal. So, I returned to him something that one of his children must have misplaced."

Persig scowled. What was the woman babbling about? He didn't like it when she took it upon herself to act independently. The Master had warned him about her growing unpredictability. If they hadn't needed her to fill the High Matri's seat, she would have been taken north before now.

"Stop glowering, brother, you worry over nothing," Enaju snapped. "I went along with your idea to separate Sa Chelka and the dark skinned mutant woman from the others—so that you could see if our young K'San

Tragar would entrap himself, when offered the bait. I chose to do the same with the Meh'gach K'San. I sent him Chelka's armored apron to see if he would snap at *my* bait."

Enaju folded her arms across her chest and looked smugly down her nose at her younger sibling's startled face. K'San Yargal is being watch, so K'San Drucas has assured me. If we can force him to make a move before his plans are in place then we will have him, and break the back bone of this so called kashallan alliance."

Damn her; she could ruin it all if she misjudged him. Persig took a deep breath, allowing his emotions to cool. "I understand your reasoning, dear sister," he said carefully, "but I still don't like it. The Ghostland troops should be here soon—perhaps we should have waited."

"And the Solstice Festival will be here soon as well," Enaju reminded him. "Since K'San Drucas captured that bunch of mutants; the other traitors and their Khutani-bred allies have been very careful. The Hunting packs have not been able to catch any more of them. They are hiding in their burrows, like cave rats. It's time to stir them up a bit, or be put under siege ourselves at Solstice."

"Very well, perhaps you're right." He sighed, and glanced sideways at K'San Drucas. The man shrugged, but offered no further comment. Persig's jaw clinched. At times like this the Segoi K'San was as unreadable as stone. That one too would have to be taught his place soon.

Lately he had been allowing his mask of subservience to slip, without caring how he revealed his true feelings. *He seems so sure of himself*, Persig thought, *I wonder why*. Had the Master shown him special favor of late—given him special orders, perhaps? Persig inwardly shuddered; no, that was impossible.

Deciding to change the subject he turned to the Warlinga and asked, "And what of K'San Tragar, has young Tobrach gone to see the woman?"

Keeping his head crest in a neutral position and his facial expression bland, Drucas nodded. "Yes, he has, Ata, and more than once. He has bribed the watch officer, with my knowledge of course, to ensure that some of his kinsmen are included in each posting outside their door. To discourage my men from visiting the Sa, no doubt." Drucas's lip curled;

expressing his contempt for such sentimentality. "He has also brought her extra food and a blanket to cover herself."

Enaju laughed. Her eyes bright with satisfaction, she set down her tea bowl and gave him a patronizing look of approval. "Well done, K'San. It would seem our young Tobrach is quite smitten with her, and that might also be to our advantage."

Drucas stared at her coldly; saying nothing. Then becoming aware of Ata Persig eyeing him with a speculative expression, Drucas curled his lip in a defiant display of contempt.

"When K'San Tobrach thinks I am occupied with other matters—and doesn't know what he is doing, the three of them have long visits. Whether he is plotting their escape, or just amusing himself I can't say. But he *is* being watched at all times so I will know if he tries anything," Drucas assured them complacently.

"Has he made any attempt to contact Blue eyes and his Caltia 'mate?'" Persig asked.

"No, Ata. I made sure he found out where we are keeping Blue Eyes, but Tobrach has been much too careful for that."

"I have already discovered that he is no drunken fool like his kinsman Gormach," Enaju observed, "but what we need to know—and soon—is whether he is loyal or a rebel."

Persig snorted, setting down his book and pouring himself some tea from the pitcher. "I doubt if he is loyal to us, Sister Dear. The question is rather, will he be like so many of these degenerate slaves, too weak and cowardly to make a decision, or will he have the courage to betray us to the mutants and their new allies?"

Persig glanced at the Warlinga, inviting his opinion. Drucas's head crest rose. He shrugged. "The man is young, untried, and very idealistic. Under Gormach's tutelage the rest of his clan have become fat and lazy. Tobrach and his men are no real threat to us."

Then he gave them a feral smile; his tail lashing the rug behind his stool in agitation. "When it is time, he will either submit to me, or Tragar's border keep will need a new K'San."

Enaju nodded. "Then I will leave such matters to you, K'San." Picking up a pile of documents from the table she began packing them in a leather bag on the floor beside her chair. "If you will excuse me, I have to get ready for the dinner tonight." She glanced at Persig and Drucas; they took her meaning and rose to go.

OUTSIDE IN THE HALL, Drucas left Persig with a contrived excuse about needing to attend to other matters. Seeing the priest's startled expression almost made him laugh out loud. Avairei Slime. Persig would be wondering all evening what he was doing—planning.

Well, let him wonder—both of them. It would do them good. He was sick of their smug looks and condescending manner. His tail lashed the air as he stalked off towards the abandoned wing where his prisoners were being kept. Red eyes smoldering, Drucas clenched his jaw, trying to suppress his mounting fury. Damn these sniveling little Avairei with their slimy plots and counter plots.

Though he had controlled his fury when Persig ordered him to separate Sa Chelka from the others; he had been hard pressed to contain his mounting rage sense then. Every time he saw the priest and his haughty sister, his claws tingled with a desire to rip open their furred throats. The image of their dark blood fountaining out, under his claws was so real; he could almost smell its pungent scent, and taste its saltiness upon his tongue. Ah yes, when it was time; his revenge would be so sweet.

Away from the more populated parts of the keep, the fungus lamps were placed further apart, causing his shadow to appear large and menacing as he moved deeper into the darkness. He smiled to himself, remembering.

As an act of defiance, he had taken not only Chelka, but the larger of the mutant females as well. When Persig angrily cursed him for his disobedience, Drucas had calmly told the incensed Ata that he wanted the woman as a gift for the master. She was strong and would probably breed healthy children.

Persig dropped the matter, but Drucas suspected that the priest knew he was lying. The mutant would make a good breeder, no doubt, but his real reason for taking her was to act as a sort of chaperone for her comrade. Knowing that, because of the Avairei's meddling, that half-bred Begta,

Tobrach was seeing—and perhaps even touching Chelka's unaproned flesh made him seethe with resentment. Chelka would be his when the time came, and this other's growing attachment to her enraged him beyond measure.

Oh, the woman must learn her place. She needed to be broken to his will—which was why he encouraged his men to humiliate and torment her; but that didn't change the fact that, in his mind, he had already marked her for his own. The Avairei were not going to kill her with the others; he would not let them. She was his—his alone.

The room his hunters took over as their headquarters was a dingy place not much bigger than a cell. It stank of dead fungus and dust. A few battered stools, a rickety wicker table and two glowing lamps were its only furnishings. Drucas's unexpected arrival interrupted a noisy dice game in progress among the guards and their officer.

At his appearance in the doorway, the officer in charge jumped to his feet with a yelp. The two hunters playing with him, hastily hid the evidence of their sport in the shadow of an overturned stool. Rising, the three men stood, with head crests lowered, their eyes watching him warily. Tail flicking, the officer bowed. "K'San?"

Drucas surveyed them coolly, giving them no indication of his mood. After letting them squirm for a while he addressed the hunter in charge. "What is there to report?"

The man bowed again. "Not much, K'San. Blue Eyes has eaten. He remains weak, but is no longer vomiting up what his wives feed him."

Drucas's lip curled, thinking of the big mutant. Traitorous Pervert. "And the women—has the Tragar K'San been here again today?"

The officer's tail curled and uncurled in an agitated rhythm. He glanced at his two comrades, then back to Drucas's stern face. "He came but a few minutes ago—we thought—we didn't expect you," he said slowly. "I suspect his cousin stationed down the hall outside their chamber saw you arrive; he will be gone soon—shall we take him?'

As Drucas considered, the muffled sound of a woman's laugh came to them in the sudden quiet. Then he heard a male voice speaking to someone in an urgent murmur. A moment later stealthy footsteps hurried down a side passage.

Drucas's jaw tightened. Inwardly he seethed. So, his captives found their stay in this prison amusing did they, well not for long. He was tired of playing the Avairei's little game. Tobrach was no fool; he was too careful to incriminate himself by trying to rescue the women. No, the three of them were getting far too cozy with one another for his liking. It was time to change the game.

"No, let him go. But from now on you are to refuse K'San Tragar admittance to the women's cell. Nor are his men to help with the guard duty, and the prisoners are not to receive any extra 'gifts' unless *I* approve—do I make myself clear?"

"Yes, K'San. It will be as you say. I will let my Hunt Leader know your new orders."

"Good. Tell the Hunt Leader when your shift is over, to increase the watchers assigned to follow K'San Tobrach. Perhaps he will be more likely to make a mistake if he is denied his little pleasures, hmm?"

The hunters grinned; the play of light and shadow in the tiny room, making their expressions appear unexpectedly ghoulish.

Drucas's face remained unmoved, his hard eyes watching them with an unblinking red stare that had them shifting nervously within moments. At last he turned, and strode out into the hall. From the corridor he could still hear the sound of the women talking quietly to one another. His head crest flattened.

In his mind's eye he could see the Meh'gach woman, wearing his brand and lying bound and helpless at his feet, her lithe un-aproned body, inviting him to take her. She was his, no other man would have her; he would see to that. There were ways—things he had learned while in the Ghostlands—magics that would bind her to him, body and soul.

Taking the lamp from the bracket by the door, he unbarred it and stepped inside the women's cell.

The women were sitting companionably next to one another, their backs up against the pitted wall. Chelka's bound hands lay on her thighs, her head turned to the mutant female who was feeding her some treat that the Tragar filth must have brought them.

When he entered, they looked up, surprised, blinking in the lamplight. Drucas hung the lamp on a peg and walked over to them slowly. He saw the mutant slide a bag into the moss at her side. He smiled, showing his fangs. "No need to hide your treats. I am pleased to know that you are enjoying the entertainment I have provided for you so much."

Looking at their startled faces made him laugh. "Did you think I didn't know?" His feverish eyes focused on Chelka's face and he clucked his tongue in disgust. "Stupid Woman, haven't I told you that the affairs of men are beyond you?" He curled his lip with contempt. His eyes flicked to the mutant female, then back to Chelka. "Women Warriors, bah!"

The dark skinned female tossed her head and bared her own teeth. "Meet us in single combat, K'San. Give us back our weapons, and free us—if you aren't afraid, then you will see if we are warriors or not."

The Warlinga's head crest flattened, coming closer, he flicked the tip of his tail playfully across her chest. She fell back letting out a grunt of pain, a long purple welt rising on her naked skin. "You have a sharp tongue," he told her conversationally, "a most undesirable characteristic in a slave."

"I'm no one's slave," she said, her dark eyes smoldering with defiance.

He slapped her again, this time a little harder. "You belong to me—for now. Later, perhaps I will give you as a gift to my Master. There is always a need for a strong female of breeding age in the Ghostlands."

"You have to get me there first, K'San," she said gasping for breath, "and that won't be easy."

"It will be as easy taking you north as it was bringing you here, never doubt it," he told her, and had the satisfaction of seeing her shudder as she realized the truth of his words.

"Drucas dismissed the mutant and returned his attention to Chelka. "It would seem that your visits with that Tragar Filth have given you a false sense of hope. But neither your precious kashallan alliance, nor the K'San of Tragar can save you. You belong to me—not to that slimeworm. When I take you north with me; you will learn who is your master."

Chelka looked up at him, her expression suddenly as hard as his own. In a voice harsh with her resolve, she said, "I don't belong to you, or any man. I will never let you take me north, K'San Drucas; I promise you that. I will die first."

Drucas cursed, by the Fires she would learn. Seizing her roughly by her bound arms he jerked her to her feet. Startled, Chelka tried to pull away, but his grip on her only tightened. His voice quivering with his pent-up rage, he said, "You insolent little Khutani-Bred Slave, I have had enough of your defiance. You are mine. Mine!"

Wrapping his tail around her struggling body he pulled her close against him. Looking down at her he curled his lips back to show his fangs. Chelka bared her own teeth and made a lunge for his throat.

Drucas swore and slapped her head sideways. Chelka grunted with the pain, then jerked her head back for another strike. He was ready for her this time and clamped a hand around her muzzle, squeezing her mouth closed. Chelka let out a strangled curse and bucked. Drucas tightened his hold, pressing her firmly against him.

"Stubborn Witch, I can see that you still haven't learned who is your master." He laughed softly, his claws digging into her scaled flesh. "But I shall enjoy teaching you, I think. We shall begin your instruction now."

Drucas raised his free hand and extended a clawed finger. He showed her its razor-sharp tip. "In the North there are ways to protect a man's property, and make a woman biddable. You belong to me, it is time you learn that fact."

Muttering Umwira words under his breath, Drucas placed his claw upon Chelka's forehead and began carving a binding sigil into her flesh. Chelka shuddered, her eyes becoming unfocused as he continued to mutter the words of his spell. He could feel her resistance crumbling. Soon she would be his—

Suddenly a wash of smelly liquid splashed over his back, breaking his concentration. Drucas roared, and flung the helpless woman from him. Whirling round he saw the mutant standing with the emptied chamber pot in her hands. "You Traitorous Witch!" Drucas lashed out with his tail, knocking her sprawling.

When the beating was over, he leaned against the wall by the door, chest heaving, and tried to get himself back under control. Both women lay huddled in bloody heaps. They were unconscious, but still alive. The magic had been spoiled—for the moment, but there would be time on the way north to strengthen the bond. For now it was enough that they both wore his brand; all who saw them would know they were his property now. Tobrach Tragar would never have her—never.

Chapter Ten

As the russet twilight deepened a tall head-crested figure stepped through the carved doorway of the inner keep out into the evening gloom. Paying no attention to his ever-present shadow, the Warlinga strode boldly across the open square; the ground mist coming off the lake, clinging damply to his legs. Across the courtyard someone laughed boisterously in the Warlinga barracks. Over by the outdoor kitchen the flames of a cook fire silhouetted a cloaked figure scolding a crouching Begta slave.

Oblivious to any distractions the Warlinga looked neither to the right or left, seemingly intent only on his destination. Furtively keeping to the shadows the watcher followed, as silent as a wraith.

Understanding where his quarry was bound at last the watcher paused by the outer wall, his tail curling and uncurling with his excitement. They would have him now. His K'San would be most pleased when he made his report. Ducking into the deeper shadows beside a storage shed, the watcher peered around the corner cautiously.

It was as he suspected, the man he followed was going straight to the guesthouse of the suspected rebel leader. He would wait just a little longer, to make sure that his quarry remained within the dwelling, and then he would go and tell the watch officer.

Suddenly from behind him unseen hands drew a leather thong tight about his throat. The watcher gagged, his hands clawing at the cord choking off his breath. He writhed, arching his back, hoping to throw his unknown attacker off balance. Before he could loosen the man's grip, however; another figure loomed out of the gloom beside the struggling pair.

The watcher's bulging eyes flicked to the newcomer, hoping for rescue. Then he felt a long bladed metal knife slip between his ribs and find his heart. As the blackness enfolded him, the watcher cursed himself for his carelessness. He should have realized that this was a trap. Never before had his quarry been so obvious about his movements; he should have checked for other enemies lurking in the shadows.

YARGAL TOOK ANOTHER swallow of his mushroom beer and stared balefully at the unwrapped leather bundle lying on the table beside him. He could feel the liquid he'd already consumed, churning in his gut. More of the frothy brew would only sour his mood even further, but he took another large swallow anyway. He needed something to deaden his fear and control his smoldering anger.

The package had appeared in his suite during the afternoon; while he was at council. When he'd opened the bundle—saw what it contained, his heart had nearly stopped beating in his chest. Quickly rewrapping the thing; he had demanded to know from the servants and his hunters where it came from and how it got on his table.

Normally no one paid much attention to who came and went from the Meh'gach apartment when its K'San wasn't at home, so it wasn't surprising that no one seemed to know how it got there.

Yargal's eyes searched the room as if he could find the answer to his question on the braided carpet, or among the simple furnishings of his living chamber. His red eyes glared at the newly whitewashed walls. If Eilith had come with him this time, the place would be bright with the Accavett's colorful tapestries. But she had not come, and the reason for her absence only made the beer in his gut ferment into an even more indigestible mass. Damn the Dingay to the black pit of oblivion.

Like everyone else in Riath, Yargal was aware of the titillating rumors spreading like blight through the harvest. It was whispered in the keep and the market town beyond that the High One had rooted out the Traitorous Slime who were plotting with the Caltia witch to destroy them all. Some even claimed that high up in the abandoned passages of the keep K'San Drucas was holding Umwira demons prisoner. At the Solstice Festival, all would be revealed, and the evil ones punished for their crimes.

He had tried to dismiss the gossip as just another Dingay trick to undermine the kashallan alliance's attempts to unite the clans against them.

By sending him this little package, however, Enaju had assured him that one of his worst nightmares was coming true.

Reaching out a trembling hand, he folded back the outer wrapping and touched one of the apron's over-lapping bone scales, then drew his hand back hastily, as if it had burned him. *Oh, My Wild Foolish Daughter, what have you gotten yourself into by following that brash young Kashallan?*

He flexed his claws, taking some satisfaction in their strong sharp curves. How sweet it would be to feel them tearing open the throat of that abomination that called herself the High Matri. For the grief and sorrow she had caused, she deserved to die most painfully.

"K'San?"

Yargal looked up. A young man from his hunting pack was standing in the doorway.

"What is it? I thought I left word that I wasn't to be disturbed unless it was important."

The Warlinga bowed. "Yes, K'San, you did, but K'San Tobrach Tragar is here. He says it's urgent, he has a message—"

Message indeed, Yargal thought. *Tragar filth, the whole lot of them were a bunch of drunken degenerates. Like his kinsman Gormach he is probably Enaju's slave. Now he is here to report back to her on what effect her latest outrage against my clan is having on me.*

Quivering with rage, he stood up and roared, "Tell the half-bred son of a Begta to get out of here before I have him torn apart. If Enaju Dingay wants to give me any more 'messages' she can come do it herself."

Yargal's hunter started to bow, then let out an angry growl as Tobrach himself pushed his way past him and strode into the room. With a curse, the hunter lunged for the uninvited visitor, bawling for the guard as he sprang.

"K'San Yargal, please listen to me," Tobrach cried. He dodged out of the first hunter's reach, but there were more of Yargal's men pouring into the room now. Twisting aside to avoid a crushing tail blow Tobrach felt claws digging into his shoulder, throwing him off balance. He stumbled, ducked another tail blow, then Two guards caught him, gripping his arms tightly. Tobrach writhed, but his captors had him and were hustling him towards the open door. His red eyes pleading, he looked back at Yargal and said, "K'San, please. I do have a message for you but it isn't from the changelings, as you think! Enaju Dingay is my enemy too."

Changelings!

"Wait," Yargal bellowed. The guards paused and looked at him, head crests dipping in confusion. Yargal grimaced; he could feel his stomach knotting in pain. He belched, then with a muttered curse, he motioned to his men. "Bring him back; I will speak to him."

Keeping a watchful eye on their visitor, the hunters escorted him back into the room. Though still loosely restrained, Tobrach had ceased to fight and now stood quietly.

Yargal's angry red eyes bored into the other man. "You say your message isn't from the Dingay, Tragar Filth, but why should I believe you?"

Tobrach's head crest flattened at the insult. Biting back harsh words of his own he gritted his teeth and met Yargal's glare. "Don't judge my house by the actions of one man, K'San Yargal. I am not my cousin Gormach. Before the Sorins I knew of the Kashallan—and swore to serve him. I have risked much to come to you tonight, please let me speak."

Yargal considered him a moment longer, then motioned for his men to release him. Waving for Tobrach to be seated and have some beer, he returned to his own stool, picked up his bowl and drained it. "All right, I'll listen, but I won't guarantee I'll believe you," he grumbled.

Stepping away from the guards Tobrach bowed then sat. "Fair enough. I came here to deliver a message, what you do with that information is your business," he said stiffly and helped himself to the offered drink.

Pouring himself more of the brew Yargal eyed his unwanted guest. He hated to admit it, but the man wasn't turning out to be what he had expected. Tobrach was tall and well-built for one of his race, but more importantly his mind was alert and clear.

Under Yargal's provocation, he had kept his temper. Though young, he carried himself with an air of assurance well beyond his years. Vaguely he recalled the Kashallan or Aju'an mentioning something about this one, but Yargal couldn't quite remember what had been said. Perhaps he *was* telling the truth.

Suddenly spying the abandoned apron on the side table, Tobrach let out a long sigh. Glancing up, he caught Yargal watching him. He turned back to the apron, and when he looked at his host again there was pity in his eyes. "I thought the Dingay wanted to keep the identity of their captives a secret, in spite of the gossip. But it would seem they have chosen to let you in on their little enigma.

He tapped the bone scales with a clawed finger. "As her father it was done no doubt to add to your torment. I am sorry, K'San. Chelka has told me of the cruelties committed upon your house. We weren't sure you would believe me, if I came to you—but since you know, that she has been captured, it will make my job a little easier. K'San, it was Chelka herself who sent me."

Head crest raised in surprise, Yargal leaned forward, questions tumbling out of his mouth. "You have seen my daughter? How is she—what have the changelings done to her? And, what, by the Great Hunt Leader, was she doing to get captured?"

"Yes, I have visited her. She is—better; I have seen to that. K'San Drucas's men aren't tormenting her any more, I assure you. I am under suspicion myself, so my power is limited, but I will do all I can for her, K'San, I swear it to you." Tobrach touched the long bladed Speir'dina knife at his hip for emphasis.

"What have they done to her?" Yargal growled.

"They haven't tortured her, as they have the Kashallan and his wife Amril Caltia," Tobrach said. Head crest flattening he took a long drink from his bowl and looked away.

When next he spoke, his voice had a flat quality to its tone that belied the agitation of his lashing tail. "When I first went to see her, the men of K'San Drucas's hunting packs had taken away her apron. She was—unclothed.

"With K'San Drucas's approval, any man, who wished to could enter her cell and see her—touch her." He flushed a bright green and buried his face in his bowl of beer. "That was the pretext I used to gain entry to her cell, too. Oh, she didn't trust me at first either—thought I had come there like the others.

"But the Speir'dina woman, Sa Marti remembered me. Your daughter is very brave, K'San, Drucas Segoi has tried to break her spirit—for what reason I don't know, but she is strong, a true credit to your clan."

Yargal's heart gave a lurch. *Oh, my daughter, I wish this hadn't happened to you, but they will pay, my dear, they will pay.* Out loud he asked, "Tell me what has happened, and who has been captured?"

Briefly Tobrach related what the women had told him about the trap, their capture and the events that followed until the time when they were separated from the Kashallan. "So you see, K'San, how very important it is to get the news about this new Umwira poison out to our allies," Tobrach said.

"The Dingay plan to try all the captives at the Solstice Festival. When they do, if the Kashallan is still alive, with the symbiont made helpless, all the people will see is the host. They will believe the lies of the Dingay. He will be just another Umwira mutant, not a kashallan at all. They will not believe us—and our support will dwindle down to nothing. Then we can be destroyed one by one."

Yargal scratched his jaw with a clawed finger. Yes, most likely the man had it right. That would be just like the Dingay. This ruse would explain their seeming ignorance of the alliance and its activities. The changelings knew—had probably known for quite some time. They, and their foul master were merely sitting back and waiting for them to walk into their snare.

And like that poor, brave kashallan, they would have done just that, without this timely warning. "But what of the Kashallan?" Yargal asked urgently. "You say he is here, have you seen him?"

Tobrach's head crest flattened; he sighed heavily. "No, and that worries me, but I dare not go to him. I am allowed certain 'liberties' in the hope that I will incriminate myself I am sure. My visits to your daughter could be excused as merely curiosity.

"But taking an interest in the others—that couldn't be explained away so easily. It shames me truly that I can't help him, that I must stand by when I know he and the young Ata are being cruelly treated, but I dare not, K'San, or I will join them in a cell. I will be of no use to anyone if that happens; can you understand?"

Yargal saw the pain in the man's eyes, and understood his shame. Wasn't he in a similar position himself? He nodded slowly. "Yes, K'San, I see your point, and I approve. You are wise to keep your freedom as long as you can. The Gods alone know when you may be needed."

"Thank you," Tobrach murmured, and took a long swallow of his beer. When he had composed himself again he set down his bowl and changed the subject. "There is another thing that worries me. I've been wondering why Combaron was so insistent that I come to Riath at this time.

"I had planned to go north after the renewal to hunt the Hated Enemy, and he practically put me under arrest to make sure that I returned with him. Knowing as I do now about the changelings, I can see why it would not have been in their Ghostland master's best interest for me to do that."

"And if they planned to send a force south over the Jeban pass your absence would further their plans as well" Yargal said thoughtfully.

"That is true enough, K'San, but I thought of that too." He gave the older man an ironic grin. "Being considered a drunken, lazy, half-bred Begta can have its advantages. Unknown to the Dingay, I left orders with my Hunt Leader Warega to be on guard just in case. The man served as a lad with Gormach's illustrious father, so he knows what to do. Far better than I would," he ruefully admitted.

Yargal's lips twitched and he poured his guest more beer from the pitcher. "That was most wise. You have told me many things of interest, K'San Tobrach, but why have you come here to tell me this tonight."

"Because the Solstice Festival is near, there isn't much time, the Khutani, and the alliance need to be told about this foul poison. Sa Marti thinks the changelings plan to empty the drug into the pools, so they can kill the Holy Ones with crossbow and spear once they are rendered helpless."

He touched the bone apron again. "Now that Enaju has sent you this she will be watching you very carefully. If you don't leave now—tonight, you may never have the chance."

"We are being watched already."

Tobrach gave him a toothy grin and stood up. "Yes, I know, as am I. But my men have taken care of that little problem for the moment, so if you are quick..."

Yargal rose too, giving orders for his waiting men to get ready. "Will you not come with us?"

Tobrach shook his head. "No, K'San, I can't—I won't leave Chelka as long as there is a chance I can save her. I will remain here and pray that I keep my freedom."

Yargal studied him with new respect. "Such an act may cost you your life," he warned. "If your hunters have killed the watchers, they may blame the deaths on me and my pack, but be careful, K'San, they may suspect you had a hand in our escape nonetheless."

"I don't doubt it, but I accept the risk. And don't worry about Sa Chelka. If necessary, I will give my life to save her, I swear it to you. I will stay. Go, K'San, please, while there is still time."

Yargal gave him a deep bow. "I misjudged you, Tobrach of clan Tragar, thank you."

Outside in the courtyard the twilight had deepened into night. Tobrach paused in the shadows, allowing the mists to enfold him in a clammy shroud. He waited listening. K'San Yargal had been quick, he doubted that anyone was aware of his departure as of yet. That was good, he had accomplished the errand Chelka had given him. Tomorrow he would tell her that her father was gone.

Tobrach swung round at a slight noise behind him. "San Cousin?"

He peered into the gloom trying to make out who had called him. The man stepped closer. "Chi'am, what are you doing here? I thought you were on the watch detail outside Sa Chelka's cell."

"I was supposed to be," Chi'am said, "but when I reported for duty I was told that our help would no longer be needed."

"What?"

Chi'am nodded. "When K'San Drucas came there this afternoon; he changed the orders. The women are refused any more visits from anyone, and our help with the guard duties is also unwanted."

Tobrach cursed. What had caused this change in plans? Had he done something to betray himself? No, he didn't think so. He'd been very careful. But if not that, then what had caused the Segoi K'San to make his unexpected visit this afternoon, and then change his orders?

"K'San?"

"Hmm?" Deciding he would have to think about this later, he turned. In the direction his hunter was pointing. Coming towards them across the courtyard was another of his men and a smaller heavily cloaked figure. When he was near enough to be heard if he spoke in a low murmur, the Avairei lowered his hood and said, "K'San Tobrach, it grows late. The High One will be at the dinner party soon, and you should be there before her arrival."

Tobrach bowed to the Maveth Ata. "I am coming, Ata."

The priest nodded, then glanced at the darkened Meh'gach apartment. "Are they gone?"

Tobrach sighed. "It took me longer than I had hoped to convince him, but K'San Yargal has gone, yes."

"Let us pray, that his escape will work to our good," the priest said, glancing off into the darkness. Then he sighed and turned back to the Warlinga, motioning for him to follow him across the courtyard. "And now, Friend, we should give some thought to your own reason for being so late."

Tobrach grunted and fell into step beside the smaller man as they headed toward the lighted hall, where other groups of Avairei and Warlinga were now entering. "Any suggestions?"

In the lamplight streaming through the open door ahead, Tobrach saw the priest's eyes gleam with mischief, and he smiled, his teeth a creamy white contrast against the satiny fur of his dark face. "As a matter of fact I do. At your grandfather's request, we have been discussing your upcoming marriage to Sa Seya Dasani."

Tobrach's head crest rose in surprise. The priest laughed and stepped into the hall, a bemused young man at his heels.

Part Four: Riath Festival

Chapter One

"Ayi-ya! The enemy has found us. Awake!"

Nathan's eyes flew open. "What—" Throwing off his blanket, he sat up, fully awake. Around him in the darkness the night exploded with the sounds of hand-to-hand combat.

<<Kasha?>>

Ignoring Corha's frightened wail in his mind, Nathan flung himself to one side as he sensed a dark form looming over him. He rolled, feeling the brush of the spear aimed at his back whistle over his head. Still down Nathan kicked upwards, and brought the reinforced toe of his combat boot into the side of the Warlinga's knee as he lunged forward to make his kill.

There was a gratifying crunch of bone and the man sprawled, crying out in surprise. Nathan grunted and heaved himself to his knees. Drawing his machete, he groped for the dazed man's head crest, found it, then jerking the head back he slit the lizardman's throat in one swift motion.

<<I am with you, Warrior, if you need me,>> the colorless voice of Maker Qwaltamis said into his mind. <<Don't worry about the Shalla, I will see to it for now.>>

<<Right.>> No more enemies to deal with for the moment, Nathan cautiously got to his feet. He peered into the gloom wishing the infer-red adaptation to his eyes that the Maker mentioned was completed.

Yargal and his men had arrived at Shaden not long after Nathan-Corha was deemed well enough by the Maker to return to the keep above. After Yargal delivered his message to the kashallan and a council of the alliance, it was decided that it was time to gather their supporters and head for the Capital.

The Solstice was fast approaching and they needed to be there in force before Enaju could stage her mock trial and set the rest of the Yeyen Banai Valley against them. With that in mind they had set out with a barely

healed Nathan-Corha to rendezvous with the hunting packs gathering at
Serath Keep to await them.

They had camped only a few hours ago in this tiny grove on the border
of Serath lands hoping to catch a little sleep before traveling on to the keep
in the morning. How by all the Gods had the enemy found them so soon
after leaving Shaden Keep? Evidently K'San Yargal's flight from Riath had
forced the changelings to take the offensive.

Well there was no point in groping around in the dark, if they were
going to make a fight of it, they might as well have some light. Bellowing
out a warning, Nathan drew his sidearm, leveled it at the dying campfire
and fired. With a roar white-hot flames fountained into the air above the
hearth, illuminating the struggling men with a daytime radiance.

Caught off guard by the light, many of the enemy hesitated, giving their
opponents a momentary advantage. The light illuminated several knots of
struggling Warlinga, teeth bared, tails lashing the air with the whistling
sounds of whips. Picking up the dead Warlinga's spear Nathan looked
around him warily, anticipating another attack.

Then Aju'an and Mar were beside him, bursting out of the shadows
with cries of alarm. Without thought the three readied their spears and
assumed the battle formation that they had practiced so diligently over the
Sorin season at Ticca.

Nathan's body vibrated with the power of the adrenaline rush flooding
through his system. With the Khutani's help Nathan moved with a grace of
a dancer and a speed that matched the heightened reflexes of his Warlinga
companions. As a team, Nathan in the middle, they flowed across the camp,
turning back the enemy spear thrusts and tail swings, stroke for stroke.

At last it was over, the Riath hunting pack routed. Nathan leaned up
against a tree trunk and sucked in great lungfuls of air. He was trembling
all over, as the aftershock of his exertion and the Khutani's adrenaline rush
coursed through his body.

Aju'an laid a hand on his shoulder. "Are you all right, kashallan-Nathan,
are you hurt?"

Still breathing hard Nathan shook his head. When he could speak a
moment later, he pushed himself away from the tree and looked around.

"I'm all right, but we'd better see to the wounded, and then get out of here—"

"Medic! Oh help, kashallan, someone. It's San Oglas, he is bleeding again."

Nathan-Corha swore and looked around for the source of the voice. Was that Tli who was calling? At last spotting the frantically waving Loti near the edge of the grove, the three men hurried over to him.

Neyal, the Meh'gach's old priest had gotten to the injured man before them. Crouched beside the Speir'dina, he was busy plastering Oglas's torn side with a heavy coating of yellow kavay, when they arrived.

Nathan-Corha looked down and asked the priest, "Is he hurt bad?"

Neyal shook his head, not looking up from his work. Nathan grunted, then scowled at Oglas. The man had his eyes closed, his lip between his teeth, and the freckles on his cheeks standing out like splatters of mud against his pale skin. "You would be an amadan and come along when I advised you not to, you stupid shit."

"It's nothing, Kashallan, really, I just tore my side open a bit fighting off one of the big brutes that was after the Loti." Oglas gave him a crooked grin, but Nathan wasn't fooled. He could see the pain in the man's feverish green eyes.

"Mm. Neyal, make sure to give him something for the pain as well. I don't want the amadan to fall off the Loti when we move out. Do you have the orange kavay in your bag, or shall I make some to give him?"

Neyal glanced up, met the Kashallan's gray eyes, and then looked down quickly. His hand trembling slightly, he withdrew another jar from his bag. "I have some, Holy One, you needn't trouble yourself," he murmured.

"Thank you."

Startled, the priest looked up, then dropped his eyes and opened the jar. Scooping some of the thick salve onto a finger, he rubbed it into an open cut on Oglas's arm. Within a few moments, the wounded man visibly relaxed, closing his eyes and letting out a long sigh of relief.

As they stepped away from the priest and his patient, Tli said, "San Oglas was very brave, Holy One. The changeling's hunters wanted to take us with them, but we wouldn't let them." Tli proudly showed him the piece of heavy tree root that he still carried like a club. The other Loti clustering about them murmured their agreement, shyly displaying their own weapons for his inspection.

"They were very surprised that we fought them," Wabin agreed, "they hadn't expected that—them San Oglas came with his magic—and they ran away."

<<Truly, Chosen, your people bring change to our troubled world—Loti fighting, Avairei warrior medics—what will it be next?>> the Maker said, its mental voice sounding a bit testy.

<<As my friend Dunnagh has said many times, amla, when you brought us here for your children you got not only a host but my people's alien ways as well. We can't help but be models for other Timornans who see us and want to experiment with our new manner of doing things.>>

<<Mm, so we are learning.>>

<<Amla, are you angry with my Kasha and his kin?>> Corha asked, a note of worry in the young ones mental voice.

Qwaltamis rumbled a mental laugh. <<No, Little One, I am not. I am just getting too old and set in my ways for my own good, that's all—don't fret.>>

Wabin and Tli exchanged worried glances then looked down at the ground. "Did we do something wrong, Holy One, we didn't mean to offend—"

Kashallan-Nathan blinked. "Offend? No you haven't offended us, you did well," Qwaltamis intoned. Nathan's face smiled. "Your words surprise me, Young Loti, that is all. You weren't bred for such combat, but I am not angry." Nathan's smile widened, and he patted Tli on the shoulder to reassure him. "And I am very glad you didn't let those Warlinga kill or take you. I would not have enjoyed walking the rest of the way to Riath, I assure you. When Neyal is finished here, help him get San Oglas back to the fire, then go with the priest to help with anyone else who may be wounded."

Tli bobbed his head, his feathery tail swishing with his newly appointed importance. "Yes, Holy One, I will do that."

Then the Maker turned to the disappointed Wabin and the Warlinga. "You three find the enemy casualties. If they are dead, drag them to a place where I can taste them—if anyone is alive bring them to me so I can question them. I'll be by the fire when you need me."

Nathan-Corha returned to the fire and sat down cross-legged, on the ground. He sighed, feeling drained and exhausted. His body was still going through the transformation process, and even with the Maker's added strength he felt worn out after such a fight. He would like to sleep, but that was impossible, they needed to take stock of the damage done by the attack then move on in case another of the Segoi's hunting packs stumbled upon them.

He cradled his hands in his lap, looking down at them anxiously. His tentacles were forming and after this little party—they were hurting something terrible.

Nathan glanced up as someone stopped beside him. Ross held out a carved flask and an empty bowl. "You want some of your formula?"

Nathan-Corha nodded. Ross sank down beside him, uncorked the bottle, and poured some of the rich blue liquid into the bowl. Setting the bottle and bowl down in front of him, he took out his dagger and cut a shallow wound in his left arm above the wrist. Picking up the bowl again, he allowed his blood to drip into the mixture.

Nathan-Corha eyed the process hungrily, the pungent scent making his mouth water. When he judged the man had given enough, he reached over, took Ross's arm away from the bowl and spat a cauterizing agent onto the bleeding wound. Ross winced at the sharp pain, then looked down at his arm. The blood was already stopped, the cut beginning to heal. Startled, he glanced up and met Nathan's eye. "You didn't have to do that," Nathan said. "I could have taken it as it was—I fed not long ago."

Ross shrugged. "I know, but I thought you might need the Gift after the fight." His voice trailed off and he looked down at his arm once more.

Nathan sighed and picked up the bowl. He took a long drink, allowing its rich taste to linger on his tongue. Remembering how Dunnagh used to put up such a fuss about his vampiric diet his heart gave a lurch. Would he ever see his dear love again?

Taking another drink he said to Ross, "I guess I did, so thanks. But, Ross, you don't have to do this or feel guilty about me, you know. I told you before I was marked—I knew this would happen someday—so stop trying to make it up to me—if that's what you're doing."

Ross looked into his iron-gray eyes and nodded. "Yeah, sure."

Nathan gave him a crooked grin and took another drink of the formula. He had always wondered how Dunnagh had been able to drink the disgusting stuff; now he was finding out that having a symbiont in his middle meant a whole lot of things were different, including the taste of food. He sipped again—not half bad.

"Besides, I can't afford to have you get too weak to fight, now can I?" He glanced down at his sore hands. The two middle fingers on each hand, were swollen and misshapen by the tentacle adaptation process now under way. "My hands aren't going to be much good for shooting a beam rifle, once we get to Riath.

"With Oglas's wound reopened again, I'll be counting on you, hmm? So, next time I need the blood gift, let one of the Warlinga, or the priest make the offering. They were bred for that purpose."

Ross nodded, stood, his face expressionless. "Yes, Sir, uh, Kashallan, I'll go help Aju'an."

Nathan-Corha nodded and took another drink of the blood-laced formula. When he was finished, he set down the bowl and rose, determined to throw off his weariness like an unwanted cloak. He'd sleep on Tli as they traveled, like Dunnagh always used to do. Dunnagh. Gods, Nathan hoped they'd get to Riath in time. If something were to happen to him...

<<I'm here with you, Kasha, you're not alone anymore—and I'll always love you,>> Corha said into his mind. <<Don't be sad—and besides, our amsi will be all right, our amla said Maker Gladdris will help him until we get there.>>

Nathan smiled and unconsciously patted his middle. <<I know Little One, I know, don't worry about me too much, I'll be all right.>>

As he was about to move away, he saw Tli carrying Oglas in his arms toward the fire. Nathan went over and helped the Loti ease the man down into a comfortable position, and cover him with a blanket. Oglas was already dozing so they left him and headed towards the outer perimeter of the grove to find the Warlinga.

Inside the shadows of the great tree, Tli put a hand on his shoulder to stop him. "Kashallan-Nathan, is the elder still with you?"

"Yes, Tli, I am here," the Maker intoned in its hollow voice. "What is it?"

Tli curled a clawed hoof in the dry leaves, unsure how to begin now that he had the Ancient's attention.

"Speak, Young One, I will not bite you."

Startled, Tli let out a nervous laugh. "I'm sorry, Ancient, I was just thinking—the Warlinga and Avairei don't know about it, but we Loti have our own secret network. We travel back and forth from our villages over pathways that the others rarely use, or don't know about. If the enemy is searching for us on the more traveled routes, I could lead you on one of the hidden pathways."

"Hmm. That is an interesting offer; but why tell me now? We could have saved ourselves some trouble and lives if you had told us about this before."

Tli scuffed at the debris again, his tail swishing. "It's sort of a secret, Elder. I'm not supposed to tell, but I don't want Nathan-Corha to be killed or injured, so I thought I'd better mention it."

"Mm. Did you tell Dunnagh-Tani about this 'secret network?'"

"I believe he knew, yes." As the Maker's point registered, Tli gasped.

Nathan-Corha laid a hand on his shoulder. "I'm not implying that his capture was in any way the fault of the Loti who guided him. He could have been followed whatever route he took.

"But sometimes a more isolated trail can be more dangerous than a well-traveled path. I think our time for concealment is ending, but I might need this network of yours to run messages to gather the clans. Would your people do that for us do you think?"

Tli brightened. "Oh yes, elder, if you asked them; they would do it."

Nathan slapped him on the back. "Good. When we get to Serath Keep you can alert your Loti kin to be ready."

"Kashallan-Nathan?" Varrod approached and bowed. "We have done as you commanded, Holy one. If you will follow me I will take you to where we have laid the enemy dead."

Nathan-Corha grunted, rose, and fell into step beside him. "Any taken alive?"

"One, kashallan, but we didn't watch him carefully enough. When we carried him to lie by the others, he seemed unconscious, but he awakened.

He clawed open his own throat and bled to death." Varrod glanced at the kashallan anxiously. "I am sorry—"

"Never mind, tell me about our own losses," Qwaltamis said.

"This night has proven to everyone that it is a good idea to have a 'medic' go along with the hunting packs." Varrod looked at the Speir'dina host with open admiration. "Without the priest's medicines, we would have had to kill two of our own hunters. As it stands now we have two dead and five injured. The two worst ones will be of no use as fighters for the moment, but they will recover. Perhaps we should leave them at Serath Keep along our way."

The kashallan grunted. Coming up to the place where the dead lay, Nathan-Corha motioned for someone to hold up a torch so he could see the bodies. All were Warlinga—at least in appearance; he would soon find out if they were more than that. Grim-faced he knelt, dipped a finger in each man's blood, and tasted it.

<<Yes, Child, it has been many years, but it is as Dunnagh-Tani claims—these Warlinga have the taint of the Umwira about them. All but two are changelings.>> Qwaltamis said into both bondmates' minds.

"The Maker says most of them are changelings," Nathan-Corha reported to the waiting Warlinga. Stepping away from the corpses he motioned for his followers to return with him to the fire.

When they were seated in a make shift war council, Yargal bowed his head to Kashallan-Nathan. "Ancient One, Kashallan, this attack must have been due to my carelessness. In spite of all my efforts K'San Drucas must have had us followed. Unknowingly we have brought them to you, and I am shamed, because such a mistake could have cost the young bondmates their lives."

Nathan's face grimaced; then Qwaltamis said in its colorless voice, "You did right to leave the capital and come to us, so save your regrets for later, K'San. How they found us is of no concern at the moment. And now that we have been discovered I believe it is time to declare ourselves openly.

"No more sneaking down the back roads, jumping at shadows. The Solstice is near, we must send word to our allies to join us. When we leave Serath Keep we will travel the main roads openly."

Chapter Two

<<I t's the longest day of the year, Kasha, did you know that?>> <<Yes, I did know, little one.>> Forgetting about Corha for a moment, Nathan muttered to himself, "I just hope it will be long enough to do what we have to do."

<<Kasha? I can taste your fear. Are you worried about our amsi?>>

Nathan sighed. This bond thing was so hard to get used to. <<Yes, Shalla, I guess I am.>>

<<Me too,>> came a frightened little voice into his mind.

Nathan stroked his middle then cursed as the beam rifle slung across his shoulder slipped down, to poke him in the hip. He straightened and re-settled the thing upon his back. Corha was so young—too young for him to be getting it upset by his worries.

<<It will be all right, Shalla, don't fret yourself because of what you're tasting from me. I'm just being stupid. We humans are like that, we think about things and get to worrying. Remember, our amla told us that Maker Gladdris is there with him. The Maker won't let anything happen to him before we get there.>>

<<Oh. Do you really think so?>>

Well not really. Shit, how to answer that one? He would like to believe it, but he was still scared. And, if he lied about how he really felt to ease Corha's mind the symbiont would know. Was it like this for Dunnagh and the young Tani, when they were fleeing Sulas? Probably.

<<I'd like to believe that everything will work out, Shalla. I know you can taste that I am afraid, but the alliance is doing all that can be done, so we will just have to help each other to stop tormenting ourselves for no reason, right?>>

<<...Right.>>

Last night the leadership of the kashallan alliance had stayed at one of the Maveth clan's Sun-time houses near the southern end of Lake Riath. Twice more on their way to the capital, they had been attacked by K'San Drucas's packs. In spite of the danger, their numbers grew; the news of their coming having spread through the countryside before them. By the time they reached the Maveth home, they were a force to be reckoned with, and the raids had stopped.

Grabbing a hasty meal, the Kashallan and his followers were on the move again in the predawn gloom. Silent as wraiths they moved along the lakeside trail, heading like so many other pilgrims toward Riath. But unlike the others, their faces remained stern, thinking about what was to come. There would be no festival celebration this day for anyone.

When they came to an outcropping of shale overlooking the lake, Nathan asked Tli to step out of the line of march. Hoping to see Riath Keep, he squinted into the salmon-colored mist shrouding the lake. Veiled in a halo of opalescence, Timorna's red-gold sun was just lifting itself above the purple horizon. Beautiful. Leaning forward he touched Tli on the shoulder. "I can't see anything through the fog. How much farther is the Capital, do you know?"

Tli pointed to a shadowed cliff looming out of the mists across the lake. "The keep is on the far shore, Kashallan, see?"

"Mm, there's something over there—maybe, but I can't make it out." He turned back to the Loti. "You must have very good eyes if you can see anything more than a lump of gray shadow over there."

Tli chuckled. "No, I can't see any more than you can, Holy One, but I know it's there. The land is very low and flat around most of the lake, but on the north shore the hills sloping down from the Rim Wall are a little higher, and made of old stone. The Keep of Riath was carved out of that far cliff next to the shore."

Nathan peered into the fog, but even with Tli's guidance he couldn't see much more than the dark silhouette of a large cliff thrusting up into the morning sky. "I'll have to take your word for it."

"Riath is there; we will see more as the mists clear off."

"All right, the keep is dug into the cliff, but how big is the town that surrounds it? Do a lot of people live there?"

Tli scratched his jaw considering. At last he said, "San Nathan, I think things must be very different in your old home. Do a lot of people live in towns there?"

Startled Nathan said, "Yes, they do. Some are very big; we call our big town's cities. Don't people live in towns here? I mean, why call Riath the capital if a lot of people don't live there."

"Mm. Those cities must be a wonder to see, but here it's not like that. Riath Keep is our capital because of the ceremonies held there. It has never had a large population, though it is said that its tunnels go a long ways back into the hills. Mostly it is a place where the High Council meets and the great yearly festivals are held. All the clans have sun-time houses along the lake, or apartments in the keep itself, but mostly we come on the holidays, for the ceremonies and the fares; only a few live here year round."

"Mm, that is very different. I guess I expected a bigger place, but it makes sense. With little stone to build for the Sorin Season, people couldn't remain here during the Confinement."

Tli nodded, then beamed. "But when we *do* come, there is so much to see and do—there are games and markets and the dancing—so much fun." Then his face fell. "But not this Solstice, I guess."

Nathan patted his shoulder. "No, not this Solstice, Friend."

As they watched the sunrise, the disembodied cadence of high pitched chanting came floating out to them through the fog. Nathan shuddered in spite of himself. The morning hymn to the Mother, he'd heard it before at Ticca; but today its mournful sound reminded him of a Caldoni lament for the dead.

"Kashallan?"

Aju'an was striding up the line of march towards him. When the Warlinga came alongside him, the kashallan asked, "What is it, trouble?"

"No trouble, but my father and the Imas, think we should take the inland road the rest of the way. The mists will be thinning on the lake soon. If the guard at the keep sees us coming too early, they may speed up the day's proceedings, rather than waiting for noon as is the custom. Do you have any objection to this change?"

Nathan-Corha shrugged, and touched Tli's flank. They began walking again along the weedy trail. Feeling the presence of Qwaltamis in his mind once again, Nathan closed his eyes and consulted with the Maker. A moment later he opened his eyes again and said, "We have no objection, whatever you feel is wise, though it hardly seems to matter does it? They know we are coming anyway."

Aju'an smiled, showing his fangs. True, but at least this way we can keep them guessing for a little while longer."

The Kashallan chuckled and waved him on. "So we may, lead on then."

As they turned away from the lake, Nathan looked back at the reedy waters, a frown crossing his face. Addressing the Maker he asked, <<Amla, if there wasn't any place around here suitable for building clan keeps, why settle here at all—I mean why make Riath the capital?>>

<<Because of its central location, and because of the rich farmlands that are at the south and western sides of the lake. The River Magre pours into the lake from the north bringing with it silt and the rich kavay waters from the Broken Lands.

<<The soil is good, and with the Rim Wall to protect it, it gets very few of the Sorin storms. In the old days, we thought it best to have the people spend the Sun-time near the fields, then return to the keeps in the hills for the Sorin confinement.>>

<<That would make since. Are there any towns or cities on Timorna?>>

<<No. not in the way your people define them—not since the Great Wars.>>

<<Oh.>>

Even though it was early, the main road when they reached it was already clogged with families traveling to the Capital for the celebration. Loti peasants with their shaggy coats shorn, walked with bundles strapped to their backs, talking excitedly in low voices with their families and friends. Here and there a carved litter bore an Avairei personage decked out in bright colored kilt and the family jewels. Surrounding the litters, the rest of their households and their Warlinga escort sauntered displaying their own ceremonial finery.

The people fell silent as the grim-faced, heavily armed Warlinga at the head of the alliance procession took their places among the throng. Making no secret of their identity now, Nathan-Corha, Oglas and Ross rode with their flat alien faces plain for all to see. When they rode by the celebrants lined up along the side of the road to watch them pass. He heard the word kashallan spoken in awed tones many times as the people saw him.

They were collecting quite a following this morning. Not only the rebel Warlinga clans marched at his back now, Loti peasants and a few Begta joined their ranks as well. Whether the crowd came along to fight beside them, if it came to that, or just to witness the show when they reached Riath, he wasn't sure.

Nathan glanced over his shoulder trying to see through the dust cloud that was building up around them. Somewhere in the throng Ima Ngeal, Urinia, and Arishim rode in their Loti born litters. He had wanted the women to stay at Shaden until this mess was settled, but they refused.

"You will need us," Urinia smugly told him. "And, how would it look if we stayed behind to hide at Shaden, after calling the clan leaders here to see you and Dunnagh-Tani?" Her eyes flashing with indignation, she answered her own question.

"I'll tell you, Young One. It will look like we don't really believe in what we have been saying. It will look like we are cowards, afraid to face the Dingay with our accusations—that's what. We are coming."

When Nathan still tried to argue, Ngeal had looked him squarely in the eye and addressed the Maker directly. "Maker Qwaltamis, surely you can understand and see the wisdom in our action?"

And, of course the Maker had; so Nathan had been overruled. The women were here—somewhere. Probably talking to as many of their fellow travelers as they could along the way.

When the Avairei clans joined the march yesterday, Urinia had proven that her presence was indeed necessary to insure Avairei continued support of the alliance. They had made their point, but this morning he made them promise to stay well back in case there was fighting, and that would have to do.

Ignoring for the moment the curious stares of the people along the road, Qwaltamis looked out through Nathan's eyes at the cultivated lands they were passing with some satisfaction. For the first time in many centuries one of its kind was viewing the surface world. It saw the fertile fields of lamra and masa roots and the dahalli groves for which they had labored so hard.

In its coils were stored the memories of another time, another world—but that was long ago, and there was no sense dwelling on the joys and sorrows of the past any longer.

For too many centuries the Makers had allowed themselves to be lulled by their dreams. They had abandoned their creations. Slept, while the hated enemy grew strong, and look what had happened. They were now in danger of losing everything once again. It was time to put the dreams aside and live once more in the now.

Though the Yeyen Banai was nothing like it had once been before the Great Wars, the Maker was pleased. In the absence of their stewardship the land, at least, had continued to prosper. Thanks mostly to the gentle Loti and their care. Oh, there was much that needed Khutani attention, but there were many good things to be proud of as well. All along their journey Qwaltamis saw evidence of the Loti's love of the land.

Of the four bred races, the Loti alone continued on with the task the Khutani gave them, in spite of the contempt they were shown by their Warlinga and Avairei "masters." Too bad the others hadn't followed the path they had been shown so well. But all that was going to change, the balance must be re-stored, and many weren't going to like the changes that were coming.

Reaching out the host's hand Qwaltamis patted the Loti he rode on his shoulder. "Your people have done well in our absence, Timornshaya," the Maker's hollow voice intoned, "I am pleased."

Tli bobbed his thanks. Suddenly shy he said, "I am very young, and don't deserve that ancient title, but I am honored that I was chosen to carry you and the kashallan to the capital. I will tell my elders of your praise when I get home."

"See that you do, because it has been well earned."

AT LAST IN THE DISTANCE the high stone walls of the fortress came into view. Spreading out like a vibrant carpet, the tents and thatched awnings of the fair lay on the mossy ground outside its main gate. People in their holiday finery already wondered among the booths. Down by the lake, a crowd was gathered around a large roped off oval. Inside Two Warlinga squared off for a match. Further down the shore the excited shouts of children at play could be heard over the adult's deeper voices. Nathan's heart gave a lurch. Children! Gods, how he hated this.

They were almost there—surely the keep knew the alliance was coming by now. Did they have time to get some of their own troops inside before they were discovered by K'San Drucas's hunting packs? That was hard to believe. Maybe the open gate was a trap. Damn, what were the changelings planning—and what would the fiends do to their prisoners if the alliance attacked?

Shit, who could say. They might as well go ahead with the plan as they had arranged. Turning to his Speir'dina companions Nathan said. "You two still want to go ahead with your idea?"

Oglas laughed. "Of course, we wouldn't think of letting such an august personage as yourself go to a gathering like this without announcing your arrival proper like."

"That's if the Elder agrees," Ross said hastily, watching Nathan's expression.

Qwaltamis chuckled. "I have never heard these musical instruments of your people, but the Chosen assures me that the sound is most pleasing. And, disconcerting to an enemy," it added dryly. "So, in this case, Young Ones, your Elder, does agree. You may begin."

Chapter Three

Drucas bowed. "Your will, Ata I will bring them."

"See that you do, K'San Drucas," Persig said, his eyes hard. "All of them, do you understand me?"

Drucas's head crest flattened. He returned the Ata's stare sullenly. Without another word, he spun round and stalked out of the chamber. *The sniveling, filth-eating, half-bred slaves—how dare they!* Oh, he would enjoy the deaths of the verminous traitors today—but not the woman—she belonged to him.

Once outside in the corridor his face and head crest position assumed their usual bland facade. The only thing that gave away his anger, was the rapid flicking of the tip of his tail as he pounded down the hall. Enaju's spies were everywhere, he would have to be careful for a while longer, but then...

They couldn't have her—By The Fires, they could not. Oh, he would remove her from her cell all right, and the mutant too, so she couldn't be made to talk. But he wasn't going to take them to the outer court to be placed on trial with the others. Blue Eyes and his Caltia and mutant wives would have to be enough to sway the people to the Dingay cause.

Enaju and her brother wouldn't dare confront him openly about his failure to bring the women, and later— Drucas smiled to himself. Who knew what might happen *later*.

When the Master's warbands arrived, there might be some surprises in store for the "High Ones." For now, however, he would hide the women in another part of the abandoned tunnels. Tonight, while things were still unsettled, he would send the women north, through the secret passages, with a few of his most trusted men. The simpering weaklings would be furious with him, but no matter. He would blame the women's disappearance on the Tragar slime—and *that* would get rid of another thorn in his side.

And K'San Yargal? If the man and his brats lived through the day, he could hardly speak out about his missing child, now could he. He would join the traitors on the stakes, if he did.

Fortunately for him, Persig hadn't seen the brands that he'd marked the women with—if he had, there might have been trouble over it. Umwira magical sigils, they would have been hard to explain away to the Council, if Chelka were to ever be placed on trial.

It had been a dangerous mistake to allow his temper to cloud his good sense, when he'd marked them. But as he'd hoped, the Avairei were too busy with their own slimy schemes to pay any more attention to their captives. All they cared about now was that the prisoners remained safe, and alive, so they could be paraded in front of the Council for this mock trial of theirs.

Well, Blue Eyes and the other two weren't in very good shape, but they were alive. Drucas stepped into the guardroom. Head crests raised and eyes alert, his men were waiting for him. Like the good mewling slave Enaju assumed him to be, he was here to fetch her meat.

"EXCUSE ME FOR A MOMENT, Ata, K'San, I see my brother over there and I need to speak to him." Barely acknowledging their startled bows, Enaju hurried across the tiled floor to intercept Persig before he could walk out into the sunny courtyard.

Resplendent in his ceremonial blue and gold kilt and cloak, he saw her coming and waited, his face impassive. Turning her back on the crowd milling about the chamber when she was close enough to speak in a low murmur, Enaju hissed, "My spies are saying that there is a new kashallan coming with the rebels. Is that possible?"

Persig's eyes widened slightly, then his face assumed its usual benign mask. Taking her arm he led her away from the sunlight, into the shadow behind one of the open doors. "We are in a public place—what, by the Fires are you doing drawing attention to us like this. Are you losing your nerve?"

"No I am not losing my nerve, but if this is true—"

"Calm down, sister dear, or you will start a *new* set of rumors yourself. The rebels are coming, true, but they couldn't possibly have a new kashallan with them—there wouldn't have been time to call another from Ticca, or create a new one, so relax.

"K'San Drucas assures me that in spite of the Meh'gach's escape, everything is going well. They have only made up that story to keep their supporters loyal, but there is no truth to it."

He chuckled softly, and waved to someone over her shoulder. "They probably hope to rescue this one before their lie is detected. What a surprise will be waiting for them when they discover that Blue Eyes can no longer perform upon command."

Enaju allowed her lip to twitch, then her look grew stern again. "Don't patronize me, Brother. There is something wrong; I can feel it. Where is K'San Drucas?"

"I sent him to collect the prisoners and ready our defenses, he will be here soon."

"But what about this new kashallan, shouldn't we—"

Digging his claws into her flesh where no one could see, he said, "Get a hold of yourself, Woman, would you shame our Master and his trust in you?" Then in a carrying voice he said, "Come, dear sister, on this most joyous feast day let me escort you to your chair in the courtyard so the festivities can begin."

As they headed out into the open court, he murmured so that only she could hear. "The walls of Riath are thick and high, no rebel mob can tumble them no matter how they try. Stop worrying over nothing. We will triumph, the Master has sworn it."

DUNNAGH DROWSED, HIS half-awake mind returning once again to thoughts of Sairsa, Pela, and the babies. He floated in a sea of happy memories. Pela combing and braiding his long red hair, baby Joran's silky red fur nestled in the crook of his arm—and, Sairsa, her green eyes and sweet red lips smiling at him from her pillow. The taste of her was so sweet upon his tongue. He could almost feel the soft warmth of her skin and the sleeping baby Tameh between them. By all the Gods of his people, he missed them so much.

"Dunnagh-Tani, are you awake," Ellis murmured.

"Mm, sort of, why?"

"There's something going on out in the hall. I thought I heard Marti's voice cursing a few moments ago."

Clawing his way out of his daydreams, he listened. Yes, there was something going on out there. Though he strained his ears, he couldn't hear any women's voices amidst the clatter of weapons and the joking banter of the Warlinga.

Ellis touched his arm; he could feel her hand trembling. "What do you think is happening?"

"I don't know."

Beside him Amril moaned stirring restlessly in his sleep. Easing himself to a sitting position, Dunnagh stroked his consort's ragged fur, crooning to him in a soothing voice. Amril relaxed under his touch and slipped back into his dreams.

Ellis sat up too. "Well, whatever it is, I hope it doesn't concern us."

He chuckled softly and reached for her in the darkness, pulling her emaciated body against him. She wrapped her arms around him and sighed. "Don't bet on it."

Suddenly the door to their cell was flung open and several large Warlinga stepped into the tiny room. Amril cried out and sat up abruptly, rubbing his eyes. Dunnagh and Ellis turned their faces away from the torchlight. Ellis uttered a low curse. "You were right."

The Warlinga officer looked down at them his lip curling with contempt. "Get up, Filth, this is your big day."

The prisoners stared up at him stupidly, blinking in the light. The Warlinga swore and motioned for one of his men to come help him. Unhooking the Kashallan from his tether against the wall they bound his hands tightly behind his back and hustled him out into the hall.

"Where are you taking him, Umwira?" Ellis screamed lurching to her feet and staggering to the end of her own tether.

The Warlinga laughed. Then one of the remaining guards slapped her to the floor with his tail and stood over her, a shadowy menace in the gloom. Reaching down he jerked her to her feet and tied her hands behind her back too. "You'll know soon enough, Mutant Witch," he taunted, "because you and the Caltia pervert are coming along too."

Giving them no time to resist the Warlinga half dragged, half carried their bewildered prisoners down several gloomy corridors, through a large, brightly decorated audience room and out into the golden light of a warm afternoon.

Outside in the courtyard, the people assembled for this event fell silent with gasps of horror. Coming up to the prisoners, K'San Drucas motioned for his men to take them to a wooden platform set up in the middle of the open court. Dunnagh and his companions were hustled up the short flight of stairs and tied securely, with their hands above their heads to a stout frame that ran the length of the structure.

The Warlinga tying him, looked him in the eye, grinned and jerked his bound arms up a little higher, then left him with his back arched, gritting his teeth against the pain. Dunnagh swore in Caldoni, which only made the man's smile widen. Damn the Black-Hearted Devil, now he would have to stand on tiptoe if he didn't want his arms to support his full weight.

After the man jumped down, Dunnagh strained, testing his bonds. As he expected, they were tight; he wasn't going anywhere. He sighed, not that he could escape even if he was free. He felt so weak, if he wasn't hanging here like meat for the butchering, he probably would fall on his face.

On either side of him Amril and Ellis were tied in a similar manner. Farther down the platform, two more ropes hung awaiting other prisoners. Dunnagh stared at them in confusion for a long moment, trying to make sense out of this new riddle. Then he understood. Those two ropes were for Marti and Chelka—but if so, where were they? Had they escaped—not likely—but if not that, what had happened to them?

Dunnagh watched K'San Drucas cross the courtyard and shuddered, remembering all too well the pain he'd endured at the man's hand. He felt a cold chill of dread run down his spine—would he hurt him again? His eyes flicked to the empty ropes. That black-hearted devil, what had he done to the missing women?

Dunnagh had no more time to wonder for at that moment a shell horn sounded and a procession of high-ranking Avairei came out of the keep and headed for another awning-covered platform directly across the courtyard from where he stood. He recognized the male half of the couple in the lead. Ata Persig, so the woman with the gleaming metal headdress and long flowing cloak on his arm must be Enaju herself.

Inside his middle he felt Tani stir uneasily. He sensed his bondmate's fear, and wished he had some way to comfort It.<<Kasha? I'm frightened,>> a tiny mental voice said into his mind. <<Will Ata Persig hurt me again?>>

<<I don't know, little one, try not to think about it. Just rest now.>>

<<I'll try.>>

Dunnagh looked away, hoping to spare Tani the sight of their enemies for the moment. So, this was Riath Keep. Right now they were in a large open courtyard, crowded with people all dressed in their ceremonial finery. In the middle of the far wall to his right, he could see the main gate standing wide open.

From the fairgrounds came music and the boisterous talk of people enjoying themselves. As the onlookers filed into the courtyard, they fell silent; gawking at the starved and battered prisoners with openmouthed attention.

Once again the shell horns sounded. Dunnagh turned back to the dais across the court from him in time to see the first ranks of the procession take their places on the waiting chairs. *Ah, today must be our trial—what a laugh.*

Dunnagh scanned the faces of the people on the dais and in the crowd nearest to the platform. When this day finally arrived, he'd hoped to find K'San Meh'gach, and other members of the alliance here to rescue him. His heart sank. Maybe they were here, hiding, waiting their chance, but at the moment, he didn't recognize anyone in the sea of faces staring up at him so intently. Where was Yargal, dead, or in a cell too?

As he continued to scan the courtyard, the gray pelted woman in the ornate headdress caught his eye. As if she understood what he was looking for, she curled her lip in a contemptuous smile, her eyes as hard as black pebbles.

Dunnagh met her stare and held it.

"The High Matri and her Council," Amril murmured.

Bobbing his head, Dunnagh lifted his lips and gave her a toothy grin.

Enaju's eyes widened then her expression hardened at his impudence. While keeping her eyes fixed on him, she said something to Ata Persig seated on her right. When Persig glanced over at him, Dunnagh's grin widened and he nodded to him, too. His eerie blue eyes watched them intently, his face as uncompromising as their own.

Persig turned, spoke to his sister, listened to her answer, and then stood. When the assembly quieted, he held out his hands in a blessing, then addressed the Council and the populace. "Good people, honored councilors, I bid you welcome. The Solstice Festival is one of the most sacred ceremonies of our year. When the sun is at its peak in the sky, it is our custom to give thanks to the Great Mother, The Great Hunt Leader and our breeders, the Sacred Khutani.

"This year our holy rites will not be performed until the terrible evil that has come among us has been cleansed from our land. Only then are we free to honor our Gods and the Khutani in the manner they deserve from us." Persig swept his hand dramatically towards the bound prisoners upon the platform.

"We must rectify this abomination and punish those who have committed it, or the Gods, and the Khutani, will no longer bless us with their favor."

The crowd murmured, shuffling their feet nervously.

Out of the corner of his eye, Persig watched the members of the High Council. They were listening, but most wore the benign masks of those used to concealing their thoughts.

"Look at them, good people, foul mutants, demons from the north. They were sent here by their wizard master to destroy us. With the help of their traitorous Caltia allies, they defiled Sulas and now they have come into the Yeyen Banai to continue their devastation. Oh, look upon the face of the Hated Enemy," Persig said, his voice dripping with contempt. "See the loathsome brute and his wives."

He paused; a buzz of angry talk began to spread through the crowd. Before the din could get too loud, he held out his hands once more for silence. The talk quieted to a low rumbling. "Ah yes, good people, his wives. Here is an Avairei Ata, given by his sister, the witch, Sagas Caltia, to this mutant demon as his 'wife.'

"A young Ata given in a mockery of true marriage to this creature, to satisfy his unnatural perversions!" Persig glared significantly at several members of the High Council. Addressing them directly, he said, "Take a good look at the corruption that has been allowed to fester among us. Look my K'Sans, Imas, look at them—do you still counsel forbearance for the Caltia Clan?"

Evidently, Amril's capture had been a much more closely guarded secret than his own imprisonment, judging by the shocked faces Dunnagh saw among the councilors. Damn them, they were using the lad's relationship to him, as another vicious maneuver in their deadly game. He should have realized what a coup this was for the Dingay—he should have insisted that Amril stay at Ticca.

With Sagas safely out of reach, the old witch, Enaju must have laughed till she peed herself, when she realized that Amril in women's dress was an even better ploy than Sagas herself might have been.

Amril heard the angry talk and met the crowd's hostile stares bravely at first, and then feeling the heavy weight of their contempt, he began to falter. He shuddered, and looked down at the ground, sobbing quietly with his shame.

"Amril, my Dear One, fight his Umwira mind magic. Don't let him win. You know what he says is a distortion of the truth. You have nothing to be ashamed of, don't cry."

Turning his angry blue eyes back to the changeling Dunnagh bared his teeth and said, "Leave him be, Umwira Changeling Slime. You are just toying with him to heighten the crowd's interest, but it is me that you really want to see dead. So get on with it and stop the charade."

The crowd gasped, Dunnagh turned on them contemptuously. "You're all a bunch of half-bred degenerates—how dare you judge Amril? Let me tell you that the Maker Dievris approved of the mating. Have you grown so insolent as to question the will of a Khutani Maker?"

Into the stunned silence, Persig laughed loudly. Hopping down from his place among the Councilors he stalked across the open space between them and climbed the prisoner's platform. "Lies. Do you expect these people to believe such nonsense?"

"I can expect anything, Ata, they listened to you didn't they?"

Coming closer to Dunnagh, Persig smiled, then slapped him hard across the face. Dunnagh grunted, losing his footing, his body swinging slightly from the blow.

"Those are brave words from a creature that will die soon. Will your words be so insolent when K'San Drucas peals your naked hide from your bones?"

"Husband, please, don't make them hurt you for my sake. I'm not worth it," Amril said, his voice still quivering with his sobs.

"You Black-Hearted Devil, leave them alone." Ellis looked out over the crowd, her blood-caked hair and sunken face making her feverish eyes look enormous. "What's the matter with you people? For seven hundred years, you pray for a kashallan to come among you, and when the Khutani bring one to you, you're too stupid to know it."

"Be quiet, Mutant Witch, or I will have one of the Warlinga teach you to mind your tongue."

"Joan, do as he says," Dunnagh said quietly. "No point making this any worse than it already is. They won't believe us anyway."

Persig smiled again. Then speaking so only the prisoners could hear, he said, "How very touching, each of you trying to divert my anger onto your own head. But silence is wise counsel." He looked significantly at Amril and Ellis. "I suggest you heed it."

Returning his attention to Dunnagh, Persig said, "Yes, you are right, Traitor, why should I waste my words on the Caltia pervert. It *is* you who I want." Without looking at the populace, he raised his voice once more. "So, Demon, let's discuss, *your* crimes."

Facing his audience again he stepped back and pointed. "Look at him, Good People, this flat-faced ugly mutant. This foul creature and his kindred killed several young Atas then despoiled Sulas, yet he claims to be no mutant but a sacred kashallan." Persig laughed, inviting his audience to join him.

The crowd growled in outrage.

"A sacred kashallan! That's what the mutant witch called her mate. Does she think we are all fools, to believe such a lie? The Bebech are dead—there are no kashallans."

Pointing a clawed finger at Dunnagh's chest, Persig shouted, "If you are what you say, Begta Vomit, then prove it. Where is your Shalla? I see only an ugly Umwira mutant here before me, prove to me and these good people that you have Khutani favor as you claim."

Ignoring the gloating priest for the moment, Dunnagh turned his glacial blue stare on the High Council, and said, "The Khutani called to you, but only Sagas Caltia would listen, only a Caltia Ima was brave enough to defy the Dingay and bring me to the Khutani to make the first kashallan bonding. Take me to the pools right now, if you don't believe me.

"If I am an Umwira, as the Dingay say, then surely they will kill me. Take me to the Khutani, let them be my judges—not you."

The crowd fell silent, confused. Then a low muttering began; the people mulling over his words among themselves.

Persig swore under his breath and slapped the Kashallan hard across the face with his claws extended. Dunnagh turned spitting blood, several long scratches appearing on his pale cheek and jaw. "Be silent, Umwira Filth," Persig roared. "How dare you defile the sacred ones by speaking of them like that."

Under his breath Persig hissed, "I should have had the Warlinga cut out your tongue, Traitor. Your wit is quick, but you won't win your freedom so easily."

Persig turned back to face the Council. Some of the unaligned members were looking worried. "Fellow Councilors, people of Timorna, this foul creature is a demon wizard. Who knows what evil mischief he might do if allowed to go down to the pools.

"Remember Sulas. We dare not take that chance. He must pay for his foul crimes, and *we* will be his judges."

Closing his eyes to blot out the sight of that gloating face, Dunnagh focused his awareness inward, trying to re-establish his link with Maker Gladdris.

The crowd fell silent, waiting.

Persig smirked. "I am going to enjoy your death, Traitor, and it pleases me even more that you are aware of your failure. Ah, but think of your death by my hands as a blessing. I'm sure your own master would have given you a much more painful end for your failure, hmm?"

THE PRIEST WAS BEGINNING his final argument to the Council, when he stopped in mid-sentence. Outside, an eerie wailing could just be heard above the noise of the fairgrounds. The sound seemed to be coming up the main road towards them; gaining in volume as they listened. In the courtyard, people murmured to their neighbors and craned their heads, trying to see out the open gate.

Persig raised his hand for silence. It wasn't long before even the noise of the fair quieted, everyone listening to the unearthly moaning. Enaju rose glancing out the gate. Finding nothing unusual, she caught K'San Drucas's eye and mouthed a question. "What's going on?"

He returned her look and shrugged.

Into the silence, Dunnagh laughed. "Worried, Ata Persig, Ima, you should be. Want to know what that noise is? I can tell you, it's the sound of the Caldoni drum and pipes. My kin and the Kashallan Alliance are coming."

At that moment someone on the wall shouted. The people in the courtyard looked up; the guards were staring in fascination at something, not visible from the ground.

"What?" Drucas shouted.

One of the men pointed down the main road. A pack of well-armed Warlinga was racing at full tilt for the open gate. Drucas pushed through the crowd bawling orders. To the sentries on the wall, he roared, "Close the gates. None of that rebel slime is to enter this keep, do you hear me? Close the gate!"

Stepping close so only Dunnagh could hear, Persig hissed, "The gates of Riath are strong, the Alliance won't save you, you know. You are a dead man; I will personally make sure of that."

"I'm sure you will try, Ata," Dunnagh said keeping his voice as low as the priest's. "But you had better look to your own health, the gates of Riath will not stop them, I promise you."

Chapter Four

Nathan swore under his breath as he saw their advanced patrol beaten back and the heavy gates closing ahead of them. Maybe they should have waited on the pipes till they were closer—had some of their people inside. Nah that probably wouldn't have worked either. K'San Drucas, or somebody else would have recognized them, and closed the gates anyway. Oh, well they would just have to do this the hard way.

Holding up his hand he bawled for the column to halt. From the walls the Warlinga looked down and jeered. Nathan sighed and directed Tli back out of range as a rain of rocks and other missals came pouring from above.

Ross and Oglas stopped playing, handing their instruments to their Loti companions. In the silence, his hunting pack turned their excited faces toward his, awaiting their orders.

Maker Qwaltamis said, <<I will be with you, Chosen, should you need me, but it is you who is warrior trained, I will let you proceed as we planned.>>

<<Thanks, Amla, and, believe me, I am glad you are here with us.>>

Motioning for the members of his Hunting pack to join him, he instructed Tli to move a short distance away from the main group.

When they were clustered around him, Nathan said, "Since they've closed the gate before we got our people inside, we'll have to use the backup plan. We blow out the gate. Once we're inside—well, we take that as it comes. But remember, our first priority is to rescue the prisoners, next is to kill or capture as many of the changelings as we can, understand?"

They nodded.

Nathan looked down at his aching hands, and grimaced. He would have liked to be in on this part himself, but that wasn't going to be possible, so no sense fretting about it. Sighing, he took his beam rifle off his shoulder and tossed it to Aju'an.

The Warlinga caught it, giving him a broad grin.

"You remember what I showed you; think you can shoot that?"

Aju'an's grin widened. "I remember, I will do exactly as you told me."

Nathan grunted, and turned his attention to his other two riflemen. Ross was a good shot and looked alert and ready, Oglas on the other hand, seemed a bit shaky. He could tell the man was in a lot of pain—even without tasting him. But he had refused to be left behind with the injured. "You gonna make it? Do you need—"

"I'll be fine," Oglas said, "I don't need your help—I can do my job. Save your strength, the prisoners may need it more than me."

"Right." Turning to Mar he asked, "You got the package from my pack?"

For answer Mar held up a small canister.

"All right, When Oglas and Aju'an start firing at the Warlinga on the wall, it will be your job to run in and set that thing on the ground by the gate. Put it just down where the two halves come together. Then get out of there, understand? It's not a big charge, because we don't want to hurt a lot of innocent people, but when Ross hits it with a beam, the gate is going to blow open."

Mar nodded, and tucked the Speir'dina magic into his belt pouch. Nathan next turned to Varrod, "When the gate blows, you lead the first hunting pack inside."

Varrod lifted his lip to display his fangs. "It will be my pleasure, Kashallan."

"Right. Depending on what we find we'll spread out and search for our people and attack any of K'San Drucas's men who get in our way. Any questions?"

They shook their heads, tails lashing with excitement.

"All right, let's do it."

AS THE HEAVY GATES slammed shut, the people in the courtyard fell into a stunned silence, huddling close to one another. Shuffling uneasily, they glanced from the prisoners to the Warlinga massing in the middle of the courtyard. A child began to cry. Several of the Avairei, not on the Council, prayed in a low, monotonous drone; their words distorted by their mounting fear. Atop the wall the guards shouted and jeered, picking up rocks and other debris, which they hurled down upon the hunting packs of the Alliance.

The crowd edged away from Drucas's men, who watched the gate, readying their weapons for a charge. Eyes wide, they looked longingly at the inner sanctum, but several grim-faced Warlinga with their spears aimed at them, blocked that escape route.

Persig took in the scene and cursed. Stepping away from the prisoners, he let out a loud mocking laugh. Staying on the platform where he could be seen, he said, "Good people, no need to worry. Our Warlinga will protect us from the evil of the North, and the rebels who have been deluded by their foul, Umwira sorcery.

"The walls of Riath are strong, and its gate high and thick. Let those poor deluded fools hammer at it all they want—they will give up in defeat, before the gate will open to admit them. There is no need to fear—"

Persig broke off, staring upward. Above the wall by the gate several flashes of light criss-crossed the sky. Suddenly a Warlinga screamed. Bursting into flame, he pitched from the walkway, falling in a shower of sparks to the courtyard below.

The crowd screamed and panicked. Wild-eyed Loti kicked and bucked, running madly around the square, trampling anyone who got in their way. Warlinga roared, lashing out with tail and claw, at anyone who came within reach. Twice more the flaming corpses landed among them, increasing their fear.

Having a good idea of what Nathan was planning next, Dunnagh shouted to the people. "Get away from the gates! My men have no desire to kill the innocent. Please move away!"

BOOM!

Persig gaped, incredulous. The huge gates of Riath slammed into the walls on either side of the gateway with a crash that shook the ground about them. Breaking its bonds upon impact, one of the mighty stone doors toppled into the courtyard with a loud reverberation. Dust and tiny rock chips fountained into the air. The crowd shrieked, bolting for the inner sanctuary; trampling the Warlinga stationed there.

Before the echoes of the opening had died away, Varrod led his hunting pack into the chaos, shouting the alliance's war cry. Drucas Segoi's men met them and the courtyard erupted into snarling knots of lizardmen engaged in hand-to-hand combat.

Still on the platform, Persig gazed wide-eyed at the battling men. His body trembled. Swallowing a curse he swiveled round to face the Kashallan, hatred smoldering in his cold black eyes.

"Your wizard is very strong in the old magics, I will grant you that, but you have shown your power too soon, Traitor, my Master too can wield the ancient weaponry. We will destroy you, all of you."

"I keep trying to tell you, Changeling, I have no wizard master. The only fealty I owe is to the Khutani."

The priest laughed. His hand still trembling a little, Persig drew a dagger from a sheath at his hip and showed it to him. "Your kin may triumph today, but you won't live to rejoice in the victory, I promise you that." Stepping closer his lips pulled back into a feral grin. "You say the Khutani own your loyalty, Lying Slime, then let them save you," he taunted.

The Kashallan focused his eyes on the priest's hand, his lips tightly shut. Beside him he heard Amril and Ellis screaming for help, but he paid them no attention. He would not let this loathsome creature see him cringe. He would die knowing at least that his people would triumph this day—that would have to be enough.

Suddenly the Kashallan felt as if reality was shifting. The air around him and the Changeling seemed to thicken. The sounds of the battle going on around them were muted, his far-vision blurred. He shuddered, unexpectedly finding it hard to breathe. What was happening?

Persig's eyes grew round with terror. Then the form of Maker Gladdris materialized in the space between them. The image of the Maker coiled itself protectively around the bondmates, raised its head and hissed menacingly at the startled priest.

Persig stumbled backwards, dropping the knife in his panic. Gladdris bared its teeth and lunged. The changeling screamed and stepped backward, arms wind milling. Losing his balance, he sprawled on the ground below the platform. In the next moment, he scrambled to hands and knees.

Before he could climb all the way to his feet a clawed hand grabbed him by the hair and jerked him the rest of the way up. Persig spun, then froze as he stared into a pair of hard red eyes. The man smiled displaying his long fangs. "Going somewhere, Ata?" Tobrach said. "I think not."

Persig spasmed as the Warlinga's Speir'dina blade slipped between his ribs. When the Umwira lay dead at his feet, Tobrach kicked the corpse aside and leapt onto the platform.

Gladdris hissed a warning.

Tobrach froze, staring at the Maker. "Honored Elder, the changeling is dead. I mean the Kashallan no harm. I am Tobrach Tragar. I have taken the oath."

Gladdris relaxed its hostile stance and allowed its image to fade. To the Kashallan it said, <<I will leave you in the care of your Warlinga now, child. Tell them to bring you to the pools. I will be waiting to care for you.>>

When the image was gone, Tobrach took a deep breath and hurried to the Kashallan. Lifting his bloody knife he began sawing at the ropes that held up the sagging man.

Dunnagh breathed a sigh and fell forward into the Warlinga's arms. "Tobrach?"

"Yes, Kashallan it is me. Don't talk now. We will get you to the pools soon, hold on."

"Pools. Yes, I should go there." He smiled weakly up at the Warlinga, his eyes dull now with exhaustion and pain. He laughed, the sound a dry rattle in his throat. "All those months ago when Gormach took our weapons from the Begta, I never thought I would be as glad of it as I am now. When did you get here, Old Friend?"

"Hush now, don't try to talk. I will tell you later."

Tobrach glanced around anxiously. There were still a lot of people milling around by the entrance to the keep, and there were knots of fighting men between here and the inner sanctum. What should he do?

"K'San Meh'gach has told us of your bravery, young Warlinga, now I can see that for myself." The Maker Qwaltamis said in its colorless voice.

Startled Tobrach looked round. A Speir'dina that he remembered from the Tragar slave pens was climbing onto the platform beside him. He blinked. No, the man was more than a warrior now—he could feel it—and that voice. With his awareness heightened for battle as it was, he could see the Maker coiled around the aura of the brown-maned Speir'dina—now that he focused his attention on him.

Still addressing the Warlinga Qwaltamis said, "You have done well, young Tragar, K'San Yargal has told us that when you had the opportunity to escape you chose to stay behind to be of help to this young one and Sa Chelka." The man's gray eyes flicked to the changeling's corpse, then back to Tobrach's face.

"Though I would have preferred to give that one a more *prolonged* end, I am very grateful that you were here to prevent him from killing this kashallan. It would be a shame to lose him now."

Speechless Tobrach bobbed his head.

Unaware of the newcomer, Dunnagh stirred and looked up at his face, a worried question in his eyes. "Tobrach? I almost forgot—where are Chelka and Marti?"

"I don't know, Kashallan, and I am worried. I thought the changelings planned to put the women on trial with you—that's why I stationed myself so close to the platform, once I saw that K'San Drucas's attention was directed elsewhere."

Tobrach's eyes flicked nervously around the courtyard, as if somehow he might find his love in all the mayhem. He looked at the two kashallans imploringly, his heart and loyalties torn.

"Give Dunnagh-Tani to me, K'San, and go find them," Qwaltamis intoned. When Tobrach hesitated, the Maker held out the Speir'dina's arms and urged, "Don't worry about this young one, look about you, there are others here who will help me with him. Go."

Tobrach glanced around. Yes, the Elder spoke the truth. A Speir'dina was holding the yellow-maned woman, and another was taking down Amril Caltia. Several more of the Meh'gach hunters now surrounded the platform in a tight formation, their spears up and ready. Tobrach helped the host ease the Kashallan into a sitting position, then stood and bowed to the Ancient. "Thank you, Elder."

DUNNAGH GAZED AT THE well-loved face of his friend, his eyes moist. "N-Nathan? I dreamed—I thought I saw—"

Nathan sat down beside him and took him in his arms. He smiled, displaying his sharp, Khutani teeth. "I know what you saw, Amsi, I saw you, too." Then letting go of all his fear and worry, he kissed him.

When they came up for air, Nathan ran his hand down Dunnagh's haggard cheek and shook his head. He looked terrible. Gaunt as a skeleton, hair matted and filthy with dirt and dried blood, eyes dull with exhaustion. Nathan's heart gave a lurch. "Dunnagh, you stupid shit, that was one of the most brainless ideas you ever had, and right now I don't know whether to kiss you some more, because I'm so glad to see you, or kick your ass for being so—so heroic and, stupid!"

Then sobering he said, "But I'm not going to do either, because as my amla has reminded me, there will be a better time for our reunion later."

"Oh, Nathan—I think T-Tani might be dying." Tears coming to his eyes, he clung to his old love, trembling. "Please hold me; I'm so frightened."

Nathan hugged him fiercely, silent tears running unnoticed down his face. Trying to keep his voice from betraying his own fear, he said, "Hush now. It will be all right; don't take on so. My Amla is right here with us, and we will get you and Tani to the pools as soon as we can. Maker Qwaltamis is worried about Tani, too and wants to taste you—then take you, Amril and Ellis down to the pools.

"But I'm afraid we will have to do this tasting the hard way." He held up a hand with its swollen two middle fingers, for Dunnagh to see. "My tentacles haven't finished growing yet, so I'll have to bite you, but I will be gentle, I promise."

Dunnagh closed his eyes, letting go. "I'm so tired; it doesn't matter. Do what you need to, Amsi, I won't mind."

Chapter Five

As the gate burst open, and the Alliance's hunting packs poured into the keep, Enaju knew she was caught up in her worst nightmare. The Hated Enemy's magic would destroy them all. They had failed the Beloved Master, and there was nothing she could do about it now—but run. Damn Persig, The arrogant fool—she had tried to warn him. The evil was all around them; she had felt it, but would he listen? No, he laughed, said she'd lost her nerve—worthless, half-bred slave!

With no thought for her brother and his fate, Enaju through off her headdress and robe of state, abandoned her dignity and ran. Before the way inside was totally jammed by the milling crowd, Enaju knew she must get back into the inner keep, if she was to make her escape. The traitors and their Caltia supporters would kill her—most painfully, if they caught her. There was another way out of Riath—a secret way, known only to a few—if she could just get to it...

She would grab a few things, then wait for K'San Drucas, or some of his men in the tunnels, below the inner keep. Enaju shuddered; the Master wasn't going to be pleased with her. Unless his warbands were well on their way south; they might lose the entire Yeyen Banai Valley to the traitors. She cursed and quickened her pace. His enemies were far more powerful than they had assumed. He had to understand—it wasn't her fault...

Returning to her suite, Enaju went into her bedroom, and threw open the chest where she kept the ritual accouterments of the High Matri's office. Tossing the priceless objects unto the floor she snatched up the pack at the bottom of the chest and laid it on the bed. Hurrying into the outer room, she grabbed what she could in the way of food and supplies, then hurried back into the bedroom.

Throwing these things on the bed too, she rolled the blanket around them, and tied the bundle with one of her long sashes. With the roll under her arm, Enaju crept back into the outer chamber, and peeked out into the corridor. She hadn't much time—the enemy filth would be looking for her soon.

From somewhere far away, she heard the echoes of Warlinga roaring and spears knocking together, but here in this inner hallway, all was still quiet. Enaju stepped out into the hall, heading away from the noise and the chaos.

Turning into a deserted corridor, not far from her suite, the changeling headed into the gloom—away from the inhabited portions of the keep. Snatching up a glowing fungus lamp, Enaju breathed a sigh of relief and moved further along the dusty passage. No one would think to look for her down here.

These ways through the hills were a closely guarded secret, known only to a few. With all that was going on up above, it would be quite some time before anyone thought to look for her here—if anyone was left alive, who knew about these passages, that is.

Enaju moved down the tunnel as silent as a wraith, listening. In the darkness she felt the ponderous weight of the stone looming over her, wanting to crush her. She shivered. Long dead Khutani ghosts flowed through the shadows. Slithering through the darkness, they followed her—coming ever closer—their teeth bared to take their revenge. When they caught her...

Enaju shuddered, and quickened her pace.

Then she slowed again, chiding herself for her foolishness. She was no weakling, afraid of shadows, she had traveled this path under the rock many times as had the other changelings when going back and forth on the Master's business. Why was she frightening herself with such notions now?

Suddenly Enaju froze. Was that the sound of Warlinga voices? She listened. The darkness and the echoing passages through the bedrock often distorted sounds, but the voices seemed to be coming from ahead of her, not from behind. She waited—listening—till she was sure. Yes, the sounds were definitely coming from up ahead, and there was no way her enemies could have anticipated her flight and gotten in front of her.

Enaju breathed a sigh of relief and stepped boldly forward. These Warlinga had to be K'San Drucas's men. Turning a bend in the passage she saw their lights up ahead and hailed them. When the men stopped, Enaju hurried forward to join them. Coming up to the pack, she blinked in surprise. It would seem that not only some of the Segoi's most trusted men had escaped, K'San Drucas himself was here—and, damn his scaly hide, two of the captives.

Enaju scowled and stepped forward, her rage sweeping away her momentary hesitation. Confronting the Warlinga commander imperiously, she glared up at him and in a voice as cold as the stone about them, she demanded, "I should have known when you defied our orders and didn't bring these two." Her lip curled with contempt. "Stolen away by the Tragar K'San indeed."

Her eyes raked coldly over the bound women. They were leaning heavily against the wall at the moment, heads down catching their breaths. At the sound of her voice, they looked up. Enaju frowned. What was that on their foreheads, dried blood? Enaju raised her lamp and took a step closer. When she recognized what the marks actually were, she hissed in surprise and rounded on the Warlinga.

Spitting out her words in a barely controlled rage, she said, "You half-bred slave of the slimeworms, how dare you!"

Enaju flung out her hand. "Leave them; they will only slow us down."

K'San Drucas Smiled, giving her an impressive display of his fangs. "They will not slow us down any more than you will yourself, Ima. Should I leave you to the tender mercies of the Khutani as well?"

Suddenly he seemed to loom over her, a menacing shadow in the darkness. Enaju swallowed and instinctively stepped back. Then angry with herself for her momentary display of weakness, she laughed. "What are you babbling about, you Stupid Warlinga, we have no time for this—we must escape and get to the Master. Tell your men to kill them and be done with it."

Drucas's head crest flattened. From the shadows some of the pack growled, a low menacing sound. His eyes alight with malice, Drucas's grin widened. "You are right, Ima, the Master must be told—and quickly. The Sa is a Warlinga, she can keep up with the pack. And if the mutant falters, we will kill and eat her. So you see there is no need to worry; they will be no trouble."

He laughed softly and stepped a little closer. "Ah, but you on the other hand—puny, sniveling half-bred slime that you are—how will you keep up with the pack, hmm? How Ima, tell me, how?"

Enaju stepped back a pace. "Where is Ata Persig?" she demanded.

"Dead. Like your entire weak degenerate race should be. You and your brother Persig have cost us Riath with your bungling. I will make sure the Master knows of your disgrace, Slave."

Enaju opened her mouth to protest, but no words could get past the lump that suddenly closed her throat. She had always been afraid that someday he would turn on her, and now that day had come.

Throwing the glow lamp in his face, Enaju bolted back down the tunnel. With a roar of fury the Warlinga batted the lamp aside and bounded after her.

Enaju had time for only a short run before she felt the Warlinga's claws sink deep into her shoulder. Enaju screamed, the sound high pitched and wild, like an animal that feels the hunter at its back and knows its death has come.

Spinning her around to face him Drucas grinned, red eyes glowing in the lamplight, like twin flames of hatred. Enaju screamed again. The pungent scent of her bladder releasing its contents, was a choking miasma in the gloom. Drucas wrinkled up his snout and laughed. "As I said, a mewling weakling."

Enaju swore at him and struck out with her own claws in a frenzy of desperation.

Drucas laughed again and held her at arm's length. Turning to his men, he said, "My, my such a frantic little cave rat. Shall we leave her for a wandering tribe of Begta to find? I'm told they enjoy such tasty morsels as rats."

The pack laughed, and added a few suggestions of their own as to what their K'San could do with her.

Suddenly bored of toying with her, he said, "I've waited for this day a long time. You arrogant, bumbling fool you deserve nothing better than a slave's death. Still, I wish there was more time to show you the true measure of my regard. Too bad, but as you said, we must warn the Master."

Drucas pulled her to him and tore open her throat, with one quick movement of his head. In his arms she spasmed once then sagged. Placing his mouth over the wound he drank in the warm rich fountain of her blood. When he had had enough he tossed aside the limp corpse and turned to his men. "The slave was right, we need to get out of here." Pulling on Chelka's tether, he stalked off into the gloom.

AS TOBRACH HURRIED across the courtyard, he could see that the fighting was almost at an end. The rebels had most of the keep's defenders that were still alive, herded together in one corner of the courtyard near the Warlinga barracks.

Feeling the knot of worry tighten in his middle, Tobrach hastily scanned the survivors. Where was K'San Drucas? It didn't take him long to realize that neither Enaju nor the Segoi K'San were here any longer. Without Drucas to guide them, it was no wonder that the abandoned men of the hunting packs had given up so easily,

But where were they? Surely they hadn't run out into the fairgrounds where the rest of the Alliance's force was searching for the enemy clan members. No they must have gone back into the keep. And their only reason for doing that would be if there was an underground escape route, somewhere in the bowels of the cliff.

That would make sense he reasoned; how else could the changelings get information back to their wizard master in the north than through such a conduit. And, if there was such a passage, then that meant they were in great danger—especially if his guess about the Ghostland warbands heading south this season, was correct. Motioning for a few of his men to follow him Tobrach bounded up the stairs and headed into the keep.

As he passed through the gaping doors, he heard K'San Meh'gach and the Serath clan leader urging the terrified bystanders to go out onto the fairgrounds. They promised the wounded that the Avairei, healers among the Alliance, would see to their injuries. They also announced to the bewildered crowd that a large open-air meeting would be held soon, so that the Alliance could explain why it had been necessary to attack the keep.

Tobrach dismissed them from his mind—he had worries enough of his own at the moment. Once inside, and away from the chaos of the public rooms, he paused. Where should he begin his search.

Turning to his Second Hunter, he asked, "Did you check the cells once the Segoi Warlinga were gone to the trial?"

"Yes, San Cousin, we checked all the rooms in the abandoned passage where the prisoners were being held. There was no one there, not even a man left on duty for pretense. I also had the cousins check other passages, but they found nothing, the dust hadn't been disturbed by recent tracks. Wherever they took them, they aren't up there any longer."

Tobrach lashed his tail in agitation. If not hidden away up there, where had the Warlinga taken them? Remembering what Marti had secretly told him about K'San Drucas's interest in Chelka, he reasoned that the women would be wherever the Segoi K'San was. Had he been fool enough to try to take her north with him?

Enaju and K'San Drucas were gone, but he wasn't sure if the changelings had left together, or if, they independently decided to save their scabby hides by running. Drucas would be harder to trace, since his apartment wouldn't be in this part of the keep—and he doubted if the man would go there anyway.

But he needed someone to show him where the escape route was, and the one most likely to know was Enaju Dingay—provided that he found her, before she made her own escape. Quickening his pace, he decided to begin his search with The High Matri's private suite. If Enaju was still there—well, she would tell him what he needed to know.

Stepping boldly into the suite Tobrach glanced around hurriedly. The room was empty at the moment, but it had been left in a chaotic state not long before. A wide-open cabinet, a tipped over chair, spilled pitcher of spiced tea on the rug, it would appear that the changeling had been here and fled. Muttering a curse under his breath, Tobrach motioned for two of his men to search the entire suite. Where had she gone from here? By the Great Hunt Leader—he flexed his claws in frustration. A picture of his beloved being cruelly tortured by the Segoi K'San, came unbidden into his mind.

"K'San?"

Tobrach looked up. One of his hunters beckoned to him from the hall. Stepping back into the corridor he noticed another of his men holding a frightened servant by her braided hair. Eyes wide and trembling, the girl lulled in the big Warlinga's grasp, mewling softly. Tobrach hurried over to them.

"She was hiding in the next room, Cousin," the hunter explained. "I thought I should bring her. But when I called to her to come out, she tried to run away."

Tobrach scratched his jaw, studying the Avairei. She looked vaguely familiar, but he couldn't single her out from the small army of young Avairei who were sent to Riath each Sun-Time to attend the High One and her Council. Perhaps she *was* one of Enaju's maids. Well, whoever she was, she might have some valuable information—if they could get it out of her, in her present condition. At the moment the girl was petrified, and his man's harsh treatment was making things worse.

Motioning for his cousin to ease off, Tobrach crouched down till he was at her eye level. "Don't be frightened, Little Sister, my kinsmen meant no harm. I'm K'San Tobrach. Surely you've seen me around the keep these past few weeks. I know I've seen you, though I don't know your name."

The young Avairei sniffed, visibly relaxing as his soft tone of voice and gentle words had their desired effect. "I'm Shina, K'San."

"Ah, and you are one of the Ima's maids, aren't you?"

The girl nodded.

"Well, Shina, with all that has happened, my men and I are worried about the good Ima's safety. We've come looking for her, but her suite is empty. We need to find her. It's very important that we do that; do you understand?"

"Yes, K'San Tobrach."

"Do you know where she has gone?"

"N-no, but I did see her—I called out to her. She didn't hear me. Oh, K'San Tobrach, you must help her, she is all alone, and the rebels will kill her if they find her!" The girl broke off, bursting into tears.

"Yes, I'm sure they will. That is why it is so important that we find her. Can you help us?"

Tobrach shifted impatiently. Nearby he could hear his men cursing Avairei frailties under their breaths. He looked over at them flattening his head crest in a silent warning. They quieted. He returned his attention to the weeping maid—had she heard him through her tears? If he wanted more information he would have to proceed carefully.

"Shina, listen to me. I want to help, I want to find her, but I don't know where she's gone. You have to help me, tell me which passageway she took when she left."

The Avairei stopped her sobbing and pointed to a darkened corridor leading into a less used portion of the fortress. "She went that way, K'San. She seemed very frightened. I guess she's trying to hide till K'San Drucas can kill all the rebels and restore order."

"Mm, perhaps." Standing up, he motioned for his men to follow him. Leaving one man on guard outside the suite, Tobrach loped off down the indicated passage.

The maid had told them the truth. When the hall they were traveling down forked, the outline of an Avairei's footprints was plainly visible in the dust of one of its branches. Holding his lantern low to the ground, he picked up the pace. They'd wasted too much time already; they must find her.

The pack loped along at a steady ground covering rhythm. They were traveling, as he had suspected, deeper into the bedrock of the hills, but the tunnels were wide and the slope gradual, with no crevices or rockslides to hamper their progress. *Very well maintained*, he thought, *even though there is rotting fungus and slime pitting the walls. Yes, very well maintained, considering that few people knew these passages existed anymore.*

Suddenly one of the men at the back of the line whispered a warning. Tobrach stopped, the pack crowding close to shield him. "What?"

"Someone is coming—behind us."

The pack froze, listening. It was hard to tell in the echoing blackness, where the noise was actually coming from, but it was definitely another pack of Warlinga traveling fast, and making no secret of their progress. As best he could tell, the noise seemed to be coming from behind them. Had the Segoi pack learned of their coming and taken another route to come back around and attack them from behind? No that was unlikely; there hadn't been any side passages crossing this one in quite some time now.

"They are coming up behind us fast," his Second said. "What do you want to do?"

"Cover the lamps and we'll conceal ourselves around that last bend in the passage. Let's see who they are first, before we rush into an attack." The pack crouched and faced the passage down which they'd just come. Hands on their spears, they waited.

Catching sight of the approaching lights on the opposite wall, Tobrach stepped out into the passage. Edging forward cautiously, his men at his back, he uncovered his lantern and let the light reflect onto his face. In a low but carrying voice, he said, "This is Tobrach of Clan Tragar. Who follows on our trail? Come ahead without fear, if you be friends."

The strange pack halted. Then the man in the lead held up his own light, showing his face. "It's Aju'an Meh'gach, K'San. Maker Qwaltamis has sent us."

Tobrach relaxed, lowering his lamp. "Come ahead."

Aju'an grinned and came forward. "Your kinsman on guard back at Enaju's suite said you had gone this way. I'm glad we found you, K'San."

Tobrach frowned. "Why were you looking for me, K'San Aju'an?"

"The Maker was worried that in your concern for my sister, you—uh—might not have gone after the enemy fully prepared." Aju'an's eyes assessed the Tragar force. "It suggested we come along to help you."

Tobrach's face greened and he dipped his head crest in embarrassment. He glanced at his men seeing them as Aju'an had. In his haste he had only taken the time to collect a few of his people, before beginning this hunt. He had been a fool; he had no idea how many of the enemy were down here, he could have gotten himself and his kin killed to a man and still not have rescued Chelka.

He bowed. "The Maker is most wise. I would welcome your help. And, of course, you must be as concerned about your sister's safety as I am."

Aju'an nodded, and motioned for his men to fall in with the Tragar pack as they headed down the deserted tunnel.

They hadn't gone much farther when a terrified scream echoed back to them from the blackness. The sound was still some distance off. The

Warlinga quickened their pace, their quarry wasn't far ahead now. Not long after the first outcry, more screaming came from the blackness ahead.

His heart in his throat, Tobrach broke into a run. It was impossible to tell from those cries who it was. All he *did* know was that, whoever was screaming, was in pain and terrified. He prayed it wasn't Chelka or the Speir'dina woman, Marti.

Slightly ahead of him as they rounded another bend in the passage, Aju'an slowed, holding up his lantern to alert the pack. "What is it?" Tobrach murmured, straining to see into the gloom beyond. Without answering, Aju'an pointed to a gray lump on the floor ahead. Holding his lamp aloft, he peered into the gloom, then hurried foreword swearing under his breath. Tobrach and the pack followed.

Tobrach's nostrils flared at the scent of fresh blood, and urine. Aju'an bent and turned over the crumpled body sprawled in their path. Seeing that the corpse was an Avairei, Tobrach breathed a sigh of relief, then his head crest flattened as he recognized the identity of the corpse. Enaju Dingay.

"It would seem that our enemy has taken care of one of our little problems for us," Aju'an observed.

Tobrach snorted, crouched down and touched the corpse. "This is a fresh kill, the changeling and his pack must be close."

Aju'an bared his fangs in a feral grin. "Then let's go find them, my hunters."

Taking the beam rifle off his shoulder, he motioned for the pack to follow him as he broke into a run. Raising their voices in a bay of triumph, the combined Tragar and Meh'gach pack raced down the tunnel after him.

DRUCAS HEARD THE BAYING pursuit and slowed. He listened for a moment then swore. Damn the rebel slime to the Poisoned Fires, they must have followed the stupid Avairei's trail. Barking out a command to his men, he gave a savage jerk on Chelka's leash and picked up the pace.

"K'San, they are gaining on us," a hunter near the rear shouted.

Drucas swore and jerked on the tether. "Run you Khutani-bred slave!" The rebels were gaining on them; the women were slowing them down. He hated to admit it, but weakened by their imprisonment there was no way that the women could keep up with a pack in full flight.

Drucas's arm jerked as once more the woman he was dragging stumbled and fell. Snarling with rage he yanked viciously on the lead. "Get up you sniveling weakling, or I'll—"

"Or what, you'll kill me? Go ahead, Umwira, I'd rather die than mate with you," she spat. "Go ahead kill me, because I'm not running any farther."

"K'San we must leave them, the enemy is too close." His Second glanced anxiously down the tunnel, then back at his leader.

"No, she is mine," Drucas snarled. Looming over the fallen woman he reached down and jerked her roughly to her feet. "You belong to me and you *will* come."

Suddenly a man at the end of the line screamed and burst into flame. "K'San please!" his Second cried.

Drucas cursed and waved his men on. Pulling her close he stared into her face red eyes ablaze with fury. "You belong to *me*, Woman." He shook her. "Me, do you understand?" With a clawed finger he traced the sigil on her forehead, reopening the partially healed wound. "I've placed my mark upon you. That sniveling little half-bred son of a Begta won't keep you, remember that, Witch. I'll come back for you, and when I do, I'll kill him, and anyone else who gets in my way. There is no one in your puny Kashallan Alliance who can keep me from what belongs to me." Then shoving her from him, Drucas sprang after his retreating men.

WHEN SHE WAS SURE THEY were gone, Chelka put her hands against the wall and clawed her way to her feet. Somewhere in the darkness nearby, she could hear Marti gulping in great lungfuls of air. She swayed, then steadying herself she took a few tentative steps towards the sound. "Are you all right, Marti?"

"I've been better—are they gone?"

"Yes."

"Good. Help me up, will you."

Chelka groped, following the sound of her friend's heavy breathing. Finally she encountered a stretched out leg by her foot, reached down and grasped the Speir'dina's arm and hauled her to her feet. Leaning against the wall Marti bellowed, "Hey, Boyos, over here. What took you so long to find us?"

"Chelka," Aju'an shouted.

"I'm here too, Brother."

In the light from their bobbing lanterns she saw her brother, Tobrach, and the hunting pack racing towards them. She looked at Marti's bloody face in the growing illumination and her head crest fell. She touched the sigil on her own forehead; her hand coming away wet. She shuddered.

<<You're mine.>> Drucas's voice whispered in her mind.

<<No,>> she told him, but she could feel the coils of his magic tightening their hold upon her. <<No,>> she said again. Chelka turned her head away from the approaching men, hiding the mark of her shame as she pressed her face to the pitted wall.

THE LIGHT THAT SHOWED the women their rescuers, also illuminated them and their battered condition to the approaching men. Naked, caked with grime and dried blood they were a pitiful sight. Aju'an slowed, waving for the pack to continue the chase. Damn the Umwira changeling, he'd pay for this. The women were leaning up against the wall of the tunnel, faces turned away from the light. Around their necks they wore tight collars, long braided leashes hanging down from a center ring stitched into the leather.

"Chelka?" At the Sound of Tobrach's voice Marti turned and smiled at them, but Chelka remained with her face turned away.

Aju'an came closer, in a soft voice he said, "Chelka, what's wrong?"

With a sob she turned to him; letting both men see her clearly for the first time. Aju'an froze, his mind reeling. He saw her un-aproned body, then he noticed the strange, bloody sigil drawn upon her forehead. "Oh, Little Sister, what has he done to you?" he breathed.

Chelka swayed a hand going up to touch the still bleeding mark on her face. Her eyes crying out her mute appeal, she looked from her brother's bewildered face to Tobrach.

Aju'an looked away, confused. Tobrach's jaw tightened, his tail lashing in a savage rhythm. Aju'an turned his back on the women, and said to Tobrach in a low voice, "What is that mark on her forehead, do you know?"

Startled Tobrach turned to him. "Don't you?"

"No, damn it, tell me?"

"It's an Umwira sigil of personal ownership. Sa Marti wears one too, though it is hard to see under her hair. At your end of the Yeyen, maybe the Hated Enemy doesn't use such marks, but the Ghostlanders do. Drucas has marked her in blood and with his magic too, most like. He did it so that we'll know that she belongs to him—and he'll be back to claim her."

Ignoring Aju'an's angry cursing, Tobrach went to her. Holding open his arms, he said, "Chelka, My Dear One, you're not his slave—not now, or ever. Fight him. You've done nothing to be ashamed of." With a strangled cry Chelka buried her face against his chest, her body trembling.

"We have lost them, Hunt Leader," Mar called out from the darkness up the tunnel. Stepping into the pool of their light, he said, "The passage forks ahead—they split up—I came back for orders."

Aju'an glanced up the tunnel, then back to his sister and Tobrach. "Tell the men to come back, we have the women, there will be time enough later to explore these passages and go after the Changeling and his pack. We'll go back now."

Mar bowed, then disappeared back up the passage. When he was gone Aju'an looked once more at his sister. Tobrach had taken off his festival cape, wrapped her in its folds, and was crooning something soothing next to her ear.

From nearby Marti gave one of her throaty laughs. "Chelka may not be as happy to see you as she is her love, Aju'an, but by all the Gods of Caldon and Timorna, I'm delighted to see your scaly hide, believe me." Then to his surprise, she flung her arms around him and gave him a big hug.

Part Five: Riath, Harvest-Time

Chapter One

<<C hosen, arouse yourself, the council is over.>>
<<Mm, good, that means we can go back to the pools now, right? I'm starved.>>

Qwaltamis gave a mental chuckle. <<Yes, my child, when you return to the pools, I will be there in the flesh, waiting for you. I will feed you and then we will rest together.>>

<<Good, and maybe this time we can really get a good rest without someone calling you to settle another crisis.>>

The Maker laughed. <<There is much that needs our attention, right now, but when the troubles are over; it will not be like this.>>

<<No, I suppose not.>>

AFTER THE HIGH MATRI'S death and the battle during the Solstice Festival, the whole Yeyen Banai Valley was plunged into chaos. Many of the Avairei and Warlinga clans who had allied themselves with the Dingay out of fear, or personal gain, found it impossible to believe that the Dingay had tricked them for so many years. Fighting had broken out in some areas, between the clans supporting the Kashallan Alliance and those still clinging desperately to the Dingay cause.

These desperate clans refused to believe that the High Matri and her brother were changelings, even though Neyal Dingay and other Dingay clan members who had taken the kashallan's oath, swore to the truth of the Alliance's claims. Hunting packs from Riath had had to be sent to quell the disturbances. The leaders of these unbelieving clans were brought forcibly to the Capital where they were taken to the Khutani to be tasted.

This process had been going on for several ten-days now, and Nathan, as host for both Maker and symbiont child was right in the thick of it. If

Dunnagh-Tani, or one of the kashallans from Ticca could have been there to share the load it wouldn't have been so bad. But Dunnagh-Tani was far too sick, and the other kashallans were too far away to help.

It was going to take a long time to get everything worked out, but at least they were making some headway. But it was an exhausting process that was fraying Nathan's nerves, and he was glad they would be leaving as soon as Dunnagh-Tani was well enough to take on the tastings and oath takings.

As a warrior, he would have liked to follow the changelings' trail immediately after they fled Riath, but that had been impossible. His Shalla was far too young to make the journey, even if the Maker hadn't been needed in the capital. Corha needed the nurturance of the kindred in the pools. Like Dunnagh before him, he was going to have to get used to his new role in Timornan society.

And because of the link the Maker shared with him, much to his disgust, Nathan had been forced to sit through endless council meetings, while the Elder's advice was sought. This afternoon unable to stand it any longer, he had begged Corha and their amla to leave him out of the shared link so he could have some peace.

The council meeting was indeed over. Most of the members had already gone or were in the process of leaving. He yawned, stood up, stretched, and headed for the door.

<<So, what did I miss in the council meeting today? Did they finally get the argument settled about whether to let the Speir'dina and the other species have representatives on the council yet?>>

Corha gave him a mental chuckle. <<If you wanted to know so badly, Kasha, you should have listened, hmm?>>

<<Ha, ha, very funny! Now answer my question.>>

<<Oh, all right. Yes, Kasha, they did—and you were right, all that wrangling was very tiresome. But High Matri Ngeal made the settling of that question, her first order of business this afternoon. Clan elders Arishim and Bennett will represent the Speir'dina, the Loti and Begta will have to choose their representatives later.>>

<<Mm, boring was the word I would have used, Shalla, but I'm glad that's settled, I would have hated to sit through another long drawn out meeting where that was the main topic of discussion.>>

<<You have our amla to thank for that, Kasha,>> Corha said proudly. <<When amla pointed out that in the past, all the intelligent species were represented on the High Council, no one dared argue any further against it. Though, I did hear several members grumbling about including the Begta.>>

Nathan snorted. <<Well the little furballs take some getting used to, but they're not so bad.>>

<<Mm, I think a few of them are coming along as guides for the hunting packs aren't they? So I will get to taste them, won't I?>>

<<Yeah, maybe, though they probably won't stay with us once we get up into the Ghostlands, they usually run when there's fighting to be done,>> Nathan grumbled.

<<They weren't bred for fighting, Silly. That's what Warlinga are for,>> <<Right.>>

<<And, besides, Kasha, that's why our amla is going with us. In its memories are many things that no one in the south remembers about the Ghostlands and the Umwira. We won't need the Begta—our amla can even speak their language. Though if what Dunnagh-Tani says is true about the Umwira having some of the old weaponry we will need your kin as well to come with us.>>

<<That dear, Shalla, is already being arranged. I think the message went out with that last caravan to Ticca. Dunnagh told us he was sending a letter to his wives and to Hunt Leader Tizu, remember? We'll meet them at our old base camp, in the Broken Lands. When we've combined our forces, then we'll head north.>>

<<Mm.>> After a long pause, Corha said in a tiny voice, <<I would be very frightened if you and amla weren't going with me.>>

Nathan laughed. <<You wouldn't even be going, if I wasn't.>> Then sensing his bondmate's real concern, he sobered. Gods, this was so hard—he had to keep reminding himself that Corha in many ways was still but a very young child. And right now faced with the prospect of traveling with a warband into hostile territory, where anything could happen, it was understandably afraid.

<<I'm sorry, Shalla, I was only teasing you, and I know what you mean, and to tell the truth, I'm a little bit frightened too. I'm glad that Amla Qwaltamis will be with us, too.>>

"Kashallan?"

What now. Turning round he saw Aju'an, with head crest lowered hailing him. The kashallan stopped. The Warlinga left his family and hurried over to him. Nathan eyed the group in the far corner sourly. Tobrach Tragar, K'San Yargal and several other Meh'gach family members were over there, and judging by their expressions, it wasn't a happy gathering. He sighed.

When the Warlinga was close enough Nathan gave him a crooked grin and asked. "What is it, you in some kind of trouble? Your father doesn't look too pleased."

"He isn't, but it's Chelka he's angry with—and maybe Tobrach for encouraging her—not me this time." Aju'an's tail tip curled and uncurled with his agitation.

"Mmm. And, I suppose you figure if I go over there, everybody's going to forget about their troubles and get happy, hmm?"

Suddenly becoming very formal, Aju'an gave him a deep bow, and addressed the Maker. "Maker Qwaltamis, my sister is determined to go north with the hunting packs. She is adamant. She says she will follow on her own, if we refuse her—and my father is furious, because he thinks that Tobrach, and Sa Marti, are encouraging her.

"My father is threatening to break off the marriage contract and lock Chelka up in the accavett if she doesn't abandon this plan. Elder please talk to her, we need your advice in this matter desperately."

"Very well, I will come, if you think it will help," Qwaltamis said.

As they approached, the group fell silent, looking expectantly at the kashallan. K'San Yargal, as Aju'an said, seemed about ready to burst apart, he was so angry. Chelka was dressed in her warrior woman's apron, and was carrying her spear. Which, Nathan noticed with some amusement, she held tightly, as if daring someone to try and take it away from her.

Lately she had taken to wearing a finely woven headband across her forehead, to hide the sigil that the changeling cut into her flesh. As a warrior woman, Chelka was becoming quite the celebrity. Just like at Ticca, she had many admirers, which seemed to embarrass her as much as it pleased her. He'd seen other young Warlinga wearing headband similar to hers, though he doubted if most of them knew the real reason why she wore it.

His mouth twitched as he saw that Tobrach too was wearing a headband, which didn't seem to have improved Yargal's opinion of the young man any, for he kept glancing at the band and scowling.

The kashallan bowed to K'San Yargal, then addressing Chelka, the Maker said, "Your brother has told me the problem, you wish to join us when we go north, is that correct?"

Chelka bowed. "Yes, Elder, that is my wish."

The kashallan next turned to K'San Yargal. "And you, K'San do not wish it?"

"No, Elder, I do not. Such a hunt is far too dangerous for a woman and—"

"Father, please—"

The Maker held up Nathan's hand for silence. "What say you, K'San Tobrach? As her intended, and as one of the Hunt Leaders of this hunt, I will hear your opinion next."

Tobrach hesitated before replying. He glanced at Chelka's green-flushed face, then looked away, his head crest lowering. At last seeming to come to some inner decision, he said, "If she comes with us, she might be killed, or captured. I don't want to lose her, but I also understand her reasons for wanting to go. She has the skills and the training, so there is no reason to refuse her. If she wants to come, I will respect her decision and allow it."

"Mm, and what about you Aju'an?"

Aju'an sighed, glanced at his father then murmured, "I don't like it either, but she can come, if she wants—"

Yargal's head crest shot up in outrage. "No," he roared. "I say no! A woman's place is in the accavett. That is how it has always been, and should always be—you young people have no respect for tradition—"

"K'San," Qwaltamis said, "you requested my advice in this matter did you not? Please allow me to give it."

Yargal bowed deeply, his face greening, his head crest dipping with embarrassment. "Forgive me Elder, I meant no offense."

"There is nothing to forgive, your concern for your children is admirable. Unfortunately you are wrong, the accavett is a relatively new tradition. It was suggested to your people just prior to the plague, and it was never our intention that it should become such a rigid institution. At that time many women joined the hunting packs. Which alas, the Hated Enemy took advantage of.

"Because they don't use the red kavay, there has always been a fertility problem among the Umwira. That's why they raid our settlements to steal women and slaves. At the time of the plague, Warlinga females were a particular target for their malice. The wizards wanted them, because of all the intelligent races the Warlinga are the largest and fiercest. With captured Warlinga females, the wizards bred a race of monsters that they could then send back south, to despoil our lands."

Qwaltamis fixed Nathan's cool gray eyes on Chelka and continued. "The danger of being captured, then forced to mate with unnatural creatures is the real reason why women of your race were discouraged from joining the packs—not because women were unsuited. As you yourself know from personal experience, that threat has not changed. If you go with us, you must understand fully the risk you face and the added danger you will place upon the men who hunt with you."

Chelka's eyes widened and her flush deepened. Glancing at each hunter in turn, she looked into their unreadable faces and began to tremble. Letting out a strangled cry, Chelka dropped to her knees in front of Nathan-Corha. Tearing off her headband, she looked at their stern faces, her eyes imploring. When she had her emotions under control enough to speak, she touched the sigil on her forehead.

"Look at me," she challenged, "take a good look at what he did to me! You don't know what it was like—any of you. He humiliated me, made me feel like I was a thing, a piece of property, a something he could use and discard at a whim. He hurt me, over and over again—I hate him! He must die—and I want to see it. He deserves to die, not only for what he did to me, but also for what he did to Dunnagh-Tani, Amril, and the Gods alone know how many others.

"I hear their screams echoing in my mind, waking or sleeping. I can't just stay here and work on my embroidery while I know that K'San Drucas and his cursed master are alive and able to do more harm. Please, kinsmen, Elder, I will try not to be an added burden, but I have to go, can't you understand?"

Nathan-Corha nodded. "Yes, Child, I can understand. You are very brave. If the other members of your pack are willing to carry the added burden you place on them, I have no objections, if that is what you choose to do."

Chelka looked into each man's face in turn, and after a moment's hesitation; they nodded their agreement.

With a muttered curse about the young, Yargal threw up his hands in defeat and stalked out of the council chamber, leaving his children staring after him.

OUTSIDE IN THE CORRIDOR Nathan breathed a sigh of relief and asked the Maker, <<How much of a risk is she, really?>>

<<That is hard to say. There are many possibilities. Under the right circumstances she could be a powerful lure to tempt the changeling into acting foolishly. We will have to make allowances and wait and see.>>

After a long pause Qwaltamis said, <<When there is more time I want to examine the Umwira sigil. I may be able to lessen its power—>>

"Nathan?"

Nathan-Corha sighed. "Oh shit, now what," he muttered, and quickened his pace, pretending he hadn't heard.

<<Now what indeed, Warrior?>> A mental rumble of amusement from the Maker, <<You recognize that voice as do I. You will not dissuade her by walking faster. Give in gracefully, Young One. She is a fine example of the females of your species, do you not agree?>>

<<Elder, please,>> Nathan said, but he stopped. Still with his back to her, he could hear her hurrying footsteps as she ran to catch up to him.

<<Your heart may dream of another, and wish it to be otherwise, but this is Timorna, Warrior, and you, like all the Speir'dina will be bound by

the breeding practices of your new home, just like any other Timornan. When the trouble is ended, you like your love, Dunnagh, must wed and sire many children. I tasted this woman during her healing, and I find her a suitable match for you. Why are you so indifferent to her?>>

Nathan squirmed. Timorna, yes damn it; it was Timorna, and he supposed he would have to do his duty—eventually, he thought privately. But he couldn't think about that right now. An image of Dunnagh's face rose unbidden to his inner vision and he quickly banished it too. He didn't want to think about him either; everything was so crazy.

Nathan was saved the necessity of answering Qwaltamis's question, for at that moment Marti came up to him. She put a hand on his shoulder and when he turned, she gave him a toothy smile. "I'm glad you heard me; I wanted to ask you something."

"What?" Coming fully round to face her, Nathan blinked. Instead of her usual raggedy Lann Gheal uniform, she was wearing a blue Avairei woman's kilt. Bare above the waist her well-rounded breasts with their erect brown nipples poked out from under a green cloth cloak.

The effect was somewhat spoiled by the long machete and holstered sidearm on a heavy leather belt around her waist, but the outfit was stunning and, much to the Maker's amusement, Nathan felt a tingling in his groin in response.

Marti, like Chelka, hadn't been tortured much during her confinement, so once she was rested and eating properly again, her health had improved rapidly. Her face was still a bit gaunt, but her cinnamon-skin had lost its unhealthy ashy look and her curly dark hair was growing out nicely, after they'd had to shave it. Also, like her friend, Marti wore a brightly-colored headband across her forehead to hide the Umwira sigil.

Noticing his surprised look, her smile widened, and she twirled around so he could get a good look. "Pretty, eh? One of Ima Ngeal's daughters gave me the new clothes."

"Yeah, nice—but not very practical if you're still planning to go with us on the hunt with us."

She gave him a disgusted look. "I won't be wearing this when I leave, Nathan. We're all getting new clothes and leather armor made for the trip, just like you."

"Oh."

"So. Would you like to take a walk with me down by the lake? We still have time before dark."

Nathan shivered; that tingling was getting stronger. "Uh, no. thanks for asking—it sounds like fun—but not right now. I'm, uh, getting hungry and I need to go down to the pools. Maker Qwaltamis is waiting for me."

"Oh, that's all right; another time then." Before he could pull away, Marti tucked his arm in hers and headed off in the direction of the pools' entrance. "I'll walk with you. I don't mind. Riath's pools are very nice too. I haven't been down there since my healing—and Maker Qwaltamis is such a kind and wise creature. I'd like to say hi again."

In his mind Nathan heard the Maker's rumbling laugh again. He stole a glance at Marti's mischievous black eyes, and hastily looked away when he saw her watching him. "Uh, Marti, it's been a long day, and I really am getting tired, couldn't we do this another time?"

"Do what, Nathan?"

"Never mind."

He sighed and continued walking. Nearly as tall as he was himself, she matched his pace with an easy flowing grace. He saw people they passed nod a greeting and give him a knowing smile. Grudgingly he had to admit that they probably made a fine looking couple together. He sighed. Timorna.

"Nathan, how is Chelka? I was actually looking for her when I came here today, but when I saw her over there with her family—and her father looked so angry—I thought better of joining them. Then I saw Aju'an come for you, so I stayed around to ask you what was going on."

"Chelka wanted to go with the hunting packs going North, and her father threatened to break off the marriage contract and lock her up in the accavett. They wanted Maker Qwaltamis to come settle it."

"K'San Yargal didn't look very happy when I saw him storm out of the council chamber. Didn't he like what the Maker had to say?"

Nathan laughed. "Not really, Maker Qwaltamis and the rest of the Hunt Leaders said she could go."

"Good, she needs to go, but—"

There'd been an odd tone to her voice when she said that, Nathan shot her a questioning look. Marti walked on in silence for a while, deep in thought. They were nearing the stairway down to the pools. Nathan glanced at her uneasily. He really was getting tired. Was she serious about coming with him? "But, what?"

"Has she told you about the dreams yet?"

Startled out of his own thoughts he stared at her and shook his head. "What dreams?"

Marti gave him a troubled look. "I wished she'd taken my advice and told you—I shouldn't be the one to tell you about this."

"Come on Marti, spit it out—what dreams?"

"I guess they're more like nightmares, actually. The changeling did something to her when he put that mark on her. He comes to her sometimes at night, and torments her."

"Has she spoken of this to Tobrach or her family?"

"I don't think so. She's been trying to fight him on her own. I only know because I was sleeping in her bedchamber one night when she woke up crying. I've been trying to get her to tell the Maker—I thought that's why she came up to the council chamber—because you were there." Her lips curved into an ironic little smile. "I guess her father cornered her first."

Nathan sighed and stepped into the stairway, pulling her along with him. There was no help for it now. "I wish she would have told me. This seems like something important. You better come and tell the Maker what you know."

Leaning closer she slipped an arm around his waist. "Yeah, I guess I better." She gave him another toothy smile, but the worry still lingered in her eyes.

Chapter Two

Dunnagh-Tani looked down at the trembling Avairei kneeling before him. He tried to smile, but his face felt wooden; he was getting so tired. He sat in a comfortably padded wicker chair in a small audience room just beyond the High Council's chambers. The Council was still in session, the occasional murmur of their voices coming to him through the closed door on the far wall.

It was a hot Sun-time day outside. The outer doors had been left open, and a cool afternoon breeze was blowing in off the lake. In the courtyard he heard the sound of children playing, and Warlinga practicing. Dunnagh glanced wistfully towards the door, but the room he was in opened onto an inner corridor. He couldn't see them, but he wished he was free to go for a walk down by the lake. It would be good to feel the sun on his face.

Hopefully this man was the last of today's batch. "Don't worry, Ata, the kashallan link isn't painful." Reaching out, he took the man's hands in his, then extending his tentacles, he showed them to the nervous Ata, then formed the link.

Still trembling the priest look down at their hands, and said, "Holy One, my family and I are totally loyal—I assure you."

"I am glad to hear that, but my Elders have required all to swear. This tasting and oath taking is no reflection on your honor, I assure you," the Kashallan said. "After seven hundred years, my kin feel it is important for us to taste as many people in the valley as possible. With our new knowledge, we will know better how to serve you in future."

He gave the Avairei a crooked grin. "And as you have also heard, this test will root out any changelings that may try to hide among us. If you are honest with me, you need have nothing to fear."

"I-I am no changeling, Holy One, truly."

The Kashallan motioned with his chin towards Neyal Dingay standing unobtrusively by the open door, waiting to escort the man out; when they finished. "You see Ata Neyal over there, he is an example in point. My kin and I have accepted his oath, no matter what crimes some of his relatives have committed. Just relax, Ata, I will be through in a minute."

The Avairei glanced at Neyal. "It's so hard to believe, Holy One, new kashallans, High Matri Enaju a changeling—so hard."

"Mm." The Kashallan closed his eyes. When he opened them again, he said. "I find none of the taint about you, Ata, so we can proceed with your oath, if you are ready."

After the man left, Dunnagh-Tani stood and stretched. When Neyal returned to the room, he said, "I hope that is the last of them for today, Neyal, I'm getting quite tired."

Neyal bowed. "Yes, Holy One, it is. Shall I send for some food and someone to give you the blood gift?"

Dunnagh-Tani glanced towards the closed door at the far end of the room. "I want to go back to my rooms first, Ata, and Amril can arrange it. You've been doing more than your share these past few ten-days; go get some rest yourself. Tell Mar where I'll be if anyone wants me." He gave the priest a tired smile. "But also tell him not to disturb me, unless it's urgent. I want to take a nap."

Neyal bowed again. "I'll tell the Warlinga, Kashallan, but it is my pleasure and my duty to serve you. Your wife is still not fully recovered; I will see to your meal."

Dunnagh sighed then nodded.

NATHAN-CORHA KNOCKED on the doorframe of the audience chamber, and then stepped into the room. Disconcerted, the Dingay priest bowed, his eyes flicking from one kashallan to the other, like a mouse caught between two cats. "I will see to your meal, Holy One," he murmured, then with eyes cast down, Neyal scurried past Nathan-Corha and out into the hall.

Nathan-Corha stared after the departing priest, then shrugged and came the rest of the way into the room. "What's with him?"

Dunnagh-Tani smiled at his friend. He looked at the now empty doorway and sighed. "Neyal's a bit nervous, that's all. He's been a big help to me since we've been here, very forthright about airing Dingay secrets. We might not have caught several changelings without his help. He feels it's his duty to make up for what has happened in any way he can, but he's also very uncomfortable around us, too."

Nathan-Corha grunted. "So he should be, after what he did at Meh'gach."

Dunnagh-Tani nodded. "Well, there is that. But as far as I'm concerned anyway, he made up for it by helping me, several times over. I never thought I'd say it, but I kind of feel sorry for him—he tries so hard. It's sad really."

Nathan grimaced. "You always were too quick to forgive, Dunnagh. Me, I don't think it'll hurt him one bit to squirm a little longer."

Dunnagh laughed and slapped him on the back. "Come on, I need to get out of here, before the council meeting in there breaks up, and they think of something for me to do. Let's go back to my room, I'm tired."

Outside in the hall, Nathan-Corha fell into step with the other kashallan. Dunnagh had regained some of the weight he'd lost during his ordeal, but he still looked like a man recovering from a major illness. They'd had to cut off his long red braidlets, and now his hair hung in a soft cap of russet waves around his ears.

It seemed funny to see him like that. Not since he was a lad and his sister, Siobhan-Ru'a, cut off half his hair in one of their games, had he seen his friend with such a short cut. It seemed weird, to see him in such a childish style. It was a jarring contrast when compared with the tracks of pain etched into his sunken cheeks and the dark circles around his eyes.

"Why are you looking at me like that, Nathan?" Dunnagh-Tani said quietly.

"Because you look like shit, that's why."

Dunnagh chuckled. "Most of the time I still feel like shit, too, so I'm not surprised you'd say that."

"Dunnagh, seriously, you don't look too good, are you sure you should be up and doing so much? While I'm still here I could have been doing more of the tasting and oath taking like I did at first. My Amla and I –"

Dunnagh-Tani patted his shoulder, and opened the door to his quarters. "I know, Mo Hara, but you've had other things to do. I'm all right—truly." He ushered the other kashallan into the room and motioned for him to take a seat. "Don't start mother-henning me. The quicker I finish taking everyone's oath, the quicker I can go back to Ticca and be with my family."

Dunnagh-Tani's suite was beautiful, Nathan thought. Its cream colored walls were hung with geometric weavings of rust, brown and shades of blue. A large green braided rug covered most of the floor and thick golden cushions nestled in the frames of fine wicker furniture. This apartment was in the upper corridors of the keep. An open window facing the lake let in a cool breeze and offered a striking view of the surrounding countryside.

Dunnagh-Tani crossed to the window. He leaned on the sill for a moment taking in several deep breaths, and he sat down heavily in a chair beside him and leaned back with a sigh. "I really miss them you know. The babies must be so big by now. The way things are going, it'll take months, to finish here." He sighed again. "And, with you heading north soon..." Dunnagh's voice trailed off, not looking at him.

Nathan-Corha shuddered. Just a moment ago there had been such an expression of sad longing in Dunnagh's blue eyes that made him want to cry. Reaching out he took the Kashallan's hand, extended his own tentacles, and formed the link. "That's sort of why I came to see you, Mo Hara," he said gently.

Dunnagh-Tani looked down at their joined flesh. He blinked rapidly for a moment; then reached out with his other hand and established a link of his own. "You're leaving then?"

Nathan-Corha nodded. "Tonight. We decided to go in secret, just in case there is still a spy or two that haven't been discovered yet. We'll take the underground passageway, same as the changelings did. This is the last free time that I'll have to come and see you."

"Then this is good bye."

"Yeah, I guess it is. I wish it could be otherwise. I hate leaving you when you're still weak like this."

"I'll be all right, Maker Gladdris and my nursemaids won't let me do anything stupid—this time."

Nathan-Corha laughed, but his heart wasn't in it, and they both knew it. "It's about time somebody made you behave. But I do hate to leave you."

"I know. Thanks for coming to tell me." He blinked and a large tear landed on the back of Nathan's hand. Dunnagh stared at it stupidly, blinked again, and then looked away.

Nathan choked back a sob of his own. Through the link they shared, he knew how deeply Dunnagh was affected by his news. Gods, he wished it didn't have to be like this.

In his middle Corha stirred, anxious and a little frightened by the flood of emotions it was tasting from the two hosts and Tani. <<It's all right,>> Nathan soothed, <<don't be afraid, Shalla, we Speir'dina are an intense lot at times. Ask Tani; your cousin knows how crazy we can be—don't fret, Little One.>>

Out loud he said to the other kashallan, "Dunnagh—Amsi, don't do this to yourself. We'll be safe enough. And we'll be back soon—you haven't lost me. Like you tried to tell me, we'll be even closer, when I come back."

Dunnagh-Tani swallowed, then released himself from his portion of the link. Looking away, he shook his head, but he still continued to cradle Nathan's hand within his own. "No, you're wrong, My Heart. I *have* lost you, and for good this time."

Nathan laughed nervously. "Dunnagh stop it. What are you talking about? When I come back, we'll go back to Ticca and—"

Dunnagh shook his head again. Raising Nathan's hand to his face, he studied the elongated middle fingers where Nathan's tentacle casings had now grown. He stared at them for a long time, turning them at different angles in the lamp's silver-green light. At last he said, "I know you'll be safe." Then bringing the hand to his lips he kissed the fingers tenderly. "But when you come back, it won't ever be the same for us."

To spare Corha, Nathan released his own link and pulled his hand gently out of Dunnagh's. Oh, Gods, this hurt, how had they managed to make such a mess of their lives—and their love. "No. I guess it won't."

Dunnagh cradled his own hands in his lap, and stared down at them blindly, tears gleaming on his cheeks. When at last he could speak, he said in a voice thick with emotion, "All those months I teased you about becoming a kashallan—I dreamed how good it would be, how much more we could share—just like in the old days when we were young and swore the warrior's oath together. Those were good days; do you remember?"

"Yeah, I remember. They were good days—the best."

"The best. She warned me you know." He grimaced. "Probably laughing right now. She's got her revenge."

What is your love made of, I wonder? Time will reveal that. Which one of us will truly betray him in the end, hmm? Think on that, Kashallan—which one of us shall bind him, out of love, to a course not of his choosing?

"Dunnagh, you're not making any sense. Who?"

"Tess-weh. She told me—that first morning, on the beach. I was so angry—and afraid for you. I hurt her—made her angry—and she told me—I didn't want to believe it, but she knew."

Nathan felt a cold chill run down his spine. In his middle the young symbiont wailed, and he rubbed a hand across his middle in a soothing gesture.

Dunnagh saw the gesture—he gave his friend a sad ironic smile—alien, not human. "I've been a fool, Nathan, I got my wish, but in doing so, I see that I will lose you, and forever this time."

Nathan sighed. "Dunnagh, stop it. We still care for each other—that hasn't changed—and you *were* right, with our bondmates to share with us—it will be even better—just like at Shaden Pools. I was a little pissed off with you at the time, but now I see what you and Tani were trying to show me—and it will be just like that always."

"Oh, Mo Hara, you don't see it yet do you? Yes, when we *meet*, the sharing will be all that I promised, but they won't let us stay together—not now, don't you understand? There is so much work that needs to be done, Nathan. As another kashallan—our duties will keep us apart. We may not see each other for months, or even years at a time after this is over. My amla told me some of what they plan for us..."

Nathan sighed and looked away. Dunnagh was right, he hadn't thought of that. The Elders, would probably send them to different parts of

Timorna, when this Umwira thing was settled—if they lived that long. They would probably make him marry Marti—and maybe others, and start his own family. Shit! Of course they would."

<<Our amsi is right, Kasha,>> Corha said. <<I can taste your sadness. I wish we could stay with Dunnagh-Tani too, but don't be too sad, you will always have me, and I love you, too.>>

<<Yeah, I know, and I love you too, Shalla.>>

At a faint knock both men straightened, faces taking on bland masks. A moment later Amril came in balancing a tray in one hand. Bumping the door closed with his hip, he set the tray down on the sideboard and smiled. "It is good to see you Kashallan-Nathan; Neyal told me you were with my husband."

Nathan-Corha smiled too. "It's good to see you too, Amril. Are you feeling better, how is your leg?"

Amril shrugged. "Better, I guess."

Nathan rose. Looking down into Dunnagh's stricken face he murmured, "I should go."

"Is there something wrong?" Amril looked from one Speir'dina face to the other, a frown creasing his furred brow. "Should I leave, so you can be alone?"

"No, no."

"Then stay, please, Nathan-Corha, Neyal told me you were here. I have brought enough refreshments for all of us."

Nathan-Corha shook his head. "Thanks, Amril, but I should go. The hunting packs are leaving Riath, and I have a lot to do before tonight."

"Oh." He looked from one man to the other again. "I had no idea it would be so soon."

Dunnagh-Tani rose. Stepping close, he touched Nathan's cheek with tentacles slightly extended. "Take care of yourself, Amsi."

Nathan-Corha choked, then gathering him into his arms, he kissed him. "Take care of yourself, too," he said close to his ear.

"I'll try, My Heart, I'll try."

Nathan-Corha embraced Amril quickly, then without a backward glance he opened the door and was gone.

—————✝╲╲╘╫————

WHEN THE DOOR CLOSED behind Nathan-Corha, Amril listened to the silence and sighed. He limped over and set the tray down on an end table beside the Kashallan. Filling a bowl with formula, he sat down beside his consort, and handed it to him. "Drink this, My Husband."

Dunnagh-Tani took the bowl automatically and drank. When he had finished he handed back the bowl. "Thank you." After that he sat just staring at the tapestry on the opposite wall tears running unheeded down his face.

Amril sipped, his spice tea, watching him silently grieve. What should he do—what would Pela, or Sairsa do if they were here? He was so tired—they both were tired. Putting down his bowl at last he rose. Taking the Kashallan's hands in his own, he gently urged Dunnagh-Tani to his feet. "Come, Husband, you're tired, let's lay down together. I will give you a massage."

Obediently the Kashallan followed him into the next room and sat down on the edge of their bed. Amril took off his kilt and crawled in behind him. Kneeling at Dunnagh's back he began kneading the taught muscles of his neck and shoulders.

As Amril's skilled hands unknotted his muscles Dunnagh sighed. A while later he said, "Nathan and I grew up together. We were so close, we've always been together—and now—he's a kashallan, and it will not be the same any more. They will take him away from me now."

Amril grunted, and continued to work. Sometime later, Dunnagh-Tani spoke again, this time changing the subject. "Amril, there will be another caravan going to Ticca soon, you could go back—be with Pela. Would you like that?"

Amril allowed his fingers to slow, thinking. By the Great Mother, how he missed her. All those long agonizing days in that cell; he dreamed of her constantly. Her warm brown eyes, her soft fur, the way her braidlets clicked together while they made love. Oh, he wanted her so much, but this sad, lonely man needed him right now. He couldn't just abandon him; not after all they'd been through—not after what Dunnagh-Tani had done for him.

Ever since he learned of Pela and Amril's love, this kashallan, half Khutani, half alien other, had done all he could to ensure their happiness. And during their capture and imprisonment, how many times had Dunnagh born the pain that should have been his, diverting the changeling's anger onto himself to spare Amril what he could.

As much as he missed her, he couldn't live with himself, if he went to Pela now and left Dunnagh-Tani here alone. He was the wife of the first Kashallan—no; he couldn't leave him.

Coming to an inner decision that he had been considering for some time, Amril set aside his fear, leaned forward and kissed the Kashallan tenderly on the neck. Then allowing his hands to slide forward he next slipped them under the Kashallan's kilt and resumed his massage. "No, Husband, I want to stay with you. We will go back to Ticca together, when our work here is done. I can wait."

The End

The *Tales of the Kashallans* is continued in Book Six: *Blood Magic's Snare*

Additional information for the Tales of the Kashallans series

NOTE TO THE READER: it is my hope that by reading the text of these fantasy books, the alien words peppering the writing are clear on their own. But for those readers who enjoy such things, and those who may get confused from time to time by the many foreign words from the various races and cultures on my imagined world Timorna, I offer the following notes to aid with clarity.

Best wishes and happy reading!

Celu Amberstone

Pronunciations of unfamiliar words:

Consonants

The sound [ch or kh] represents the ck in the word lock [lahkh].

Other consonants are pronounced like in English.

An apostrophe in a word represents a glottal stop.

Vowels

A – like father AI – like in ice AY – like in way

E – like in ate EI – like in island

I – like in see

O - like in low

U – like in too

Y – like in eat

H – when next to a vowel shortens and softens the vowel sound

Timornan words (general)

Timorna [tim-MOR-na] – The name of the uncharted planet where this story takes place.

The Great Destruction – A nuclear holocaust that almost destroyed life on Timorna, thousands of years ago.

The Burning Times – A time when the radioactivity was at its highest, just after the destruction.

Sorins [SOR-inz] – A weather condition in which the wind blows straight out of the north, picking up radioactive dust and other harmful substances as it heads south. During the Sorin seasons all life must seek shelter, or go dormant, to survive.

KHUTANI [KOO-TAH-NEE] – The ancient eel-like symbiotic race living on Timorna in its deep undergrownd waterways, who were responsible for storing the genetic patterns and keeping life alive during the Great Destruction and the Burning Times that followed.

Amla [AHM-la] – The term used by the Khutani and kashallans to refer to a parent.

Amsi [AHM-see] – A Khutani term used to address a peer of its kindred.

K'amsi [k'AHM-see] – A Khutani term of respect for an elder of that race.

Sh'amsi [sh'-AHM-see] – A Khutani term used to address a younger sibling.

kashallan [kah-SHAH-lan] – A host-symbiont bond. A partnership between two intelligent beings sworn to serve as guardians and healers of the planet Timorna.

Kasha [KAH-shuh] – The intimate name a symbiont in a kashallan pair uses for its host.

Shalla [SHAH-luh] – The intimate name a kashallan host uses for his symbiont.

The Kashallan – This term refers to a particular pairing, that of the human, Dunnagh Kai, and Tani, the Khutani symbiont. They are the first bonded pair in over seven hundred years.

Bebech [BEH-bech] – A native race that served as hosts of the Khutani, who were killed off by plague.

kavay [kah-VAY] – A blue substance created by the Khutani that when introduced into a living organism makes its survival possible on Timorna.

kavay alignment – The process by which the body is metabolically changed at such a deep level that, once alignment occurs, a constant supply of kavay must remain in the diet, or death will occur.

Sweh'an [SWAY'-ahn] – Another type of host-symbiont bond, this time between a mortal host and a spirit being from another dimension that will use its powers to aid a host, in exchange for possession of the host body at agreed times, so that it can experience a physical reality.

H'an [h'-AHN] – The host for a Sweh'an spirit.

Swe'a'sa [SWAY'-ah'-sah] – The intimate name the host uses to address her Sweh'an spirit companion.

H'an'si [h'-AHN'-see] – The name the Sweh'an spirit uses to address its host.

Cha'Han [CHA'hahn] – The Avairei priest who is bound to the Sweh'an bonded host as her companion.

Ba'etchat'seh [bah'-AYCHAHT'sah] – The Timornan version of a padded cell, used to discipline the Sweh'an when its behavior while taking its pleasures becomes too troublesome.

Wa'chassey'ul [wa'-CHSAY'-ool] – A Warlinga bound by magic to the will of the Sweh'an as both lover and mortal guardian.

AVAIREI [AH-VYE-RAY] – One of the four intelligent species bred by the Khutani. A furry, bipedal race with cat-like features and a long mane. They are the priests, scholars and healers of their society. Their function is also to care for the Khutani in their underground pools, and to distribute the medicines the Khutani make for the creatures they introduced to their world after the Great Wars nearly destroyed all life on Timorna.

Ata [AH-tuh] – (Father) A term used when addressing a male Avairei.

Ima [EE-muh] – (Mother) A term used when addressing a female Avairei priestess.

Ima Matri [EE-muh MAH-tree] – The priestess who is head of a Avairei keep like Sulas.

High Matri – The head, and ruler over, all of the Avairei family clans.

Ata Leyas [AH-tuh LAY-ahss] – (Healing Father) The male Avairei who is second in command of the religious hierarchy at a keep.

WARLINGA [WOR-LING-ga] – Another of the intelligent species bred by the Khutani. Large two-legged lizardmen naturally endowed with teeth claws and long muscular tails. Their function is to be warriors and hunters. They were bred especially to protect the Khutani-held southern lands from the Umwira, the mutated remnants of the original people who caused the Great Wars.

Chi'awari'ga [CHI'-ah-WAHR-ee'-gah] – An ancient Warlinga ceremony of single combat to settle a feud or other dispute.

Accavett [ah-cah-VET] – The women's quarters in a Warlinga keep.

Sa [sah] – A title of respect for female Warlinga.

San [sahn] – A title of respect for male Warlinga. The terms Sa and San are also used for humans as well because many of them are warriors, too.

LOTI [LOW-TEE] – A third intelligent species. They resemble centaurs with long, shaggy fur. Their function is to farm and care for the land of Timorna. They are also artisans, weavers and craftsmen.

Timornshaya [tim-morn-SHY-uh] – A term of respect offered to the Loti people.

BEGTA [BEKH-TA] – THE last of the four intelligent species created by the Khutani. Small, woolly-furred simian-like people with long arms. They live in the wilder regions of the south. The Begta are an outcast people, hunters and gatherers, who are notorious thieves. They are despised by most other Timornans, and often hunted for food, or sold as slaves.

Domail [dough-MAIL] – A Begta victory dance.

Begtanshay [BEKH-tahn-shay] – A term of respect given to the Begta people by the Khutani and the kashallans in earlier times.

UMWIRA [OOM-WEER-UH] – This is a name given to the mutated descendants of the planet's original intelligent inhabitants by their enemies. Also known as the Ghostlanders, they are the people who were responsible for the Great Destruction. They are the sworn enemies of the Khutani and wish to destroy all that the Khutani have created, so they can reclaim the more favored lands in the South.

Clans of the Western Umwira – The Western Clans are related to the Ghostlanders and descended from the original inhabitants of Timorna; being exposed to the poisons of the north and west where they live, they have mutated and interbred with slaves taken from the Khutani-held lands, so that they don't resemble the peoples before the wars.

The seven clans are: Blue Stone, Sand Mountain, Bitter Water, Red Wind, Rock Salt, Green Clay, Twisted Grass.

Plants and Animals on Timorna

taba worm [TAH-buh] – A long, thin worm that lives among the liru reeds, in both the Swamp and the Broken Lands. Eaten by the Begta. The appearance of a bowl of taba worms is rather like blue spaghetti.

gumati [goo-MAH-tee] – A frog-like creature with four hopping legs, living in the Swamp. Eaten by the Begta.

budasen [BOO-dah-sen] – A stork-like creature with long neck and legs. It has big paddle feet for running across the surface of grassy ponds. Not a bird; it has scales, and can't fly.

pomong [puh-MAHNG] – A lizard-like predator with a long, sharp tail. It preys on the budasen.

snayga [SNAY-guh] – A small predator that swims in large schools. Eating habits like the piranha of old Earth.

vistri [VIST-tree] – A six-legged scaly predator about the size of a large dog, and like dogs hunt in packs. Very dangerous.

winglah [wing-LAH] – Any large creature of the western lands that has through the generations mutated into a dangerous monster because of exposure to the Sorins.

obeylem [oh-BAY-lem] – A large plant-eating creature, living in the Swamp. It has six limbs (four long legs for walking, two short arms for grabbing food), also a long tail and neck. Hunted for their meat.

bolacht [BAh-lach] – A herd beast introduced by the Khutani to meet the needs of the Speir'dina. Provides meat milk wool and can be ridden as well.

madag [MA-dag] – Timorna's answer to a herd dog. Looks something like a small armored dinosaur. Can fight vistri, but gentle with humans and other Khutani-bred races

shri moss [shree] – A short yellow moss, growing everywhere as ground cover.

liru reeds [LEER-roo] – A tall, brown bamboo-like plant growing in the canyons of the Broken Lands and parts of the Swamp.

kavalpa trees [kah-VAHL-puh] – Tall, black trees like weeping willows that usually grow up around a spring or other water source. When their long branches touch the ground, they root themselves, thus forming, over time, large thickets that give shelter to many of Timorna's inhabitants.

masa root [MAHS-suh] – A plant with a large edible root, eaten by most Timornans. Cultivated by the Loti.

lamra [LAM-ruh] – A corn-like grain developed from the liru reeds. A staple food in the diet. Cultivated by the Loti.

dahalli [Da-hal-lee] – A thorny shrub that can grow quite tall with purple broad leaves and bright orange berries that are sweet.

clamisa – A mutated form of masa root growing across the Shallow Sea in the West. A staple of the western Clans

oko – A small armored predator in the western lands it looks something like an armadillo. Thought to be sly by the Western Clans.

dhuura – A sea creature found in the Shallow Sea. It also is a food staple for the Clans of the coast.

leongon – An armored shark-like predator in the Sea.

nagril – A nearly transparent jelly/shrimp-like creature that feeds much of the sea life on Timorna.

cobura – A furred sea animal.

aluutae – A reed/grass-like plant growing in the West used for basket making.

Land features

Ghostlands – This is a wide peninsula of barren land that connects the Favored Southern land with the blackened and radio-active northern continent. Living mostly underground this is the land where a cabal of techno-wizards has control of what is left of the old technology. They also have tremendous Psy powers which they have gained through exposing themselves to mutations sought in the poisoned places in their land.

Broken Lands – A region of canyons and mesas where some of the Begta bands live, and where the humans set up their base.

Yeyen Banai [YAY-yen ban-EYE] – A large valley surrounded by a high rim of mountains. This is where most of Timorna's Khutani-bred population lives.

Rim Wall – The mountains encircling the Yeyen Banai.

Jeban Pass [JAY-bun] – The main route from the Broken Lands through the Rim Wall to the shelter of the Yeyen Banai Valley beyond.

The Great Swamp – A low-lying stretch of land to the south of the Broken Lands. Very dangerous to travel, since it is pockmarked with poisonous pools, and subject to constant earthquakes.

Lake Ticca – A large lake at the edge of the Great Swamp, out of which the Shaden river flows. In its center is the island fortress of Ticca keep.

Shaden Falls [SHAY-den] – The portage around this waterfall is the main southern route from the Swamp through the Rim Wall to the Yeyen Banai Balley.

The Shallow Sea – The straight between the land of the Western Clans of the Umwira and the northwestern edge of the Swamp.

Timornan Keeps and Fortresses

Avairei keeps:

Riath [REE-ahth] – the capital

Sulas [SOO-luss]

Ticca [tee-KAH]

Shaden [SHAY-den]

Ha'limra [ha'-LEEM-rah]

Warlinga fortresses:

Tragar [TRAh-gar]

Meh'gach [MAY'-gakh]

Caldoni words adopted into the Timornan language

Speir'dina [SPEER'-din-uh] – The term chosen by the humans to refer to themselves after they accepted that they had become a part of Timornan society. Literally it means sky people.

Teh'lach [TAY'-lahkh] – A pseudo-family group among the followers of the Kashallan, containing members of several different species.

Speir'van [SPEER'-vahn] – Literally, "sky-woman." Used by the Speir'dina as a term of respect for a high-ranking human woman, such as Sairsa the first kashallan's human wife.

OTHER CALDONI WORDS and phrases

Caldon [KAHL-don] – The world where Dunnagh and many of the Lann Gheal armachda are from.

Cumarsaid [KOO-mar-sayd] – A trance-like state in which the practitioner opens his awareness to communicate psychically with other life. This discipline was practiced as part of the ancient Caldoni warriors' training and is still taught today.

Lann Gheal – A term meaning "Bright Blade," it refers to a mercenary organization formed on Caldon. Their purpose is to keep alive many of the ancient warrior traditions of their race. They are not for sale to the highest bidder in a conflict, and will only fight for what they believe to be right.

armachd (plural: armachda) [ar-MAKHT, ar-MAKHT-uh] – Warrior.

Geish (plural: Gessa) [gaysh, GAY-suh] – A charge or compulsion laid upon someone that binds them to do a certain thing. A Geish is usually of divine origin, but also can be laid by one person on another.

Fir Gall [feer gahl] – A foreigner.

mo – This word means "my," but when used with other words often changes the sound at the beginning of the next word.

Cara [KAH-ruh] – Friend. mo hara [moh HAH-ruh] – My friend—my love. Mo hri [moh hree] – My heart. Mo gra [moh grah] – My love.

Ce'awn [kay'-OUN] – A chieftain. mo he'awn [moh hay'-OUN] – My chieftain.

Ceartachd [Keer-takht] – A word meaning the "rightness" of a thing.

Ca'companachta [kah'-kom-pah-NAKH-tah] – Literally meaning "battle companions," it is a relationship of lovers who also fight together.

Bacach [BAH-kakh] – An unlikable person, an evil man.

Amadan [AH-muh-dahn] – Idiot; can be used affectionately or as an insult.

Dina [DEE-nuh] – People.

kina [KEE-nuh] – Kin or kindred.

le'ayn [lay'-AIN] – Twin. Literally, "half of one."

shenahi [SHEN-ah-hee] – Ancient Caldoni storyteller or bard.

Pibroch [pee-BRAHKH] – A musical instrument like a bagpipe.

Faltia, cuj milla faltia [FAHL-tee-uh, coodge MEE-luh FAHL-tee-uh] – Welcome, a hundred thousand welcomes.

go ra my get [GOR-rah-MY-uh-get] – Thank you.

Ru'a [ROO'-ah] – "The red." It refers to a person with red hair; for example, Dunnagh Ru'a (Red-haired Dunnagh.)

colcannon [kohl-CAN-nun] – A native Caldoni dish made with potatoes, cabbage, and onions.

Don't miss out!

Visit the website below and you can sign up to receive emails whenever Celu Amberstone publishes a new book. There's no charge and no obligation.

https://books2read.com/r/B-A-YGQM-CGESB

BOOKS 2 READ

Connecting independent readers to independent writers.

Did you love *Prey of the Umwira*? Then you should read *Refugees and Other Stories*[1] by Celu Amberstone!

[2]

Shape-shifting beings and magical powers move in the natural world, and curious humans find unexpected roles to play in these stories from a celebrated author. Selkies and dragons have their tales to tell here. Ghosts and aliens with their own agendas and a troll interact with humans in stories that reference myths in new ways. Here, the reader will find reverence and reflection as well as adventure, and even humour.

Refugees And Other Stories is a collection of stories by author Celu Amberstone. Previously available only in anthologies and magazines, these stories are gathered together here for the first time. Drawing on her Indigenous and Celtic heritage, Amberstone writes powerful fiction subtly different from the usual science fiction or fantasy adventures. The introduction to her fine collection of stories is written by author and professor Dr Allan Weiss, whose specialization is in Canadian Literature.

---

1. https://books2read.com/u/mvoAlj

2. https://books2read.com/u/mvoAlj

Amberstone integrates her Celtic and Indigenous heritage into these stories. Her characters (whether human, alien, or mythic beings) are strangers in a strange land, at the intersection of the real world and words of magic – and if that makes you think of Heinlein and LeGuin, you are on the right track.

Amberstone's seductive and enthralling stories employ fantastic elements to balance the joy of kinship with the devastating effects of colonialism. A must-read collection! - Dr Joy Sanchez-Taylor, author of *Diverse Futures*, and professor of English at LaGuardia (CUNY)

"Refugees," by Celu Amberstone, throws readers on an emotional roller-coaster ride within a refugee culture that has been rescued, transplanted, and controlled by ambiguous benefactors from a post-apocalyptic Earth. - Quill and Quire

Amberstone's tales reflect real-world challenges and what it takes to overcome them. - Dr Allan Weiss, author and associate professor of English and Humanities, York University.

Also very strong is Vancouver Island writer Celu Amberstone's tale of human refugees living on an alien planet under the supervision of alien Benefactors ("Refugees"). Amberstone does a nice job of painting the shades of gray in her paternalistic society. Humans who have lived on Tallav'Wahir for centuries lead peaceful and happy lives, but they are utterly dependent on aliens to make all the decisions about what is in their best interests. And when a new shipment of refugees arrives from a dying Earth, their assumptions and their security are badly shaken. - Donna McMahon for *SF Site*

The benevolence of an alien race that helped them come to this place, and requires their obedience to rules, is questioned over the course of the story, as is whether harsh decisions aimed at ensuring humanity's survival are an acceptable price to pay. - James McGrath, reviewing "Refugees" for *Journal of Postcolonial Theory and Theology*

Also by Celu Amberstone

Renewal
The Prophecy of Manu
Teoni's Giveaway

Rituals
Blessings of the Blood: A Book of Menstrual Lore and Rituals for Women
Deepening the Power: Community Ritual and Sacred Theatre

Tales of the Kashallans
The Dream-Chosen
The Hunted Kashallan
The Outlawed Bond
Uncertain Refuge
Prey of the Umwira
Blood Magic's Snare

Standalone
Refugees and Other Stories

About the Author

Celu is of mixed Cherokee and Scots-Irish ancestry. Celu Amberstone was one of the few young people in her family to take an interest in learning Traditional Native crafts and medicine ways. This interest made several of the older members of her family very happy while annoying others.

Legally blind since birth, she has defied her limitations and spent much of her life avoiding cities. Moving to Canada after falling in love with a Métis-Cree man from Manitoba, she has lived in the rain forests of the west coast, a tepee in the desert and a small village in Canada's arctic. Along the way she also managed to acquire a BA in cultural anthropology and an MA in health education. Celu loves telling stories and reading. She lives in Victoria British Columbia near her grown children and grandchildren.

About the Publisher

Kashallan Press is an independent publisher releasing books by author Celu Amberstone. Among her books are critically-acclaimed works now re-released by Kashallan Press, and new works showcasing her talents in writing both fiction and non-fiction.